THE FIRST PAIR OF
THE ZEPHYR SERIES

The Gantlet

HIS STORY

J. JAMES WHEELING

FEATHER
WATCH
PRESS

Feather Watch Press, LLC
www.jjameswheeling.com

Hardcover ISBN: 978-1-968526-03-0
Paperback ISBN: 978-1-968526-04-7
eBook ISBN: 978-1-968526-05-4

Cover and book design by Jess LaGreca, Mayfly book design
Map illustrations and design by Map Hero

Library of Congress Catalog Number: 2025913430
First Printing: 2025

Dedication

I dedicate this story to all those, famous or unsung,
who, through humility and kindness, contribute
to the world by letting their true hero emerge.

A Note to the Readers

The book you are holding (or listening to) has taken fourteen years to complete mostly because I had to learn to write correctly and I strive for historical accuracy. When this story's inspiration first came to me and I accepted the challenge to steward it into being, I began by alternating chapters between the man's story and the woman's story which are happening, more or less, simultaneously. As the story matured, it became clear that it had become too vast for one book. I was advised to divide it into two books and created *The Gantlet* and *Kismet*. It makes no difference which one you start with but, if you want to know the whole story, my advice is to enjoy both books.

This first pair signals the beginning of the Zephyr series. The stories begin in Boston with the California gold rush in 1849 and will run through the Silver Panic of 1893 in the Red Mountain Mining District in the San Juan Mountains. All will be released as pairs and I anticipate there will be multiple pairs to get this magnificent story to its end.

Buckle up, it's going to be a fun ride!

Contents

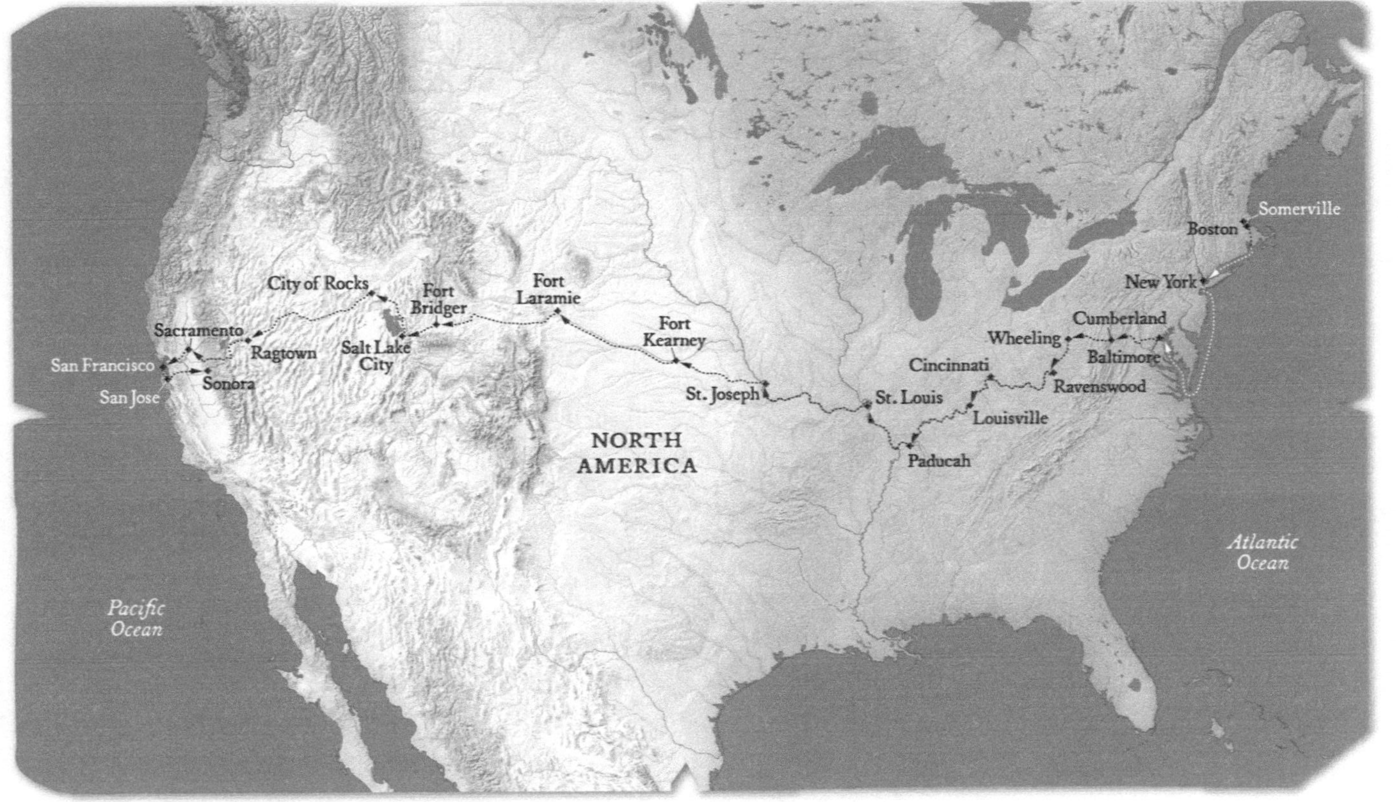
Somerville
Boston
New York
Cumberland
Wheeling
Baltimore
Ravenswood
Cincinnati
Louisville
St. Louis
Paducah
St. Joseph
Fort Kearney
Fort Laramie
Fort Bridger
City of Rocks
Salt Lake City
Ragtown
Sacramento
Sonora
San Francisco
San Jose
NORTH AMERICA
Pacific Ocean
Atlantic Ocean

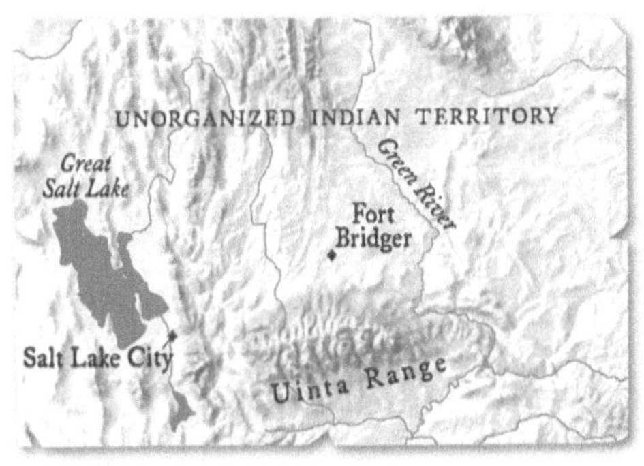

Prologue

JANUARY, 1850

FORT BRIDGER

UNORGANIZED INDIAN TERRITORY

*I*t had taken weeks for Louis Vasquez to coax Dash Truepenny's buried memories to life. But what else are they going to do during the long, cold January evenings? In the windowless, cramped storage shed Vasquez had let Dash use as his home since his arrival four months ago, only the wind's whistle forcing snow under the door is audible.

A solitary candle sits on the wood stove, radiating heat. The candle's glow is enough to illuminate the delicate tendril of blue-gray smoke sporadically puffing from a pinhole in the stovepipe. The space reeks with the commingled funk of musty burlap, dried animal hides, wood smoke, and human body odor. Not that either man notices.

His story finished, Dash looks into the candle's glow for a reaction from Vasquez. The trapper-turned-merchant's balding head bows toward him in deep concentration. Dash realizes this is the first time he has told his entire tale to one person. To have the saga out in the open brings a bloom of relief to his soul.

Dash studies the man who has shown him unusual compassion while recovering from his injuries. The thought makes Dash self-consciously tip the damaged side of his face into the dark shadows.

With his rough-skinned hands chafing slowly around each other, Vasquez speaks softly, "I've known some hard times, but Dash, yours is the darndest."

After a few moments, he continues, "I'm wonderin' if you know what a gantlet is?"

Dash considers the question. A style of gloves is all that comes to mind, and he's confident that isn't the answer Vasquez wants, so he slowly shakes his head.

Vasquez responds, "Way back in time, in the old country, a gantlet was a way for newcomers to be tested as worthy of joinin' a people's clan. If the fella could survive the abuse of the gantlet, then he was deemed suitable."

Dash lets this sink in. All the incidents, from the moment he fled for his life to his spontaneous decision to go west and then his unlikely survival, flash before him with a new light.

"Here's my thinkin'," Vasquez continues, "you've been runnin' the West's gantlet. Each of the trials of your westbound trip was a test of your strength and determination. Can't say if the West is done with you, but, my Lord, she's doled you some terrific punishments."

Dash doesn't argue with his assessment but wonders just how much longer he will be punished for doing the right thing.

"I'll leave you to your thinkin' Dash. Just remember, yours is a new life. Not to say it's goin' to be easy, but you'll never be what you were. A man your age taking on the responsibility of a baby is goin' to change you. But Bridger sees somethin' in you. I'd take full advantage of his teaching. It could be your future."

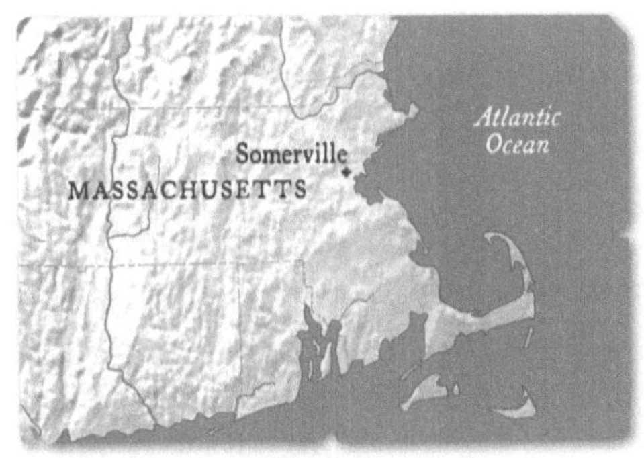

Chapter 1

APRIL, 1849

SOMERVILLE, MASSACHUSETTS

The mornings had been the worst. From the moment he stirred from his sleep, impending dread built when Donovan realized he had to face another day of psychological and emotional peril in his father's office. It hadn't always been this way. There had been a time, about five years ago, when his father, William O'Creigh, had encouraged him and showered all manner of anticipatory praise on him, admitting openly that Donovan was the future of the family business.

"While your brothers are older and should inherit the quarry, I see you being the brains behind our business. Your skills with the ledgers and seeking prospective business opportunities are far more important than their brawn. Once you're done with your education at Harvard, I can transition you into a role suited to your new skills and the company's future."

Donovan recalls being so flattered by his father's praises, the words buoying him above the sneers and off-color comments of his brothers, Angus and Thomas. Like peas from William's pod, they were taller than average, wide-shouldered, and strong from their labors in the quarry. They towered over Donovan, who took after their diminutive mother, Betsy. Donovan's younger sister, Nell, was the mirror of Betsy, making the family an odd diploid of its parents.

Nell was sweet and kind, a sensitive soul who detected Donovan's moods, sometimes without him even knowing he was having one. He remembers her entering his room, her soft brown curls bouncing, and her fawn-colored eyes gazing at him as he sat at his desk with his books. Only a year younger, she longed for the education he was promised and frequently read over his shoulder while he studied.

Able to carry on a decent debate over the subjects he was studying, they would get lost in their conversations until summoned to the table by the dinner bell. Donovan fondly remembered many delightful discussions with Nell. Her perspectives were authentic and pure, unlike some of his teachers' opinions.

Donovan and his school buddies had signed up for the Harvard entrance exams with the grand plan of going to school together. Only days later, Donovan came down with a strange fever that caused him to miss the exam. After weeks of bed rest, he was finally feeling stronger. But when he tried to stand, he fell onto the floor in a heap. After several attempts, the doctors realized the blurriness in his left eye was causing the balance problem, and his blurred vision gradually doubled. The only remedy for a return to a sense of normal balance and sight was to cover his left eye with a patch.

"O'Creigh, keep your son away from any labor that might cause a strain. We don't know what has happened, but it is likely the fever has caused some kind of brain damage. Keeping his eye covered will allow him to walk around, but the chances of him being fully functional are grim."

The doctor's words, while whispered, had announced the moment William's hopes and dreams for his youngest son evaporated. It had been a slow process of decline, and his father had shown some pity at first. But as the months had turned into years, William had become increasingly resentful and openly hostile toward the same son he had once considered the family business's savior. Now considered a disappointing burden, William's communications to his son were with contempt and malice.

While Donovan's friends all went on to Harvard, his family relegated him to clerking in the family's office. Some of his friends had been well-suited to the rigors of academic life, Hugh and Wilton specifically, but Ezra and Gus had struggled and come to Donovan for tutoring. Without his father's knowledge, Donovan spent those years acquiring an alternative education, which he managed to do without any complications as long as he kept his eye covered.

Bored with his role as a clerk and gaining weight from being banned from physical activity, Donovan had taken an interest in the newest technology of the telegraph and Morse code. Eager to find a vocation that could liberate him from his father's grasp, he had thrown himself into the process of learning to read and translate the long series of dots and dashes. Forced to put up with the callous treatment of his father and brothers during the day, Donovan pined for the quiet time of his room and the challenge of learning something new.

In the third year of his friends' Harvard education, two pivotal events had happened. First, Hugh, his best friend from primary school, introduced him to Lillia Soilleux. Donovan felt captivated from the first moment their eyes met. Many young ladies were put off by his eye patch—some stared when they thought he wasn't looking, while others just refused to look at him. Not

Lillia, though. She had smiled sweetly at him with no hesitation, holding his gaze with conviction.

As they spent more time together, he told her of his interest in Morse code, and she eagerly asked if she could learn it with him. They spent every opportunity together practicing tapping and decoding each other's phrases. Donovan remembers those days as the brief spark of light in an otherwise gray tempest of life with his father.

The second revelation from that period of his life was when Donovan noticed odd notations in the company ledger books, clearly made after Donovan had completed his end-of-day summaries. Curious but not willing to mention it until he understood more, he did nothing. Then one night, Donovan had forgotten his Morse code book in the office and returned to fetch it. He arrived and found William giving low-toned directives to his brothers, who then rushed brusquely toward him as he stood inside the office's doorframe.

"Outta the way, Donnie," one of his brothers hollered as he shoved him aside.

Tempted to turn back rather than face his father, Donovan chose to fetch his book. He saw William quickly penciling something into the ledger before slamming it shut.

"What do you want?" William demanded.

"I left a book behind and came back for it. Where are the boys going in such a hurry at this hour?"

"None of your concern. They're doing whatever it takes to help keep this business profitable. It's astonishing I once thought you'd be the answer to our future but, as it turns out, it's those two brutes."

Donovan offered no response as he grabbed his book and turned to leave. William caught his sleeve to stop him.

"What do you have there?"

"Just a book I'm reading."

"Show me."

Donovan hesitated, considering his father's reaction to the book's topic. His reluctance prompted William to grab it away aggressively, his expression growing cold as he flipped through the pages.

"What do you hope to accomplish with this?"

"Just curious, that's all."

"Is our family business not enough for you? Need something else to occupy your time?"

With a contemptuous expression on his face, William thrust the book back to Donovan.

"You're such a disappointment, Donnie. When I think of how high my hopes were for you. . . I doubt you'll ever bring value to this family. You'll probably be nothing more than a parasite."

The encounter with his father left Donovan feeling so wounded he couldn't face him for weeks. He worked on his Morse code outside of the house, while tutoring his friends on their third-year exams. He continued with his clerking duties to justify being fed and housed but was more determined than ever to find a vocation of his own.

Just as Donovan was determined to find a way out, William doubled down and kept him from having any time at all for pursuing outside interests. His father increased his time demands in the office, often filling his day with mundane and duplicitous tasks. Then he gave him errands to run, seemingly against doctor's orders, making sure every waking moment was taken up with family business.

Despite William's efforts, Donovan found spare moments to spend with Lillia. One afternoon, they sat together on a park bench among a cloud of autumn leaves that fluttered around them. Donovan faced Lillia admiring the graceful curves of her cheekbones which drew his attention to her perfectly shaped lips. He held a slate and was supposed to be transcribing the code she was diligently tapping out but had yet to make a mark. When her tapping stopped, she stared into his eyes and he was helpless to defend his adoring gaze.

"It's just . . . you are so beautiful, Lillia. I'm finding it hard to concentrate."

He reached out to stroke her cheek with the back of his fingers, moving his hand to her chin and delicately lifting her face to his. Leaning in, the two enjoyed a slow, gentle kiss until they heard the familiar voice of Donovan's best friend, Hugh, calling out from across the park.

"There you are! I've been looking all over for you. I've got this great idea for a winner-take-all wagered race to California between us and some loud-talking Yalies. One group heads to California overland, the other around Cape Horn. First one there wins the whole pot. Wondering if you'd like to be on our team, Donovan?"

Lillia and Donovan exchanged glances before Donovan looked up and grinned slyly at his childhood friend and said, "Actually, Hugh, Lillia and I have decided to get married."

"That was quick! I knew the moment I met Lillia, she was the girl for you. Smart not to let her get away."

Donovan and Lillia shared a smile at Hugh's comment before Donovan asked, "When are you thinking of launching into this race?"

"Once we finish school, April or so. There are rumors of easy gold! Don't want to wait too long."

"Turns out, we hope to marry about that same time. Going to have to forgo your offer, but thanks for thinking to include me. Sounds like a grand adventure. How many are going?"

"I'm still gathering the group, but I've got Ezra, Wilton, and Samuel, as well as Gus, although he's dragging his feet about the money. Not surprising. He says he has a buddy who works on the docks who thinks he can swing the expense. His brawn'll match your brains."

"How much is it going to cost?"

"My Yalie friend thinks we should make the wager one hundred dollars. From what I've been able to gather, it is likely to cost us each between three and four hundred for expenses. If we can get enough to make the wager a tidy sum, we'll have something to work with when we get to California. Still plenty of things to work out, but it sounds like the Yalies are up to giving it a go."

"Pretty rich for my blood, old friend. I need everything I've saved for Lillia and me. I'm taking a job in a telegraph office once I'm fluent in Morse code. I'm done working for my father."

"Oh, I don't want to be around when you tell him. He's likely to . . . no matter, you've earned the right to make your own decisions, whether or not he sees it that way. I'm happy for you both, disappointed but happy. Regarding the race, if you change your mind, you know where to find me."

With that, Hugh bounded back to his pack of friends. Donovan and Lillia watched him through the falling leaves until Lillia broke the silence.

"California seems like a world away. What makes him think they're just going to make the jaunt there, win the money, and find gold lying around?"

"Hugh's a great friend, but he's never known disappointment or hardship. He can't imagine things not working out. His parents worship him and his younger siblings, showering them all with love. I'm sure they've never heard a cross word from either of them."

Lillia noted Donovan's wistful expression.

"As will our children. Although, I don't expect answering their every demand to be to their benefit. Disappointment builds character. Showering them with love won't be difficult."

Donovan felt a deep rush of pleasure at the admiration and affection toward the woman sitting across from him.

"I'm fortunate Hugh introduced us."

Lillia giggled softly.

"We're both lucky. We each make the other better and that's how it should be. Now, one more practice message before you take me home?"

"Certainly. Although make it a little easier this time. I still struggle with 'x's and 'y's."

Now, a week before their marriage, a heated conversation thunders from behind the closed doors of William O'Creigh's study. William's loud voice could easily be heard in the hallway, and Donovan recognized his father's irritated tone. The other voice, regrettably familiar, belongs to Malbon Kinkade, a pasty-faced, self-righteous Boston philanthropist who uses gaudy flamboyance to disguise his advanced age and wealth.

Kinkade, a self-promoted benefactor of the poor and destitute, had convinced William to invest in immigrant tenement houses around the Fort Hill area. This meant more frequent visits to the O'Creigh home lately, and at every visit, Donovan tries to escape his oily presence.

But on this night, Donovan eases up to the doorframe, his curiosity getting the best of him as the two business partners continued their argument in the study.

"The last one you brought me was feeble. Never thrived no matter what I did. I had no choice but to put her out of her misery," Kinkade said.

"What, exactly, does that mean?"

"I simply deprived her of air. It was quite easy, really, she wasn't strong enough to resist me for long. Now then, I must have another. I think I'd rather have a pair . . . siblings, so they can console each other after an episode."

"Good God, man, what are you doing?" Williams asks, exasperated.

"I might get a tad exuberant. I mistook the last one's shrieking as enjoyment. Alas, an error. Can you find me a boy and a girl? That would be perfect."

William's sigh is audible even through the door.

"Malbon, your untoward dalliances pose a threat to my reputation. You've got to use some restraint."

"Don't be absurd. No one would dare doubt my front. Besides, the Irish are scurrying around our city like rats. Their filth and disease threaten humanity. I'm simply doing my part to thin their ranks while satisfying my personal needs."

"Until you get careless. What happens when someone traces their disappearances back to our tenement house or, specifically, me?"

"You have my pledge of protection."

Donovan listens as William's voice breaks the silence, his tone low and even.

"It will cost you more. The search will be extraordinary. And it won't be immediate. My boys are in upstate New York on a delivery for another client."

"I'll pay you ten times the normal if you bring them to me tonight."

Donovan listens for his father's reply, which comes uncomfortably quick.

"It's time my youngest son learns the world's ways. Been sheltered too long. He's not remotely as intimidating as the other two, but his bulk will be enough to be convincing. This job will take finesse and persuasion—fortunately, he's got both. The doctor has warned against exertion, but there shouldn't be . . ."

Shocked by William's quick reversal to Kinkade's offer, as well as his role in their plan, Donovan feels his blood run cold. When he hears them approach the study door, he slips silently down the darkened hallway. Once William closes the home's front door behind Kinkade, he turns back.

"Donnie! My office, now."

Donovan lingers for a few moments before feigning his rush to the doorway.

"Yes, Father?"

Striding toward his desk, William blindly tosses words over his shoulder.

"I've got an urgent errand for you. Normally, I'd ask your brothers but, given the demand, I must trust you to fulfill the task."

Donovan follows his father toward his desk, a mix of curiosity and dread pulsing through him. At his desk, William slides open a desk drawer and retrieves a torn scrap of newspaper. After a brief scan, he faces Donovan and thrusts the paper in his direction.

"This is an advertisement used by the arriving emigrant Irish intending to locate friends or family already here. Take the Lowell train into Boston. You'll find this woman in our tenement building across from Fort Hill along with her two children. Your task is to impersonate the agent of her sister who has placed this ad. Offer her this money . . ."

William hands Donovan a generously full pouch of coins.

". . . and explain she has to make a choice: her children's well-being or reuniting with her sister."

"I . . . I'm buying her children? Why would she agree?"

"Tell her they will be cared for by a generous and kind benefactor, rather than dying in poverty. Deliver the children to this address in Charlestown."

William flings Kinkade's calling card at Donovan.

"This errand must be completed by midnight tonight so use the Maine railroad to get to Charlestown. Be discrete. Return home and say nothing to your mother or sister. Not a word, understand?"

Still absorbing the task being asked of him, Donovan hesitantly studies the money pouch and the two pieces of paper in his hands. When he starts to form a question, William interrupts.

"What, son? Too good to take part in the family business? Follow my instructions and this will be another step toward convincing me of your usefulness. Do I make myself clear?"

Incredulous, Donovan levels his good eye into a targeted stare.

"Don't worry, Father, your instructions are perfectly clear."

Donovan hastily leaves the room, his mind whirling with the implications of his father's directive. He feels certain this isn't the first time his father has provided children to Kinkade and who knows what other unsavory clients. As he pulls on his coat, he now understands the additional entries in the quarry's ledger books were for the sale of human beings.

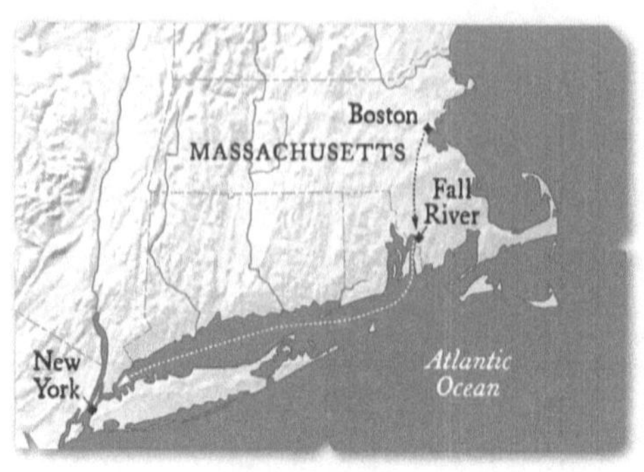

Chapter 2

APRIL, 1849

BOSTON, MASSACHUSETTS

April's crisp night air chills Donovan on his way through the streets of Boston to Fort Hill. When he arrives at the dimly lit tenement house, he quickly rereads the newspaper scrap.

Nora O'Doyle of Baltimore seeks information about her sister, Evelyn O'Doyle and children. Last known to have boarded a ship for Boston in Liverpool. Please contact Father O'Roarke at the Catholic Church on Boston's Main Street with any information.

Donovan looks up at the tenement's front door, takes a wavering breath and steps forward. The unlocked door swings heavily inward on its hinges, a blast of malodorous human stench billowing in its wake. Frantically groping his coat pockets for his handkerchief, Donovan paws the cloth over his nose and mouth before stepping inside.

He finds himself in a great hallway with doors in varying degrees of openness. From within drift the murmurs of muted conversations, the occasional child's cry, and low sounds of discomfort. Approaching the first open door, he sees haunting shadows of people lit by inconsistent candlelight. The room is strewn with soiled bedrolls. Cowering in the corner are five hollow, expressionless faces.

"Do any of you know of Evelyn O'Doyle?"

All wordlessly shake their heads. Donovan moves to the next room. His eyes water and he mashes the handkerchief tighter against his face. Room after room, his single question goes unanswered. Forced to take the stairs to the second floor, a distant burst of pitiful wailing punctuates his arrival on the top stair.

He works his way down the hall until he comes to the source of the keening. The room's occupants shrink back when Donovan's shape fills the doorway. That is when he sees the two children huddled around a figure curled on a bedroll, their pitiful sobs continuing in low moans.

"I'm looking for Evelyn O'Doyle."

The children's cries hiccup to a sudden stop as they look up at him, tear tracks running down their dirty faces.

A voice from the shadows says, "'Tis her there, on the pallet. Just took her last breath. The wee mites 'ave no one now."

Donovan freezes. He had been prepared to fulfill his father's demand, heinous as it was, but this is too much. Kinkade's slimy voice and William's belittling of his hesitation fill his memory.

He turns to leave. At the room's doorway, William's sneering expression fills his mind's eye. Then something snaps. Unsure if it is the years of demeaning treatment or the lies and deception recently revealed, but at that moment, he decides he will no longer compromise his morals to make things right with his father.

He turns back to the pathetic children clad in tattered clothes. He drops the handkerchief and reaches for their bony wrists, taking one in each hand. The children do not resist against his gentle, upward tug to their feet. Rushing away from the scene of their dead mother, he holds his breath and pulls them down the stairs toward the front door.

When they emerge from the building, Donovan unashamedly gulps for fresh air. The children stumble after him to the street, where he stops and casts his gaze skyward. He hears a sniffle and looks down at the children.

"We are going to find your aunt in Baltimore. My name is Donovan. You are . . . ?"

The children stare at him unblinkingly until the boy speaks up.

"Me's Quinn, and that's my sister, Molly."

"Alright, Quinn and Molly, we've got to find someplace where I can think."

Donovan ponders briefly before saying, "I've got just the spot."

Gripping their little hands, he walks resolutely away from the tenement house toward the only place he knows he can go to come up with a plan. His mind reels with his options and lands on only one, audacious and irrevocable.

When they push open the pub's door, the light, and noise from inside indicate a party is going on. Hugh is leading the celebration, but when he sees Donovan, he makes his way through the crowd toward them.

"Donnie, what are you doing here? Whose are these? Is there something you need to tell me . . . ?"

Donovan pushes Hugh aside at the last suggestion, interrupting him.

"They are . . . well, they are, I suppose, my wards, for the moment. I must get them to their aunt in Baltimore. You are still leaving for California tomorrow, correct?"

"Yes, but how did you . . . how will you . . . what about . . . ?"

Without answering, Donovan moves the children through the crowd. Finding a booth, he guides the children into it before turning back to face Hugh. Donovan's right hazel-green eye stares into Hugh's kind face, his sweet, gap-toothed smile slightly askew after having had a few pints of beer. The normally well-coiffed mound of strawberry blond hair flops loosely across Hugh's light-brown, freckled face. While Donovan thinks of how best to explain himself, the fine red hairs of Hugh's eyebrows arch like startled question marks at the delay.

"I can't tell you the whole story right now. Suffice to say, I need to get these children to Baltimore as quickly as possible. I can tell you I've discovered a horrifying secret my father has kept from me, and I have betrayed him by taking these children and his money. The consequences of my actions will, no doubt, be quite grim."

Hugh spends several moments considering this revelation. Donovan knows he can trust Hugh, a better friend to him than anyone, other than Lillia. He knows Hugh, no doubt, is also formulating a plan and he prays it is something realistic.

"Does Lillia know of your circumstances?"

Donovan slowly shakes his head.

"When is your wedding?"

"Next week. We are waiting for her uncle to arrive from the Mediterranean."

"So, you could be back from Baltimore in time. But then there's the issue of your father. The way I see it, chum, you've got to get time and distance between you and him. Lillia is going to be disappointed, and you've got to convince her you're doing a gallant thing. The wedding may have to be . . . postponed, somewhat."

Donovan knows Hugh is right about his father. After the last five years of abuse and humiliation along with tonight's revelations, Donovan suddenly craves distance. But Lillia? He can't risk getting her or her family involved in this mess.

While Donovan ponders his circumstances, Hugh leaves to order food for the children. When he returns, he slides into the booth next to Quinn and engages the boy in small talk while casually using his own handkerchief to tenderly clean the boy's face. Donovan watches how easily his friend manages conversations and bites his lip with envy. Donovan recalls Hugh's unique position, the oldest of six children; this recollection sparking an idea. Before he can speak it, voices bombard him from behind.

"Are ya here to join us on our grand race to California, Donnie?"

Donovan turns to see the familiar faces of Gus and Ezra, the two friends who he had tutored through Harvard. As a tray of warm drinks and food arrive to the table, Hugh pushes it toward the children, both now sporting remarkably clean faces.

"Eat whatever you want, Quinn and Molly. Donnie and I have some talking to do."

Donovan and Hugh leave the children, their starved eyes bulging at the feast before them. As the friends head toward the greater group, another friend from school, who had studied law and followed in his father's practice, steps forward. Wilton's heavy-lidded eyes loom uncomfortably close to Donovan's face as he breathes out his question, both actions signaling he, too, has had one too many ales.

"Donnie, you goin' to explain what's goin' on here?"

"We are trying to figure out how to get Donnie and the little ones to Baltimore and back before his wedding next week. It's not impossible, but it's going to be expensive. For the same amount, we still have one spot left on our California race team. What kind of money do you have, Donnie?"

Donovan's money belt is stuffed tight, and he recalls the exact, and still shocking, amount within it but hesitates to reveal the sum.

"How much is it going to take to join your team?"

"One hundred dollars for the wager plus another four hundred for trip expenses."

Hugh smiles coyly anticipating Donovan's rejection of the massive sum. When Donovan doesn't flinch, he continues.

"We won't know our route until we flip the coin in New York City, but I'm partial to going overland. With that in mind, I've made up a starting plan. We leave from South Station on the first OC train headed south for Fall River at first light tomorrow morning. Then we catch a steamer to New York City, meet up with the Yalies, and flip the coin. After our route is determined, we'll set the terms of the wager and the race to California begins.

If we are lucky enough to not be sailing around Cape Horn, my plan is to sail to Baltimore and catch the train to Cumberland. From there, well, I haven't been able to think that far ahead only that we are headed west to the Promised Land."

Donovan's earlier idea sparks to life, an outrageous but not completely impossible idea. With as calm a voice as he can muster, Donovan asks, "Sounds like Baltimore is right on your way. Since I'll already be with you, I should probably just join your team."

His statement causes an immediate uproar from the celebratory teammates now surrounding Hugh and him. Heavy-handed claps fall on his back while showers of splattered ale fill the air around him. He sees the familiar faces of Gus, Eddy, Wilton, and his free black companion, Samuel, along with an unfamiliar face of who he guesses is Gus's dockworker friend, Luther. He shoots a look at Quinn and Molly's startled expressions, unable to disguise their food-filled cheeks.

"I'll need to write a farewell note to Lillia."

"You're actually goin' to leave her behind?"

All ears lean in for his response.

"Boys, I'm in a tight spot and need to disappear for a while. I'll explain later, promise."

Nervous tension crackled through Donovan on the morning train to Fall River while Molly and Quinn had slept, curled around each other like kittens. Certain his father or brothers would have emerged from the shadows at the Fall River train station, Donovan had kept his vigilance. When Hugh triumphantly had announced he had found a New York City bound steamer for them, Donovan was overcome with relief.

Now, aboard the steamer, Donovan feels his fear of his father wain, only to be replaced with stabbing regret for what he has done to Lillia. For authenticity, his note to her was in Morse code and its message was brief, direct, and a whooping betrayal. He feels his chest tighten when he remembers the passionate conversations they had shared about creating a life that would support and encourage each other's unconventional perspectives and talents. He wants so badly to give that life to her. But with his new knowledge of what kind of life his father had to offer them, he can't abide exposing Lillia to it. His departure, abrupt and illogical, is for the best. He is certain of it.

Someday, he hopes he will look into the warmth of her brown eyes and tell her the full story, and why he couldn't let her link her fate to his and his morally bankrupt family. He feels the warmth of tears welling when he recalls the note's words.

> Dearest Dot . . . Learned illicit family business . . . Must
> flee Boston . . . For your family's safety say nothing to my
> father . . . Meet me in San Francisco . . . Please . . .
> Love Dash

Hugh's holler breaks through Donovan's fitful rest and signals their arrival at Manhattan Island's waterfront. The Bostonians eagerly crowd the ship's railing until the dock lines are secured, Hugh leading the rollicking pack down the steamer's boarding plank toward their reunion with the rival team from Yale on the steps of the Bank of Albany. Donovan is grateful when Gus offers to carry Molly so they can keep up.

Once on the bank steps, Donovan hears a voice call out, "Hugh! What took you so long?"

"Benjamin, isn't geography taught at your fancy school? It's a lot farther to New York City from Boston than New Haven, chum."

Hugh introduces his friend before he presents each Bostonian. After Benjamin rattles off the other Yalies' names, he turns to Hugh.

"Best make sure everyone knows what we have concocted, don't you think?"

"Alright then, here it is, boys," Hugh says. "We are going to flip a coin right now. Heads, the Bostonians sail to California. Tails, the Yalies sail to California. Whomever doesn't sail takes the cross-continent route, however they choose. First team to California wins the race's wager to do with as they wish."

With that, Benjamin flashes a bright ten-dollar gold piece and flips it dramatically into the air. Donovan watches the coin's rotations with held breath, praying he doesn't have to spend the next five months on a ship.

When the coin clatters on the ground, a loud cheer goes up and Benjamin calls out, "Yay! The Yalies are sailing to California! Fortuitously, we've already booked passage on the ship *Night Call*. She sails at sunset today without stopping until Rio de Janeiro, Brazil. Too bad you boys will still be stuck figuring out a way to leave New York City."

"Don't get too cocky, my friend. We still have our business with the bank about how to get the wager to California. And don't worry about us; we'll make the same quick progress as you."

Hugh's statement throttles some of the Yalies' excitement, but Donovan breathes a sigh of relief knowing the Bostonians are committed to the solid ground of the overland route to California. Before the two leaders enter the bank, Hugh approaches Samuel.

The legal courier to Wilton Bailey's solicitor father, Samuel has been educated at the coloreds-only Smith School on Beacon Hill and is highly respected for his literacy and skills at easy conversation. Samuel also has a keen awareness of his surroundings in situations where his free status could be compromised—a skill Donovan appreciates now more than ever given his new knowledge of the O'Creigh family business.

Hugh speaks loud enough for Donovan to hear, "Samuel, I have an idea for you while Ben and I are inside."

After a quick consultation, Hugh enters the bank while everyone else waits in a park across the street. After an hour, the doors burst open, and the two leaders huddle their teams in respectful distance from each other.

"Well, what happened?" Gus asks.

Hugh spits with uncharacteristic disgust, "Did you know there are no banks in California? Not one! After hearing our idea, the bank officers lectured us like we were fools but suggested using one of their junior bank officers as the wager's courier.

But there's a hitch—in return for guarding our money to California, we have to fund the courier's passage; the winners agree to make him a percentage partner, and if neither team claims the wager by May of '51, the courier gets the whole pot. It seems like a steep price to get our money to California. But we're returning in a few hours to meet the courier and sign the papers."

From the corner of his eye, Donovan sees Samuel approach Hugh, his sides heaving. Curious, Donovan subtly adjusts his position to hear the last of Samuel's report.

"... leaving at the same time," Samuel whispers heavily.

"Perfect!" Hugh exclaims before hiding his outburst and whispering, "They won't expect that, will they? Just the way we need to start off. Keep 'em off-balance."

Returning to the park after eating lunch, Donovan observes Luther, the most unfamiliar member of the Bostonian team, while they wait for the bank officers. Taller and with shoulders once again as wide as his own, Donovan doesn't doubt Luther's strength and is quite glad Luther is on their team.

A pair of bank officers appear on the bank steps and begin introductions of a well-dressed man to the Yalies.

"Looks like that's our man," Gus says. "Best go get a measure of him."

As they approach, Donovan hears one of the bank officers say, "I'll arrange for the signatures, collection of the wager, and Mr. Wellingham's passage fee. Give me ten minutes."

An irrational ache suddenly grips Donovan's gut. New York City is one of his father's favorite haunts. Given his well-placed connections, if any evidence of Donovan's escape route is leaked, there's a good chance he'll hear of it.

When the junior officer steps closer to Donovan, he makes a quick assessment of him. Clearly, the man is well-to-do. His clothing is of the latest fashion, clean and tailored to fit him perfectly. Dark brown hair curls across his forehead and gives him a tossed look in contrast to the crisp lines of his attire. Clean-shaven, Donovan quickly notes the cleft in the man's chin and as they make eye contact, the man's smile reveals matching dimples in both cheeks.

"Howard Wellingham. You are?"

Donovan knows he has to respond. To not shake the man's hand would make a scene. He extends his hand, gesturing to the children as he mumbles all of their names.

"Children? On an adventure like this?" Wellingham questions.

"Going to Baltimore . . . to their aunt's . . . just to Baltimore."

Wellingham lingers, staring at Donovan, his attention focused on the eye patch.

"Aren't you concerned about the strain of this trip on your well-being?"

"Not at all," Donovan says through tight lips.

"Ah, yes, well, you've more courage than I. Good luck in your quest, O'Creigh."

Turning to the children, Wellingham bends low and peers into their eyes saying, "You'll like Baltimore. It is a grand city."

Donovan flashes a nervous smile, his mind whirling with this encounter's implications. If his father interrogates this man, he could identify Donovan by his eye patch. His father will learn where he took the children and know he is bound for California. This one meeting may have ruined everything.

Gus speaks up, "Mr. Wellingham, how are you going to beat us to California with the wager?"

Wellingham stands and turns his gaze from the children to Gus and says, with a gentle chuckle, "You're not the only one in a hurry to change their life."

The original bank officer returns and gestures for the teams to come inside the bank. Keeping the children at his side, Donovan enters and finds a bank secretary leaning over a wide ledger on a desk with a small trunk positioned to his right.

Forming a single file line, each contestant deposits their wager money plus a percentage of Wellingham's passage fee into the trunk and states their name for the secretary to record beside a numerical figure. Frantic to disguise his true identity in case someone were to inspect the ledger, Donovan holds the children back until they are last. His puzzling pays off in an inspired flash.

He places the money pouch in the trunk and maintains a sober expression as he gives his alias—Dash Truepenny. Given his circumstances, the use of Lillia's pet name for him is crucial. The bank secretary's eyebrows lift at the unique moniker, but Donovan quickly guides the children out into the late afternoon sun just as the Yalies bellow, "To the *Night Call!*"

Prompted by their departure, the Bostonians eagerly gather around Hugh who grandly gestures and says, "Follow Samuel. He has the plan well in hand."

Luther hoists Quinn onto his shoulders and Donovan gathers Molly into his arms as the eager Bostonians mob behind Samuel. Making their way through several back alleys, Samuel veers the group toward the waterfront. They burst from a narrow street and are greeted by a forest of ship's masts. Samuel smiles and points.

"There she is, second from the right of the steamer."

It takes a moment for it to sink in and Gus caws first.

"What, we're on the same ship?"

"All of us," Hugh says, laughing. "But what the Yalies don't know is her captain has just learned of family trouble. He has changed his original route to see what he can do to help—in Baltimore."

As they run to board the ship, Wilton asks Samuel, "How did you know?"

"Once Benjamin told us about their passage arrangements on the *Night Call*, Hugh sent me to do reconnaissance. When I found the ship, I started conversations with some of the crew. Nice fellas, eager to get to California, only going to stop in Rio de Janeiro and Valparaíso. Said their ship hailed from New York City but their captain's home is in Baltimore. I got to thinkin' their captain needed a reason to stop there, even if it was just for a brief visit."

"But how'd—?"

"I penned an urgent note from his family and paid a kid to deliver it to the captain. As long as we pay him deck passage, we're Baltimore bound."

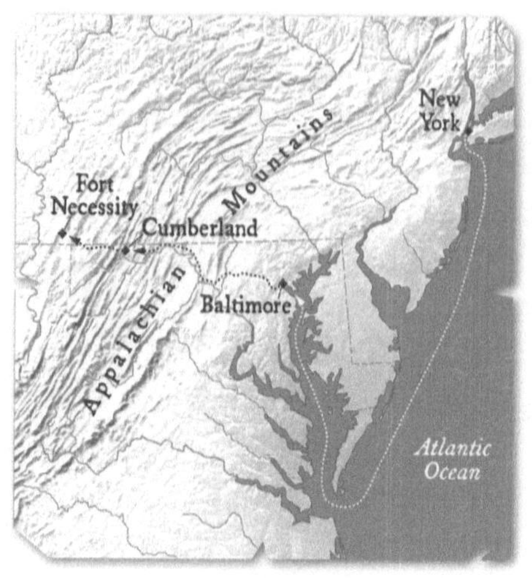

Chapter 3

APRIL, 1849

BALTIMORE, MARYLAND

A heavy cloak of fog greets the *Night Call* when they arrive at Baltimore's wharf. Donovan's sleepless night makes him groggy as he escorts the children to the address given in the "Missing Friends" advertisement scrap.

After his brisk knock and an inordinately long wait, a woman swings the door open and with it, the smells of a fish house. Pungent though it is, Donovan is sure the children are as hungry as he and hopes the woman will not only be the children's long-lost aunt but, out of gratitude, will offer them all sustenance.

To his utter devastation, he learns the children's aunt left for the West only a week before. Whoever this woman is, she wants nothing to do with two more mouths to feed. As the door shuts on them, he looks into the children's wasted faces, now blank of emotion. When the trio return to the Bostonians, one thing is clear: the children are not welcome to join the Bostonians' brotherhood. Hugh's firm statement is made quietly.

"Donnie, take them to the church. We've got to get going."

Donovan stares at the ground in turmoil. He may have rescued them from a life of hell with Kinkade but, without a refuge, his efforts, not to mention his own life-altering actions, will have been for naught.

"We are catching the B & O train to Cumberland. Don't miss it," Hugh says.

Donovan guides the children to the town's tallest building, its spire piercing the morning's low-hanging clouds. Around the church's side, he finds the priest's quarters and knocks on the door. When the door opens to reveal a portly middle-aged man, Donovan spills their whole story short of how close the children had come to being slaves to immorality.

To Donovan's relief, the priest tells him of the church's orphanage. When it is clear he is leaving them, the children grip his legs, a surprising but logical act given their brief association.

Trying to ease their fears with a quick appeasement, Donovan bends to their level and says softly, "Molly, Quinn, Father . . ."

Realizing he doesn't know the priest's name, his attempt is temporarily curbed until his puzzled expression prompts the priest to offer, "Father O'Leary."

"Father O'Leary is going to make sure you have food, clothes, and a warm bed. Then he'll find a family who will love and care for you. I'm sorry we missed your aunt. I'm certain you're in a better place than in Boston."

Turning to Father O'Leary, Donovan says, "Thank you, Father. They need so much, and I can't help them."

"Perhaps," Father O'Leary starts, his eyes downcast and crinkling gently, "your conscience would be eased by a donation?"

Donovan takes a ten-dollar coin from his money belt and hands it to the priest. As he rushes down the steps, he is grateful that no cries break through the liberating silence.

Donovan glances at his slumbering traveling partners, the westbound train's rhythmic sway having had its effect. Turning his gaze to the blur of the passing spring-greening countryside, he quietly ponders the life-changing decisions of the last forty-eight hours. Interestingly, relief and shame merge into justification. His father got what he deserved for resorting to such a horrific business.

He lifts the railcar's small window and welcomes the blessedly soft breeze across his scruffy whiskered face while it casually flips his hair's loose brown curls.

"Ah, the zephyr wind. It will be in our faces for the duration of our journey."

Donovan looks over his shoulder to see Hugh smiling while enjoying the same breeze.

"Zephyr?" Donovan asks.

"Yes, well, while you've been tapping out your Morse code dots and dashes, I've been buried in classical literature. Zephyr is Greek for the wind coming from the west. It's usually considered gentle and warm but could vary in aggressiveness. I think we should consider it a good omen, chum."

Donovan turns back and hears Hugh settling in the railcar's wooden bench with a series of thuds and thumps. He credits his friend's suggestion of joining the race for having saved his life, yet another debt of gratitude owed. He wonders how many debts a friend can stack up before he becomes a burden.

The town of Cumberland presents itself in early evening, the train's fluid sway slowly grinding to a halt at the station. Donovan's stomach pinches with hunger and he hopes the comfort of a bed will ease the kink in his neck. As the group leaves the railroad station, Wilton asks a passing lady for a boardinghouse recommendation. Smiling broadly, the woman points to the main road.

"Follow this road. There's a sign for Miss Myrtle Brownstone's. It's real clean and has good food."

At the boardinghouse, Wilton and Hugh inquire about accommodations while the rest wait outside. Countless wagons roll past, pulled by horses or oxen, most clearly preparing for westward travel.

Gus coughs out his disdain, saying, "That looks like mighty slow going to me."

Wilton and Hugh return to announce there are enough beds for everyone after Wilton fabricated the charade about Samuel being his personal man, requiring he stay with him. Donovan knows little of Wilton's arrangement with Samuel except that Samuel had handed over his own money for the race's wager.

Hugh and Donovan's room has two narrow beds with thin mattresses, yet they're decidedly plush after the ship's deck and the train seat. Before they are called to supper, Donovan lies down for a few moments, relaxing and stretching his neck and shoulders.

Kitchen smells saturate the dining room before Miss Myrtle and a young girl bring out bowls heaping with pot roast, potatoes, onions, carrots, gravy, and yeast rolls. After a quick blessing, the boarders filled their plates. Donovan looks around, noting that all look well-fed and from comfortable positions in life. He wonders if any are also running from demons or chasing dreams.

As soon as dessert is served, Hugh uses his spoon to direct Donovan's attention to Luther and an older man seated opposite them. The fellow shows all the signs of having led a difficult life. One of his most distinguishing features is an unruly thatch of white hair and an unusual scar running under each eye and across the bridge of his nose. His ruddy complexion suggests he spends his life in the elements and his thick, knotted fingers confirm a hard existence. The man looks away from Luther to address the others.

"My name is Zeke Bolton. Thought I had drivers and loaders lined up, but they're chasing the same elephant as you boys. Left me in a bind, they did. I imagine if I drove the lead wagon, a general knowledge of driving would be good enough. I'd consider a straight trade—all of you to Brownsville for help with loading and driving."

Donovan waits, wondering who will ask the group's burning question. Finally, Ezra blurts, "How long to get to Brownsville in a freight wagon compared to a stagecoach?"

"Can't go as fast as a stagecoach, loaded like we'll be."

Wilton scans the table before asking, "Speed is important to us, but what's a stagecoach going to cost?"

"A stagecoach'll cost about three dollars a person. But they stop in every town and hamlet. Of course, we'll have stops to rest the horses. Either way, it's seventy-five miles over mountains and through valleys. If we drive from sunup to sundown and take a one-hour break at noon, we'll be there in three, maybe four days. Stagecoach won't get you there much before. Won't have an outlay in food and lodging. I'll provide food and the wagons'll make a decent enough roof."

"What're you hauling?" Luther asks.

"Basic supplies, iron strapping, and nails for the merchants in Brownsville to make barrels and crates. Takin' some lighter sacks and bundles'll fill in the gaps so's the weight is distributed evenly. Easier on the animals that way."

"When will you be ready to leave?"

"If I can get drivers, in the morning. There's goods here in Cumberland still to be loaded, but once we're balanced, we're moving. With an early start, could be to Frostburg before noon."

"Give us a few minutes to talk it over?" Hugh asks.

"Sure, boys. I'll play a hand or two of cards before I lay down my head."

With that, the group leaves the table and heads to Hugh and Donovan's room to confer. On the way, Donovan asks Ezra about the old man's offer. His reply is pragmatic.

"As long as it gets us farther west, can't beat the price."

"If something goes wrong," Donovan counters, "we're obligated to him."

"We'd have the same problem if we took the stage, except we'd be helpless until another came along. Or we'd have to walk and have wasted our money. At least we'll have the equipment for a repair. Plus, no cost in lodging. That'll appeal to Gus."

As they enter the room, they find the debate in full swing, Wilton's voice raised above the others.

"I don't like giving up our freedom to move fast just to save money."

"What freedom?" Hugh asks. "We're at the whim of the stage schedule. Any problems along the way become ours. We could easily spend twice if we end up having to change stages in other towns."

Offering his words slowly, Luther says, "That kind of freight isn't goin' to bring much risk. We get the wagons balanced right, we should make good time."

"I say the benefits outweigh the risks," Gus says.

Donovan adds, "And boys, we better get comfortable with risk."

His comment ends the discussion. They take a quick vote and Hugh leaves to tell Mr. Bolton they will take him up on his offer.

Bolton's shrill whistle pierces the morning air, the massive horses' muscles tensing at his signal. Leaning into their harnesses, the immense freight wagons creak forward and lumber out of the warehouse yard toward the National Road. Between and among a baffling quantity of freight, the Bostonians find their seats and are westbound again.

Donovan's seat is on a nail barrel in the back of Samuel's third-in-line wagon. He feels the chill of a morning breeze on his face as the wagon crests the tree-covered hillside of the western Maryland wilderness. Rolling along on the National Road, he peers closely at the tightly fitted, crushed stones constituting the road's surface. Unlike the familiar Boston cobbles that would have shaken his teeth loose at this speed, this surface makes the ride as smooth as still water.

The approaching staccato clatter of shod hooves interrupts his observations. It's only the fourth day of his escape, and panic fills his mind. A posse of five riders race past the wagons. Samuel's team shies and the lumbering wagon lurches toward the road's unstable edge. A chill racks Donovan as it occurs to him these men are bounty hunters.

Gus, holding tight to the wagon seat next to Samuel, shouts at Donovan, "What was that about?"

"Don't know, went by too fast for much of a look."

The small wagon train rounds a bend and reveals an idyllic village, the sign announcing it's Frostburg. After stopping to rest the horses and stretch their legs, Bolton's shrill whistle slices through the air signaling their departure; the next stop is Grantsville.

Gus announces, "Bolton says it's another twelve miles ahead. We need to hurry so we don't pull in after dark."

Before the wagons pick up speed, a sudden commotion comes from a brick building in Frostburg's town square. Donovan recognizes the same mob of riders that had passed them earlier. The five men's long black coats flap as they run to mount their horses. They spur their horses aggressively back the way they had come, the horses' shoes scraping against the hard roadbed.

He feels a flush of relief. Every yard of distance between them eases his anxiety. And yet, the threat is real. He knows his father's relentless nature, and if he's caught and brought home, life will not be worth living.

As the afternoon wears on, the horses' pace slows which forces Bolton into more frequent stops. During this hiatus of quiet, Donovan hears the rush of water—like rapids, or maybe a waterfall.

Just as Bolton's departure whistle pierces his concentration and the wagons lumber forward, he hears the clatter of approaching horse hooves and calls out a warning.

"Coming up on your left, Samuel. The same crowd of riders."

"What the—"

Before Samuel can finish his sentence, the lead rider overtakes him and gestures to stop the wagon. Once all the wagons had been halted, the lead rider announces they are on the trail of a runaway and demand to search each wagon. Sure they are looking for him, Donovan's muscles tense and he decides he's not going without a fight.

With no alternative, Bolton motions for compliance. Samuel grips the horses' lines firmly while Gus and Donovan dismount and untie the load cover's securing ropes. Trying to conceal his identity for as long as possible, Donovan does his best to duck and dive scrutiny. He pulls back the canvas cover with shaking hands while surreptitiously scanning his surroundings trying to form an escape plan in this unfamiliar wilderness.

An alarm sounds from Bolton's wagon. The rider who had been watching Donovan spurs his horse toward the call.

Confused, Donovan leans over to see Bolton's wagon surrounded on three sides. The lead rider holds a pistol on Bolton who is struggling to control his horses against the noise and yelling.

Suddenly, a rag-clad boy bursts from under Bolton's wagon cover. He tears across the adjacent open field, legs churning wildly, his pale bare feet flying through the grass and mud. His surprise exodus affords the boy a brief advantage over the horsemen, but it isn't long before the hunters disappear from view behind a steep hillside.

Stunned by the incident and relieved he is not the bounty hunters' target, Donovan's legs wobble. He and Gus leave Samuel holding the horses' lines to confer with Bolton. They find the old man, rigid in his seat, thick fingers fidgeting aimlessly with his horses' lines.

"Mr. Bolton, shall we tie down and get started again?" Donovan asks.

"No use gettin' in too much of a hurry," Bolton spits out with agitation. "They'll be back. It'll take valuable time waiting, but I'd better answer those vermins' questions or face some kind of warrant."

"Sir," Hugh asks, "did you—"

Bolton waves off the question.

"Know what you're goin' to ask. The answer is no, I didn't know the boy was there. Guess he got in overnight. What'd I've done if I'd found him? Turn him in? I would not have. He might be twelve, thirteen at most."

Sticky silence hangs among them.

Bolton finally gestures with a flick of his left hand and says, "Make use of the time we're sitting here to give them horses a drink. There's a path to the river on the left of that bridge."

Each holding a leather feed bag, Hugh, Wilton, and Donovan scramble down the hillside.

Dipping into the water, Hugh asks, "What do you think has happened?"

In answer, a pair of gunshots pierce the afternoon calm. Donovan's head jerks up to see Hugh and Wilton's wide-eyed expressions. Water slops from the buckets as they rush back to the horses. It isn't long before the bounty hunters charge toward them, rigid in their saddles.

Donovan sees their frustrated expressions as they roughly heave back on the horse's reins. Mute, the riders fan out among the wagons.

When a rider approaches Gus, he spits, "Did you do what you came to do?"

"The louse got what was comin' to him," the rider snarls. "Teach him to run off and leave his responsibilities to the others."

"Are you paid to hunt him down?"

"Nah, don't get paid less'en we bring them back alive. We got our shots off and waited to make sure he didn't come up. Boss'll catch hell from the master." He shrugs. "Don't come home empty much but it happens."

The leader hails his posse. The men wheel their horses around in the opposite direction and ride away. As they pass, Donovan thinks of his brothers—unpleasant men in an unsavory occupation.

"Did they give you any trouble?" Gus asks Bolton.

"Not much. Said I should be more careful," Bolton snaps. "Tell you what, let's get a mite farther down the road. There's a stable where we can unhitch and water the horses. This distraction has rested the animals, but the drivers deserve an early break. Won't be but another mile or so. It's not Grantsville, but not far off the mark."

The Bostonians unharness and water the horses at the abandoned corral and stables while Bolton builds a cooking fire and prepares their supper. When their chores are done, they gather around the fire.

"Boys, you gotta believe I had no idea that young'un had stowed away. In all my freighting days, nothin' like it . . . I can't believe those fellas shot him. Guess he didn't hold enough value to keep up their hunting."

After a moment, Wilton says, "I'm betting they missed. I'll lay money down the kid got away."

"I agree with Wilton," Donovan says. "From where they shot, the gun's ball wouldn't have the velocity to kill, especially after hitting the water."

"Hope he kept his wits about him," Ezra says.

"Are we crossing the river again, Mr. Bolton?" Wilton asks. "Maybe we can find the kid's body and give it a proper burial?"

"Nope, headed north tomorrow. Need to get to the Youghiogheny River ferry. Whether we cross the river tomorrow or the next morning will depend on traffic. If we keep up today's pace, disregarding the interruption, we'll make Brownsville in three more days."

While they wait for supper to cook, the Bostonians set up their bedrolls under the wagons. The day's warmth fades with the dusk, foretelling a chilly first night under the wagons. Back at the fire, Donovan joins the others in devouring Bolton's bacon, biscuits, and dried fruit. While not the quality of food he is used to, he's satisfied enough to rest.

Retiring for the night, it isn't long before the forest throbs with snores emanating from under Bolton's wagon. Joining his comrades under the other two wagons, Donovan is grateful for the distance.

"Anyone want to bet on the kid surviving?" Luther asks in a low voice.

"I'll take you two-to-one he made it," Hugh says.

"But how are we ever going to know?" asks Ezra.

Luther winks. "I have a feeling if he found us one time, he'll look to hitch on with us again. Just you watch."

Later that night, while Bolton's snorts shred the night's stillness, Donovan wakes to a different sound. Footsteps? Craning his neck toward Bolton's wagon, he catches a brief glimpse of a ghostly white foot lifting off the ground. He considers investigating but realizes he doesn't need to—the kid is back.

Donovan awakes to the pristine silence of the forest—for the first time in nine hours.

Approaching the wagon master, the old man looks up and says, "Cold one last night. S'pose nights'll warm as you boys head west."

Donovan nods. As he tosses broken sticks at the fire, he asks, "What do you think the odds are that the runaway survived his ordeal yesterday?"

"Oh, don't know. Guess it'd depend on how much strength he had after all the running. If he was fresh, say, a day or so from escaping, he might'a been strong enough to swim the river, if he wasn't hit."

"What would you do if we were to come upon him again?"

After a brief hesitation, Bolton sighs and says, "Guess my perspective's different than most. I indentured myself to find this country's promise. My sister and me. She died on our way over. Since I owed for both passages, I had to work twice as long. Given his desperate jump from the cliff—I s'pose I'd have pity on him. He'll be written off as a bad debt when them bounty hunters make their report. Good enough for me."

Heartened by his response, Donovan confides, "Sir, I believe we've a fugitive among us—again."

The old man looks up, his eyes wide with disbelief while cracking a crooked grin. "You don't say. You was checkin' if we were thinking the same, eh? I reckon we'd best get him warmed up."

Walking toward the lead wagon, they decide a casual, but louder than normal, conversation about a warm breakfast would be the best lure. Donovan talks about the bounty hunters boasting they had killed the boy. While loosening the canvas cover, Bolton continues with an offering of sanctuary if they were to come upon him. Their strategy works like a charm.

Thumps come from the wagon's front corner. When the canvas cover begins to ripple, the men share a grin. Timidly, the boy peeks out.

"They's gone, really? Gived up on me?"

"Yeah, son," Bolton says, "you have nothing to fear from us."

The boy scoots onto the wagon's tailgate and dangles his feet, a quiet struggle for trust raging across his face. His decision made, he reaches for his torn right sleeve, cautiously peeling the fabric back. An ugly slash of red shows where the bullet had grazed his mouse-shaped bicep.

Bolton leans in too hastily to inspect and the boy leaps off the tailgate, ready to sprint. Bolton holds up both hands in surrender and says, "Whoa now. Just wanting to see to you."

The boy scowls even as he cautiously offers his arm. Following a quick examination, Bolton fetches a small leather sack containing a generous pile of soft rags and a square tin.

He treats the wound with brown salve, wraps it in a clean bandage, and orders, "Now for the feet."

Becoming more trusting by the minute, the boy produces his left foot first. Donovan is shocked to see the skin of the boy's sole hanging in rotting shreds. Rather than gawk at the putrid sight, he leaves to check the fire and his companions.

He finds Luther stretching his large torso with gusto in the building fire's warmth. After a few minutes, Hugh, Ezra, and Gus arrive after having fed the horses. Samuel and Wilton are the last to make their sleepy faces present at the fireside.

"Hugh," Donovan calls with a grin, "how much was your bet last night?"

Their curiosity piqued, they follow him and find the boy, his expression set with stubborn determination. Bolton grips his foot, slathers brown goo onto his sole, and then wraps it to match the other dangling foot.

"What happened to your feet?" Donovan asks.

"Lime dust. Ate through my shoes, before startin' in on my feet."

Proudly, Bolton says, "Let's see you walk in those bandages."

The boy scoots off the gate, wincing with anticipated pain. But the bandages soften the ground's blow. He takes tentative steps before relaxing and nodding in gratitude.

"Much better, sir."

"Well, boys, meet our newest member," Bolton announces. "Don't want to know his real name, so I suggest we call him Homer."

The boy thinks for a bit before saying, "Feels good on me, I'll take it."

The Bostonians and Bolton hitch the horse to the wagons before heading toward the Youghiogheny River ferry. As they finish loading the wagons, Homer pulls Donovan to the side.

"Mind if'n I ride under the canvas? Don't want no one seein' me, if you take my meanin'."

Donovan nods toward the wagon and says, "I understand more than you'll ever know."

Bolton's departure whistle snaps the teams into the morning's traffic. By early afternoon, they join the serpentine line of westbound travelers at the Youghiogheny River ferry. The air is filled with the din of vendors hawking wares, laughing children, and barking dogs. When the ferry operator calls for the next wagon to board, a cacophony of impatient commotion erupts as the travelers organize themselves.

Bolton's wagons are forced to wait until late afternoon for their turn to cross. When their lead wagon drives onto the ferry, Donovan is alarmed when the wagon's weight submerges the ferry deck to its edge in the river's current. One false move will be catastrophic. Despite Donovan's concerns, Bolton's wagon crosses followed by Luther's, and neither are lost. But when Samuel slaps the horses' lines for their wagon to board the ferry, panic rises in Donovan's chest. He hears the ferry workers' groans and labored breathing as they pull the heavily braided guide rope. He forces himself to look at the passing scenery rather than dwell on the uncertainty of their circumstances.

Realizing he had been holding his breath, Donovan gasps for air when the ferry slams into the opposite dock signaling their arrival. Samuel expertly drives his team off and joins the others. They continue down the road until the green expanse of Fort Necessity lay before them.

Bolton's whistle signals their halt before he hollers, "We're here, boys!"

In the old fort's meadow, the wagons form a crescent with enough room to unhitch the teams. While Bolton sets up the fire ring, the Bostonians fall into their chore routine. Occupied with their work, only Bolton notices another company of wagons pull up across the creek from them.

Following their supper, Bolton makes his way to the wagon company. Donovan watches him address a man he assumes is the company leader, returning later to satisfy the Bostonians' curiosity.

"Seems these folks are headed to the same place as you boys. Going to be plenty crowded in California."

"Are they driving their wagons all the way?"

Bolton raises a skeptical eyebrow at Gus's question and replies, "Said they are boarding a steamer, wagons and all, that'll take them to St. Louis."

"How many wagons are in their train?" Wilton asks.

"Eight families in all, been on the road for a week. Best get to checking our wagons for grease before the light quits us."

Donovan sets up the horses' picket line while the others perform the necessary checks and lubrications. Distracted by the adjacent families' chatter and activities, Donovan stops his work and focuses on the closest one.

A young woman, with her back to him, vigorously chops something. The mass of auburn hair piled on her head wobbles from her effort. He sees a tall fellow sneak up on her and slip his arms around her waist, burying his face into the nape of her neck. Her shriek becomes laughter as she turns to embrace him.

Turning away, Donovan is suddenly overcome with loneliness for Lillia. Counting on his fingers, he realizes tonight would have been their wedding night. Her haunting image fills his mind, and he wonders what she is doing in the wake of his departure. Certain his father had no compunction against interrogating Lillia and her parents about his whereabouts, he cringes at the thought.

His note had asked her not to reveal his destination. All too familiar with his father's manipulations and torments, Donovan prays Lillia had the fortitude to keep his secret. But Lillia was the strongest woman he had ever been around, her staunch integrity a trait he genuinely admired. She knew how his father had treated him. She would protect him. Even if she might not ever see him again.

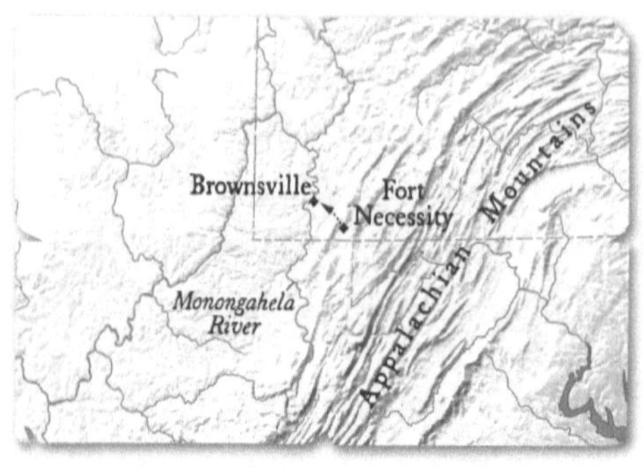

Chapter 4

APRIL, 1849

FORT NECESSITY, PENNSYLVANIA

At dawn, Donovan rolls out from under the wagon and heads toward the creek, a bucket in his hand. The early morning mist whispers into his face as he submerges the bucket into the water. His gaze casually follows the water's path until he sees he is being observed by another at the same chore. Recognizing the tall man who had loved on the auburn-haired woman the night before, Donovan nods before turning to leave. The tall man speaks in a low muted tone.

"Say there, a word?"

Halted by the question, Donovan slowly turns.

"Certainly."

The stranger asks, "What are you hauling there?"

"Materials for the tradesmen in Brownsville," Donovan replies.

"You work for the freighter?"

"We're trading our labor for passage to Brownsville. Heading to California from there."

The stranger chuckles, "So are we. Where's home?"

"Boston area. You?"

With a quick hand gesture the stranger says, "Some are from the country east of Cumberland, most are from Baltimore."

At the mention of Baltimore, Donovan's mind's eye flashes back to the newspaper advertisement, the fish woman telling him the children's aunt had left a week ago, and finally, the look of despair on Quinn and Molly's faces as he left them on the church's doorstep.

When he realizes his long pause, he asks, "What's your route to California?"

"Leader says the best time'll be made by taking a steamer from Brownsville down the Ohio, over to the Mississippi and north to St. Louis. We'll be on the steamer for a month. Then it's across the great western wilderness. You?"

"Not sure. Waiting to see what our options are in Wheeling. My name's Donovan O'Creigh. Call me Donnie."

The tall man offers his hand.

"Wallace Gutherie. Friends call me Ace. You are goin' overland from Brownsville to Wheeling?"

"Yep, we're in a hurry," Donovan replies.

"I do like the idea of speed but couldn't convince my girl to travel light. Has to have her things. After cuddling up last night, I don't regret the compromise."

Ace flashes a wink and a mischievous smile before asking, "How did you get your eye patch?"

"I'd had a fever, then things went blurry. I couldn't stand without dizziness; doctor's only solution is to keep it covered. Folks still stare, but I've had time to get used to it."

"Just curious. Nora says if I don't tend my curiosity, it'll be my ruin."

"Nora?" Donovan asks.

"My wife."

Donovan nods slowly, his mind suddenly engaged, before saying, "I'd better get back. We'll be breaking camp soon."

"Me too. Nora'll be wondering what happened to our coffee water."

Ace gives another wink and leaves. Donovan watches him go as a flush of recognition rushes through him—the name from the newspaper advertisement!

Could there be two Noras from Baltimore?

Back at the breakfast campfire, Donovan shares his new information about St. Louis being a month away by river. When the Bostonians cast side glances, Bolton offers his opinion.

"Considering how far you'll get by river, a month ain't much. Steamer'll be expensive. Wonder if piloting a flatboat down the Ohio wouldn't be a better fit."

Hugh asks, "What can you tell us about piloting a flatboat?"

"Nothin' to it. Stay in the river's middle, steer clear of sawyers, shoals, and steamers. No complicated equipment . . . only a rudder, two poles, and two sweeps for steering. And you can travel at night when there's a full moon. Night traveling will guarantee you got the place to yourselves. Steamers don't dare navigate at night."

Bolton pauses to look at the Bostonians' faces, a conspiratorial grin spreading across his face before he says, "Here's the ringer . . . for the money you'll spend owning a flatboat, someone in Memphis'll pay the same, if not more, for its lumber. You could haul freight too. Sell it all in Memphis and buy tickets on a St. Louis-bound steamer. Something to think about."

Bolton tosses the contents of his cup into the grass and packs up.

"Going through Unionville today. Looking to sleep in a proper bed tonight, all of us, my treat. Brownsville will be tomorrow and you boys will take off from there."

Eager to be on their way, the Bostonians rush to pack up and hitch the teams to the wagons. Once they are rolling down the road, Donovan sees the Baltimore company wagons fall in behind them like obedient children. They travel all day with no event except for the developing bank of dark clouds boiling in from the west.

Unionville, Virginia, reminds Donovan of Cumberland. Vibrant merchants, intent upon capitalizing on the westbound emigrants, preside over shops bulging with necessities, their tempting displays spilling out through open doors. At a stable on the city's outskirts, Bolton dismounts and ambles to the Baltimore company's lead wagon, the late afternoon light casting his shadow in long light. From his position, Donovan easily overhears Bolton's plan.

"Stabling our horses here and spending the night in one of the town's boardinghouses. Farther through town, there's a field where you can camp. Intend on leaving here at dawn to get to Brownsville by noon tomorrow. What I'm sayin' is, if you want to continue with us, watch for us driving by at first light tomorrow mornin'."

Once the Baltimore company passes by, Bolton arranges for the horses to be boarded in the livery before directing the Bostonians.

"You boys unhitch the horses, store the harnesses inside and then meet me and Homer at the boardinghouse across the street."

When they arrive at the boardinghouse, they are pleased Bolton has arranged for everyone to have their own bed. They also learn Homer has had a bath and received a new set of clothes, including boots, one size larger to accommodate his bandaged feet. Impressed by Bolton's generosity, Donovan becomes more curious about Bolton's childhood and what brought him to the life of a freighter.

Bolton's abrupt rap on their door jolts Donovan and Hugh from their deep sleep. Slow to rise, they join the others outside the boardinghouse, where they are greeted by a fine mist and Bolton sipping coffee.

"Picked a good night to sleep indoors. Afraid today's traveling is going to be miserable. Best invest in hats and overcoats, boys. They'll likely come in handy in your travels."

After the Bostonians make their purchases, they quickly hitch the wagons and set out, the Baltimore company falling in line behind them. Donovan sees everyone has their rain gear on and offers a wave to Ace, who grins widely out from under his dripping hat brim. When Nora is nowhere to be seen, Donovan assumes she has opted to stay dry in the wagon's bed.

It rains all day and the traveling is slow. When they arrive at Brownsville, the clouds are lifting and the late afternoon sun makes steam rise from the road. Bolton pulls into a warehouse area, dismounting to talk to the Baltimore company leader.

"There's a good spot over by Redstone Creek. From there, you can take the road to Pittsburgh and catch the next steamer to St. Louis."

Ace drives his team past Donovan and leans out.

"Nora'll cook you and a friend supper, if you're of a mind to find us."

Donovan nods and says, "That'd be my pleasure."

The Bostonians spend the rest of the day's light unloading Bolton's wagons. Before they leave to shop for horses, tack, and supplies for their cross-country ride, Homer announces he has decided to go with the Bostonians to Wheeling. Bolton is visibly disappointed.

"Guess you'll be needing a horse and some tack. Let's get you set up."

"Why do you bother with a boy like me?"

"When I finished my indenture, a man gave me a hand up. I wouldn't be where I am today without his kindness. Hope you'll do the same when the time comes."

Finished with their shopping, Donovan and Hugh leave to find the Baltimore company. The roads are slick with deep mud and potholes and the creek is swollen. Its soft earthen banks slough off into the current.

At the confluence of Redstone Creek and the Monongahela River, they follow the creek's precarious bank. Donovan approaches the water's edge and washes the mud from his boots but hesitates when he sees the water's fomented state. An odd sound makes him look across the muddy, roiling water. Donovan turns back to Hugh, his head cocked confirming they both heard the odd sound over the raging water's rolling rumble.

Higher on the bank than Donovan, Hugh sees an arm waving above the water's wakes and yells, "Someone's fallen in! We're their only chance!"

Donovan, his muscles tensing under his girth, feels a rush of energy.

"Hurry! Cut a tall sapling. I'll go after them."

Hugh races toward the forest, while Donovan pulls off his boots, his bare feet tingling in the cold, muddy water as his toes grip tight to the smooth river stones. Pushing aside his earlier concerns, he steps into the swirling water, the current instantly ripping at his legs. Ten feet from the bank, the swirling water goes from his ankles to his thighs.

Hugh returns with a sapling, extending its trunk to Donovan's outstretched hands. Holding the sapling over his head, he scans the water's roiling surface. Seconds later, he sees flailing arms coming toward him. He inches out against the water's aggressive pull until only a few yards separate them. He lowers the sapling from above his head and extends it toward the passing person.

"Here! Grab hold!"

Close enough now to see a woman, her acknowledging eyes widen with fear. She shifts toward him, outstretched fingers spread desperately toward the sapling's leaved branches. The sapling's leaves drape like a curtain between them and he only knows her grab is successful when her momentum threatens his balance.

The woman's weight slowly pulls the sapling through his grip, and the branch stubs on the sapling's trunk lacerate his palms. He releases the sapling only after he feels her arms wrap around his ample torso. Reaching his arms around her shoulders, he instantly knows her.

"Nora!" he says.

She struggles against the current, mumbling, "I must . . . I must . . ."

"Hold still. I'll get us to shore!"

"No! Wait, I must . . ."

When an enormous weight lifts, Donovan wonders if she has succumbed. Then he sees her calico skirt balloon and swirl gaily away in the somber current.

Her thick Irish accent blossoms when she exclaims, "Now we be makin' some progress. Good riddance to tha' damn skirt! Almost got us killed."

With Nora still clinging tight, he wades from the waist deep water toward Hugh's waiting hands. Suddenly, Nora stops and stares at Hugh.

"'Fore I leave the drink, might I 'ave your coat?"

Donovan frantically waves for Hugh to give up his coat. Shirking it off, Hugh hands the coat to Donovan, who holds it up while Nora slips her arms into the sleeves. Satisfied, they continue their struggle up the creek bank.

Once they are on solid ground, Hugh rushes away, leaving Donovan and Nora to collapse with exhaustion. Breathing heavily, Donovan rolls his head toward Nora, who is on her back, her pantaloon-covered legs and booted feet sticking immodestly out from under Hugh's coat.

He turns away until he hears Hugh's excited voice exclaim, "Here they are!"

A rush of footfalls crash through the bushes and Donovan sees Ace standing over them with a wide smile on his face.

"Woman, how am I going to keep you if you insist on taking off your skirts in front of other men?"

His clothes cling and hang like weighted sacks as Donovan squish squashes beside Ace to the campfire, Hugh and Nora following close behind. When Nora disappears to change, Ace offers Donovan a blanket to wrap up in while draping his wet clothes over a bush to dry. When Nora returns, Ace asks the pertinent question.

"Wife, how did you come to be bobbing down the creek today?"

"Lost me footin' when I was a goin' for a bucket o' water. Shoulda never gotten close, once I saw its murky nature."

Donovan sees Nora's gaze suddenly shift.

"Oh, the bucket . . ."

Ace wraps her in a hug, saying, "Don't worry. You gave our babe its first taste of swimming. You're a strong gal. I'm proud of your quick thinking, but I'm equally beholden to our courageous friends here."

Nora wipes the tears from her eyes with her apron and turns to Donovan and Hugh.

"If you'll stay for supper, I'll be gettin' right to it. Ace'll spin some of his tales for you."

"Only if you'll let us help get some fresh water for supper," Hugh says.

"Let's see if we can borrow a water bucket from someone," Ace says.

The two leave Donovan to feed the cook fire while Nora deftly cleaves off thick slices from a whole ham.

"How is it that you have ham?" he asks.

Tossing her words over her shoulder, Nora replies, "Ace cured a couple for us. Need to finish 'em 'fore St. Louis. Me mum taught me two lessons . . . eatin' well brings a healthy babe, an' a man whose belly's full is a sight more agreeable to a woman's asks."

He observes Nora as she prepares their meal, the unruly curls of her piled hair fall in wavy wisps around her face and shoulders. Quick and confident in her skills, she smiles at him. With that simple expression, Molly and Quinn flash into his memory.

Could she be . . . ?

Before he can ask, Ace and Hugh return.

Setting a full bucket of water down at her feet Ace says, "Here you go. There's plenty so you aren't tempted to go for another swim. Donnie, let's warm by the fire while Nora works her magic."

At the fire, Ace spins his tales. Nora chimes in as she moves to and from the cooking fire, adding, ". . . lost me whole family, save a sister. Hoped she'd make the trip, but I'd not heard nary a thing from her 'fore we left Baltimore."

Donovan's expression goes passive, her words confirming the familial tie he had suspected. When Nora serves the men their meal, Donovan eats quietly while Hugh and Ace exchange stories.

". . . that's when Donnie here waded out into the murk and fished Nora out with the sapling. Still can't believe she held on!"

Shy at Hugh's words, Donovan stands to take his plate to the rinse bucket, saying, "Thank you for supper, Nora. Ham is a delicious treat."

He leaves the campfire to change into his damp clothes. When he returns and hands Ace the blanket, Ace shakes his free hand.

"I owe you a debt of gratitude."

Donovan replies, "Hope it isn't the last time we share a campfire."

"Good luck to you, fellas. Safe travels and don't take all the gold before we get there."

Stepping into the near black darkness, Hugh and Donovan hurry back to the boardinghouse.

Between steps, Hugh asks, "Donnie, what made you go after her?"

Donovan is quiet for a moment.

"Honestly, Hugh, I'm not sure where the courage came from. Same as when I saved those children in Boston. It just came over me."

"The boys aren't ever going to believe this story!"

Donovan laughs with him and says, "I doubt they will."

Surrounded by the din of music and laughter from Brownsville's saloons and dance halls, Donovan puzzles on the question nagging his consciousness. Why could he find the courage to save Nora but not to ask her about her niece and nephew?

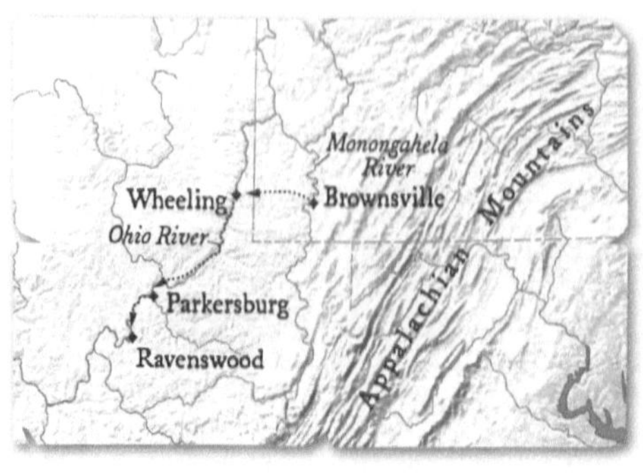

Chapter 5

APRIL, 1849

BROWNSVILLE, PENNSYLVANIA

Lively debates fill the two-day horse ride from Brownsville to Wheeling. At the heart of them is making their choice between taking a steamer versus piloting their own flatboat. Their impasse centers on two divergent but related priorities: expense and timing. Forced to compromise until they get to Wheeling, the group rises early on their last leg of the trip.

They arrive with enough light to stable their horses, secure rooms at a boardinghouse, and answer their dilemma once and for all. Splitting into two groups, Donovan joins Gus and Ezra to explore the flatboat idea while Hugh, Samuel, Luther, and Wilton inquire about steamer information. When they rendezvous for dinner at the boardinghouse, Hugh starts with a disappointed admonition.

"The steamer is expensive, but even more important, we'll have to wait around for the next one bound for Memphis."

"Not only will we have a three-day wait," Wilton adds, "there's no guarantee there'll be room for us."

Gus shares his team's better news.

"We found a flatboat builder who has offered to let us buy one for the combined value of our horses if we'll help him finish the four boats he has under construction."

The flatboat choice is undeniable and, thankfully, uncontested.

Their arrival the next morning is met with the ear-splitting noise of ringing hammers and mallets even before they crest the bank above the flatboat construction site. They find the owner, Bert Smythe, a heavy canvas apron stretched across his wide girth, already barking orders at his laborers. Donovan sees the four vessels under construction, the men working at a feverous pace. After introductions, Gus is the first to initiate.

"What's our role, Mr. Smythe?"

Smythe wags a callus-encrusted finger at two wide-bedded wagons opposite the group, their longer-than-normal bed designed for hauling great lengths.

"If you can keep those full of lumber and rolling in regularly, we'll make quick time."

"Where's the mill?"

"A mile down the road. Ideally, as soon as one is unloaded, the next one needs to be pulling in full. Four of you drive and three stay here to unload to the workers."

Samuel and Luther immediately assume their roles, Gus and Wilton joining them. After the wagons leave, Smythe motions to Hugh, Ezra, and Donovan.

"While you're waiting, I'll show you around."

They struggle to match Smythe's long strides and pass several smaller construction activities. At an enormous pile of cut saplings, Smythe motions to the men aggressively stripping off the bark.

"Support studs as well as poles, sweep, and rudder handles."

Continuing to the flatboat construction site, they find two boats flipped and floating in the river shallows. Men are pounding hemp cording into the plank cracks with blunted mallets before applying a generous amount of thick, waterproofing resin. As the group passes, Donovan's foot slips and he stumbles into a resin pot, the hot resin spilling onto a worker's hand. After a howl of pain, the worker irrationally lunges toward Donovan. Just as quickly, Smythe's massive hand shoots out, gripping the worker's neck.

"'Twas an accident, fool. No need to unhinge. Soak your hand in the river for a few minutes. Then get back to work."

Releasing his grip, Smythe leaves the worker gasping and shooting an angry side-eye toward Donovan. Hardly older than the Bostonians, the young man's expression is a smear of anger and despair. He has unusual scars that splotch across his face and neck while uneven tufts of hair stick out from under a worn knit cap. Familiar with public embarrassment himself, Donovan hesitates, searching for words to apologize, but finds none.

Just as Smythe shows the Bostonians where to stack the planks for easy access for each boat's foreman, the first wagon pulls up and they rush to work. By midday, stripped to their undershirts and suspenders, Donovan stops to wipe his brow, wincing at Hugh.

"Have you ever worked this hard?"

"Honestly? Never. I'm a pastor's son. My father only required me to do house chores."

"Me neither. My mother would faint away if she saw me working like this."

After lunch, the rate of delivery slows. By quitting time, the last two boats are ready to flip. The Bostonians watch as the eighteen-by-seventy-foot structures are lifted up and over, using levers and ropes. The workers call to each other as the tension shifts from one side to the opposite, before the flat surfaces spank against the water signaling success.

The Bostonians share grins all around. While tired from the unfamiliar physical exertion, Donovan joins the others on their walk back to the boardinghouse with pride swelling in his chest. After all the years of being told he was incapable of labor, he wishes Lillia could see him now.

Bolton's suggestion for hauling income-producing goods has completely taken root in the Bostonians' minds. At the supper table that night, they discuss what freight they should float to Memphis.

"What about lumber? It can't spoil and it's bound to be valuable," Luther suggests.

The boardinghouse host enters with another bowl of potatoes and overhears their discussion.

He says, "I've got a farmer friend who has some baled wool he'd sell you. Probably has other goods like bacon, barreled pork, apples, potatoes, maybe some beans. I can ask him when we see each other tomorrow, if you'd like."

Grinning at their good fortune, the Bostonians nod and accept his offer.

Over the next two days, their responsibilities shift from lumber deliveries to cording and resining planks to hauling clay to seal the cabins' floors. Between their chores, they purchase fifty ten-foot planks and all the farmer's wool and farm goods. At the end of the third day, Smythe approaches the exhausted Bostonians.

"Well, fellas, tomorrow we'll install the stove and its pipe, the hawser cleat, the rudder mount, and the sweep locks. Once those are done, the boat's all yours."

"Mr. Smythe, we've got lumber and freight to round up. May we borrow the wagons after work tomorrow?" Luther asks.

"Happy to help. Couldn't have finished so fast without you boys."

That night at the supper table, Wilton asks their host about navigating on the Ohio River.

"Check with Rot McNally at the mercantile. He's old but used to run the river regularly. He'll have some advice."

Homer arrives to remove plates when Gus asks, "Homer, what are your plans?"

Waiting until the boardinghouse host leaves, Homer says quietly, "I'm . . . I'm stayin' here. Folks've offered me a job. Beats the lime pits! I think they like me."

The Bostonians raise their glasses to his news but only Donovan notices the boy's hesitant grin.

By noon, the Bostonians have finished all the installations. Assignments in hand, they scramble into action. As part of their original agreement with Smythe, Hugh and Donovan bring the horses to his corral and load their tack on the boat. Samuel and Luther take the others in the wagons and head to the lumber yard and the farmer. By evening, the flatboat is loaded including, to everyone's surprise, four kegs of whiskey purchased by Wilton. When eyebrows raise, Wilton tries to explain.

"You never know, boys, these may become as valuable to us as the lumber."

With their wealth loaded, they plan to spent the night aboard. Ezra and Gus go to the boardinghouse to fetch the group's belongings, returning with Homer. He is full of questions and observations as he explores the boat, and Donovan notes a shine in the boy's eyes when he strokes the smooth wood of the rudder's great arc. He wonders if the boy is having second thoughts.

Once Homer leaves, they review their supplies. Donovan is relieved to see that Luther, Wilton, and Gus have all purchased weapons: one rifle and two pistols. Gus also produces a lantern and curiously, a grappling hook.

"The man at the mercantile said a lantern will help other boats see us if we run into fog. And the hook? Seems to me like a good idea, just in case."

Donovan leans in to Luther.

"Did anyone get river advice from the fellow at the mercantile?"

"All McNally said was to keep in the river's deepest part and we'll make out just fine."

Satisfied with his reassurance, Donovan, Samuel, and Wilton bed down on the boat's deck while the others take advantage of the cabin's four interior cots.

Restless all night, Donovan is jerked awake by a faint splash in dawn's foggy light, initially discounting the sound as a fish rising. Curiosity overwhelms him and he takes a quick peek over the boat's railing, which reveals nothing unusual, and he turns back. Just as he turns, an abrupt rush of air whistles past his temple followed by the clatter of an object shooting across the boat's deck. Cautiously rising above the railing's edge, he surveys in the shoreline's direction and sees the twisted face of the angry resin worker through wisps of fog.

Indignant, Donovan hisses, "What is wrong with you?"

The worker's reply sends chills up Donovan's spine.

"Best ask the question of yourself. Ain't nothin' you and your like can do 'bout it now. You are goin' to be in for a wild ride, for sure, you fat ol' dandy boy!"

With that, the worker vanishes into the shoreline's thicket, the fog providing ample cover. After a frenzied search of the deck, Donovan finds a broken mallet handle and is puzzling over the object and the worker's oblique threat when the rest of the Bostonians gather around.

Unnerved, Luther whispers, "Let's shove off. We've got enough light to get a head start on these other flatboats."

Agreeing, everyone is spurred into activity. Given the fog, Gus proudly produces his lantern, announcing, "Who knew we'd have to use it so soon?"

The lantern's amber glow produces only a dull smolder against the dense fog. Warning bells ring in Donovan's mind and he wonders if they are being manipulated into rushing their departure regardless of the hazardous conditions.

Before he can voice his concerns, the hawser's loop is off the dock post. Luther and Ezra stab the guide poles into the river's soft sediment and heave the flatboat toward the river's current. Donovan feels the flatboat's bottom leave the silty riverbank and they are free.

"Wait! Wait!"

Through the shrouds of fog, Homer appears, a knapsack bouncing on his shoulder, hobbling toward them. Luther and Ezra make a futile effort to halt the boat's progress by poling against the boat's forward momentum, but the current has taken hold.

Focused on Homer, a slight movement catches Donovan's attention. His eye follows a thin cord rising out of the water. He traces one end to the massive dock post they had just left. Slowly rising, he sees the other end looped around the weak junction of their rudder paddle and the rudder arm. When the cord's slack is used up, it will tear the rudder apart. Now he understands what was meant by "a wild ride."

Homer waves frantically toward them, only a few feet from the dock post where the cord is tied. Instantly, Donovan knows Homer is their only hope to avoid sure disaster.

"Homer, cut the cord! See it? There, tied to the dock post! Cut it or it will rip our rudder off. Please, Homer! Find something and cut it!"

Donovan's words skip across the water's surface like stones, and he only knows Homer has heard them when he sees Homer slowly turn toward the dock post. His eyes turn and with agonizing sloth, follow the cord as its tautness builds. Finally, he drops his knapsack and fumbles with the knot before producing a large kitchen knife.

Donovan watches Homer, knife poised, stare out at the flatboat, his face etched with regret. The flatboat is now in the firm grip of the river's current, the straining cord fully visible through the wispy fog. Now that the implications are clear to everyone, the air bursts with urgent calls. With a deliberate downward arc, Homer's knife cuts through the cord, his action producing a high-pitched ting.

A cheer ricochets off the blanketing fog. Donovan sees Homer triumphantly raise his arms before he sags to the ground in defeat.

Rather than technique or experience, nervous tension navigates the Bostonians to the river's center. Hugh mans the rudder from the cabin's roof, Donovan and Ezra take the poles, Wilton and Luther are at the sweeps, and Samuel finds his place at the bow on lookout while Gus keeps the coffee coming from inside. The fog lifts after several hours, and they're alone on the vast plane of slow-moving water.

Hugh calls out confidently, "Bolton's right, there's nothing to this!"

His bravado is shattered by an unseen steamer's whistle and the Bostonians scramble to attention, frantic for their first encounter. With excruciating slowness, the flatboat lumbers to the right shore while everyone focuses on the twin billows of black smoke rising above the treetops.

When an oxbow in the river forces the majestic steamer to swing wide, the Bostonians can only gawk at its comparative scale. The steamer's pair of paddle wheels, mounted on opposite railings, create twin troughs that fan into an alarming wedge behind the vessel.

Donovan quickly notes the danger and is sure their humble craft won't stand a chance against getting swamped if the wake hits directly. As Luther and Wilton strain on their sweeps, the massive steamer passes without acknowledgment to the flatboat's presence. When the lumbering wake hits them, the flatboat creaks through the rough pitch and roll. Everyone finds a grip and holds tight, only daring to breathe when the flatboat returns to level. Only after the steamer is well beyond them does a celebratory cheer rise up.

Ezra yells, "I hope they're all that uneventful!"

"Did you see the power coming from those paddle wheels?" Wilton exclaims.

Donovan silently watches the steamer disappear around the river bend, his mind filled with the wonder of it.

As they work their way back to the river's center, Donovan shifts his attention to the untamed flow of the current. Nothing keeping it or restraining it, just free to flow at its own pace. A new feeling suddenly washes over him, one he doesn't ever remember feeling—freedom. He has no one monitoring him, yelling at him, telling him what to do. He is choosing his own direction, deciding how his time is spent. He owes no one anything, except to be a contributing member of this team. It is a feeling he could get used to.

He turns his face to the warm sunlight with renewed spirit, willing it to burn away the worn shell of his past life. He knows he will never go back.

When the visages of his mother, Nell, and Lillia fill his mind's eye, a twinge of despair twists through him. A burst of regret makes him squeeze his eye shut. He wishes he had had time to say goodbye to them. Especially to Lillia, knowing that a coded note was hardly what she deserved.

When he slowly opens his eye, he sees Hugh staring at him.

"What's that silly grin doing on your face? You thinking of something or . . . someone?"

"I'm thinking about how grateful I am to you for helping me get on with this new phase of my life, Hugh. I owe you. When we get to California, we need to create something good for ourselves. Something we can be proud of and pays us back for the trials we've suffered through."

"Sounds good to me but, chum, you've had way more trials than me. I can feel the relief for escaping your father, but don't you worry about Lillia and what she's going through?"

Donovan considers his words carefully before saying, "I can tell you this as my best friend. We would have made our marriage work but in truth, we were rescuing each other from our respective situations. I wonder which has made her the most upset . . . me not marrying her or me not taking her away from what she calls 'New England's suffocating society'?"

"Yep, she is a bold spirit, that one. That's why I thought you'd be so good for each other. She would draw you out, and you would free her from her hated societal conventions. Any chance you'll go back to her?"

"I'll not be going back. If she doesn't come to San Francisco like I asked, I doubt we'll see each other again. But I promised her I would look for her in San Francisco, and I intend to keep that promise."

Both silently acknowledge the truth of Donovans's statement, until Hugh asks, "So what are you going to do with your Morse code in California?"

"I don't know. Can't help but think it will be a handy tool at some point."

Hugh laughs and croaks, "Yep, once we find all the gold, you'll have something to fall back on to make a living! Better than being a preacher's son. All I can do is talk anyone into anything."

Dawn finds Donovan at his position at starboard sweep, wanting to build his confidence before the river traffic becomes thick. He flexes his fingers around the smoothly drawn handle, raises the great paddle out of the water, and strokes above the waterline anticipating its power.

By the time they approach Marietta, Ohio, all manner of vessels cover the Ohio River's surface in confused congestion. Eventually, the Bostonians figure out the rules of maritime traffic right-of-way. When they finally float past the city, they are relieved and ready to relax. Hugh, enjoying the luxury of his rotational day off, reclines on the wool bale next to Donovan's sweep and dozes in the warm sun. Lethargy does its magic and Donovan watches Samuel, at bow watch, also succumb. Still nervous in his sweep role, he splashes water on his face to ward off any drowsiness.

A distant steamer's wailing whistle snaps the entire boat crew to attention, and they begin evasive maneuvers to the right shore. As they cautiously round the river bend, a sign announces the town of Parkersburg. When they see the steamer is still docked and boarding passengers, Hugh reclines onto the wool bale and grins up at Donovan with a lazy smile.

"Relax, Donnie, we'll be well beyond them before the steamer leaves."

Donovan winces when the steamer's whistle shrieks a final deafening departure announcement and notices black smoke billowing from the twin smokestacks. The flatboat passes by close enough to observe passengers waving and calling out to loved ones on shore as the boarding plank is lifted. Now past the upstream-bound steamer, he turns his back and sends his attention downstream, heaving a sigh of relief.

In the next moment, a thundering force thrusts Donovan over the boat's railing, his hips catching between the railing and the sweep's handle. Using the sweep's handle, he lifts himself upright. When he lifts his head and looks over his shoulder, he sees the once glorious steamer listing awkwardly, its lifeless hulk engulfed in flames, and desperate people jumping into the water from the second and third decks.

The water is littered with the bodies of people who, only moments ago, had been waving goodbye. Steamer debris mingles and swirls with floating bodies, their mouths open and wailing, or face down, hair and skin smoldering on their skulls. At the shoreline, he watches men plunge into the river to drag out the injured while women busily tear at their underskirts to create bandages.

Donovan's gaze falls on a stream of dark liquid pooling at his feet. Self-scanning, he finds no pain or injury. He drops his sweep and rushes up the roof ladder to find Wilton missing. From the ladder's vantage point, he can now see the dark liquid's source. Hugh, still in his earlier calm repose, has a jagged shard of smokestack metal piercing his torso, his life's blood pulsing onto the flatboat's deck.

The sight of Hugh propels all to the ship's railing in a frantic search for Wilton. From the corner of his eye, Donovan sees Samuel signal toward the stern. Without hesitation, Luther dives over the railing into the murky water. Donovan arrives at the railing to see Luther lift Wilton's limp head above the surface and drag him toward the flatboat. With a powerful hoist, Luther lifts the flaccid body upward. Donovan joins the eager hands as they struggle to haul Wilton over the railing.

The jagged bone shards mashing against a torn artery in Wilton's left arm are the obvious injuries. Ezra tears off his shirt, tying it tightly above what is left of Wilton's elbow. Heading to the cabin for blankets, Donovan returns to see Wilton shaking uncontrollably and coughing up gushes of muddy water. Ezra grabs a blanket and wraps it tightly around their injured friend.

Unable to help himself, Donovan's gaze turns outward and sees the flatboat is adrift, spinning in a lazy arc, captured completely by the river's current.

He yells, "The flatboat is out of control!"

He rushes back to his sweep while Luther climbs the cabin ladder and wrestles the rudder from the current's grasp. By syncing up the sweeps, they slowly arrest the flatboat's spin. When centered in the river again, everyone emits nervous energy, their motions animated to match their loud voices.

Donovan had read accounts of steamer boilers exploding. In most cases, the steamer's boiler had exploded when it had run dry or was too hot and water had been added carelessly. But he had never expected to witness such an event in person.

Thickening dusk makes the village of Ravenswood's riverbank sign hard to read. The Bostonians maneuver the flatboat to the southern shore, upstream from the town's riverfront. Ezra leaps into the river shallows with the hawser's looped end in hand and ties up to a well-worn stump. As the flatboat whiplashes in the current, Gus joins Ezra and the pair race toward town.

Soon, a lantern bobs in their direction with Gus and Ezra in the lead. At the bank, Donovan sees a man holding the lantern in one hand and a leather satchel in the other. Ezra and Gus wait on shore as the doctor wades through the river's shallows, the dim lantern light exposing his intense expression. Once aboard, he wordlessly enters the flatboat's small cabin where Wilton lies on a cot.

When the doctor emerges moments later, his hasty retreat foretells the grim truth. Donovan watches as Luther and Samuel help Wilton off the boat and into Ezra and Gus's waiting arms. The four escort Wilton away, leaving Donovan behind. He lights the lantern, his mind flooding with a mix of anxiety and sorrow.

They had covered Hugh's body with a blanket, but in the rush to get help for Wilton, had not yet considered what to do with his body. Donovan hangs his head and tears fill his eyes. How would they find their way without Hugh's confidence? Donovan had only ever felt as good as Hugh believed he could be. The same could be said of the others. How could they go on without him?

Shame for his personal selfishness racks through him. As he wipes his eye, he hears Hugh's voice whisper, "Suck it up, Chum. There's more to you than you know."

In the dim light of dawn, Donovan wakes to Samuel's soft voice saying, "Need to visit the doctor's office today. Couldn't tell us anything last night."

"We need to bury Hugh, Samuel. And we need to get his money belt off him before we do. He would want us to use it to get to California. I just don't know if I can . . ."

"Don't worry, Donnie, I'll get it."

When Samuel returns, they distribute the coins between them, counting out enough to pay for Hugh's burial. As carefully as they can, they wrap Hugh's corpse in his bedroll, lift him off the flatboat, and haul it to the undertaker with instructions for it to be buried in Ravenswood. As Hugh's best friend, Donovan pens a quick note of condolence to Hugh's family. Still cautious about leaving any detectable trace of himself, he signs Gus's name and hands the undertaker the envelope with a coin for postage.

Leaving the undertaker, they visit Wilton at the doctor's office. After the surgery to amputate his damaged arm just above the elbow, Wilton is asleep when they arrive, and the doctor gives them his prognosis.

"He's going to live but won't be going with you. Too much risk of damage. Wanted you to have this . . ."

He hands Donovan a dictated note and he reads it aloud, "Take half my money and consider me a partner in whatever you end up doing in California."

Returning to the flatboat, they solemnly lift the hawser and push off. From his position at the bow, Donovan makes out a conversation going on between Samuel and Luther at their sweep positions.

"We had an arrangement."

"What kind of arrangement?"

"If anyone tries to take me, he had papers naming me his personal man. Without Wilton . . ."

"We'll stand up for you, Samuel."

"Haven't you noticed? We're floating on the River Jordan, one side holding men in bondage, the other side free. Bounty hunters prowl the southern side for any Black man they can steal away. Without Wilton's papers, I've got no proof I'm not a runaway. There's nothing you can do if they try to take me."

"We'll make up some new papers."

"With what?"

Donovan turns to join the conversation.

"Hugh had a journal and ink in his bag. I can work up something that looks official. Who is supposed to be the . . . owner?"

"Donnie, you look more the part than anyone."

Donovan's apprehension prompts Samuel to continue.

"A Black man has to be constantly on his guard. Please, Donnie, even though it's a hoax, I need the protection."

The trio goes quiet while Donovan ponders Lillia's abolitionist passion and her Unitarian Church's role in the Underground Railway in Boston. Then he considers the real likelihood of his father and brothers' nefarious business as bounty hunters, including the ambushing of freedmen and selling them into slavery. A defiant thought spurs him on, and he bobs his head toward Samuel.

"I'll do whatever it takes."

As his teammates rest outside that night, Donovan lights the lantern inside the flatboat's cabin and writes an official-looking document making himself an unwilling owner of another human being. A late-night breeze causes the document's edges to flutter. He stops his work and smiles at Hugh's explanation of the zephyr wind and hears the wind say, "Way to go, chum."

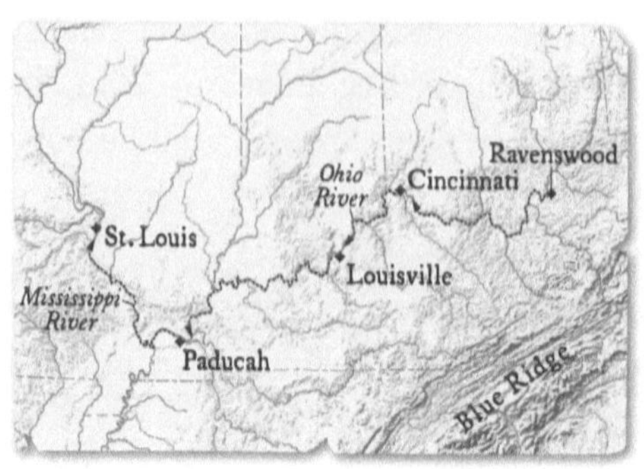

Chapter 6

MAY, 1849

OHIO RIVER

By mid-afternoon the next day, the river's stagnant air is choked with humidity. The current swirls languidly around Donovan's sweep and he wonders where Hugh's zephyr winds are when they need them. At the same time, he notices the river's traffic shifting rapidly toward the riverbank. Gus sees the shift too.

"Where's everybody going?"

In answer to his question, a distant thunder boom breaks the stifling calm. Unable to see beyond the tree line, the Bostonians look at each other in bewilderment until another clap of thunder spurs them into action.

"Best take shelter along the riverbank!" Luther yells.

Frantic, they do what they can to move the lumbering flatboat toward the port-side shallows. Ezra jumps off the bow, hawser loop in hand, the heavy-braided hemp line snaking behind him as he searches for something substantial to throw the loop over.

Even though the sun still shines, the distant rumbling continues. The Bostonians rush to secure the rudder and sweeps between the cabin's port side wall and the lumber pile. The sky goes dark just as they roll the massive wool bales over their valuable navigational tools. The branches of the riverbank's great trees drape protectively above them, and it is only when the wind picks up that they hear the storm's roar.

"Inside the cabin! Hurry!"

Heeding Gus's call, they scramble inside and throw the door's heavy bolt.

Scurrying to the cabin's fortified corners, Donovan hears Ezra mutter, "Dear Father in Heaven, please let the hawser knot hold."

As the roar continues to build, the once-protective trees creak their protests against the howling wind gusts. Donovan feels the cabin's corner post strain against its anchoring mortise, followed closely by a deafening crack from the starboard side just before he is forcefully thrown to the deck.

Sprawled and gasping for air, he hears the cabin's plank walls splinter. The normally windowless room is filled with wind gusts and balls of hail. Through the cracked lumber, he sees the coarse bark of a tree limb crushing the cabin wall opposite him.

Still prone, Donovan feels the boat's deck rise. It strains upward before rebounding with a loud splash. After the third rise and fall, he hears Gus swear loudly.

As suddenly as it began, the violence ends. Still skeptical of their safety, no one moves. When water gently lapping against the flatboat's side is the only sound, Ezra stands and steps through the rubble.

Trying the door, Samuel lifts his head and says, "No good. Doorframe's smashed."

Ezra slices through the door's rawhide hinges with his knife and pushes the door out. Once outside, Donovan sees heaps of debris caught in the current of the serenely flowing river. The flatboat sits akilter, the port side front corner pinned into the riverbank by the fallen tree. A great limb fans its branches and leaves in a filigree over the boat's deck and its contents.

Donovan assesses the damage quietly. It is clear the tree's trunk had acted like a counterweight to the wind's gusts that ultimately prevented the boat from flipping. It was the tree's secondary limb that crushed the cabin wall and, while a challenge, will be easier to lift off than its adjacent trunk.

"What a mess," Gus mumbles.

"Yes, if not for those few inches, our trip would have ended abruptly," Donovan replies.

The Bostonians spent the rest of the day clearing the hail and debris from the boat's deck. All evening, they formulate a plan for removing the limb holding them hostage, their only chopping tool being a hatchet.

"Do you think my grappling hook could help?"

Donovan turns to Gus and grins, "Your grappling hook may be just the answer!"

The Bostonians put their plan into action at first light. Luther uses the hatchet to hack away the moderate-sized limbs. Samuel and Ezra plunge the limbs into the soft riverbank along the tree's trunk per Donovan's directions.

"Gus, fasten the grappling hook to the limb on the cabin. Then throw the line over to Luther on the riverbank. Luther's going to pull on the hook's line while Ezra and I lever the trunk up with the limbs stuck in the riverbank. You and Samuel use the poles to pry the flatboat away from the bank as the tree lifts . . . hopefully."

The Bostonians take their positions, and Luther takes hold of the hook's rope before barking the cadence, "One, two, three . . . lift!"

His command is followed by a cacophony of accompanying groans.

After several group attempts, the limb budges and Donovan shouts, "Stay with it! There's movement!"

Their efforts continue with a red-faced Luther heaving mightily. Finally, the flatboat's trapped corner inches free, the force shooting the flatboat out into the river's shallows. Everyone on shore cheers while Gus and Samuel rush to pole the flatboat back to shore. Luther retrieves the grappling hook and joins Ezra and Donovan on the riverbank.

"How'd you know to do all that lifting and levering?"

Ezra answers for him.

"That's what Donnie does best. Whenever we had a difficult mathematics problem at Harvard, I'd take it to Donnie. He always had a way to figure it out. I looked so good the next day in class."

Luther looks at Donovan with a surprised expression.

"You weren't with these guys in Harvard?"

"No," Donovan replies, "I was too sick to take the entrance exams. Then I couldn't see for a while. But I got a secondhand education when I tutored Ezra and Hugh."

"If it wasn't for Donnie, I wouldn't have finished," Ezra confirms.

Donovan keeps his surprise in check. He knew Hugh had struggled but had had no idea about Ezra.

As the flatboat glides into the current, Samuel comments, "However it came to be, I sure am glad you knew how to get us out of that fix."

Donovan shakes his head at that, knowing full well that Hugh—wherever he is—had a hand in the rescue.

In the river's middle again, other vessels pass by like nothing had happened the day before. Before long, the outskirts of Louisville show the storm's true path. Piles of planks lay where a barn had been. Unusual debris hangs from twisted and deformed trees.

Surveying the shoreline, Luther lets out a low whistle.

"Sweet Jesus, I doubt we'd a made it if we'd been any closer to the storm."

By the time Louisville's riverfront comes into view, the late afternoon sun bears down on them. Eager to repair their cabin and replenish provisions, they find a place along the dock to tie up. Gus, Ezra, and Luther leap off the boat, leaving Samuel and Donovan to assess the damage.

Donovan notices a lone steamer docked opposite from them. No smoke comes from its stacks. As he studies it, he sees a man walking toward him. Moments later, he recognizes the man and grins widely.

"How did you get so far ahead of us?"

Ace stands beside the Bostonian's vessel, running his hands along the railing and says, "Can't say. Been looking for your face on every flatboat we passed. Good thing I was lookin' for your face though; wouldn't have recognized you otherwise. Lost some weight in the last few weeks?"

Donovan shrugs saying, "Hadn't really noticed but now that you mention it, my pants seem to be pretty loose. Are you on the steamer docked ahead?"

"Yup, that's ole *Buckeye Belle*."

"You don't sound too enamored."

"She's stout enough. Captain's havin' trouble with the crew. Drug a couple of fellas off by their collars before the storm. Left us sayin' he had to find replacements. Hasn't returned."

Samuel and Donovan exchange glances before Donovan tells Ace what happened in Parkersburg. Ace bows his head before saying, "I'm so sorry to hear the news about your friends. Hard to understand what the Lord has in store for us, isn't it?"

Donovan nods in agreement just as Gus, Ezra, and Luther return.

Gus sets down the heavy box of nails and a hammer and says, "How 'bout we spend the night here and let off a little steam?"

Donovan looks from one to the other of his comrades. Everyone returns his gaze excitedly except Samuel.

"I'll stay with the boat."

Ace smacks the flatboat's railing with his open hand.

"Fellas, I have an idea. I can't stray too far in case our captain shows up and wants to leave. But I'm bettin' we're here another night. And I owe a favor to Donnie for saving my wife in the creek. If you boys provide the space, I'll drum up some entertainment."

Ezra looks at him with a wary expression before asking, "What kind of entertainment? I'm needin' music and some dancing."

"I best not say 'til I know but I'll get something cookin' while you fix that cabin roof. I expect there's some musicians who'll want to use it for a stage."

As Ace quickly returns to the steamer, Gus leans over to Donovan and says, "Him owing you a favor couldn't have come at a better time."

Freshly fueled by Ace's enthusiasm, the Bostonians make their repairs, finishing as the sun's last rays light the sky in crimson and rose. Before long, Ace and Nora lead a procession of four musicians and five women toward the flatboat.

Seeing Nora's face for the first time since the campfire dinner at Redstone Creek, Donovan is suddenly possessed with the need to tell her the truth about her sister and children. Spurred by Ace's earlier comment about mortality, he decides to not let this opportunity pass without sharing his knowledge with her.

The musicians hop up onto the cabin's roof and strike up a dance tune. Nora's advancing pregnancy doesn't keep her from dancing with all the Bostonians at least once and with Ace every other time. As the evening wears down, Donovan decides he should broach the subject with Nora on his last dance with her.

Fretting to put together his explanation in short order, he takes Nora's hand and spins into the group.

"Nora, there's something I need to share with you. I'm not sure how to go about it, though."

"Whatever 'tis, Donovan, I'm a good listener."

"You mentioned you've been waiting to hear from your sister, Evelyn. I have some bad news."

Nora's feet slow as she gapes at his use of her sister's name. Taking her from dancing to a wool bale along the railing, they are joined by Ace, a concerned expression on his face.

"What's going on here?"

Nora looks at her husband and whispers, "Seems Donovan here has something to share about my sister, Evelyn. Out with it then, Donovan."

Nora's directness makes Donovan's mouth go dry until he blurts, "Well, I found a woman with two children in a boarding-house in Boston. She had an advertisement in her possession that I think had been placed by you. When I found her, she had, well, she had just passed. From what, I do not know. Her children, Molly and Quinn, were crying beside her. I knew they had no one else."

Recognizing the children's names, tears cascade down Nora's cheeks. Through them, she mutters, "What did you do with them babies?"

"I took them to Baltimore to find their aunt. When I went to the place listed in the advertisement, the woman there said the sister had left a week before, headed west to California. I didn't know what to do so I took them to the local church's orphanage. I gave the priest some money to help with their expenses. It was all I could do."

Ace wraps Nora in a strong hug as she sobs into his chest. Both men stare off, equally uncomfortable with feminine distress.

"Nora," Ace says. "Listen to me. We can turn around right now. They will still be at the church orphanage, even after a few weeks, I'm sure of it. We can set out again with another company next spring."

Donovan watches Nora's face as she considers Ace's selfless offer. He would not be surprised at all if she took him up on it, but he couldn't quite read her expression.

No one is more shocked than he when she says, "No, Ace, we aren't going to turn around now. We've got too much planned. When we get to California, I'll use the same church network to send for them."

Donovan wishes he could be more helpful but knows there is nothing he can do.

"I'll leave you folks to talk this through. I know this news is awfully painful, but I thought you should know. I'm so sorry."

"Donovan, I appreciate you tellin' me about my sister. She's in heaven looking down on us now. You left the little ones in the best place you could, and I'm obliged to you."

Donovan moves away from the couple and finds a quiet place to watch the last few dances before the steamer folks leave, their lanterns bobbing away like giant fireflies.

Dawn's first light is escorted in by the peace-shattering thump of boots on the Louisville dock and a gravelly bark of, "Permission to board!"

Several loud raps on the flatboat's railing accompany the gruff demand, jolting the flatboat's occupants to attention. Instantly, Donovan is paralyzed with the irrational fear of finally being tracked down by his father and brothers.

Luther moves first, rummaging through his personal bag's contents until producing his pistol and maneuvers to the door. Donovan cautiously peers over Luther's shoulder as he cracks the door enough to push the pistol's barrel through the slot.

There are five men clad in dusty traveling clothes, weapons visible in their waistbands. None are Donovan's brothers.

The gruff voice bellows again, "Lookin' for three negro runaways. Tracked 'em to this riverbank. Thinking you got some stowaways aboard. Lookin' to make sure they ain't tryin' to hitch a ride. Let us board. We'll poke around, and you'll be on your way, quick like."

Luther eases the door open and steps onto the deck, his pistol trained on the leader. The rest of the Bostonians remain anchored in place.

"Three you say. Boys, let's show 'em there are no runaways on our boat."

Obediently following his directive, the Bostonians step from the doorway.

Luther asks the leader, "Where do you suggest we 'poke'?"

"If'n that's how you want to go 'bout it . . . start with them wool bales."

Nothing had been replaced after the party, so they scoot the wool bales back to the boat's center. The five men post themselves along the dock for the flatboat's entire length, peering down suspiciously. Clearly unsatisfied with the results, the leader barks again.

"Alright then! How 'bout you let us board and check alongside the outside railing? They's like ticks when they's desperate."

Donovan shoots a look at Luther, whose grip on his pistol has not loosened.

"Boys, take the poles and scrape the boat's edges down deep in the water. If there's something holding on, the pole will tell you. You men just stay where you are and watch for a smooth drag."

Samuel and Donovan both grab a pole and head to the bow. Opposite each other, they start to drag the pole toward the stern. Donovan watches the men's eyes as they examine the pole for any irregularity, exhaling when he reaches the stern without a bump. When Samuel has the same result, Luther turns to the leader.

"That pretty much tells the tale. Probably sprouted gills and are swimming to the free side of the river, while you're here wasting our time."

"You ain't got no secret compartments in that deck of yours, do ya?"

Luther continues to train the pistol on the man's chest.

"Nope, not on this flatboat. Headed to California, not spiriting anyone to freedom."

The leader nods in Samuel's direction and growls, "You, boy. You got papers?"

Samuel visibly gulps as Donovan fumbles in his pocket for the freshly folded piece of paper. Offering it to the man, he says hoarsely, "He's mine."

Donovan grimaces at the taste of the foul words. The leader waves off the offered document while saying, "Just checkin'."

Stuffing the paper back in his pocket, Donovan realizes this ruffian probably couldn't read it anyway.

The leader gestures to his men and they step away from the flatboat and Luther's pistol.

"You boys watch out now. There's all manner o' trouble in these parts for ignorant folk."

Once the bounty hunters are out of range, Luther uncocks his pistol. He sits heavily on a wool bale and takes a deep breath.

Everyone is quiet until Samuel asks, "How'd you know?"

"No one boards the boat. I overheard some old men talking yesterday, could've been river pirates."

"You think those guys were pirates?"

"Not worth taking a chance. Louisville has become a hub for sending slaves down to New Orleans. When those who've sold their slaves try to return to Kentucky, the pirates rob them . . . or kill them if they put up a fuss."

Luther's expression brightens when he lays the pistol on the wool bale beside him and says, "Hope you boys don't mind me taking control of the situation."

Ezra exclaims, "No, Luther, keep the pirates off our boat any-time you think it's necessary!"

"I vote we get on our way. I've had enough excitement," Gus says, and everyone works together to replace the remaining cargo.

Ezra hauls in the hawser and Luther unties the stern line before hustling up the ladder to the rudder. Donovan pushes the flatboat from the dock with a pole and they are underway.

Passing the *Buckeye Belle*, Donovan catches sight of Ace on the stern deck, holding a tin cup and admiring the enormous paddlewheel. At Donovan's hail, Ace raises his cup in salute and Donovan wonders when he'll see him next.

Pole position on a flatboat in the middle of a river is hardly strenuous. Between boredom, the Ohio River's muggy air and the already annoying itch of his wispy beard sprouts, Donovan unconsciously strokes his jawline. After a while, his rubbing matches the rhythm of the frogs and cicadas along the riverbank as their hum and chirps grow in the fading afternoon light.

Gus casually leaves his bow position and tosses his fishing line over the railing. Ever since Ravenswood, Gus had tossed in a line and frequently provided fish for their evening meals. Donovan watches the line get grabbed by the current and feels his belly rumble in anticipation.

He is not the only one. Gus's fishing line cues Ezra to leave his port side sweep and build a fire in the stove. Donovan muses at this friend's newly acquired cooking skills. It seems Ezra enjoys preparing their meals, something no one would have believed had they not embarked upon this adventure. But then, none of them would have believed half of the things they'd already endured.

From his overhead rudder post, Luther suddenly hisses.

"Donnie, look! Off our starboard aft corner."

Donovan scans the water from the railing. Seeing nothing obvious, he looks up at Luther and shrugs, puzzled.

"In the water, next to the boat's waterline. Three of 'em."

Donovan fixes his gaze on the waterline close to the boat. Through the swirling water and the sunset's reflection, he spies three evenly spaced reeds piercing the waterline.

Acknowledging the sight, Luther says, "This morning's visit may not have been without warrant."

"What do we do now?" Donovan asks.

"Can't stop."

"We can't let them cling to us like this. Got to get them on deck."

"How are you going to do that?"

Donovan contemplates Luther's question and then ties a piece of sackcloth to the end of his pole. He gently plunges the pole's cloth-covered end down into the water and waves it back and forth for a moment. After several attempts, there's a tug on the pole.

The dark top of a man's head rises up through the swirling water. It pivots toward Donovan, the whites of the man's eyes bright in the shadows. Donovan smiles and gestures him up. Without rising any further, the man reaches on either side of him and pulls two smaller heads to the surface. He sees their expressions are laced with distrust and fear.

Donovan extends his hand, using the other to brace against the railing. With great exertion, the big man lifts his small companion toward it. A boy of about ten years vaults into Donovan's grasp. Hoisting the dripping boy over the railing, Donovan sets the gasping boy against the cabin wall.

When Ezra emerges from the cabin, he exclaims, "What the . . . ? Mighty big fish, Donnie."

By this time, Donovan has the next young man's hand gripped and is doing his best to haul him aboard. He judges him to be a teenager, bigger and stronger. Ezra returns with blankets while Samuel helps Donovan aid the big man's arrival over the railing.

Samuel kneels down by the dripping trio and says, "My name's Samuel. This is Donnie. We are going to California. Are you hungry? Something to drink?"

The big man looks at Donovan and Samuel. Then he nods, remaining focused on Samuel.

Samuel gives Donovan a gentle nudge and whispers, "I'll stay with them. Ezra's making coffee."

Donovan enters the cabin and grabs three cups. Pouring coffee into them, Ezra asks, "Do you think they're who the bounty hunters were looking for this morning?"

"Haven't learned yet."

When he returns, Donovan offers the cups of coffee and notices the big man's shaky grip.

"Mighty grateful. Name's Absalom. These'uns my sons, Philip and Thaddeus."

"Were those men after you this morning?"

"Yes, sir. Been chewin' our dust for days. Came close to catchin' us a couple of times. The Lord mus' believe in our freedom 'cause each time somethin' come along an' saved us."

Samuel asks, "How'd you come to be in the water by our boat?"

"T'was after the twister. We was runnin' for cover and there your boat is, big tree holdin' it down. We slipped alongside hopin' the Lord would give us the strength to hold on. You boys were so busy getting the tree off, you didn't notice. Decided to see where you was goin'."

"You've been in the water for two days?"

"No. While you was havin' your shindig, we snuck onto the riverbank and dried out. Went back in at dawn this mornin'. Pushed back when your poles went by. Good thing or them devils would've had us."

Donovan gestures toward the cabin and says, "How about you go inside by the stove? We've got a full moon tonight, so we aren't stopping. Ezra will get you some beans when he's got them ready."

Absalom nods and leads the boys through the cabin's doorway. Donovan climbs the ladder to Luther and asks cautiously, "What do we do now?"

Luther whispers, "Tell you what we aren't going to do . . . we aren't stopping on the left side of the river. What did you find out?"

"Been with us since the storm. Used us as a shelter and then decided to hang on. Those bounty hunters almost had them."

Absalom and his boys stay tucked away in the cabin while the Bostonians float beneath the full moon's bright guiding light.

Toward dusk of the next day, they venture out and Absalom asks Samuel, "Any idea of where we are?"

"Don't know exactly, must be getting close to the Mississippi," Samuel replies.

"We need to get gone. What's that north shore called."

"I'd guess it's Indiana, but it might be Illinois."

"That'll do. We'll be free if we get to either. Yes sir, we are almost there."

Due to a blanket of thick clouds thwarting any night traveling, the Bostonians agree to tie up on the north side riverbank. While void of bounty hunters, the north side has fewer tie-up stumps and more hidden sand shoals. Absalom and Philip leave the cabin and lend their strength to help get the flatboat off several shoals before they find a secure place to tie up.

Once secured to the bank, the Bostonians rush to make camp in the dying light. A fire on the bank is a luxury and they build it large and bright. Absalom and the boys help them gather firewood, and Donovan detects levity in their expressions, wondering if it's because they're finally on dry land or because the land is free soil.

Enjoying the fire's warmth after their meal, Gus blurts, "Absalom, what happened to the boys' mother?"

Samuel snaps back quickly, "That's none of your business."

Absalom looks from one Bostonian to the other with a stone-sober expression before saying, "No, it ain't your business. But you boys, like my boys, need to know. Life is cruel. Things'll happen with no rhyme or reason. You'll have to stand up and get on with the life the Lord gives you."

Absalom pauses for a deep breath.

"These boys' momma was sold down the river to N'Orleans. Ain't a thing I could do. That's why we ran. Willin' to die gettin' to freedom. Thanks to you, we's one step closer. Like to ask for one more day's distance from them's that's chasin' us 'fore you let us off."

Absalom's words render the Bostonians mute. Donovan considers the truth of Absalom's words compared to his recent tragedies. His father's ugly secret, Hugh's death, Molly and Quinn as they knelt over their dead mother, and finally, Lillia's innocent, smiling face.

Get on with the life the Lord gives you, indeed.

The following evening, Absalom, with Thaddeus on his back and Philip at his side, slip into the dark water and swim toward the north shore. When Absalom and Thaddeus stagger onto dry land and Philip emerges a little further downstream, everyone is relieved. Donovan watches with an odd pang of sadness, as they slip silently into the riverbank's vegetation. The three runaways now join the list of people who have touched him on this trip who he might never see again.

The May sun shines bright when the Bostonians lash their flatboat to another in a wide part of the river. Both crews lean against their railings to chat while the rudder men maintain their positions.

Donovan hears one of the other crew say, "If you play your cards right, you could get a St. Louis-bound steamer to give you a tow. I ain't never been on a tow but I heard of it bein' done."

Another crew member adds, "And all your goods will be worth double upstream from what you'll get for 'em in Memphis, for sure."

Judging by their expressions, Donovan can tell Gus, Ezra, and Luther like the idea.

"Double?" Luther says under his breath. "That'd make all the trouble worth it."

Gus asks the other crew, "What kind of steamer has the ability to tow a flatboat?"

"A sternwheeler's what you're lookin' for. Them that you can get directly behind. Sidewheelers'll get too off-kilter."

They continue their conversation on other topics for a while, before unlashing and drifting apart. It isn't long before Gus can't contain his enthusiasm.

"What do you think, Donnie?"

"No doubt those steamers have enough power. I just can't figure out how we'd attach our hawser directly behind their paddlewheel."

Ezra chimes in, "If we could double our money, we'll get to California in style! Don't forget, we're still in a race and need to find the best horseflesh there is. Maybe we could even afford to own two animals if one wears down."

The dilemma of how to hitch a towline dominates their conversation until Paducah comes into view, a day and a half later. As the last town before the confluence of the Mississippi and the Ohio rivers, it's their last chance to explore their options before making a decision. At the river dock, Ezra and Gus rush off to get a valuation of their load. When they return, Donovan can tell by Gus's slumped shoulders and trudging gait that they don't have great news.

"Paducah's only going to give us half of the load's value of Memphis, which is a quarter of its value in New Orleans. Next steamer bound for St. Louis is due in two days. Maybe we'll get lucky, and the captain will consider a tow."

Everyone digests this news until Samuel says, "If the steamer doesn't offer to tow, I vote we go back to our original plan: float to Memphis and buy tickets to St. Louis."

Donovan scans his companion's faces before saying, "I agree with Samuel. Still not confident I understand how we'll actually hitch the towline, but I'm willing to hear what the steamer captain's ideas are."

After two days of impatient waiting, a steamer's whistle howls through the humidity. The Bostonians spring to life, eager to approach the boat's captain. They watch as the *Mischief* docks downriver and Luther, Gus, and Donovan rush to meet it.

The captain's girth precedes his arrival. As he steps onto the dock, his cap sits askew on his head, and he is unshaven. Donovan notices not only crumbs from the man's breakfast scattered in the folds of his captain's coat but several large stains down its front.

"Excuse me, captain. Are you St. Louis bound?" asks Gus.

"Isn't everyone?"

Luther ventures, "Would you consider towing a flatboat?"

The captain stops in his tracks. He looks hard at the three young men before asking, "How much will you pay for the service?"

"How much do you want?"

The captain rubs his whisker-thick jawline. "Seen it done but I've never done it. It'll put a mighty drag on my engines. What's your tonnage?"

Luther is quick to reply, "Not more than two. Just enough to get us some extra trip money for California."

"California! Ha! My steamer's full of folks thinkin' they'll make a killing in California."

Unimpressed by his outburst, the Bostonians stare unflinchingly, waiting for a price.

"Thirty bucks. Leave in the morning. I need a day to grease my insides and spruce up my outsides before St. Louis."

The price was more than expected. While they exchange glances, the captain starts to walk away.

Luther calls after him, "When do we tie up, tonight or in the morning?"

"Why, son, in the mornin'. I'll want you on my port side to stay clear of the shoals and sawyers along the riverbank. Pay me in the morning."

The captain walks into the crowd, his corpulent stature cleaving a path and leaving a wake behind him. Donovan is perplexed by the captain's statement about the port side. It doesn't make sense.

Luther howls, "We did it!"

"Yes, but at quite an expense. At least we won't be backtracking from Memphis."

Donovan tries to sooth Gus's anxiety.

"Don't worry, we'll use Hugh's money. But why we are to tie up to his port side instead of being towed from behind? If that is the case, we'll need more points of contact than our hawser and our stern rope."

They explain their arrangement to Samuel and Ezra when they return to the flatboat.

Donovan reconciles his earlier thoughts, and Gus notices his turmoil and asks, "Donnie, what is it?"

"There's something about this captain that I don't trust."

"Like he is a slovenly pig?" Luther suggests.

"He's the kind who would have no compunction to cut us loose in the middle of the rivers' confluence, pocket our money, and happily wave as we float in the opposite direction. If we will have no defense against the risk of that happening, we might as well save our money and float to Memphis."

Ezra is quick to say, "A few more points of contact is certainly easy enough insurance against your worries, Donnie."

With that, the Bostonians leave Donovan and Samuel on the boat while they venture into Paducah for several more ropes. Donovan watches their backs and hopes his intuition isn't right.

Theirs was not an early departure. While the Bostonians had been up since the crack of dawn, the riverboat captain moseys in after his breakfast, cleaner than the night before but still unkept. Once the boilers are heated, the great engines roar to life, and the *Mischief* pushes away from the dock with its load of firewood, goods, and passengers.

Donovan had watched the loading process carefully. He feels his neck hairs raise when he understands the captain had not balanced his load to counter for their flatboat's weight on the *Mischief*'s port side.

The riverboat casually floats to the river center while the Bostonians' flatboat eases alongside. At only fifteen feet shorter than the steamer, the flatboat's bow is pulled even with the *Mischief*'s to keep the paddle wheel area as clear as possible. Luther tosses their heavy hawser line to a deckhand at the steamer's bow, while Gus hands a line to a deckhand at the steamer's stern. Their newly purchased ropes are attached to cleats at the midway point of both vessels, giving them four points of connection.

Watching the ropes being secured, Donovan still feels uncomfortable. He paces the length of the vessel, fighting off his persistent anxiety with the captain's lackadaisical behavior. While examining the paddlewheel's construction, an antidote to his uneasiness occurs to him. He frantically rushes to find Gus just as the shrill wail of the steamer's whistle cuts through the morning air.

Bursting into the cabin, Donovan blurts, "Gus! I need your grappling hook."

"Well, sure Donnie. Why?"

"It's only a precaution, but if something goes wrong, your grappling hook could be what saves our entire trip."

Gus pulls the grappling hook and its connected line from its corner.

Donovan grabs him by the shoulder and says, "I might need your help. Come with me."

The two rush to a pair of empty cleats at the flatboat's stern. Donovan winds the hook's line between the cleats, tying them securely before winding the extra rope into a neat coil, the hook resting in the middle. Gus watches Donovan with a baffled expression.

"What has you so worried?"

"The captain hasn't balanced his load to account for towing us. If his ineptitude forces him to choose between his steamer and our thirty dollars, we'll be first to go. This is just for my peace of mind, if something goes wrong. If nothing happens, only you will know of my concern."

Two hours from Paducah, most of the Bostonians lazily watch the steamer's crew reduce the firewood pile by half to satisfy the captain's calls for more power. Luther chuckles at their frenzy.

"At this rate, we'll have to stop for fuel wood right after we reach the Mississippi."

Seated at the flatboat's stern since their departure, the grappling hook and coiled rope between them, Gus and Donovan nervously anticipate the confluence of the two mighty rivers.

When the Mississippi River's muddy eddies engulf the Ohio's clearer current, they hear the captain bellow, "More power! Give me more power!"

Donovan feels the steamer launch into the waterway before starting a great, wide, northbound arc. When the expected surge of power does not come, sweat breaks out on his brow. He watches the two tethered vessels strain against the tempestuous crosscurrent, the flatboat's deck lines growing taut. The steamer groans into the turn, its engines straining to their maximum against the Mississippi's opposing current. The flatboat's deck lines rebound, along with an impressive water arc from the flatboat's hull. The resulting splash drenches both boats' decks just before the flatboat's deck lines go taut again, narrowly avoiding a collision.

The captain calls for more power again, despite the thunderous throb coming from the *Mischief*'s engines and the paddle wheel spinning wildly. Donovan knows the overloaded bow deck has elevated the stern-mounted paddle wheel just enough to prevent the proper purchase on the river water.

As the boats' rhythmic dance becomes more exaggerated with each swing, Donovan detects the steamer's slight list toward the flatboat. Reflexively, he grips the hook and stands to take aim at the paddle wheeler's iron debris guard. At the same moment, two deckhands wielding shiny hatchets approach the flatboat's securing deck lines. His scenario is coming true. The captain intends to cut them loose.

When Gus sees them, he yells, "Throw it, Donnie! Throw the hook!"

The hatchets find their mark with a sharp flash. Without the flatboat's burden, the steamer's starboard slams back into the water. Donovan knows there's no time to waste. With the space widening between the two boats, he flings the hook toward the debris guard at the steamer's stern. The hook's treble points spin in a graceful, arcing flight trailed by the coil of its attached rope.

The hook flies true, looping itself twice around the guard's bolted metal frame. The hook's sharp points bite aggressively into the iron and the line's slack is instantly taken up with a jolt. The flatboat skitters across the water's surface like a bathtub toy, her stern becoming her bow. The captain cuts the throttle in half and the engines' roar abates to reduce their power. The redistribution of the flatboat's weight serves as a counterbalance to the steamer's overloaded bow and the paddle wheel settles evenly down into the water.

The Bostonians' cheers roar as the deckhands arrive at the steamer's stern. Helpless to rid the steamer of its parasite, the deckhands leave. Donovan studies the hook's line and determines the need for a secondary.

"Fetch the cut lines. We need to splice them together and secure another connection to the wheel guard."

The Bostonians rush to fulfill his directive, returning with the thick hawser line, its loop now missing, and the three other lengths, more than enough to reach the wheel guard from the flatboat.

Waiting to attach the second line until they stop for firewood, Donovan prepares for the captain's verbal lashing. The big man arrives in a huff, while Donovan loops the second line through itself and back to Gus to secure to the flatboat's stern cleats.

"You wily little buggers, what do you think . . . ?"

"If you had loaded your bow properly, the whole incident could have been avoided. Our evasive action has saved you from your own carelessness," Donovan interrupts.

The captain's face turns red with Donovan's truth.

"The least you ticks can do is help with the additional wood to pull your weight."

Luther calls out, "You've been paid, remember?"

Facing this further truth, the captain spins on his heel and leaves the Bostonians, who have, once again, dodged a disaster.

Chapter 7

MAY, 1849

MISSISSIPPI RIVER

The day after the flatboat's realignment behind the steamer, the *Mischief* continues its northbound slog. To amend the May heat and river humidity, Ezra and Gus playfully use the flatboat's poles to send great crescents of river water cascading over each other.

Watching their antics from the cabin's roof, Donovan hears a steamer's whistle coming up behind them. As it gains on the *Mischief*, he sees the oncoming riverboat's smokestacks belching black smoke and its paddle wheel churning furiously. When the steamer draws even, Donovan gapes. It's the *Buckeye Belle*!

He searches for Ace or Nora's familiar faces. He spies Ace leaning awkwardly against an upper deck railing post. Then he sees Nora arrive at Ace's side and Ace points in Donovan's direction. Oddly, she offers a stiff wave before escorting Ace through a doorway.

Only when the steamer passes them does he see the yellow flag of quarantine waving off the *Buckeye Belle*'s stern.

At their next boiler water and firewood stop, the Bostonians note the *Mischief*'s deckhands unloading blanket-wrapped corpses, and their own yellow flag is raised.

An uptick in river traffic signals their proximity to St. Louis. Before the sun sets, the *Mischief* prematurely docks alongside other vessels on the Mississippi's eastern riverbank. The flatboat lazily sways at an acute angle behind the paddle wheel.

The steamer captain yells, "Going to stop here tonight. Waiting until morning to dock in St. Louis. Oh, and we've got cholera on board."

The captain's three-pronged pronouncement leaves the Bostonians resigned to their fates. Their only resort is to hope nothing happens until they can get to solid ground. When Gus and Ezra race to vomit over the flatboat's railing, tangible fear washes over the others. Luther, Samuel, and Donovan let their afflicted companions have the cabin, and bed down on the boat's deck, the illness' mystery baffling them.

"The only thing we have in common with the *Mischief* is air and water," Donovan says in a muted voice. "We can't stop breathing, but we can stop drinking river water."

Luther whispers, "That means all we have for drinking is Wilton's whiskey."

The agony-filled groans of Gus and Ezra fill the air until the cabin falls eerily silent. Engulfed in the river's humidity and a growing feeling of dread, Donovan slowly falls into a tormented sleep.

"Donnie! Get up! We have to get off the boat!"

Luther's booming voice jolts Donovan up straight, acrid smoke instantly stinging his uncovered eye to tears.

"Really! Move it! We are on fire! Get your blanket and the rifle. Samuel's getting the bags from the cabin."

Jumping to his feet, the intense heat coming from the *Mischief* distracts Donovan. The steamer is a wall of flames. Remembering Luther's assignment, he staggers to the cabin, his fingers finding the rifle's smooth barrel next to the stove. Samuel emerges from the darkness with all the personal bags.

"What of Ezra and Gus? Are they coming?"

"Donnie, they've passed. We gotta get outta here or we're going to join 'em. Don't want to be here when the whiskey blows up."

Luther, now chest deep in the river, yells, "Hurry, embers are hitting our deck! The towlines are on fire, too!"

Rushing to the railing, Samuel flings the bags toward Luther with remarkable accuracy, climbs over, and slips smoothly into the water until finding the river shallows. Donovan goes over the railing but takes one last look over his shoulder.

Samuel screams, "Donnie, they aren't coming! Hand me the rifle and get off!"

Donovan tosses the rifle to him, lurches over the railing, and strains against the current to wade toward the muddy riverbank. At the riverbank, they scramble to distance themselves from the blaze while observing ships anchored or docked north of them, all on fire. People, like little ants, scurry away from the fires and crowd the riverbanks.

Scanning to their south, Donovan sees the culprit firebug, adrift and at the whim of the Mississippi River's current. Flames claw high into the night air from a once mighty steamer's upper deck while glowing embers spew into the circulating wind. Ricocheting between the darkened riverbanks, the floating inferno produces spectacular explosions after each impact before spinning away gracefully. Devastation follows in its wake.

Loud pops bring Donovan's attention back to the flatboat. Flames greedily lick up the grappling hook and towlines' braided cords until they snap. Freed, the flatboat swings out into the current. He watches helplessly as the flames greedily lick at the lumber and barreled goods they had stewarded from Virginia, now lost forever.

When a whiskey barrel explodes, liquid fire shoots across the flatboat's deck with a wondrously, bright blue flame. It's not long before another whiskey keg goes up. Donovan watches the flaming pyre float away, taking the bodies of Ezra and Gus, all of their investments, and a fair measure of hope with it. Their only possessions now are a rifle, two pistols, and the meager contents of five personal bags.

The incongruent sound of shuffling footfalls interrupt Donovan's fitful dreams. He wakes to see the disheveled form of the *Mischief*'s captain staggering toward him, Luther, and Samuel. A rude nudge with a boot's toe precedes his hoarse voice.

"We're five miles downriver and on the opposite riverbank from St. Louis. Bet you're glad to be seein' daylight."

The captain's parsimonious jab hits a nerve in Donovan. Rather than lash out, he joins Samuel and Luther in the exodus throng of misplaced travelers on the eastern riverbank. Through a background of inky dawn light, he sees distant billows of black smoke. White ash falls like ominous snow and floats on the morning breeze, all foretelling signs of a catastrophe.

Approaching St. Louis' riverfront, they realize everything has burned. Through the blue-gray haze of smoke and ashes, Donovan counts fifteen steamers still smoldering in ruins and wonders if the *Buckeye Belle* is among them.

They take their place with hundreds of forsaken travelers at the westbound ferries. It isn't until late morning before they cross. Once within St. Louis, they join the chaotic battle with travelers and newly displaced residents for life's basic needs: food, water, and shelter.

Discouraged, Samuel says, "We will not get what we need here. We need to go inland, north of the fire."

Striking a contrary path through the riverfront crowds, Donovan sees the *Buckeye Belle* at her mooring, abandoned but not burned. He quickly scans the immediate area but sees neither Ace nor Nora.

Samuel is right. The crowds thin by late afternoon, allowing the Bostonians to find bread and water. Staking their spatial claim under a tree, Luther evaluates their situation.

"Best dump out Gus and Ezra's sacks. Doubt there'll be much to work with."

Samuel does the honors. Fortuitously, Ezra's sack reveals his half-full money belt. Gus's sack reveals his pistol and some socks but is empty of coins.

Samuel disappointedly looks at Donovan and asks, "Where would he have put it?"

"Maybe he spent it. He bought the grappling hook, pistol, and lantern in Wheeling. Probably kept what was left on him."

Samuel slips Gus's pistol into his pack and Luther adds the rifle to his pack with a pistol. Because of his limited sight, Donovan makes no objection and turns away to hide a wave of despondency. He sees Nora's familiar face in the crowd, and jumps up. The crowd flow is slow, and he dodges relief wagons and wailing children. When he catches up to her, he takes her by the shoulder and turns her toward him.

He says only one word. "Nora."

She looks up into his face. Tear tracks line her cheeks. She searches Donovan's face through weary eyes before spreading her arms wide and falling into him. He catches her awkwardly and realizes she could only act like this for one reason. He hastily finds a quiet spot behind a stack of crates.

"Where's Ace? Did we . . . you, lose him?"

Unable to speak, Nora nods and breaks out into sobs before choking out, "What do I do now? He's gone. I'm having a b-b-baby . . ."

"Where are all your things?"

"They've been taken off the steamer. A family is watching over them while I figure out what to do with Ace's remains. But I have no idea . . ."

"We lost two of our own, burned along with our flatboat last night."

"Cholera, like Ace?"

"We think they passed before the fire engulfed us. We barely escaped."

"I'm . . . I'm sorry."

"Come out of this chaos. We'll discuss the situation in peace."

Donovan escorts Nora back to where Luther and Samuel are sitting and explains her situation.

Luther speaks softly, "The fastest way of dealing with the dead coming off the river is to deposit them in what they call a cholera pit. Just a group marker, no service."

Nora breaks into quiet sobs at his directness. Donovan exchanges uncomfortable looks with Luther and Samuel.

Donovan asks, "What's your company going to do?"

After a long pause, Nora responds, "We've lost twelve to cholera. Down to twenty members. There's me and one other widow."

This realization spawns a fresh round of sobbing until she finds her voice again.

"Travelin' season is passin' and we're late because the steamer captain cost us time in Louisville. With Ace by my side, I thought I could do anything, but now . . ."

Donovan braces for more sobbing but none comes. Instead, Nora rests quietly for a few minutes before taking a deep breath.

Standing, she sets her gaze on Donovan and says, "Best be gettin' back. I'm boardin' a steamer for St. Joseph as soon as I get things resolved. If you haven't made a plan, I imagine the company would welcome your help. Abernathy is fair and honest. My cryin' days are over. I'll not be givin' up. If you decide to talk to Abernathy, count on a hot supper. I've got to make arrangements for my husband."

She points in the direction of where the Baltimore company is camped before turning and disappearing into the crowd.

"Seems we're in too far to go back," Samuel says.

"How do you think the Yalies have faired?" Donovan ventures.

"Don't know, but if we've had this much trouble, I'll bet my boots they have too," Luther answers.

Donovan nods and replies, "Could be we'll beat the Yalies by just surviving."

"Maybe by joining the Baltimore company we'll give them confidence to push the tempo a little harder. If there's money to be made along the way for helping, we'll be better off than we are right now. If there's still wager money by the time we get to California, it'll be gravy. Besides, we have two years to get there. The courier can't claim it before then."

Samuel's thoughts spur them into action. They combine Ezra's money with Hugh's and Wilton's and determine it's enough for their steamer passage to St. Joseph with extra for horses, tack, and a small amount to join the Baltimore company. If they can trade their labor for their meals, it just might work.

They gather their meager belongings and set out for Nora's company camp. Early evening light glows through the smoky air. Traffic has calmed and now the only wagons passing them are hauling corpses to the waterfront. Donovan notices the bright flash of a familiar, colorful fabric in one wagon and knows Nora has handled Ace's finality.

A brilliant sunset, heightened by the particulate matter in the St. Louis air, illuminates the Bostonians' arrival at the camp. When Nora sees them from the cook fires, she rushes to them.

"You're joining us?"

"If we can afford it. Where's Mr. Abernathy?" Donovan asks.

She leads them from the encampment's center, toward a distant wagon. When they pass pots of steaming stew, Donovan's stomach growls, and he realizes their last meal had been on the flatboat. Only twenty-four hours had passed, yet their world is upside down.

They find Nathan Abernathy bent over, examining a wheel hub. Nora clears her throat and says confidently, "Mr. Abernathy, excuse my interruption."

The man straightens and smiles at her, before turning to the three young men. He extends his hand toward Donovan first.

"Nathan Abernathy, welcome."

As Donovan reaches for the man's hand, he detects a mid-Atlantic accent.

"Donovan," he says.

Then Nora interrupts anxiously, "I don't know if you remember, but these men were with the freighter who took us to Brownsville. Ace and I befriended them along the way. Ace thought highly of them and they are as eager to get to the goldfields as we are."

Abernathy accepts handshakes from Luther and Samuel, then steps back, crosses his arms, and scrutinizes them.

Nora rushes on, "They've lost some to tragedy and cholera like us. With Ace's passing, I propose they join us. They'd strengthen our ranks, and we'd give them our companionship."

"How many are there of you? What are your encumbrances?"

Donovan exchanges looks with Luther and Samuel.

"Of the seven who started, we are all that remain. As far as encumbrances, we have none. Lost it all in last night's fire."

"What means do you have for traveling? Wagon, oxen, horses?"

"We have enough money for passage to St. Joseph, horses, and tack . . . maybe more, depending on what joining your company'll cost."

Samuel's statement makes Abernathy rock back on his heels, arms still crossed while contemplatively sucking at the ends of his developing mustache.

"Our weakness is the loss of men. Two women are trying to make the trip alone, one with six children. I'd consider a smaller fee, if you agree to help these women. Do you have any weapons?"

Luther answers, "We've got two pistols and a rifle."

"Confident in their use?"

Luther and Samuel nod. Donovan adjusts his eye patch self-consciously.

"I, for obvious reasons, have never shot a firearm."

Samuel speaks up, "But Donnie solves problems. Went to Harvard."

Samuel's fib makes Donovan wince under Abernathy's fresh scrutiny.

"Can you drive a wagon, work with livestock, repair equipment?"

Both Samuel and Luther nod but Donovan admits, "I'm unfamiliar with all of that. But that doesn't mean I don't have skills to complete this journey. I'll meet the challenges as they come. What's your charge?"

Abernathy considers before slowly offering, "Normally, it would be one hundred dollars. I'll settle for twenty-five each if you'll pledge your assistance to the widows and help with herding and hunting along the way."

Less than they had expected, the three young men eagerly shake the man's hand to seal the deal.

"In the morning, I'm securing passage to St. Joe's where I will employ an experienced guide to California. You're welcome to join us immediately, starting now with supper."

Thanking Abernathy, the young men follow Nora through

the common area cook fires to her wagon. She reaches inside and pulls out three tin plates and three forks. Handing one of each to Luther and Samuel, she holds back Donovan's.

"Go ahead, Samuel and Luther. I need a moment with Donovan."

The two leave Donovan to puzzle over Nora's request. She retrieves a stained envelope from a satchel and holds it out to him.

"Ace wrote this to you. He died handin' it to me. I don't want to know what it says."

Donovan hesitates and then nods, takes the note, tucks it into his pants pocket, and she hands him the tin plate and fork without another word between them.

After they all have settled in for the night, Donovan reads Ace's dying request.

New friend Donnie, seems my days are done. My Nora's a courageous one, stubborn but stout. As my last request in this mortal world, please look after her. Get her and the babe to civilization before you continue on with your own pursuits. Sorry to leave our friendship so soon, Ace

Lowering the note, he stares into the darkness as his new reality collides with his conscience. His chest tightens at the thought he might have escaped one nightmare only to land in the middle of another. But going back to Boston is not an option. He will likely only see Lillia again if she decides to meet him in San Francisco. From a place of practicality, what business does he have parading out into the wilderness without workable skills? And now, how can he refuse a dying man's plea?

It takes three days for the Baltimore company to contract with a St. Joseph-bound steamer. In the meantime, the Bostonians

familiarize themselves with the company's men. They have an easy camaraderie with everyone, except for the three other bachelors, Robbins, Clancy, and Frank. They hail from the far western counties of Maryland, and Donovan senses a curious, if not prickly, sense of competition. Crude in their behaviors, none of them have had much of an education.

Their departure day finally arrives, and Donovan, Samuel, and Luther help load the wagons and livestock onto the Missouri riverboat. They are on the bow deck when the steamer whistle cracks the air above them. The sound triggers Donovan to think of Hugh and all the death he has witnessed in the last month. He had had little contact with death before this trip.

Samuel whispers, "Eerie, isn't it? Being on board a steamer after all we've seen."

Both Donovan and Luther nod in agreement, each lost in their own thoughts. Donovan weighs his chances of surviving this trip and concludes he has to continue because he can't go back.

From his seat at the bow, he studies the passing countryside. Oceans of waving green grasses bathe in May's warmth setting a spell over the countryside. Contrastingly, he notes the difference in the Missouri river's water, the color and consistency of brown gravy, and wonders at the cause.

His choice of seats also allows him to observe the riverboat's crew who are constantly tossing out weighted lines to measure the river's depth while keeping a sharp eye on the river's edges.

When they see anything suspicious, they yell loudly, "Planter ahead, larboard," to which the riverboat's pilot makes the necessary adjustments to veer away.

At one of these outbursts, Donovan asks a crew member, "What is a planter?"

"An underwater tree still rooted into the riverbed. A sawyer is a waterlogged tree that saws up and down in the river's current. Both will ruin a steamer's hull if hit."

He also concludes that Missouri River steamer pilots are a different breed from those on the Ohio. Steering between continually sloughing banks, old shipwrecks, and a litany of submerged or semi-submerged trees is a frightful and perilous job.

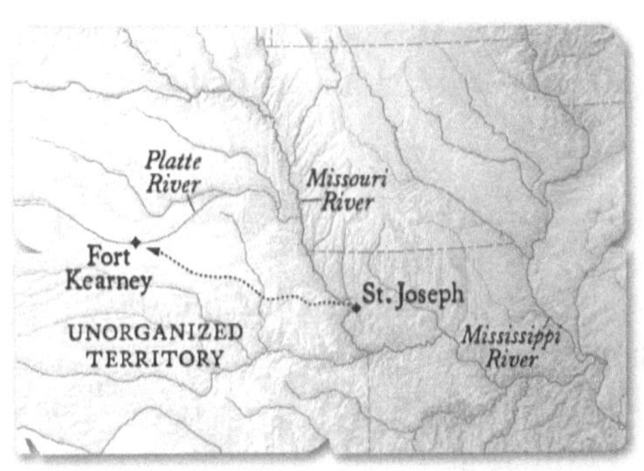

Chapter 8

MAY, 1849

ST. JOSEPH, MISSOURI

After an arduous week of riverboat travel, the pilot doing his best to navigate through one treacherous bend at a time, everyone's eager to disembark at St. Joseph. Following their arrival onto solid ground, the Baltimore company's first objective is to purchase horses and oxen. Joining several men in a visit to the stockyards, the Bostonians observe from the shadows before making their required purchases. Unfamiliar with the term "green broke," Donovan and the boys ignorantly walk their new and questionable saddle-worthy, horses back to camp.

The wagons are arranged in a circle, and the women work over the cooking fires in the center. Abernathy arrives and gives a whistle for the members to gather.

"Seems we're late. Most guides and companies left a couple of weeks ago. Without a qualified guide, we're takin' an awful big chance."

One of the company men calls out, "We're over halfway there, Abernathy! Can't quit now."

Donovan is surprised when Nora speaks up.

"Where did you inquire, sir?"

"I've been along the docks, dry goods stores, tack shops, talking to local folks as I go. No knowledgeable guide remains, I assure you."

Nora's scowl tells Donovan the answer isn't satisfactory.

"Don't you think it'd be worth takin' a gander at the vulgar side of town where an uncivilized, lonely man might be holed up?"

Donovan hears several men harrumph, before Abernathy bestows his response.

"Mrs. Guthrie, leave the search to the men. Lend your hand to the cook fires."

Donovan recognizes Nora's tight-lipped expression as the same one Lillia would wear when men were similarly condescending. She abruptly leaves the gathering and returns to the fires. He watches her engage in conversation before going to her wagon and fetching a market basket along with a black mourning bonnet.

Curiosity getting the best of him, Donovan follows her from a distance. She makes her way through several storefronts, but her basket isn't getting any heavier with purchases. After stopping at the butcher, she crosses the street and enters a boardinghouse. From behind a pile of sacked beans, Donovan watches her rush from the boardinghouse and disappear around a corner.

Forced into a near run to keep after her, he finds himself in the layman's district, home to blacksmiths, wheelwrights, stables, and a quantity of saloons. Nora is nowhere to be seen. Climbing on a crate for a better look, he searches for her dark bonnet. He sighs with relief when, through a blacksmith shop's haze, he recognizes the silhouette of a pregnant woman.

On the move again, Nora beelines to the last building on the road that abruptly disappears into the brush thicket. Donovan sees her march to the door, knock, and wait. After several minutes, a large woman opens the door. They have a quick exchange, and Nora goes into what he is sure is a brothel.

He maneuvers into position behind an abandoned wagon bed across the street from the building. After a few minutes, Nora emerges. Donovan is horrified when she walks directly toward him, gesturing for him to rise from his hiding place.

"Donnie, time to stop bein' sly. I've known of you since the butcher's shop. Grateful to know you cared to follow me, it fortified my resolve."

Donovan stands to face her, guiltily running his fingers through his hair. She takes his arm, and they begin the return walk to town.

"Well, aren't you curious?"

"Nora, I'm not curious, I'm confounded! What possessed you to go into that brothel?"

"The blacksmith told of an ol' trapper who 'as a sweet'art there.' Said I might find him sleepin' off last night's festivities. Said he might consider guiding if there's enough in the pot. I made sure the offer would get his attention. Should see him tonight about suppertime."

"Did you actually meet him?"

"Oh no, but he's there, just not decent."

"How do you know he'll take the job?"

"His sweet'art is gettin' a bonus for persuading him."

"But is he qualified? Don't we have to know he can get us to California?"

"Not my place to qualify him. Abernathy hasn't even had a conversation."

Back on the market street, Nora ducks into the shops she had visited earlier. Before long, her basket is overflowing, and Donovan is glad to be along to haul everything back to camp.

He finds Samuel and Luther at the horse picket line, and Samuel asks, "Where'd you disappear to?"

"Nora needed some help with her shopping. How are the horses?"

His partners trade glances before Luther grins and utters, "We know why we got such a good deal."

Donovan waits for more but when all he gets is Samuel's wink, he knows.

"They aren't broken to ride, are they?" he asks with a frown.

Samuel grins and replies, "Let's just say we're their first practical owners."

"Have they got wagon training?"

Luther answers, "Not too much experience there, either."

Resolutely, Donovan jerks upright and snaps, "Let's take them back. Abernathy told us we had to provide horses that could help with the wagons."

Samuel winces and drops his head to his chest before replying, "Thought of that. We went back but there were no more horses in the corral. Every last one was bought up."

"Don't worry, Donnie. We'll get them broke to work, just goin' to need a few weeks to get the job done," Luther says with a playful slap on Donovan's back.

"*Bon nuit.* Who's the chief here?"

The gruff, growling question precedes a figure emerging from the darkness. Alarming most of the company's men, Donovan quietly marvels as the most hirsute being he has ever seen walks past him. Eyebrows, beard, and matted head hair project in tufts from under an equally chaotic furred hat. Clothed in soiled leather leggings and a matching leather tunic, he also carries the longest barreled rifle Donovan has ever seen.

After stepping into the glow of the camp's fire, the man plants his rifle butt in the dust and waits for an answer.

Abernathy, dinner plate in hand, extends his free hand and says, "I'm this company's leader. Abernathy's the name. And you are?"

Donovan nervously searches for Nora, confident of her awareness of the arrival. He sees her bonnet-framed face staring at the man from opposite the cooking fire. Standing stock still, she gives no indication of her role in his arrival.

The fur man returns Abernathy's handshake with a gravel-voiced reply, "Jean Pascal Ramboulet. Been tol' you're needin' a guide to California. *Mes amis*, you're gettin' a late start. Tough to make the mountain passes before the snow closes 'em. Or," Ramboulet shrugs, "just as easy, the passes could stay open. Hard to know."

"So, there's a chance we can still make it through this year?" Frank asks eagerly.

"This country's full of surprises. Luck plays heavy here so if you're lucky, you'll get through."

Abernathy asks, "You interested in hiring on as our guide?"

"Any extra supper in your pot?" Ramboulet replies.

Abernathy motions for another plate and makes room at the fire. Their discussion takes place between the scrape of his fork against the tin plate and his slurps. Topics range from alcohol consumption to routes through the mountain passes. Agreeing among themselves that Ramboulet sounds acceptable, the Bostonians wait for the other company members to make up their minds.

Abernathy asks, "What is your financial requirement?"

Ramboulet's fork stops its scraping, and he replies hesitantly, "I wouldn't be here if you folks hadn't already offered up."

Abernathy's face clouds into a scowl, his eyes sliding around the campfire for some acknowledgment from one man's face to the next. Donovan scans for Nora, but she has disappeared. Abernathy's tone shifts to less conversational and more accusatory.

"We've not talked to any guides. Your appearance is a surprise. Who engaged you?"

Ramboulet yanks his hat off and whips his head to release a cascade of tangled mats falling to his shoulders.

"Was told there's an offer of four hundred dollars for my services, half now and half when we reach California. Plus, meals and an extra horse."

Abernathy chokes, "That's exorbitant, sir. I assure you, no one from this company was authorized to make such an offer. Further, I've heard only the best guides are worth that amount."

Ramboulet stands and replaces his hat, shoving the errant tendrils and knots under its crown. Taking hold of his rifle barrel, he ignores Abernathy's slight toward his skills and stands to leave.

"*Merci* for the meal. Goin' to have a strong word with my woman over this."

Before he takes a step, Nora emerges from the darkness, carrying a leather pouch by its strings, and says, "'Twas me who promised the payment. I spoke to your woman this afternoon. She relayed my message to come here tonight for an interview. I'll finance the payment's first half."

Indignant shock fills Abernathy's expression as he blurts, "I dismissed you from getting involved."

"Sir, we're on failure's doorstep. I found you a guide to interview when you'd no luck. I'll admit to usin' a sum for persuasion, but you'll do the hirin'. I've not heard anything makin' me believe he's not capable. Don't let your prideful stubbornness evaporate Ace's dream."

Abernathy stares at Nora. She holds the leather pouch in her hands, poised to pass it to Ramboulet. He scans the faces of the company's men lit by the fire's glow.

Abernathy says, "Aye, to hire this man as our guide. Nay, we don't."

Abernathy points to each voting man. Each man replies with "aye". Nora places the pouch in Ramboulet's weathered free hand and Abernathy seals the contract with a handshake.

Without releasing his grip, Ramboulet growls, "Be ready at first light. No time to waste."

The Bostonians silently made camp underneath Nora's wagon in the dark. Just as Donovan crouches to crawl under the wagon to join Samuel and Luther, Nora calls to him.

"Donovan, a word?"

He rises to join her, and she whispers, "Could we take a quick walk?"

"Sure, Nora. What's on your mind?"

"Things you should know about me and Ace. Things you didn't know before he . . ."

She stops talking and Donovan waits patiently for her to continue as they step away from the wagon and into the surrounding darkness for privacy.

"I came to Baltimore after losin' my whole family on the trip over from Ireland, died o' sickness an' left me with nothin'. I wandered into Baltimore after landin' in New York City and found a job tendin' store. Ace came in to buy feed for his horses. My eyes met his and it was settled. Ace gave me a family and a reason for livin'. He married me and took me away from the city's coarse life and gave me courage to go on. His dream of the West became mine.

If I can survive what I have already, I'll be makin' it to California. I just want you to know that I'll not be quittin'. No matter what the others say, I'm takin' my baby and finishin' what Ace started, doubters be damned. When I get there, I'll send for Molly and Quinn no matter the expense. I'll do my best to keep my family together."

Unwilling to argue against Nora's determined tone, Donovan studies his boot tops. The absurdity of her intentions is overwhelming, but before he passes judgment, he realizes he has no room to talk.

In the pre-dawn light, a four-legged mass approaches their camp. Eventually, Donovan determines it's Ramboulet mounted on a horse covered with the traveling gear of a man used to living without comforts. When the horse pulls up at the company's perimeter and waits, Donovan joins the others in their rush to pack and hitch horses.

Clearly impatient with the company's unpracticed sloth for departure, Ramboulet wordlessly moves to the wagon train's front. They follow his lead all day, stopping only to water the livestock and eat their cold noon meal. At day's end, the men gather to discuss their progress while the women prepare their food.

Ramboulet leads off with, "Only made eleven miles today. If you're hopin' for Scottsbluff in six weeks, we gotta do better."

Donovan observes the guide as he talks. A scar runs across his right eye which gives it a lazy look. Other than sharing the similarity of eye injuries, this man is his true antithesis. It is hard to understand how a man could let himself be so filthy.

Ramboulet pauses from his mileage report to retrieve a fat leather sack from his breast area. He opens the sack, pulls out a wad of brown leaves and jams them into his mouth. Donovan watches as his tongue works the wad around until his right cheek swells against the bulge and he talks again.

"Folks, gettin' to Scottsbluff by the Fourth of July means gettin' over the mountains before the heavy snows. Here to tell you, at today's pace, we got no hope in hell of making it."

He punctuates his last sentence by expectorating a torrent of tobacco juice so forcefully that it threatens to extinguish the fire.

"Once we get down the trail a ways, we'll see how we're travelin'. If need be and you're willin', I've a shortcut no one travels after Fort Laramie. Could take a week off the trip, but it's as dry as a virgin milk cow. Considerin' the trail before us, we'll be suckin' hind tit for livestock feed. My shortcut could save us. But it's up to you folks. Got about five hundred miles to make up your minds."

The words barely make it out of his mouth before another deluge of tobacco juice jettisons into the fire.

"Most important thing now is, we can't crawl like today. Nope, gotta whip 'er in the flanks."

Silent to Ramboulet's chastisement, Donovan and the other men exchange glances after having their reality laid so bare.

Luther and Samuel provide the morning's entertainment, showing off their horse skills while attempting to gather the company's loose cattle. Driving Nora's wagon, Donovan watches in horror. His father had only purchased trained horses, so there was never the consideration that the beast might want to kill him. Shuddering at the thought of public humiliation, he vows to ease into his relationship with the new horse.

Watching his expression, Nora senses his discomfort and asks, "Not prepared for the same wreck tomorrow morning, Donnie?"

"I've never . . ."

"Start off with a handshake."

His aghast expression makes Nora giggle.

"How would you suggest I do that?" he asks.

"Get his attention with a handful of oats. When he's through, gently blow into one of his nostrils while pattin' his neck. Givin' him a handshake, a personal greeting. He'll decide then what he thinks of you."

"How do you know this?"

"Ace used it to introduce himself to a new horse."

Her mention of Ace sets them both into uncomfortable silence.

After their evening meal, Donovan gives the handshake idea a try. At the picket line, he offers a handful of oats to his horse. The horse's velvety lips eagerly flip the oats onto its tongue. As the animal munches, Donovan runs his hand along the horse's neck, while nervously confirming he is alone.

He leans in and blows a gentle puff into the horse's left nostril. The animal stops chewing, flares its nostrils and returns a startled puff. Unsure of what to do next, Donovan pats the horse several times on the neck and leaves. A shrill whinny breaks the darkness after he has walked about ten paces and he smiles.

In hopes of avoiding an audience, Donovan rises earlier than normal. Walking toward the horses' picket line, his mouth is so dry that he has a hard time swallowing.

Grunting as he hoists his saddle onto the animal's back, the horse matches his grunt. When the saddle's cinch is tightened, the horse rumbles again. Donovan smiles nervously. So far so good.

As he had seen his father's groomers do, Donovan leads the horse around for a few minutes before checking the cinch for tightness. Sending up a quick prayer, he gingerly puts his boot into the saddle's stirrup and lifts himself into the saddle. Prepared for the animal to bolt away and heave him to the heavens, he sits rigidly, muscles tense. But nothing happens, except a deep, guttural grunt.

Relieved but still tense, he gives the horse a gentle nudge with his boot heels. The horse steps forward obediently, making a perfect left and right turn when reined. He rides away from the company while they pack up. Donovan decides using their time alone to understand each other has suddenly become important.

At a nearby creek, he dismounts and leads the horse to the water. While the horse slurps his drink, Donovan releases his tension with a loud exhale. His horse looks up, water dripping casually from his lips and grunts in agreement.

"Alright then, hello Grunt."

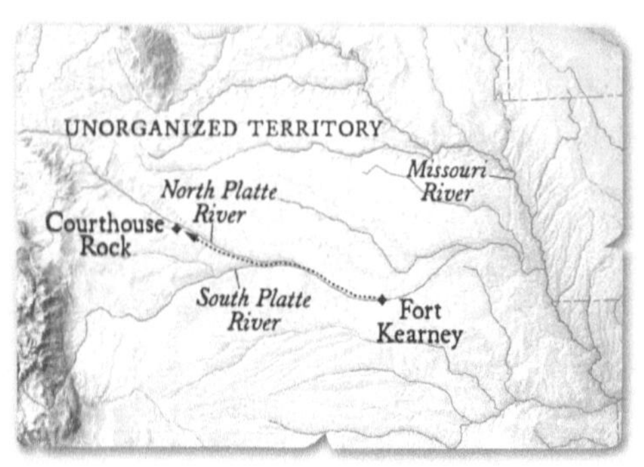

Chapter 9

JULY, 1849

FORT KEARNEY, CALIFORNIA TRAIL

ort Kearney feels like an oasis after over a month on the trail. Breakdowns of wagons and their wheels were the main culprit, many taking several days of idleness to mend. Despite not being remotely close to their goal of Scottsbluff by July 4, the women replenish their food stocks, while the men tend to wagon repairs blamed for their slow pace. After supper on their last evening at the fort, Ramboulet calls a campfire council.

"Fort Kearney's the first step, but we're still in mighty peril. Got over three hundred miles to Fort Laramie. Between us, there's Scottsbluff and crossin' the South Platte."

The now-familiar shot of tobacco juice punctuates his point.

"Been five weeks since the last company rolled through. If there's been rain, the stock'll benefit for feed. Ribadeaux's trading post may offer a few things if you're desperate, but he'll scalp you with his prices. Best get what you need here."

The travelers exchange side glances before he starts again.

"Three days from Ribadeaux's is Fort Laramie. It's your last chance for supplies. There you'll need to examine your souls and decide about that shortcut I mentioned. Spend your idle time thinkin' on the idea of spendin' the winter in Mormon Country—Salt Lake City, to be exact."

Ramboulet turns to Abernathy.

"Leave at dawn for Scottsbluff."

Ramboulet's speech motivates the Baltimore company into meeting or exceeding their mileage goal every day for the next two weeks.

Every afternoon, dark clouds emerge in the far distance, their giant billows growing to colossal heights in the northern and western skies. Today's storm looms closer than previous days and as the western winds build to a fury, the company rushes to find a camp spot. Noting the Platte River's deeply cut banks as evidence of spring flooding, Ramboulet chooses the downwind side of an adjacent high spot away from the river's flow.

"We'll wait until mornin' when the horses are fresh to cross. Them clouds and mountains is far, far off but there's been somethin' big happenin' there for days."

The company circles their wagons into a tight corral with practiced efficiency. Ropes are thrown over the wagons' canvas covers and attached to anchor spikes driven deep into the ground to avoid the wagons toppling over in the wind's gusts. With the livestock herded inside the wagon corral, fire trenches are dug and cook fires started below ground level on the leeward outer circle. The wind's assault is so extreme that even heavy iron cook pots sway on their tripod stands over the fires. Clearly the strongest wind of their journey, Donovan is impressed. Hardly the gentle zephyr wind of Hugh's myths.

While they wait for supper, Donovan, Samuel, and Luther help Widow Wilson's boys haul river water to refill every cask and empty pot they can find. Supper is consumed quickly, everyone eager to take shelter. Under Nora's wagon, the Bostonians create a saddle wall against the wind, arranging their bedrolls perpendicular to the saddles. Once the camp settles into an uneasy quiet, Donovan hears Nora rustling overhead trying to find a comfortable sleeping position given her late-stage pregnancy.

When a tremor jolts Donovan awake, he is met by darkness and calm winds. The unnaturally shaking ground is followed by an equally unfamiliar sound. He strains to peer into the night, but the new moon's darkness is complete. The ground shivers again and he scrambles from his bedroll to fetch Nora's lantern. As he lights it, the odd sound gets louder. He holds the lantern high, but its shallow arc of visibility offers nothing out of place within their camp.

Curiosity prods him forward, even though his instinct screams something isn't right. The growing rumble draws him toward the river's cut bank where he hears the low growls of grinding and gnashing accompanied by the occasional pop and scrape.

At the bank's edge, he holds the lantern out in front of him. Only a few feet away he sees a coagulation of liquid, mud, and debris swirling and gnawing along the river way. Suddenly grateful for Ramboulet's wise insistence they make camp on the high spot where they did, Donovan concludes all the low-lying areas must be completely flooded.

He turns his lantern in a quick survey. His hunch is confirmed. Helpless to do anything and knowing dawn will reveal the entire truth of their predicament, he extinguishes the lantern and returns to Nora's wagon. Unable to sleep, he resorts to wrapping up in his blanket, leaning against the wagon wheel, and listening to the water's eerie sound continuing behind him.

At dawn's first light, Donovan can't wait any longer. He rushes to Abernathy's wagon, his sharp rap on the wagon's wooden bed producing a growl from within.

"What is it?"

"Sir, you need to see. We're surrounded by water. The river's escaping its banks."

The wagon lurches abruptly. When the canvas covering over the driver's seat rips open, Abernathy's sleep-creased face emerges and peers toward the river.

"Would you look at that! Where'd it all come from? We didn't have a drop here."

By now, Ramboulet and the others have emerged from their sleeping places. Silently, they stare as the frothing current fills every low spot for miles, each high spot becoming its own island.

"Floods can come from anywhere in this country. Damn lucky we made camp where we did," Ramboulet mutters.

Abernathy climbs from his wagon and joins the gathered group, saying, "Well, yes, I suppose we should be grateful, but how are we going to proceed from here? The river is impassable."

Ramboulet looks past Abernathy toward the mountains and says, "Stuck here until the water drops. Could take days, maybe weeks. No choice but to wait 'til the rains quit in the far mountains."

"We don't have weeks!" Abernathy laments.

Donovan leaves the two frustrated men while he searches for his companions, still under the wagon.

He jerks on their boot toes and asks, "Ever wonder what it would be like to live on an island?"

Luther raises a sleepy head, muttering, "Can't say that I have."

"We're being held hostage by floodwaters from a distant storm."

Samuel and Luther scramble out from under the wagon. Nora pokes her head out from the wagon's canvas cover.

"Oh, my."

The camp is now fully engaged. A fire is built with the wood gathered the night before and the camp convenes at Widow Wilson's tarpaulin. A company man turns to Ramboulet.

"How long are we going to be here?"

After consideration and a stream of tobacco juice, Ramboulet's expression is thoughtful.

"Don't know. We're close to three hundred miles from them mountains and their storms. Been goin' on for at least three days. If it took three or four days to get to us, the longer the storms keep up, the longer we'll have to wait."

Donovan exchanges glances with Samuel and Luther acknowledging their shared reality. Another delay doesn't bode well for surviving let alone winning the race. Their survival options are evaporating, one by one.

The Baltimore company marks the mundane days on their prairie island by the recurring development of the distant, ferocious thunderstorms and the collection of driftwood for their cook fires. On the first afternoon when the distant skies are cloudless, a mild celebration breaks out in the marooned camp. Four days later, the water level begins to drop. Hearts lighten and the women talk of a true celebration. The children rush to gather driftwood for a bonfire. At dusk, the fire is lit, musical instruments are retrieved, and the party begins.

Nora's swollen belly forces a respectable distance between dance partners. When Donovan approaches Samuel for his turn to dance with her, Samuel leans in.

"Doubt she'll admit it, but she's getting tired. Tread easy."

Donovan nods with understanding and gently takes Nora's hand. After only a few steps, he sees her eyes widen as a gush of water stains her skirts.

She grips his hand with unexpected force and gasps, "Oh, Donnie. We've danced my baby into the world!"

Widow Wilson immediately makes demands for hot water

and clean rags. She looks at Samuel and Luther and orders, "Keep her standing, brace her up if needed."

Then she turns to Donovan and commands, "I need your help arranging a birthing space in her wagon."

After several trunks are pulled out, he lifts quilts and a few supplies into the wagon before she summons Luther and Samuel to bring Nora over. The three young men gently help Nora into the wagon's bed. Quick to leave, they head to the campfire where a bottle of whiskey has mysteriously appeared and is being passed around. Ramboulet, having imbibed his fair share, raises the topic of birthing.

"My first wife, a beautiful French woman, had babies so quick we only had a few minutes from the first pain before the baby arrived."

Donovan hears Robbins ask, "What happened to your French wife?"

"Left 'er and the children in France for the wilds of Rupert's Land and, eventually, to St. Louis without a regret."

Abernathy gasps, "You just left her? Alone in France?"

"Don't be gettin' righteous. Church don't allow divorce, and she could claim abandonment. She had family and, no doubt, she had a fella tarryin' at her side in no time. Worked out for both of us."

Just then, a newborn baby's wail carries across the camp and the men let out a cheer.

Three days pass and the sodden prairie stinks of decay. But the water is finally going down. Ramboulet assesses the situation with the company's men listening attentively.

"If we don't move now, we ain't gonna make Salt Lake City before the snow flies. First stop'll be Fort Laramie. It's a military post but there's a chance folks could winter over and join the first emigrant groups next spring. Won't be comfortable, but it'll be safe."

Eager for progress, the men leave to pack their wagons. Donovan decides to help Nora prepare for travel. With Widow Wilson's help and not having been pressed to travel, Nora has made a quick recovery.

He finds her outside the wagon bouncing the baby in her arms and announces, "Time to pack up, Nora. Ramboulet says it's safe to cross the river and be on our way."

"I'll not be missin' this smelly place. Dry ground and fresh air'll be a blessin'."

With the sun high and bright, Ramboulet and Abernathy organize the teams and riders, and they begin their crossing. When the first wagon accomplishes the task without encountering quicksand, everyone sighs with relief.

Once all the wagons are across, they drive as far away from the river's stink as possible before striking camp. In the last light of dusk, Donovan and the boys lay out their bedrolls under Nora's wagon. Nora returns from the campfire, the baby making audible snuffling sounds.

"Excuse me, boys, seems she's ready to eat again. Donnie, hold 'er while I climb up?"

Before he knows it, Donovan is holding a weighted nest of blankets which he awkwardly adjusts for a better grip. Samuel pushes the bundle toward Donovan's chest.

"Haven't you held a baby before?"

"Can't say that I have."

"The closer to your body, the happier they are. Put her head and neck in the palm of your hand, your other hand under her bum."

Luther joins them and asks, "Where'd you learn that?"

Samuel looks at him sideways and says, "I'm the oldest of eight. Answer your question?"

From inside the wagon, Nora calls out, "Ready, Donnie. Hand 'er up."

Donovan lifts the bundle to her outstretched hands and turns to leave, but stops when Nora asks, "Donnie, will you stay and talk to me while the baby nurses?"

Obliging, Samuel and Luther continue to the campfire while Donovan leans his back against the wagon bed. Staring out at the prairie, he waits for Nora to start the conversation.

"Donnie, what does your gut say about our chances of gettin' to California this season?"

"Ramboulet says we're going to be lucky to get to Salt Lake City, and some might consider staying at Fort Laramie."

Nora gives a long pause before asking, "How far would suit you?"

"If the weather holds, I'd consider Salt Lake City. Ramboulet says it'll be uncomfortable at Fort Laramie."

"Does Ramboulet know when we'll arrive in Salt Lake City?"

"Doesn't talk much about timing. I'd guess we'd get to Salt Lake City around mid-October."

A long silence follows until Nora asks, "We were foolish thinkin' we'd make it to California leavin' St. Joe's so late, no?"

"It was a stretch. Might have made it, if the flood hadn't happened."

"Donnie, I'm goin' to need help even if we make it to Salt Lake City."

Her words send Donovan into deep contemplation. At this point, forfeiting the race wager has to be considered a reality. If he has to start with nothing, so be it. And what of his promise to Lillia? If he doesn't show up in San Francisco by the time she does, she'll adapt and flourish without him. But it's the weight of Ace's request where his conscience is burdened. He decides it's time to share the gist of it with Nora.

"Ace asked me to get you to a safe place. I'll honor his request. California can wait."

His words bring soft sobs of relief from inside the wagon. Not wanting to intrude on her by looking in, Donovan offers his hand around the wagon's canvas. Nora takes it and her strong grip seals their agreement.

A week later, Courthouse Rock comes into view along with a shabby structure in the shadow of the great monolith.

Ramboulet growls, "Told you 'bout it before. Ribadeaux's tradin' post. Deals in desperation."

Quiet settles over the company, until Widow Wilson calls out, "After the holdup in the flood, my supplies have withered."

"If you got to go, don't go alone. Don't want no mischief stirred up."

The four women look from one to another. Nora volunteers to take her baby and go, if Donovan agrees to escort her. Making light conversation, they walk through the scrub and brush toward the building. When a shot rings out, they freeze in their tracks. When a body is thrust from the building's door, it lands directly in their path. They watch as another man walks out to the dusty pile, spews a withering French rant over it, and stomps back inside.

Donovan questions whether they should enter the trading post but Nora is undeterred. They continue, step into the low building where the reek of sour alcohol assaults their senses. Waiting for their eyes to adjust to the dim light, Donovan hears a man's voice growl from the shadows.

"*Bonjour, mes amis.*"

Donovan hesitates, recalling what little French Lillia had taught him and mumbles,

"*Bonjour.*"

"Salt and coffee," Nora says.

Her voice rings out clearly and Ribadeaux leans forward, pressing his palms against the pockmarked wooden counter.

"*Mon Dieu, ses cheveux, c'est magnifique.*"

Donovan sees Nora's cheeks flush even in the dim light and knows she understands the man's compliment. She squares herself to him, her baby in a carrying sling against her chest. Ribadeaux retrieves her requests and places them on the counter.

"*Merci.* How much?"

Ribadeaux smiles through a food-and-tobacco-juice-matted beard.

"Two dollars, *si'l vous plait.*"

Nora turns to Donovan with an indignant expression and mutters, "Ramboulet was right, the price was only a dollar in St. Joe's."

"*Mais oui*, but you are here, so you'll pay the price."

"I'll pay you one dollar."

Donovan feels his pulse race at Nora's bold defiance.

"*Ma chère*, you cannot expect me to survive if I sell everything at half price."

Nora stares defiantly at the condescending man. Swiftly, she reaches up to her hair knot and, with a dramatic flourish, pulls out the single stick holding it. The whole arrangement tumbles to her waist, covering her baby's sling in a cascading waterfall of scarlet curls. She slowly shakes her head, the buoyant tresses expanding into voluminous waves. Her sensuous display stuns both men.

"I'll be givin' you a dollar and a lock of my hair for the coffee and salt."

Nora's left eyebrow arches in a wordless challenge. Ribadeaux returns her stare. In a flash, he brandishes a polished knife, flips it around, and presents her with the handle.

Matching his bravado, Nora grabs the handle with one hand, takes a shoulder-length handful of hair with the other, and, with a broad arc, slices through it cleanly. She returns the knife to Ribadeaux along with a long lock of ringlets. Dropping a dollar coin on the counter, she picks up her items, turns on her heel, and marches out into the sun's brightness. Both men stare as she retreats, the breeze catching her flaming hair into a great billowing wave.

"*Mon Dieu*, she's a fine spirit. You're a lucky man."

Not interested in correcting the man's assumption, Donovan bolts from the trading post's dank confines to catch up to her. Beyond sight of the trading post, Nora reins in the windblown strands of her hair while waiting for him, plaiting them with deft hands.

"Nora . . ."

"Donnie, don' say anythin'. I'll not be payin' double for goods. Mine's an asset that'll grow back. Someone'll pay him double for my hair. It was a good trade, and he knew it."

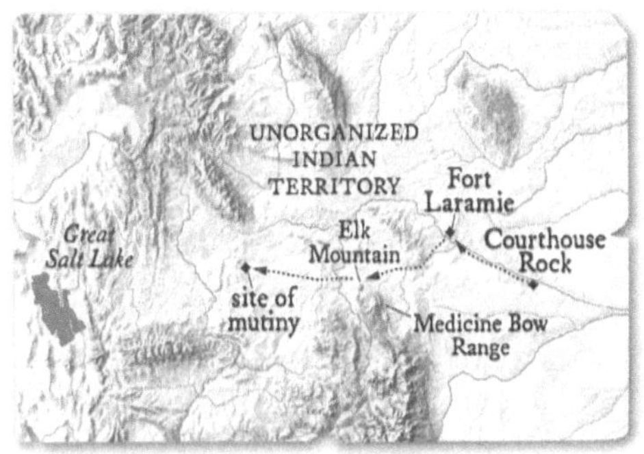

Chapter 10

AUGUST, 1849

FORT LARAMIE, CALIFORNIA TRAIL

Ten days later, the Baltimore company, miserable with fatigue, pulls into Fort Laramie under a blanket of low-hanging clouds. They had made camp and built their cook fires when the fort's commander, Major Trimmon and three subordinates officiously stride toward them from the fort's adobe walls.

Abernathy and Ramboulet welcome them to their campfire, intent on information about the western route's condition. With all the company men's full attention, Major Trimmon gives his assessment.

"There's been rain across the plains. That said, so many have gone before you, it's doubtful the grass has grown back. From here, you've a month to Mormon Ferry and another two weeks more to Salt Lake City. I implore you, for your sakes and for those who depend on you, to reconsider your plans for California this year."

A familiar hiss of tobacco juice hits the fire. Donovan recognizes this as Ramboulet's way of announcing himself.

"Been about fifteen years ago. First time the ground ever felt white man's feet. We was tryin' to outrun a storm barreling outta the northwest. Worried about stirrin' up Indians along the Wind River, so we marked a trail for Fort William to where Bridger's fort is now. Picked our way around Elk Mountain, across the plains to Bitter Creek and then to the Green. Made three hundred miles in ten days, but we was on horse. Likely no trail left, this country resents trespass. But I remember the landmarks clear 'nough. It's a fair piece but should be plenty of grass and fire-makings."

Major Trimmon's expression of doubt precedes his statement when he scoffs, "I've been stationed here a year and know nothing of this mysterious route."

Grimly, he turns to Abernathy and warns, "Measure this man's words with care. You're responsible for the souls in your company. I can escort those who want to go back to civilization. For those who wish to stay in Fort Laramie, there's enough time to prepare for their accommodation, but there'll be a fee. I assure you, going on could be calamitous."

With that, Major Trimmon and his associates turn on their heels and march across the hard-packed ground toward the fort. Judging by the company members' expressions, the major's foreboding words have sown their intended seeds of doubt.

Abernathy turns to Ramboulet and asks him to elaborate on his uncharted trail. Ramboulet explains once again and clearly offended by the major's insinuations, adds a rebuttal.

"Them mountains and rivers don't move. West is west. Been tellin' you about this shortcut since St. Joe's and now's the time for decisions. Just know, I'll not be returnin' the flame-haired woman's money because you lost your nerve."

Donovan glances around the fire searching for faces filled with confident, enthusiastic expressions. There are none.

"Somethin' ta be said for holdin' back," Ramboulet continues. "Fort Kearney would be decent enough for winterin'. Pack up next spring and head out with the first companies. No shame in bein' cautious, no shame at all."

From behind Donovan, a voice he recognizes as Cyrus Hess, the father of a large family, speaks up, "Can we have until morning to make our decision? Me and the wife need a discussion."

"Make up your minds and come prepared at dawn. Keep in mind, Ramboulet's right. We've paid our money. We'll have to come up with more if we hire on with a different company next spring."

After Abernathy's statement, Donovan hears Nora's voice call out, "What of Salt Lake City? What kind of winter will it be there?"

"Weren't no Salt Lake City in thirty-five when we crossed. Mormons may take in the needy. Got to cross through some mountains to get there. Weather'll decide our progress."

No one else speaks. Donovan is certain Abernathy and his family are going on. And he knows Nora's intentions. And where she goes, so does he. He turns to Luther and Samuel examining their expressions before tipping his chin for a private conversation. The three young men casually walk toward the camp's outer edge.

"What do you think, boys?" Donovan asks.

"I didn't expect any of this to happen, honestly. But I'm willing to make the trip to Salt Lake City and winter over there," Samuel replies.

"I've got nothing to go home to," Luther says. "I stole the money to join this race, and I'll likely hang if I return. I'm with you to Salt Lake City for the winter and on to California in the spring."

"To tell you the truth, Ace asked me to take Nora to a safe place before continuing on. I'm thinking that safe place is Salt Lake City. Maybe she will live there or she might decide to move on with us in the spring. I don't know. But I need to honor Ace's request. Hope you boys understand."

Nodding their agreement, the three remaining Bostonians bed down under Nora's wagon.

At the next morning's campfire, Abernathy assembles the heads of all the families.

"The time has come. Family heads speak your decisions. The Abernathys are going as far as Salt Lake City for the winter."

Widow Wilson and her five children decide to be escorted back to Fort Kearney for the winter. Robbins, Clancy, and Frank all signal their determination to continue, much to Donovan's disappointment. The Hess family also fall in line to proceed west. When the Bostonians are asked, Luther speaks for them.

"We've agreed to accompany Mrs. Guthrie to Salt Lake City for the winter."

The company is now made up of seventeen people: nine men, three women, four children, and a three-week-old baby.

No one argues or complains. Widow Wilson sells her thin cattle to Abernathy and her water casks to Cyrus Hess.

Before moving out, Abernathy checks each wagon for weight, explaining, "The lighter the load, the less stress on the animals."

Mounted on Grunt, Donovan joins Samuel to move the meager collection of livestock—three head of cattle—due west across the Laramie River on a well-used wagon road. When they make camp, talk around the fire is hopeful and Donovan is sure everyone is offsetting Major Trimmon's dire tone from the evening before. Abernathy gives some encouragement with the day's mileage report of eighteen miles.

Then Abernathy hastily adds, "Mind you, though, we must keep today's pace, if not faster."

Ramboulet adds, "Twenty to twenty-five miles a day, if we're to get to Salt Lake City in a month. Any dawdlin' and the weather'll trap us. Need an earlier start. Tomorrow we'll be breaking from this road and headin' down unbroke trail. It'll be slow going until we get through the mountains."

Veering south off the wagon road, the Baltimore company travel parallel to the Laramie Mountains for several days. The rising sun's warmth on their left side feels odd. It becomes clear that riding horseback across the terrain is preferable, especially when a wagon's wheels hit a hidden rock or hole. Driving Nora's wagon, Donovan hears the occasional howl of the other drivers and knows his bruised backside won't be the only one at the campfire tonight.

Ramboulet leads them through a narrow canyon, and they slip through without difficulty. The streams they cross have greatly diminished flow but provide enough to fill canteens and barrels. Ramboulet's forecast of untouched grass for the livestock in protected gullies and small meadows holds true.

Emerging from the Laramie Mountain range, they find themselves in a wide valley bordered by yet another row of mountains, the Medicine Bow Mountain range. Following Ramboulet's lead, the wagons turn northward to they cross diagonally between the two mountain ranges.

Approaching the tallest mountain they have come upon yet in their travels—Ramboulet calls it Elk Mountain—Donovan gazes up at the mountain's treeless peak. A reflexive shiver washes over him, seeing the depths of its dark, spruce-covered canyons and the mysteries lurking there.

Turning to the west, Donovan scrutinizes the arid expanse with awe. Heat waves blur the hues of purple, sage, and ochre into an indistinguishable mirage. His attention shifts to the ribbon of blue-gray peaks forming a stout barrier against casual penetration, and he wonders how far beyond those mountains Salt Lake City might be and if he will ever see it.

One thing he knows for sure, Ramboulet did not fabricate the fact that no one has passed this way with a wagon. Their progress across the gullied hills pockmarked with unforgiving sagebrush is painfully slow. The only sound, other than the constant whistle of the westerly wind, is the monotonous grind of grit crunching under their wagon wheels. Ramboulet had warned that this country is hostile to trespass and now Donovan understands.

After a week on the secret trail, Donovan watches Abernathy ride past Nora's wagon to join Ramboulet at the lead. Judging by the company captain's gestures, Donovan can tell he is worked up about something. Before long, Ramboulet spurs his horse and leaves Abernathy throwing his hands in the air in frustration. Only idly curious about his observations, Donovan rocks flaccidly with the wagon's motion, boredom his constant companion.

His lethargy evaporates when Ramboulet returns to the company's evening campfire with a stranger. Clad in buckskins and his horse similarly outfitted to Ramboulet's, the pair approach the fire and Ramboulet introduces Jim Bridger. Donovan remembers his awe when Ramboulet had first entered their campfires in St. Joseph and sees now that Bridger is a kindred soul of the wilderness. Bridger is gone before Donovan wakes.

Anxiety flashes through the company when Indians are sighted in silhouette against the next day's blazing sunset. After careful study, they breathe a sigh of relief when it's determined the groups are traveling in opposite directions.

That fact doesn't keep Frank, Clancy, and Robbins from crowing with inflated bravado, "Good thing they didn't want any trouble!"

Hearing their hoots, Abernathy shouts back, "That's enough, you idiots. No one wants any trouble, now or ever. Just keep your heads down and your mouths shut."

Like kicked dogs, the three men return to their driving, but Donovan senses their simmering contempt for Abernathy.

After crossing the Medicine Bow river's trickle, navigation becomes a constant duck and parry with gulleys and cut banks bisecting the ever-thickening, sagebrush-covered landscape. Donovan dreads Ramboulet's mileage report long before they stop for the night, certain they've missed their daily goal. He's not wrong and despair replaces disappointment.

Clancy, Robbins, and Frank utter low-toned comments mirroring Major Trimmon's doubts about Ramboulet's route. Briefly tempted to come to Ramboulet's defense, Donovan, Luther, and Samuel let the complainers mouth off, deeming them just as weary of travel as everyone else.

Following their evening meal, Mary Hess, wife and mother of the only family with small children left, complains of stomach pains. By this time in their travels, everyone knows the telltale signs of cholera so no one is surprised when each of the four Hess children follows suit through the night.

Despite Cyprus's efforts to ease their pain and coax doubtful recoveries, his battle ends at dawn when Mary succumbs. Like human dominos, each child falls too. Heartbroken, Cyrus wails, lamenting the injustice. Desperate to lay blame, he determines the cause to be the water casks he had purchased from Widow Wilson at Fort Laramie. He cracks each barrel wide open, their precious but questionably contaminated liquid sucked up eagerly by the indiscriminate parched ground.

In the essence of time and energy, the company's nine remaining men decide to dig one large grave for the five lost souls.

The hard ground defies their shovels, and the grave is shallower than any would have liked. With no substantial rocks or trees in sight, they settle for leaving the corpses unceremoniously mounded with the surrounding coarse soil.

Cyrus, imprisoned by grief, wordlessly throws gravel on the mound, his dull expression making Donovan ache with pity. Abernathy makes an attempt at saying consoling words over the gravesite before moving out. When done, everyone trudges to their wagons and hitches up.

As the wagon wheels begin their familiar crackle over the rough ground, a gray pallor settles over the company. Humbled by the speed with which Cyprus's fortune had changed, Donovan's confidence continues to wither. Cresting another hillock, he sees the ominous plain stretching before them. The impossibility of their situation makes his breath come in shallow spurts until Nora hands him his canteen.

She says, "Don't lose your faith now. I believe we're goin' to make it."

Three days after the Hess family burial, the Baltimore company makes camp.

Donovan feels Samuel nudge him and whisper, "Look, Donnie, Indians."

His gaze follows Samuel's pointed finger to see several men approaching on horseback. Their pace is slow and unthreatening but that does not slow the beat of his heart.

Despite the anxious fluttering in his stomach, Donovan says, "Better let Abernathy know."

While studying the dignified men's comportment, from behind him Donovan hears Cyrus moan lowly. He follows Cyrus's gaze and sees a portion of Mary Hess's stained dress draped across the leader's lap. Cyrus lurches toward the arriving riders, but Luther quickly intercepts and escorts the distraught man away.

As the Indians ease their horses to a stop, Abernathy and Ramboulet step toward them. The Indian leader gestures toward the draped fabric. Ramboulet waits until the man dismounts and draws in the coarse dirt, nodding when the man pulls on the fabric. Ramboulet turns back to the company.

"The Hess family grave was destroyed by beasts. The bodies were dragged out and mauled, the clothes torn off. These fellows reburied and repaired the gravesite. They want us to know they honored our dead. We should show our gratitude."

The company's women produce blankets, and the Indians seem pleased with the gesture before moving off to camp a short distance away. Following an uneasy supper, the Baltimore company bed down, their firearms cleaned and loaded. By the time the Baltimore company rises the next morning, the Indians have disappeared.

As has Cyrus.

After inspection, it's clear he walked away with nothing, just disappeared into the vast openness. Ramboulet and Abernathy briefly discuss a search but determine it to be a wasted effort. The Hess wagon is unceremoniously hitched, and Clancy takes the reins. The Baltimore company moves out, knowing Cyrus has succumbed to the hand fate has dealt him.

They make camp along a piddling creek that night where Ramboulet announces, "This measly trickle feeds the beast that marooned us on the prairie. It'll be our last water until we get to the Green River. Bridger said there'll be grass enough, but best fill your barrels and pray it's enough to get us across."

The company members' senses are so dulled with fatigue, no one reacts to his announcement. As if disappointed by their lack of response, his voice perks up.

"Our mileage today was twenty-five miles. Pretty good, considerin'."

Only a meager celebration greets his mild attempt at encouragement. From their wagons, Robbins, Clancy, and Frank angrily bark at each other. The Bostonians cast sideways glances at the arguing. Luther and Samuel's silent sullenness mirrors Donovan's despairing fatigue. But the traveling stress is affecting the other single men differently. No one dares speak to them, their combative nature intimidating everyone, even Abernathy. Especially Abernathy.

"Lookie what I found in ol' Cyrus's wagon, Capt'n."

Clancy's whiny voice gets throttled before he can finish. Robbins pushes Clancy and whatever his hand is holding behind him but not before getting the entire company's attention.

"What's going on, Robbins?" Abernathy asks.

"Seems Cyrus had some contraband stowed in his wagon. There are the parts required for a whole still and some bottled spirits hidden deep in their trunks. Clancy's a-thinkin' we might celebrate makin' our mileage today."

Abernathy and Ramboulet stand slowly, their expressions measured and unreadable. After an encouraging gesture toward them, the Bostonians reluctantly join the leaders. The whole group go to the Hess wagon and find Clancy, Robbins, and Frank standing around the wagon's tailgate. It is obvious they have already sampled Cyrus's bootleg.

"You know the company policy on alcohol. I expect you to pour it out, all of it. As far as the still is concerned, at this point, it's extra weight. Pull it out and leave it behind."

Abernathy's words flash pained expressions through the men like a hammer coming down on a thumb.

"You can't mean that, Capt'n. We were doin' fine not knowin' it was there this whole time. You never know, it might come in handy along the way."

Frank's plea is met with grim silence. Donovan watches as Frank, Clancy, and Robbins glance back and forth while Abernathy considers their words.

Finally, Ramboulet says, "There's some truth to having functional tools along the way, even if it's for brewin'. Since there ain't grains to make bootleg with, pouring out what's there is enough to put a stop to any mischief."

"Alright but find all the bootleg and pour it out."

Having delivered the order, Abernathy turns away, walking back to the fire. The Bostonians leave as a group, Ramboulet coming along but lagging behind. Donovan turns to see Robbins handing bottles to Frank and Clancy, who set them on the ground at their feet, unopened.

"Why would Abernathy leave it to those renegades to pour it out?"

Samuel's question goes unanswered until Luther and Donovan are back at Nora's wagon.

Luther rolls out his bedroll and lays down, saying, "Boys, remember those river pirates in Louisville? I've got the same feeling here. Best keep your eyes open to whatever those three are up to."

After the discovery of Cyrus's still and alcohol, the tension is palatable within the company. Suspicion lurks at every evening campfire in the coming days. Nora and Mrs. Abernathy quietly attend to their tasks but then disappear into their wagons, leaving the men to grease the wagon axles and portion out the livestock's water. Lacking any discussion points, their dire circumstances burden everyone's mind.

Tonight, Ramboulet unexpectedly says, "Goin' ahead to scout the quickest route to the Green River and its water. Could be gone overnight, maybe two. Keep goin' due west, an' I'll find you."

His abrupt announcement draws up everyone's head, revealing tired faces etched with concern. Everyone except Robbins,

Frank, and Clancy. Donovan notes the smug smirks playing across the trio's faces and realizes the truth of Luther's premonition.

Ramboulet is gone before dawn. Their usual morning routines are marked with escalating tension. On horseback, Donovan and Samuel push the three thin cattle across the sun-parched plain, while Luther drives Nora's wagon. The cattle's thirst makes them belligerent, and it's all the riders can do to keep the animals moving without exhausting their horses. Donovan notices Frank walking alongside a wagon, tallying his steps on the wagon's side. Chalking it up to boredom at first, Donovan considers that no one had bothered to track their progress in this way before. Perhaps Cyrus is not the only one losing his sanity.

When it's Donovan's turn to take the lines of Nora's horses, he climbs into the wagon's seat and is soon joined by Nora and her baby girl. Healthy and well-fed, the baby is bright and happy in stark contrast to the company's grim mood. At a stop to water the horses, Nora hands the baby to him before stepping down. The baby's weight makes him laugh out loud.

"She's getting heavier by the day. And her hair is coming in. It's just like yours."

Nora chuckles, "'Tis a blessin' and a curse. She'll have to decide. I've named her Amalee after Ace's sister. I'd like to honor him by using it."

Donovan smiles and bounces the baby playfully, her giggles lifting his mood slightly.

"It's a fitting name for such a happy baby."

After three days, Ramboulet doesn't return. His leadership vacancy causes tempers to simmer with the hot, dry wind. No one travels without watching the horizon, ever alert for a single rider coming their way. Disappointment is their only reward. Without

Ramboulet to guide them, murmurings of discontent erode their confidence.

When Abernathy announces the day's mileage of fifteen miles at the evening campfire, Frank heatedly blurts out, "I been countin' myself and we're barely making ten miles a day. You're fabricatin' just to keep us going."

"And we're not even going the right direction! No wonder Ramboulet can't find us."

Robbins's accusation adds to the already-inflamed atmosphere. Flaring tempers give way to irrational shouting. Rather than participate, the Bostonians choose to take precious water to their hobbled horses, leaving the others to volley accusations at each other.

Without Ramboulet, Donovan knows Abernathy lacks credibility and wonders if clearer minds will intervene. He engages Samuel and Luther in a strategy but is interrupted by a single, close-range shot shredding the vast prairie's stillness. Pivoting, the Bostonians see Frank lying prone and unmoving in the dust, faint wisps of blue smoke coming from Abernathy's pistol barrel.

Seconds later, a second shot cracks. This time, the Bostonians race toward Nora's wagon and their guns. By the time they arrive, an unnatural wail fills the air. Peering around the wagon's corner, Donovan sees Mrs. Abernathy cradling her son's bleeding body, her shoulders heaving with grief. Luther shoves a pistol into Donovan's rib cage.

"Donnie, take this, even if you don't use it. It may be enough to intimidate whoever has lost their mind."

Each carrying a weapon, the Bostonians crouch and move out from behind Nora's wagon. Donovan hears a shot fired from the Hess wagon. On his left, Luther flails backward and hits the ground. He doesn't move. Wide-eyed and panicked, Samuel and Donovan stare at each other as a gun battle rips between the Abernathy wagon and the Hess wagon.

Samuel and Donovan scramble toward the Abernathy wagon.

Arriving at the captain's side as he rushes to reload, Abernathy says, "They killed my boy, did you see? They killed him in cold blood. Never even touched a weapon. Just fired."

"They just killed Luther too."

Samuel's words bring Abernathy up tall with shock. The increase in his height gives Robbins's bullet just enough space to hit him square in the forehead. Tilting back like a dropped post, Samuel and Donovan stare at his dead body in absolute horror.

"What are we going to do?"

Samuel checks his pistol and then says calmly, "We're going to save ourselves. Whatever that means. We have to get a better look at where those two are holed up. Keep your pistol cocked and fire if you get a clean shot."

"But Samuel, I've never . . ."

"Figure it out, Donnie. You find Clancy, and I'll hunt down Robbins. The shots are coming from behind the Hess wagon, so I imagine that's where we look. Abernathy's pistols'll give me two shots."

With that, the two sneak around opposite sides of the Abernathy wagon, Donovan taking a moment to secure his eye patch. He finds Clancy madly tamping a rifle with gunpowder at their original wagon. Unable to avoid detection, Clancy quickly takes aim at Donovan, his face skewed with the wild-eyed expression of insanity.

Donovan raises his pistol, its unfamiliar weight making his hand waiver as he aims it. Despite his effort, the barrel wobbles and bobs ineffectively.

"You ain't got what it takes, do ya, blue blood? I'll save you the embarrassment and put ya out of yer misery."

Donovan watches the rifle barrel raise, gleaming in dusk's last light. When the expected boom happens, he tenses and falls into the desert gravel. But then he hears sounds and looks up to see Nora slipping down from her wagon's bench seat, gripping a rifle and running toward him.

"Donnie, get up. Samuel's been shot but not before Abernathy's wife took out Robbins. We've got to help him."

Nora pulls him to his feet as she runs past, and he quickly checks himself for damage. There is none. Satisfied, he follows her toward Samuel, who they find sprawled on the gritty ground with a blood stain in his left shoulder below his collarbone. Nora drops to her knees and lifts his head.

"Stay still, Samuel," she says. "Donnie, get one of my petticoats and tear it into strips. I'll need water to clean the wound and for him to drink."

Donovan obediently rushes to Nora's wagon. On the way, he sees Mrs. Abernathy crouched over her husband, the look of despondency telling her tale. Without stopping to console her, he gets to the wagon and throws open a trunk, taking the first petticoat his fingers touch. He ladles two dips of water from a barrel into a bucket. Returning to Nora, he arrives to see her weeping.

"Oh, Donnie, he's gone. He told me to tell you to take all the money and do big things in California."

Her recitation brings Donovan to his knees as darkness envelopes the fragile remnants of the Baltimore company. He suddenly feels the grip of desperation and calculates this event's calamitous effect. Their odds of survival have dropped precipitously.

Donovan digs graves all night and the next day, seven in total. With hands blistered and raw, he works with grim disdain. The fragrance of Nora's morning coffee leads him to the cook fire. Widow Abernathy wordlessly joins them, more out of habit than out of a need for consolation.

She looks at Donovan and says, "Thank you for digging the graves. It is quite a task in this unforgiving ground."

"Yes, ma'am. I'll need to bandage my hands before I bury them. Do you think you could give me a hand with the covering?"

"Of course. I must go through pockets and fetch out anything useful. Please give me time."

"Time is all we have left, ma'am. No one's driving us anymore. We just need to survive."

Donovan closes his eyes against his own violation of Samuel's pockets, remembering he carries his money in his socks. Luther had his money belt stowed in Nora's wagon along with Donovan's. Finished, he drags the corpses to their graves, one at a time. Nora meets him with two shovels.

"I'm no stranger to shovelin'," she says.

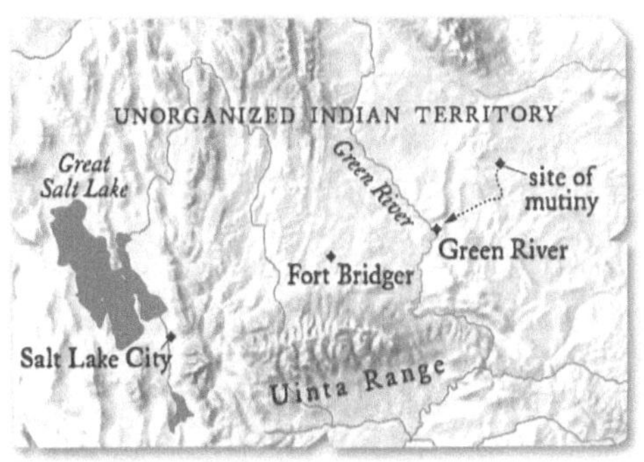

Chapter 11

SEPTEMBER, 1849

RAMBOULET'S SHORTCUT

Without the pressure of being driven, the Baltimore company's three remaining adults take their time. They spend the next few days deciding what important items need to be gathered from the other wagons. In a moment of insecurity, Donovan collects the accumulated Bostonian monies and puts it in his personal saddlebags. Despite the risk of hoarding, he rationalizes their earlier caution is no longer warranted. Surviving is.

All their livestock, except for Grunt, have scattered to the four winds. They combine their necessities into two wagons and, reluctantly, Donovan accepts he is the only one left to find the hobbled horses.

Fetching Grunt's bridle, he's grateful his horse has always preferred to stay close to humans. Easily slipping the bit into the horse's mouth, he slides the head carriage over his ears and leads him back to the wagons to be saddled. On his way, he surveys the horizon in all directions. None of the other horses or cattle are in sight.

Undaunted, Donovan saddles and mounts Grunt, setting out with several ropes looped around his saddle horn. Determined to make the best of his tenuous predicament, he makes giant, ever-expanding circles around the wagon camp. Eventually, he rides over a hill and spies three horses down in a low swale, their heads hanging low in rest. Hoping to approach without spooking them, he eases Grunt down the gentle grade. Getting closer, he sees their hobbles are intact, despite their desperate departure.

He recognizes one as the animal Robbins had ridden and remembers how cruelly the animal had been treated. The wind shifts and the horse lifts his head abruptly, its eyes wide with alarm. The other two lift their heads without portraying the same fearful energy.

Donovan carefully loops catch ropes over the two docile horses' heads and dallies them to Grunt's saddle horn. Confidence wells in him as he sizes up Robbins's horse. Clearly not as docile, he considers leaving the difficult horse behind. But another horse could increase their chances of survival.

He dismounts, holding Grunt's reins with one hand and the empty rope loop in the other.

He attempts to gently slip the loop over the horse's head, but the horse doggedly hops just beyond reach. Forced to drop Grunt's reins for more mobility, he steps toward the horse, who, in response, raises its head defiantly, flicking his head up and down in objection. His confidence slipping, Donovan gives the horse a chance to calm before trying again.

At his next attempt, he successfully gets the rope loop around the animal's neck, but when the loop's pressure tightens, the horse shrieks in terror. Connected to the frightened horse by a rope's length, Donovan resists the horse's pulls and tugs with both hands. His increased pressure only makes the animal wilder, now rising off the ground with small bucking motions, his front feet still hobbled.

Wary of frightening the other horses, Donovan toys with releasing the rope and leaving the horse to survive on its own, knowing they only really need two horses to pull the two wagons, and he already has three. But, once again, having another would provide insurance against one going lame.

Redoubling his effort to calm the horse, Donovan quietly steps toward it whispering softly while shortening the lead as he goes. The horse seems to respond to his quiet words.

Momentarily pleased with his effort, Donovan shoots a nervous side glance toward Grunt. With that slight motion, the horse shies and lifts to his hind feet. The increased pressure on the travel-worn hobbles' leather thong causes it to snap and the horse's left front hoof flares out to strike. Instantly, shooting pain explodes on the left side of Donovan's face followed by complete darkness at the ground's impact. Lying in a fast-accumulating pool of warm blood, his numbed brain faintly detects the quick clip of retreating horse hooves.

"Donnie! Donnie, wake up, please! You've got to wake up!"

Nora's voice echoes in the dark clefts and crevices of Donovan's consciousness. His feet twitch, then his fingers, knees, and elbows until his whole body spasms back to life. The gentle strokes of a wet cloth wiping his head bring comfort until bright light lances abruptly into his right eye.

"There you are! So much blood here, Donnie. I don't have enough bandages to fix you right. We'll need to be gettin' you back to the wagon for that."

"Nora? What happened? Where am I?"

"You'll have to remember how you got in this fix, but we're about a half mile from the wagon camp. Grunt and two horses returned without you. I set out following their trail and came upon you down in this draw."

"I . . . I tried to catch all three horses. Robbins's horse reared up and struck me."

"Can you walk if you lean on me?"

Donovan lifts his head, but excruciating pain forces him to immediately drop his head back and he mutters, "I don't know if I can."

"S'pose you could lie here and die, but we need you, Donnie. Don't leave us now."

Her insistent pleas bring him to sitting, despite a blur of dizziness. Taking his arm, Nora pulls him to his feet with a determined effort. Leaning in close and straining under his weight, she holds him until he finds an uneasy balance.

With infinite care, the two walk across the grainy ground, Donovan's low grunts of pain matching each crunch of their steps. When they finally arrive at the wagons, Mrs. Abernathy quickly comes to their aid. Before he knows it, his head is being carefully swabbed and bandaged, including his eyes. He is guided to Nora's wagon and laid on his back in its bed. Once the women leave, he can't help but doubt his survival.

Donovan's experience is restricted to sounds, as the bandages on his eyes and head keep him in complete darkness. Raging winds make the wagon's canvas cover pop and slap. Amalee's cries are shushed repeatedly. A surprise chill works its way along the wagon's bed, the cold seeping in against the muscles of his backside and thighs.

"Nora are you there?" he calls out.

"Yes, Donnie. Sorry about the babe. It's terribly cold all of a sudden."

"What time is it?"

"Just before dawn, I think. It's been blowin' for a while, but the cold just got here a bit ago. Can't see to build a fire."

"Is she cold too?"

"Aye, we both are."

"Come lay against me. Put her between us. We'll keep each other warm until daylight."

Nora's hesitation hints at her discomfort, but when she moves closer, he knows she sees his plan's validity. She eases into the slim space next to him, cradling Amalee between them. Instantly, Donovan feels their warmth and tries to roll onto his side. The movement causes stars to explode in his darkness.

He hollers, "I . . . I can't move without . . ."

"Needn't worry, Donnie, all's well. We'll be gettin' cozy real quick now."

Donovan feels the thrum of her heartbeat on his shoulder. Her warm breath wafting against his neck adds more intimate awkwardness.

When he shifts slightly, his movement initiates Nora to ask, "Donnie, I've been thinking on something. Wonder if you might help me sort it out?"

"Sure, Nora."

"Why do people do such things? Make decisions that put others in peril?"

Stumped by her question's expanse, Donovan silently struggles to answer, prompting Nora to continue, "I've a notion 'bout the different degrees of decisions. First, there's the daily decisions, them w'little or no true thought given. Such as whether to make coffee or change our clothes.

"Then, there's the kind that changes things, like whether you ride a horse to California or take a wagon. Headed west, no matter.

"The decision that marks your life is when you take responsibility for something or someone. Getting married. Having children. Killing someone."

Donovan feels a tremor run through him and wonders where she is heading.

"But the worst is when someone or something does the deciding for you. Something that once done, you don' recognize yourself. Like my family dyin' on the ship to America, or Ace dyin' because cholera made that decision. Me funding Ramboulet changed the whole company's future. It wasn't right for me to make that decision for everyone, was it Donnie?"

Donovan's tremor becomes a full-body prickle at her direct question.

He stammers, "Seems everyone made their own decision to continue when you paid Ramboulet. Widow Wilson did her own thinking when she turned back."

"But them boys the other night. They changed our lives by killing Abernathy over if we were heading in the right direction. What right did they have to do that?"

Donovan musters only a shrug, muttering, "Honestly, Nora, it doesn't matter anymore."

But Nora, her breath coming in shallow gulps now, doesn't stop.

"Your decision to help me is because of Ace's letter, right? If you hadn't struck your friendship with Ace, you wouldn't be considering my care, would you?"

Donovan tries to swallow, but there's no moisture in his mouth. Nora's questions have struck close . . . too close.

"Donnie, I must add to Ace's request."

"Add what?"

"If something happens to me, Amalee don't have no one in this world. If there's any way to save her, I need to know she won't be left behind. Given that you saved Quinn and Molly in Boston, I'm hoping you'll be open to the idea."

Nora's request makes Donovan's mind freeze. If he'd married Lillia, he'd be sitting in his father's office, likely miserable but content to go home to a devoted wife. Instead, he is here, wounded and lying in a wagon bed headed west, bonded by a dead man's request to a widow and her infant. And now this.

"Nora, my head hurts so bad, I don't know if I'm going to survive long enough to get to Fort Bridger. I'm pretty sure you've better chances of surviving than I do."

The wind's fury rocks the wagon with ominous power while he waits for her reply.

After several minutes, she stirs and says, "Feels like our path's gettin' dim, but I just can't give up, Donnie. I just can't."

"Honestly, Nora, I'm not sure how we're going to find our way from here."

At that, Amalee squirms between them, and Nora does her best to comfort her. It's not long before their combined warmth puts all three of them into a light, but welcomed, sleep.

Donovan wakes to a blast of chilly air against his exposed face.

He hears Nora say, "Father in Heaven. Why are you makin' this so hard?"

"What, Nora? What is happening?"

"I just lifted the flap to see the light of morning, and a storm's upon us. Everythin', and I mean everythin', is coated in an icy layer of snow. I best find Mrs. Abernathy and learn her circumstances. I'm goin' to leave Amalee with you. Please hold her close. She's fussy, lookin' for her breakfast, but I need to know about Mrs. Abernathy before I feed her."

He feels Amalee's weight lean up against his chest and then plop down gently, her head in his armpit. Frustrated by the bandage's forced blindness, he gropes awkwardly at it and lifts the right side to see enough to position the baby snugly. He hears the crunch of Nora's receding footsteps and before long, the sound of women's voices coming toward him.

"Donnie, Violet needs to join us. She's almost frozen to death. Stay where you are, and I'll make room."

"What about a fire? Surely, we can burn some contents in the other wagons."

"I'll work on a fire. But first, Violet needs your warmth."

Shocked to be in another awkward position, he gulps back his objection and repositions Amalee to the crook of his arm. Nora pulls and pushes at the wagon's contents until there is room for Mrs. Abernathy, Violet, to crawl in.

"Violet, here is my quilt. Scoot yourself into the corner next to Donnie and the baby. Donnie, it's her feet I'm most worried about. Let her wiggle 'em between your calves."

Silently complying, he feels the woman's frigid toes invade the space below his knees and does what he can to compress his calves against them. Their stone-cold feeling makes him twitch and Violet senses his discomfort.

"I'm sorry to chill you, Donovan. Nora is right, I'm near froze. If she hadn't come for me, I'd be at Nathan's side in heaven, a thought I'd prefer at this moment."

From outside the wagon, Nora grunts as she drags things to the wagon's leeward side. After several trips, he hears sounds of a shovel clanking against the ground and knows she is digging a fire pit in the frozen turf. Several minutes later, he hears the crisp click of flint being struck and her gentle coos coaxing the spark into a flame.

Finally, she yells out, "Hot damn, we got ourselves a good one. Won't be long now and I'll have hot drinks for you and warm milk for the babe. Hang on, you two! The horses stayed on their picket lines. Soon as the sun comes out, we can be on our way."

Donovan's thoughts, one minute relieved to hear of a source of warmth, now make him cringe at the idea of traveling. The monotonous chores of catching horses and driving the wagon seem like monumental tasks when he considers the continued pounding in his head.

"How can she think of traveling in this weather?" Violet demands, "I'd just as soon lay here and die."

Donovan, clearly the more injured of the two, decides against feeding Violet's depression and states calmly, "The sooner we're on our way, the sooner we get help at Fort Bridger. Nora is taking control of our situation, and we must do all we can to help her. And your feet have made improvement."

Violet jerks her feet away with a humph. Donovan turns his attention to Nora's activities outside. The aroma of coffee tickles his nose. A pot clanks. Nora hums as she works, something he has not noticed her doing before. It strikes him that in their tragedy, Nora is effortlessly shifting her role from subservient to leader. He recalls when he saved her in Redstone Creek. She had not been helpless really. She had just lost her footing, and he had arrived in time to help her out of the flooding waters. And she had shown initiative and found Ramboulet when Abernathy had come up empty-handed. And her dramatic performance at Ribadeaux's trading post was brilliant. Ace talked about how strong she was and how much he admired her for her courage and strength. Now Donovan witnesses her courage again.

Two tin cups of coffee and two bowls of porridge are shoved into the wagon bed in exchange for Amalee, whom Nora takes to the fire's warmth to nurse. Violet guides the bowl of porridge into Donovan's hands, and he welcomes the warmth. Slowly feeding himself, he finishes the porridge before Violet hands him the coffee. The crunch of Nora's footsteps announces her before her words.

"Everyone's been fed and warmed. Don't know about you two, but I'd like to move away from this place of death. Donovan, we'll be leavin' your bandages on. You rest in the back with the baby. I've got the compass. Violet, do you think you can help me harness horses and hitch up the wagons?"

"Yes. Lord knows I've hitched plenty of wagons."

"Alrighty then, off we go."

If he thought enduring the untamed terrain was difficult from the wagon's slightly sprung seat, lying prone in the wagon's bed was brutally painful for Donovan. With no way to anticipate a jolt, each bump catches him unaware. Remaining guardedly rigid, he stifles his anguished cries and lets the bandages absorb his tears. When Nora pulls up the horses, he finally lets his body relax.

He hears the canvas cover ties whistle open, and Nora's voice says, "Time for feedin' my little one. Seems Violet takes to drivin' her wagon. Acts like she wants to be in the lead, even though I've got the compass. I s'pose if she goes too far off track, she might look back for guidance. Then again, maybe not."

"Nora, how do you know where to go?"

"Before he disappeared, Ramboulet told Abernathy to head due west for two days and then start a slight turn south until we got to the Green River. Probably should'a suspected he was up to something, given those vague directions. I'm headed to the southwest. The horizon is filled with distant mountains. Wish you could see 'em, Donnie, so grand they make my heart race."

Donovan quietly considers her strategy before asking, "What does the weather look like?"

"Better than this morning. Still brisk, but the sun makes a difference. The ground is drying up before my eyes. I see a dark cloud bank north of us. Hope it's just clouds and not more snow. Seems early for snow, doesn't it?"

Donovan considers his mental calendar and asks, "I think it is September, but is it early or late?"

"My journal has us at September 16. Maybe it's normal in this wilderness, but it seems early for where I'm from."

"You're keeping a journal?"

"Have ever since Ace and I decided to make the trip way back in February. Even though I was pregnant, Ace said we couldn't wait. Had to get west 'fore all the gold was gone. Once the bug bit him, nothin' could turn his head."

"I proposed to Lillia a year ago amid a flurry of autumn leaves. California gold played no role in our lives at that point. Who would have ever known . . ."

His voice trails off before Nora asks, "Can I get you anything before we start up again?"

"A cup of water will do. Better drink it before you start driving or else I'll be wearing it."

The cloud bank Nora saw was indeed another storm. She ties the horses to the sheltered side of the wagons, and they rush to eat their supper. When the winds hit, the travelers wrap themselves in quilts in the bed of Nora's wagon to share their combined warmth. Despite the wind's howl, everyone settles into their own degrees of sleep.

At dawn, Nora scoots outside and Donovan listens carefully for her comment.

"Heavenly Father, while it's better than yesterday morn, would it offend you to give me somethin' to steer by? Really, this fog's thicker than wet wool! Likely not goin' to make much progress today."

Conflicted by her rant, Donovan senses the disappointment in her voice even as his backside's bruises are grateful for time to mend a bit. Fog, though, seems odd to be happening in a vast desert. His mind pricks with ideas for why there would be fog and then it occurs to him . . . fog happens when the air temperature is colder than water temperature.

"Nora! I think we must be getting close to the Green River!"

At the wagon gate, she pokes her head into their sanctuary and says, "Aye, I agree. But I've got no way of knowing how far it is or how we're goin' to navigate it when I can barely see my hand in front of my face. Suppose we could wait a while to see if it burns off."

"I think it is wisdom to wait," Violet says. "There's fresh blood on your bandages, Donovan. We should take advantage of our time and clean your wounds."

"I'll get the fire going," Nora says with sudden urgency.

Helpless to protest against the women's enthusiasm, Donovan lays still until asked to scoot toward the wagon gate. The effort is exhausting. He gasps reflexively when the bracing chill of the fog hits him. It is the coldest fog he has ever experienced. When the women tenderly unwind the cloth bandages from his head, the cold air creeps in with every layer removed. He grits his teeth against the pulsing pain. Just when he is close to crying out, a warm cloth is applied, and he relaxes.

"Oh, Donnie. I'm not sure how this is going to mend. Your cheekbone . . . and your eye socket . . . I'll do my best to wipe the blood away, but there's not much more I know to do."

Nora's anguished voice fades away as she gently dabs the warm cloth against his head's left side. Her efforts reopen the wound and she gasps, "Oh, no, it's bleeding again!"

"I know how to stop the bleeding. I found some of Nathan's leaf tobacco. It'll help. The only drawback is someone has to moisten it."

Donovan hears nothing until Nora says lowly, "Give it to me. I'll chew on it for a bit."

Prior to this, Donovan had been content to keep his right eye closed rather than watch their ministrations. But at Nora's announcement, he cracks it open enough to see her take a wad of black tobacco leaves from the sack and stuff them into her mouth. Chewing vigorously for several moments, she throws her hand to her mouth, spits the mass into it, and hands the tobacco to Violet. Then Donovan hears her vomit unceremoniously from the wagon's opposite side.

He feels Violet press the slimy handful of tobacco gently against his open wound and then the pressure of a clean bandage being wrapped tightly around his head. She makes several more wraps but today, she keeps his right eye uncovered.

"I figure you ought to see what is happening."

"Thank you. I'll try to be better help."

After several hours of waiting, the sun's pitiful attempt to cut through the opaque fog is enough to spur the women into action. Once the horses are harnessed, Donovan returns to his prone position in the wagon's confines and cradles a sleeping Amalee. Nora slowly picks their way to the southwest in constant consultation with her only companion, the compass sitting next to her.

Nora's horse knows it first, but from Grunt's tied position at the wagon's side, Donovan hears him snuffling the air eagerly. The horse's renewed energy has Nora straining uncomfortably on the lines. When she tries to stop the progress, the horse objects and rears in the harness.

"Donnie, somethin's come over him. I don't know what to do but stop and let him settle some. You'd best slip out of the wagon, take Amalee and her basket with you. Untie Grunt, too, just so you have him. Do your best to hurry. I'm not sure how long I can hold onto this beast."

Gathering Amalee into the crook of his arm, Donovan wiggles awkwardly toward the wagon's gate, the activity causing his head to resume its incessant pounding. Releasing the gate, he gathers the baby's basket and gently sets her into it before stepping into the whirlpool of swirling fog.

Quickly untying Grunt, he drops the horse's reins, content to let him follow. Finding his way to Nora's side, he grips Amalee's basket and notices that Violet's wagon is oddly absent.

"Where is Violet?"

"She was just slightly ahead of me. The fog has kept her from getting too far beyond my sight today. Are you right enough to walk? I'd feel better if Amalee stayed with you outside the wagon.

Been too long without water, and I think the horse is a bit crazy for a drink."

"I'll stay back with Grunt and follow you. As long as he can see you, he'll guide me."

"I wonder why Violet didn't stop when I did?" Nora asks Donovan as she slowly eases the pressure on the lines and the wagon begins to roll away from him.

"I don't . . ."

A distant crashing sound interrupts Donovan. He hears a horse shriek—a death cry to be sure—but the sound's distance is hard to judge. Through a break in the churning fog, he detects a jagged edge, and the ruts left by Violet's wagon wheels. As quickly as the edge is revealed, the fog disguises it again, flowing in a violent upward whorl of mist.

Instantly alarmed, Donovan freezes in place. Nora's horse, now confused and bewildered by the other horse's death calls, continues to dance and skittishly sway in the harness. Inch by inch, the cliff's jagged edge approaches and Donovan knows backing up the wagon is quickly not becoming an option.

"Donnie, take Amalee and back away. Don't know how long I can hold 'im . . . goin' ta try to back 'im up."

Donovan sees the horse go wild-eyed. It rears onto its hind legs, the harness straining against the pressure. At the same time, the horse's hoof impact causes the fragile bank to crack and release. Despite her efforts, the flailing horse's weight jerks Nora and the wagon beyond Donovan so quickly that his last sight of her is only her frightened expression before vanishing into the clouds below.

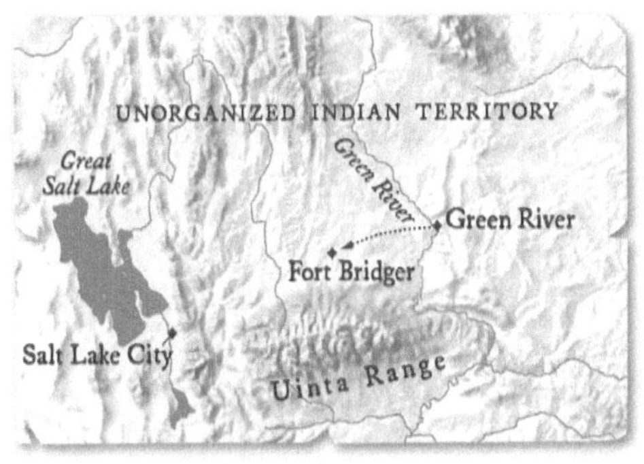

Chapter 12

SEPTEMBER, 1849

GREEN RIVER

"Nora!" he calls. "Noooorrahhh!" Donovan's voice breaks in anguish as he yells her name, over and over.

Nothing but the eerie echo of his voice returns to his ears, volleying off the hidden depths enshrouded by looming fog.

An eternity passes while he waits. The wagon had crashed with a deafening clatter. Donovan hoped that somehow Nora might have survived the impact, but the passing time makes his hopes futile.

He continues to call her name until his voice falls hoarse, his throat dry. Amalee takes up the cause and howls from her basket, the handles still gripped tightly in his hand. Suddenly puzzled about how the child could know of her mother's tragic death, it is clear to him that Amalee understands something is terribly wrong.

Man and child sob together, collapsed on the ground. After a time, Donovan senses the presence of Grunt and realizes he has only two souls in this wilderness. Deep resolve helps him stagger upright to take Grunt's reins in one hand. Holding Amalee's basket handles in the other, he walks away from the cliff.

At a safe distance, Donovan loops the baby basket's handles over the saddle horn and cautiously steps into the stirrup. His legs feel like mush, but he musters enough strength to push up and lift his right leg over the saddle's swells. Breathless from the exertion, he sits for a few moments trying to steady himself. Then he gives a gentle tug on Grunt's reins and points him back in the direction they had come, the only safe ground he is confident of at this moment.

Reaching behind the saddle's swell, he gropes anxiously for the saddlebags he remembers tying there. Their reassuring bulk gives him a whiff of calm until he realizes the compass had gone over the edge with everything else in the wagon. He is on his own, left to navigate by the sun and the stars if he and Amalee are going to get to Fort Bridger.

The sun's position tells him it's about midday. The lifting fog reveals rolling hills with deep creases that could provide cover. Amalee's whimpers tell him refuge is not her priority, eating is. By traveling toward the sun's descent for as long as he physically can or until he comes to the Green River, whichever happens first, he prays he will make some general progress toward Fort Bridger.

Amalee quiets, as if she, too, knows they must continue on their journey. But, in the back of his mind the question looms . . . even if he survives, how can he possibly care for this child?

In what seems like hours later, the fog has evaporated and the river presents itself as a twisting green serpent in a vast sea of beige sand and gravel. Restricted tightly by deeply eroded cliff walls, Grunt picks his way to the water with as much care as a thirsty animal can. At the watery edge, Donovan lets Grunt wade out knee-deep to drink his fill before nudging him to cross.

Finding a sandy bank with remnants of driftwood from spring flooding, Donovan dismounts and ties Grunt to a wild-rooted stump. He chooses to leave the baby basket's handles looped around the saddle horn and takes his empty canteen to refill it. Stiffened by the long ride, his legs regain their circulation as he gingerly staggers across the river rocks toward the gently flowing current. Once his canteen is full, he sips carefully, the water's chill on his parched throat almost making him gag while his incessant headache flares to life.

Back at Grunt's side, he leans against the horse, exhausted. His mind nudges him to make haste, but his body ignores the prod. It's the baby's whimper that sets him in motion. He leads Grunt away from the river toward the willow-infested river-bank, eyeing the sandy bank for a protected spot. Within a few moments, a suitable spot emerges from the thicket, protected on two sides by the willows. Gathering his resolve, he removes Amalee and her basket, his saddlebags, bedroll, and finally Grunt's saddle and blanket.

Knowing a fire is mandatory for their survival, he slothfully creates a fire ring, gathers driftwood, and tears shreds of cedar bark from it for tinder. With the flint from his saddlebag, he strikes a few times and successfully produces a spark into the nest of shredded cedar bark.

Once the fire is dancing, he retrieves Amalee from her basket. Keenly aware she will only survive if he can find something for her to eat, he is suddenly grateful for her ample baby fat. Sinking into the sand next to the campfire, he takes her out of the basket and is woefully unprepared for the nauseating stench of a day's worth of bodily fluids.

Despite the building chill, he removes his shirt and lays it in the sand, hastily pulling his coat over his bare torso. Once all the soiled garments are removed and tossed a good distance, he rolls the child up in the shirt and ties the sleeves tight around her.

With a stare of expectation, she whimpers until he says, "Let's see what I find in my saddlebags, Amalee."

He gropes in the bags' depths until his fingers find an unfamiliar drawstring pouch. Loosening the string, he lets out a whimper of joy when he sees a few handfuls of oats.

"Your momma is looking out for us, little one."

Using an emptied metal brandy flask, he fills it with water and the oats before setting it into the fire's coals. While he waits, he finds a handkerchief and decides she can suck the oat water from a saturated handkerchief while he eats the solids.

"It's not the grandest meal, but until I get you to something better, you'll have to be happy."

After eating their meager meal, he takes Grunt to the river for another drink and one for himself. The cold air makes the water feel warm, the perfect combination for another overnight fog event. He builds up his fire before settling into the sandy low spot with Amalee cradled in his arms under his coat and saddle blanket.

His mind returns to Nora's observations about decisions. He realizes her analysis had left out one kind of decision. She had neglected the decision of whether to fight to live or just give up. If he doesn't make it to Fort Bridger soon, that decision could be his.

The anticipated fog's chill niggles through Donovan's coat and worn trousers as he wakes. Amalee had been fitful all night, no doubt unsatiated by the oat water. He shifts in the sand and cracks open his eye to see a figure standing not ten feet from him. Wiping at his good eye, he focuses through the obscuring fog. He makes out two legs standing squarely and a musket barrel extending above the right shoulder but is still unclear as to who it is, until the figure speaks.

"*Sacre Christ*, I can't believe anyone survived the fall. An' you of all of 'em."

Ramboulet's disdain is clear. Questions flare in Donovan's mind as to where their guide has been these past days but uncertainty about the man's intentions forces him to hold his tongue.

"Best be buildin' up this fire. Looks like you did pretty good on your own last night."

"Did the best I could."

Their voices rouse Amalee and she squawks from beneath the protection of his coat and the blanket.

"*Mon Dieu*, you saved the baby?"

"As it happens, we got out of the wagon just before."

"Why are you wearing bandages?"

"Let's build the fire and I'll tell you everything. But first, I need to know where you have been. You said two days."

"S'pose you deserve an explanation."

"Considering I'm the only one left, I believe I'm owed one."

Ramboulet silently gathers driftwood sticks and kindles the fire's flame while Donovan brings Amalee out of his coat and wraps her in the blanket. Even though he is eager to know Ramboulet's excuse, Donovan keeps his peace.

"It's like this . . . I knowed them boys was goin' to cause all manner of trouble once they found them spirits. Worn down, they was. My bein' there wasn't goin' to make a difference in the outcome. 'Cept if I took a bullet. I been around this long because I can sense the devil's mischief comin' out."

Donovan lets Ramboulet's words hang for a while before saying, "Yes, well, the devil's work was complete. After the shooting was over, it was me and two women and a baby. Hard to imagine there being a worse omen for continuing, but we tried. I took a horse hoof to the face trying to catch a spooked horse. The women were driving the wagons through the fog toward Fort Bridger and before we knew it, the wagons went over the cliff."

Donovan's last words make Ramboulet stop feeding the building fire and stare into Donovan's face.

"Just went over the cliff? Didn't try to stop?"

"I don't know why the first woman didn't. Nora tried, but the horse just kept rearing and drug her over the edge while I watched helplessly, holding the baby in her basket."

"*Mon Dieu. C'est triste.*"

Amalee's needs usurp the men's conversation and Donovan asks, "Do you have anything with you she can eat?"

Ramboulet rises and disappears into the fog. He returns leading his horse by the reins and ties the horse next to Grunt. From his saddlebags he produces an arm full of goods, casually dropping them by the fire's edge. He settles a tripod over the growing fire and suspends a skin bag from it. After filling the bag with a canteen of water, he settles a frying pan into the coals off to one side.

When Ramboulet produces a cloth-covered slab of bacon and begins slicing a few chunks into the pan, Donovan's stomach roars to life. After the bacon chunks release their fat, Ramboulet carefully scrapes the fat into the water bag followed by a dollop of molasses from a small jug. He swirls the concoction with his finger, tastes it, and smiles with satisfaction.

Fashioning a scrap of tanned deerskin into a rudimentary cone shape, Ramboulet pours a small amount of the liquid into the cone. Producing his enormous hunting knife, he pricks at the deerskin until a small hole reveals a drop of liquid. Retrieving the baby, he sits and cradles her in his bent knee for support.

"Ain't your momma's milk or her titty, *ma chère,* but it's all I got."

Donovan is awestruck when Amalee eagerly suckles from the offered cone. After finishing, Ramboulet deftly juggles her to his shoulder and gently pats on her back until she emits an audible burp.

A tobacco-stained grin cracks Ramboulet's matted facial hair as he holds her up and says, "*Bon bébé!*"

The morning sun burns away the fog and Ramboulet lays a scrap of animal hide on the sand. He loosens her from the shirt and lets her stretch her arms and legs in the sun's warmth before turning to Donovan and handing him a flask.

"Your turn."

Ramboulet kneels in the sand and tugs on Donovan's bloody head wrap. Cringing with disgust, Ramboulet turns his face away and flushes the wound with whiskey. Roiling from the whiskey's burn, Donovan fights off nausea when Ramboulet pulls out his hunting knife.

"Where'd your eye patch get to?"

"Haven't had it since the horse kicked me. Suppose it's laying in the dirt somewhere."

Holding stone still, Donovan prays for a steady hand when the mountain man takes aim at the crushed cheek bone and eye socket. He flinches under the knife point's pressure while it explores the sensitive area.

Finished with his probe, Ramboulet secures the wound with torn cloth strips and says, "Your face sure gots character now. Don' look like the eye muscles were cut but won't know 'til it heals some. You gonna need someone with more doctorin' skills than me. Fort Bridger is a strong day's ride. I'll get you there 'fore leavin'. Winter's coming soon. Given your shape, best plan on hunkerin' down at the fort. 'Sides, *bébé* needs human milk, not just bacon grease and 'lasses."

Sometime in the dark night, Amalee starts wailing. Her forehead burns with the heat of fever, and she is soaked with sweat.

Donovan sees Ramboulet reach under the blanket and pull Amalee away from his chest. He forms a cradle with his arms and swishes her through the air in small arcs, but her shrieks only heighten. Ramboulet nudges Donovan with his boot.

"Get up. Breakin' camp. Gotta get 'er some help."

Finding his voice, Donovan croaks out, "What's wrong with her?"

"'Spect the change o' diet. Mine's no match for momma's milk. Gas, I 'magine."

"Will she make it to Fort Bridger?"

"Goin' to give it our best shot. The horses had rest, feed, and water. Now I'm wonderin' if you're goin' to make it, sweatin' like you are!"

Donovan feels the flush of fever in his own body, the aches that make him want to do nothing more than lie back on the ground and moan with misery. He watches Ramboulet rush to catch the horses, then saddle and pack them. Donovan forces himself to rise, but every movement makes him dizzy. Amalee continues her distressed shrieking from her basket. In dawn's dim light, Ramboulet helps Donovan onto Grunt but keeps the baby with him.

"Startin' off at a long trot. If you can't take the bouncin', slow back to a quick walk. Follow my trail best you can."

Finding it impossible to keep Ramboulet's pace, it's not long before Donovan is relying on Ramboulet's twisted, broken ground trail. When that is lost, it is Amalee's distant, pitiful wails that continue to guide him in the right direction. When Donovan finally catches up to them, they have stopped to rest Ramboulet's lathered horse. Approaching with care, Donovan listens for Amalee but hears nothing. Ramboulet snaps his head toward the west, his free hand pointing.

"*Et voilà*, Fort Bridger."

Donovan squints into the westerly wind. The sun's rays outline the thorny peaks on the mountainous horizon, promising only an hour or so of daylight left.

"Goin' to sprint to the fort so's we make it by dark. Give your horse 'is head and he'll find his way to the others. Help'll be waitin'."

With that, Ramboulet spurs his horse over the bank's edge, dramatically leaning back in the saddle, arms thrown wide, one hand loosely gripping the reins, the other holding Amalee's basket handles in perfect balance. Donovan watches them plow through the shallow river water in a glorious display of spray. Disappearing around the river's bend, he is sure the fort inhabitants will hear Ramboulet coming before they see him.

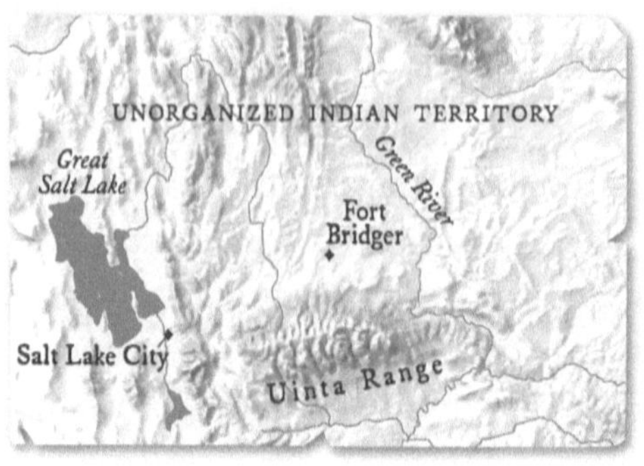

Chapter 13

SEPTEMBER, 1849

FORT BRIDGER,

UNORGANIZED INDIAN TERRITORY

With Fort Laramie and Fort Kearney as his only references of wilderness compounds, Fort Bridger's ramshackle eight-foot stockade does little to impress Donovan when he rides through the open gate at dusk. Equally unremarkable are the fort's various hand-hewn structures when compared to the military forts' efforts to precision. Be that as it may, a wave of relief flows over him to have reached this much civilization.

He and Grunt stop at the hitching post next to Ramboulet's tired beast in the fort's common ground. No one appears to greet him. His canteen is empty, his throat is hoarse, so any noise from him is out of the question. He is forced to wait on Grunt's back until noticed.

Finally, a door squeaks open. Donovan hears Ramboulet's voice and a woman's reply as a baby whimpers. Suddenly, several pairs of hands are pulling him carefully from the saddle. Donovan feels himself being carried until Ramboulet leans in close.

He says, "No doctor here but Vasquez. His wife, Narcissa'll share her momma's milk since she's got a new little one."

Donovan feels his body being laid onto a cot and tries to relax but the pain in his head is too strong. He hears the low hum of voices in serious discussion until he feels a gentle tug on his head wrap. He grits his teeth against the inevitable pain. The air fills with the putrid odor of rotting flesh. Donovan cracks open his eye. A pair of dark eyes stare out from under a thicket of black eyebrows so close to his own, he's unable to see anything else.

"By the look of this handiwork, goin' to have to talk to ole Ramboulet 'bout his doctoring methods. Seems he knows more than he lets on."

Gently, the man begins swabbing Donovan's wounded head with warm water while whispering, "Need to pay close attention to that eye socket. Don't want to lose it. Them bones'll need coaxin' to knit but you ain't got nothin' but time. How'd you come to have this mess?"

"Kicked by a horse. Smashed my face. Lost the baby's mother and the wagon over a cliff. Along with everything else, saved only my horse and the baby."

Vasquez's expression softens as Donovan's story spills from his quavering lips.

"You made it this far. Better get some food in you. I'm Louis Vasquez."

"I'm—" Donovan starts to introduce himself and then stops. His mind returns to some of the things he had contemplated while riding toward Fort Bridger. One of the most important was the promise that if he survived, he would become a new person and find a new life. That new life starts right now.

"Name's Dash. Dash Truepenny."

"Alright then, Dash, I'm going to get you a bowl of stew and cold water. After you eat, we'll get you tended to."

Within a week's time, Amalee is back to her happy self. Dash isn't as fortunate. His wound is not healing easily, and Vasquez is troubled by its stubbornness. Whenever Vasquez checks the wound's progress, pain shoots through Dash's skull.

He learns to face each day with a sliver more courage than the day before. When Vasquez arrives at his storage shed residence with another man, he feels his courage wither at the sight. He recognizes Jim Bridger from their brief introduction on Ramboulet's secret trail.

"Vasquez tells me you've got a nasty wound. Mind if I give it a peek?"

"No, sir," Dash mumbles shyly.

With routine efficiency, Vasquez unwraps the bandages along with the now customary collection of bilingual oaths at the stench. Wincing against the fresh air hitting the tender skin, Dash braces himself for examination. Bridger comes in close to study the fractured cheekbone and eye socket. Several minutes pass before he speaks.

"Son, I got a hunch this eye o' yours can be saved but it's goin' to require you to be still as a post. Can't have any wincin' or twitchin' when I come in with my knife. Don't have nothing but whiskey for the pain but with enough, you'll go still. What do you say?"

Reluctant to admit his eye's previous dysfunction, Dash decides there is nothing to lose in Bridger's attempt and says, "I'll do whatever you think I should, sir."

"Alright then, Louis, you get the whiskey, I'll sharpen my knife. Once you're good and drunk, we'll lay you back and tie you down. Can't stress enough how important it'll be that you don't move while I got my knife point in your eye hole."

The road to Dash's inebriation is lined with some freshly baked bread and an earthen ware vessel of whiskey, for which Vasquez is quick and generous. With no accumulated tolerance for alcohol, it isn't long before Dash lies prone on his cot and feels the two men strapping him down. The prick of a sharp knife point is his last sensation.

His escort back to consciousness is a pounding throb accompanied by the echoes of soft coos in the room. Dash's good eye flutters open and he sees Narcissa Vasquez holding a round-faced Amalee in fresh, clean garments.

Amalee leans toward him and Narcissa pulls her back saying, "No baby girl, your daddy has had quite an ordeal. Best just sit with me for a while."

"How long . . ." Dash starts.

"It's been hours since Bridger finished. Said it was one of the hardest things he's ever done but feels good that your eye is going to be right again. Thought I'd check in and bring your daughter to say hello."

Dash looks at Amalee while pondering the need to correct Narcissa's mistake. Finally deciding it would take too much energy, he reaches out and strokes the soft cheeks of the Baltimore company's only other remaining member.

"Must take after her mother. She doesn't hold much likeness to you, Dash."

"Yes, she's her mother's image, ma'am. Thank you for looking after her while I've been healing."

"Not to worry, Dash, she's been a joy. Louis and I have a little one, so I have lots of practice with babies. Since you'll be spending the winter with us, I imagine Amalee and Mary Ann will become playmates. Do you remember when Amalee was born?"

Dash struggles to recall until finally blurting out, "The last part of July, I think."

"Oh, they are close! Our little Mary Ann was born July 25. No wonder they seem to be identical. Except for the hair, of course."

At that moment, Vasquez enters the shed, shutting the door against a flurry of snowflakes. Narcissa smiles and lets him take her seat on the log next to Dash's cot, before bundling Amalee up and leaving. Louis sits and looks into Dash's face.

"Ramboulet is back just in time. Said he went to your wagons' crash site to see if there was anything he could do or salvage for you. I'm glad to report he found your woman's body and gave it a proper burial."

"Any salvage?" Dash asks.

"Nothin' he shared. I imagine the river washed most things away. After this amount of time, there's not likely to be anything worth saving. You're going to have to start over, Dash, with only what you brought in your saddlebags. Best face it, you're in a fix. It's damn early for the kinda storms we're gettin'. Means a long winter. You ain't goin' anywhere 'til spring. Bridger'll welcome your company, 'specially if you can contribute to livin' here. Earn your keep."

Hesitant to reveal his inadequacies, Dash asks, "What's needed at Fort Bridger?"

"How good a shot were you 'fore all this?"

Dash feels his insides squeeze tight as he says, "From Boston. No need for guns."

"Growing up in Boston give you any carpentry skills?"

"I was only a clerk but I know Morse code."

Vasquez's bushy eyebrows raise above his brown eyes as he blows through his bushy beard and mustache.

"I'd say you're a little unprepared for this chapter of your life. Once you heal, you'll have to build your strength and learn to live in this world. Do you good. How are you with horses?"

"Had to buy and ride an unfamiliar one on this trip. He's pretty good. Where is he, anyway?"

"In the corral. Not the fanciest bag of horseflesh but he's well-mannered. Eats like a plow horse."

"Nora knew horses better."

"Nora?"

Quickly, Dash considers how to absorb Nora and Amalee into his new life story without flagrantly lying.

"She was Amalee's . . ."

Vasquez misinterprets his hesitancy and replies, "It's to be understood, Dash, losin' yer wife the way you did. Horrible memory."

An awkward silence builds between them until a new topic comes to Dash.

"What became of the things I rode in with?"

Vasquez gestures with a head nod.

"Your tack's in the barn and your bags are under your cot."

Dash slowly pulls on the heavy saddlebags, his fingers stiff and uncooperative. When Vasquez sees his struggle, he leans over with one hand and pulls the closest bag out, his fingers nimbly releasing the leather latch.

"Can I find somethin' for you?"

"I . . . I . . . I just need to know what the baby and I have to survive the winter on. I don't remember what's in here. If you wouldn't mind fetching a few things."

Without hesitation, Vasquez flips the saddlebag cover open and the first thing to come out is Luther's money belt.

"Well, now, Dash," Vasquez says slowly as he admires the belt. "Maybe this here's a substitute for your lack of skills. Never considered you'd have this kinda coin."

A few days pass before there's a knock on Dash's door and a familiar shape enters the room. Dash feels an uneasy tension as Ramboulet finds a stump seat and sits, uttering a low groan.

"We need to talk. Seems I'm out my final guidin' payment and given the circumstances, I s'pose I should just get on. But Vasquez tells me you got somethin' to work with in the way of money. Would you trade me some coin for somethin' I got that's likely sentimental to you?"

The hair on Dash's neck bristles at the guide's sappy tone. Suspicious that Ramboulet might believe there was more to his and Nora's relationship, he struggles to deliver a clarifying question but not before Ramboulet pulls out a rawhide wrapped bundle and sets it on his lap.

"Wouldn't have normally done somethin' like this but when I saw her layin' there, all perfect, I just had to have it. Then I got to thinkin' it might be worth somethin' to you. If you think so, I'll take ten dollars for it."

Confused about Ramboulet's explanation and offer, Dash reaches up and slowly pulls the tight bundle's straining string. With a pop, the knot releases and the thin rawhide falls away to reveal a mass of red curls. Instantly recoiling in horror and disgust, Dash slaps the bundle away from his lap, his mind whorling with its implications.

Exasperated, Ramboulet says, "What? She don't have no use for it now! I laid your woman in a deep hole I dug myself. You should pay me for the service. The beasts had got on the other woman such that there warn't much left. But since your woman was hangin' from one of the wagon cover bows, she was untouched. I took great care in th'scalpin' though it was harder than when the skin's fresh."

"I . . . I . . . I don't want it. Take it away. I don't want it. Get out. Get out now."

Ramboulet gathers up the bundle off the floor, growling, "Tell you the truth, I'll get more than ten dollars for it when I sell it a lock at a time. Or some Indian'll likely give me ten times in trade for the whole scalp an' use it in one o' their ceremony costumes. 'Sides, a city boy like you don't stand a chance in this place. Your only way of surviving is to head back to the city where you come from and find a city girl for your little one. You ain't got what it takes."

Ramboulet stomps out letting the door slam to punctuate his point. Dash twitches with the memory of Nora's beautiful hair. How many times had he secretly admired it? Memories of Nora and Ace after Dash had rescued her from Redstone Creek and then the night they danced on the flatboat in Louisville fill his mind's eye. Remorse for everything that happened in the last six months joins with the echoes of Ramboulet's last words.

Despite the pain, uncontrolled pressure fills his head, and tears streak down his cheeks. When Vasquez comes to the shed later, he hesitates at the sounds of sobbing coming from inside and decides to wait for his visit.

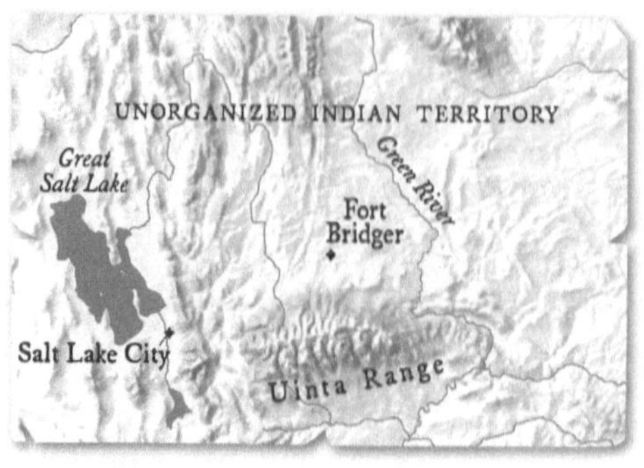

Chapter 14

DECEMBER, 1849

FORT BRIDGER,

UNORGANIZED INDIAN TERRITORY

*T*wo months after Ramboulet's grisly offer, Bridger offers to sell a rifle to Dash saying, "Ain't no way your eye is going to work, unless you give it something to do. Now's the time to start getting some learnin' at shooting a rifle. What do you say?"

Dash's intention of embracing a new life causes a slight hesitation to the idea, but he answers with enthusiasm, "Yes, I'd like to learn to shoot a rifle."

By this time, everyone in Fort Bridger accepts Dash's permanent facial disfigurement. When Jim Bridger patches Dash's right eye to force the left eye to do his seeing for him and objects come into focus, no one is more shocked than him.

His rifle purchase comes with lessons, and as the weeks pass, Bridger gives him tasks to build his confidence. Dash gains not only faith in his eyesight but strength enough to hold the long-barreled weapon level and true. Some of the fort's men, Blaze, Smudge, and Fred, take an interest in Dash's practice regimen and join him every day to encourage him through friendly competition.

After his morning chores are done, Dash meets the men outside of the fort's balustrade where they have set up a series of targets of varying sizes and distances. Since each man has to reload his rifle for every shot, the object of their practice is accuracy, not speed. As Dash becomes more comfortable, the men add moving targets swinging from tree branches. Wagers are always made; winner takes all. The day's worst performer is expected to make enough new lead balls for the next day's practice.

Being the newbie, Dash learns quickly how to make new ammunition by liquifying sticks of lead into small pots before pouring the liquid into ball forms to cool. It's not long, though, before he wins a few contests and makes fewer lead balls.

Remarkably, Dash's camaraderie with the men is not the highlight of his day. Narcissa gives him full permission to visit Amalee whenever he wants. As the winter days shorten, he's eager to visit and play with the little girl. When he walks into the room, he is never disappointed by the gleeful expression that crosses Amalee's face, and he feels his own spark of joy toward her.

They play with her modest collection of toys, and Narcissa dotes on both of them like a mother hen. There's always a napkin-covered bit of leftover pie or cake that finds its way into his hand before he leaves, and Dash is grateful for her kindness.

On his way back to his solitary cot and wood stove in the storage shed, Dash gazes at the overhead stars shining so bright in the dark sky. His eyes well with tears for all that has happened since leaving Boston and Lillia. He remains astonished that he and Amalee are safe after their traumatic circumstances. And he feels his heart swell with the feelings he has developed for the strangers who have made him and Amalee part of their frontier family.

Just after the fort welcomed the new year, a sharp rap on Vasquez's storage room door jolts Dash from his cot. Cracking the door against the cold, Bridger pushes past Dash, his moderate physique transformed by hide and fur coverings.

"Dash, I was hopin' you'd come along on a huntin' expedition. Fort needs fresh meat. A scoutin' party just arrived sayin' there's elk to our south. I suppose the snow is deep up high and pushed them down into the valleys. I'd like to see what you have for seein' distance outta that eye. No time like the present for another test."

Nervous energy floods Dash's system as he rushes to collect a similar wardrobe of warm hides and furs accumulated over the past months. He nervously stuffs a bag full of jerky and dried fruit, a blanket and rifle ammunition into his pack before following Bridger out of the cabin into the dark, frigid morning air.

The two men join Blaze, Smudge, and Fred, who are packing their bags with knives, axes, coils of rope, blankets, and several large, empty leather bags. As the youngest and clearly most inexperienced among them, Dash does his best to fight off the chill of doubt about his readiness.

The sky dawns pink against the pure, rolling white of the open plains, and Bridger leads the outfit out the fort's gate and toward the western Uinta Mountains. The men resemble loping buffalo, the dark furs draping from their ample shoulders, snowshoes slapping into the dry snow. Before long, the men push back their fur-lined hoods, steam rising from their hot heads into the chill. Dash doesn't dare unwrap the protective head scarf

Narcissa made him to prevent the cold from piercing his scar and giving him a crippling headache.

By the time the sun is at its peak, they come upon a willow-infested creek where they stop to rest and eat jerky and cold biscuits. Dash chews while listening to the men jab fun at each other. Slogging through the sea of white for a few more hours brings them to the mountains' foothills. As they climb, white-barked aspen forests finger their way into the dark, denser spruce forest. Smudge notices Dash studying the black, scarred slashes on the aspen trunks.

"A grizzly marking his territory."

After the tales of bear encounters told by the fort's evening fires, Dash feels his pulse accelerate.

"Don't worry none, Dash; they're sleepin' this time of year. We only got to be concerned with Injuns and wolves. Ain't seen no sign of either yet."

Dash nods uneasily.

At dusk, they arrive at a grove of spruce trees where heavy snow has bowed the branches to the ground. Like big badgers, the men burrow into the adjacent snowbanks pushing the snow aside until they reach dry ground, creating a large cavern.

They build a fire at the structure's outer edge and squeeze around it, eating their cold rations by the building warmth. Bridger lays out his plan for the hunt.

"We'll stalk back into these hills in the early mornin'. Won't be no wind blowin'. Elk will be close to their waterin' hole. The key is to pick an animal and focus. Don't fire willy-nilly into the herd. Don't want do too much trackin' in this kind of snow."

"How . . ."

Bridger's eyebrows raise at Dash's interruption.

"Go ahead, Dash."

Dash self-consciously looks to either side of him.

"Just wondering how we're going to get the meat all the way back to the fort with no horses?"

Fred coughs and remarks, "Why do you think we brought you along, Dash?"

Through a chorus of guffaws, Dash stares sheepishly at the men, his heart sinking. Bridger sets the record straight.

"We're the beasts of burden. We'll each lash our ropes to a quarter. Hide stays on to protect the meat while we drag it across the snow. You'll drag the goodies."

Blaze sees Dash's confused expression and says, "The organs . . . liver, heart, kidneys. All good eatin'."

Bridger says, "Dash, you need to get some experience with firin' your weapon at somethin' other than a knothole. Get your confidence up and make sure that left eye of yours is workin' correct. I want to see what your range is. It's too hard takin' the long shot at the fort."

Dash gulps back doubt as the others nod their agreement. Heartened by Bridger's confidence in him, he still has never shot at a living target before.

In the pre-dawn darkness, Dash feels the mound of sleeping men stir. Grunting and groaning, they crawl out from the snow structure and break camp without a warming fire. Bridger points Fred and Smudge uphill to the left and he, Blaze, and Dash around to the right.

When their snowshoes plop into the soft snow, Dash's tight muscles protest, and he struggles to keep up. His rifle is heavier than it felt the day before, and trip lines of bush branches lace the trail, forcing Dash into an awkward stagger. Determined to keep both his balance and silence, he persists so as not to disappoint Bridger.

Eventually, they come to a stop and Bridger waves the men closer. Gasping, Dash takes in the sight before them. A narrow mountain valley is packed tight with an enormous herd of tranquil elk milling in the pre-dawn light.

Bridger silently taps Dash on the shoulder and motions for him to set up behind a large boulder pile. Fred and Smudge arrive above them a short distance down the valley and hold their positions, while the others prepare their rifles for firing. On Bridger's signal, the two men silently set off again, their trail now running parallel to the herd. At the herd's midway, they descend through the low scrub oak, voices raised and arms waving.

Chaos erupts with half the herd bolting toward the shooters while the other half escape in the opposite direction, their long legs barely able to lift above the deep snow.

"Pick one out, Dash. Aim for its front shoulder, between the front legs or right behind the front flank."

Dash lines up the rifle's sight but the animals are in such a frenzy that he struggles to aim at just one. Calls from cows to their calves fill the air until an explosion cracks from Bridger's location. A second boom comes from Blaze's rifle. Tension crackles when Dash still doesn't have anything sighted. His chance is almost lost.

"There's one! Can't make up its mind. Hold your fire, Dash. I'll call out when he decides which way to run. Remember, squeeze the trigger like you're fondlin' a woman's breast, gentle and slow. Alright now, he's comin' our way, about a hundred yards off."

Dash sees a lone, confused spike bull plowing through the herd's broken snow trail. Its wild-eyed expression signals its recognition of its peril. It stops to call out, the hesitation giving Dash enough time to aim at the stranded elk's heaving chest.

Gentle and slow, like strokin' a woman's breast.

At the bottom of his exhale, he caresses the rifle's trigger. The rifle's recoil sends him airborne and backward. Blaze arrives to lend him a hand and, once upright, Dash peers over the boulder to see the animal flailing in the snow, its front leg dangling useless. He has only a moment to regret that his shot wasn't fatal before he hears another booming shot come from over his shoulder, its sound reverberating off the valley walls.

The animal instantly lies still, its crimson life's blood flowing onto the surrounding sea of white.

From behind, Dash hears Bridger say, "Ain't no good for the meat if they suffer."

As Bridger's group wind their way through the brush to the valley floor, Fred and Smudge arrive, whooping at their success. In addition to the young bull, there is a cow and a lead bull lying prone, the bull's antlers broad and wide showing six points on either side.

Stripping to their leather shirts, the men disembowel the carcasses with their long hunting knives. With practiced efficiency, the organs are separated from the other entrails before being tossed into a hot pile in the snow to cool. Having never seen anything like it, Dash ignorantly gawks, prompting Bridger to direct him.

"Dash, them goodies go in the leather bag in my blanket roll. Pack snow around them so they keep good and cold before putting them in the bag."

The sun is bright as the men work and sweat drips from their faces. Slowly coming upright, Bridger wipes a handkerchief across his brow.

"Goin' to have to leave the bull behind. We'll hang him up in a spruce to keep the wolves off."

Once the bull is gutted, they drag the carcass to a great spruce, its thick branches strong enough to support the carcass's hefty weight. Using one of their precious ropes, they heave the large carcass up and off the ground, securing it at about twenty feet high.

With no time to celebrate, they turn their attention to getting back to the fort. Each man loops a rope harness attached to a carcass half across his chest. Dash hauls the goodie bag full of organs over his aching right shoulder. The winter sun drops behind the western horizon, and the men move noticeably slower after their day's exertions. When they reach the willow-choked stream, Bridger holds up his hand.

"We'll camp here before the light gets away."

Each man drags his load toward the creek's edge where a snowdrift has formed along a cutback providing a natural backstop. Digging out a snow cave, the men shove the carcass halves into the void and cover them generously with snow.

"Dash, bring them goodies and come with me," Bridger barks.

Dash follows him to where the creek forms an arc and the willows are bent into a low, dome-shaped shelter. Taking advantage of exposed driftwood piles, they carve out a fire pit in the sandy creek bottom. Before long, they enjoy the warmth of a bright campfire, the wind held at bay by the creek's steep bank.

Bridger, his eyes bright with anticipation, grins widely.

"Now for the day's bounty."

Smudge presents each man with a forked willow branch. As the men sharpen their willow forks to points, Fred removes a large liver from Dash's bag and slices it into thick slabs. The men skewer the meat onto the forks, positioning their sticks above the fire's coals. The liver's juices sizzle on the fire ring's hot rocks. As the men eat and tell stories, Dash feels the comfort of a full belly. Through half-open eyes, he curiously watches the men build the fire into a raging inferno.

"Why are you building it up so big?"

Smudge turns, "You can't hear them?"

"Hear what?"

Smudge points toward the darkness.

"Listen careful, over there."

Dash turns away, straining to hear sounds in the direction of Smudge's pointed finger. Cutting through the night air, he hears the distant yips and calls of wolves.

"They'll be here soon. Don't like fire much. Need to sleep with one eye open. We don't want them buggers gettin' into our treasure."

Bridger's voice growls, adding, "Been eatin' on the gut balls since we left. Counted twelve watchin' us from the trees. Likely a few more joinin' them, itching for the good stuff. Got a lead ball here sayin' we earned that meat fair and square."

Dash is shocked by the men's matter-of-fact behavior. Tired as they are, the men retrieve their materials and set to work making lead balls. Focused on their task, an hour passes, and the fire has died down. Bridger stands up and looks into the darkness.

"They's here, boys. Best build the fire up so we can keep an eye on them."

Obediently, a shower of dry wood and willow sticks transform the coals into bright flames. A chill runs down Dash's back when the dancing flames reflect multiple pairs of canine eyes staring intently at the men. As the flames grow higher, the wolves begin to pace, stubbornly refusing to leave the opportunity for an easy meal.

"Damn Jim, I got at least twenty sets starin' back at me."

"Good news travels fast, Smudge. Forget about sleepin' tonight. If these curs are set on takin' us on, we'll need all guns firin' quick-like. May take a while to scare them off."

Dash feels his pulse quicken when the pack's leader, a massive-headed animal, boldly steps toward their meat cache, his ears forward at full attention. As if issuing a taunt, he flashes his yellow fangs through grimacing lips.

"OK, boys, now I got thirty pairs of devil eyes. If we all fire at once, that'll scatter them long enough to reload. Blaze, you load for me. Fred, you load for Dash and Smudge. Keep two or three rifles goin' steady. Keep count of them musket balls. Aim careful and we'll thin them out—'til they head back to them hills."

Following Bridger's lead, Dash kneels, left hand holding the rifle barrel, elbow braced on his knee. Aiming through the fire's flames, he studies the darkness, the glowing eyes floating before him like menacing lightning bugs.

"Dash, Smudge, I've got the leader, cocky sombitch. Once he goes, that'll take some fight outta them. This'll be somethin' to talk about when we get home."

Seconds later, Bridger's rifle booms into the darkness. Yowls of pain instantly rack the darkness as the pack's leader twitches in the snow. Determined to get a shot off, Dash squints through the thick smoke. A pair of eyes flash at the creek's bend. He squeezes his trigger, and the rifle responds. Before he knows the result, Blaze grabs the rifle away and hands him another, loaded and ready.

A rhythmic cadence of firing follows from Smudge, then Bridger, then Dash. The air is choked blue with gun smoke and death cries, both close and distant. Minutes later, Bridger raises his hand.

"Hold up, boys. Let's listen."

A slight breeze wafts the gun smoke up and away to dull silence. An armful of willow sticks flares the fire to life again. The men scan the area and when they see nothing, they ease out only as far as their fire's glow.

"I've got seven close in, Jim."

"How many balls did we throw at them, Blaze?"

"Eighteen at my count."

"The wounded ones are dangerous. Best keep our eyes peeled."

The men sigh with relief, return to the willow shelter, and build up the fire again. Too wound up to sleep, they fill the rest of the night with stories, except Dash, who, devoid of stories, keeps a nervous eye on the surrounding darkness.

The rising sun finds Dash alone in the willow shelter. When he rushes out, his right shoulder protests loudly. In his line of sight, there is nowhere without carnage. Filigreed blood trails swirl too close to their cache. Heaps of fur lie prone in their crimson halos. Dash follows the men's footsteps across the creek and up the opposite bank. Outside the bank's protection, he stops.

Before him lay more animal carcasses, the pristine snow mutilated by death throes and frantic escapes. Bridger and the others walk toward him, their heads bent low in discussion. When they see him, Bridger hails him with a wave.

"Quite a scene, ain't it, Dash? Them that could, ran off. Must've been more than we thought. We need to get on. Folks from the fort will want to come back for the pelts. Right now, I want food in my belly."

Thoroughly spent from their expedition, the exhausted men's return to camp is heralded by whoops and hollers of joy for the bounty they bring with them. Dash sees Amalee resting on Narcissa's right hip and Virginia on her other, both waving and smiling without any real understanding of why. The sight of Amalee's joy-filled face sends such emotion through Dash that he barely sets down his load before running to swoop her into the air.

"The fort will eat for weeks off all you brought back," Narcissa says excitedly.

"We have to go back for one more—the big bull. Too much to carry, but with him, we may not have to hunt until after the snow melts," Bridger announces as he passes by the happy scene.

"I hope we have time to rest before going back. I've never worked so hard in my life," Dash replies.

"Get your rest and let the others take care of the meat. It will take all of our strength to get that big bull back to the fort."

The hunters rest for five days before returning to the hanging elk carcass. Bridger insists Dash join them again, citing more hands makes easier work.

"With luck, we'll sprint the whole way and be back to the fort by dark."

Flattered by their inclusion, Dash thinks back to his earlier life, and how he wasn't allowed to have any physical exertion. A sprint in the snow on snowshoes would have been unthinkable. After all that has happened since he fled Boston, everything about him has changed. He has strength and fitness, his bulk has turned to muscle, and he has the complete use of his left eye. He slowly grins to himself when it occurs to him that no one, not even Lillia, would ever recognize him now.

As the men approach the killing field, Dash notices a dark shroud of clouds emerging along the northern horizon. When he points them out to Bridger, a deep scowl is the only reply.

The five men carefully approach the tree where they left the carcass hanging.

"Damn, there's a cat on it," Bridger growls.

Dash follows Bridger's gaze as he continues, "A mountain lion. Damn nasty critters. Not easy to shoo off when they think what's yours is theirs."

Dash wonders if they could just leave the carcass to the mountain lion and turn back, avoiding the approaching storm.

Before he can suggest it, Bridger says, "Alright, boys, here's what we're going to do. The cat is alone. They don't pack up. We got the advantage because he's up in the tree. One shot won't do it unless it's a lucky head shot. And once he's hit, he's dangerous, like nothin' you ever seen before. He'll come at us until he's dead. I don't want to bury anyone, so keep a sharp eye and be quick to reload."

Bridger pulls his rifle around from its strap across his back and loads it. Everyone mirrors his actions. As he loads his rifle, Dash studies the tree for the lion, finally making out his tawny fur through the spruce needles' dense darkness. With his eyes adjusted, Dash also sees dark gouges in the elk's muscular haunches where the lion has been feasting.

"How long has the lion been on the carcass?" he asks Bridger.

"I imagine he jumped up there when we was fightin' them wolves. Judgin' by his size, he's a mature tom. Wouldn't have left the carcass, just slept right there after fillin' his belly."

A scream announces the cat doesn't like their presence. Bridger points the men into their places.

"If we're goin' to get our meat an' get home 'fore the storm, best get to it. Blaze, you take the first shot from over there, Smudge, opposite the cat, and Fred across from Blaze. Dash and I'll stay right in the middle, in case you don't drop him. Fire one at a time, so we know if we all gotta use our lead. Whoever has the next shot, be ready. Cats move like lightning when they're mad and hurtin'. Have your knives close as well, in case you need them."

Dash feels his knees go weak at Bridger's stoic directions.

"Blaze, that storm is bearin' down. Take your shot."

Blaze lifts his gun barrel, the sun reflecting off the oiled metal. Dash anticipates the explosion and the billow of black smoke, but it's the low, pronounced yowl that tells him the cat is still alive.

"Smudge, your turn. Make it count."

Dash holds his breath as Smudge, choosing to kneel, takes aim and fires. The cat doesn't fall from the tree.

"Fred, finish him off."

Dash sees Fred shift his weight and aim at the lion's left shoulder. As Fred pulls back his rifle's hammer, the lion lets out an angry yowl and leaps from the tree to face the shooters straight on. Blood pulses from its right shoulder.

Dash has never seen a mountain lion before and based on the gasp from Blaze and Smudge, this animal is exceptional. His head is as big as a bull's and his long tail flicks with demonic irritation.

"Shoot now, Fred!"

Forced to adjust to the cat's new ground position, Fred's shot misses and blasts a two-inch hole in the spruce tree's trunk radiating a profusion of splinters skyward. The lion stands motionless, sizing up his adversaries.

"Dash, your best shot is through an eye socket, but anything around the head will do. I'll aim for the heart through his front legs. Boys, once we fire, if he doesn't drop, be ready to use whatever weapon you got."

Only Dash hears Bridger whisper, "Damn, he's a monster."

Dash sucks in his breath and lays the rifle's bead into the sight at the end of the barrel. The idea of hitting the animal's eye from this distance seems ambitious, but he aims there anyway. As he expels his breath in a low hum, the lion stares back at him, a look of resolute defiance before beginning to bound toward the men. Dash feels his heart pound as he pulls the trigger.

The great cat leaps toward Dash's shot, his massive paws extended out like razor-lined dinner plates. Bridger's rifle explodes a split second later. The immense feline's terrifyingly graceful forward arc is abruptly interrupted, the momentum reversed and the animal falls into the snow, a lifeless pile of bloody fur.

No one moves. As they stare at the lion's carcass, Dash notices each of them is breathing in shallow, rapid breaths. Bridger breaks the silence.

"Damn big animal. Knives at the ready, we're takin' this critter back with us. No one is goin' to believe it unless they see it for themselves."

With knives drawn, they cautiously creep toward the animal. This would be the animal's one last chance to inflict damage. As they surround the carcass, it's enormity is baffling, and Bridger examines it.

"Look at this scar, here."

He points to the animal's spine where four hairless scars speak of a grizzly strike.

"But here . . . this here is what we'll talk about when we get back to the fort."

He points to the animal's head and looks up at Dash, a broad grin crackling through his whiskers. There is Bridger's chest shot and Blaze's shoulder wound but, it is the hole in the left eye socket that did the cat in. Dash's shot.

"There ain't no denying it was you who took it, Dash. Mighty fine shootin', son," Bridger says.

All clap Dash on the back without too much ceremony; then they get to work on the carcass. Using their knives, they disembowel the cat to reduce the weight. Fred chops down a slender aspen trunk and they mount the animal on it by tying its paws together and running the pole through the loops.

Blaze and Smudge lower the elk carcass to the ground and quarter it. After the lion's feasting, there are only three quarters worth hauling home. Bridger and Dash take up the lion while the others strap the elk quarters to their shoulders.

"Head out boys; the storm ain't gettin' any nicer."

Sure enough, on the way home, they move through relentless headlong winds and pelting snow. Even through the raging fury, their well-packed trail holds up. They finally arrive home after dark, the blizzard now coming full force, the dim lights of the fort welcoming them like torches from heaven. While those with the elk head toward the barn and cold storage, Bridger turns away.

"Dash, you and I are goin' to haul this cat to Vasquez's storeroom. First, to drink a round to our success and second, because the smell of mountain lion will stampede the horses right outta the barn."

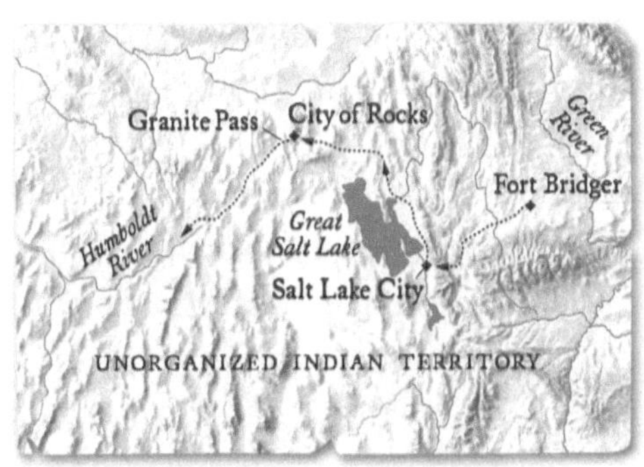

Chapter 15

JANUARY, 1850

FORT BRIDGER,

UNORGANIZED INDIAN TERRITORY

After the excitement of the hunt, Dash feels the warmth of acceptance among the fort's inhabitants. Because of Vasquez's earlier care, Dash trusts him enough to allow Vasquez to tease out the details of his life before Fort Bridger when the older man visits.

Without revealing his family's secret, the shame of leaving Lillia before their wedding or anything about the wager, Dash slowly, painstakingly, divulges the tales of the Bostonian's ill-fated journey west. Each memory leaves Dash shaken, and it takes weeks for the full saga to spill out.

After every revelation, Vasquez leaves the cramped store-room for his home with Narcissa and their children, including

Amalee. Dash feels a wave of gratitude for their generosity toward both him and the child. But, in his solitude, he is helpless from keeping the memories of leaving Boston, his friends, of Lillia, Ace, and the last images of Nora from creeping in. Despite his recent accomplishments and personal growth, he falls asleep wondering how his life would be had he surrendered his soul and values to his father.

On the night when his story finally arrives at the company's mutiny, Nora's brave effort continues, and he reveals the last time he saw her careening over the cliff's edge. Vasquez sits still, his rough-skinned hands chafing slowly around each other.

Speaking softly, he says, "I've known some hard times, but Dash, yours is the darndest."

After a few moments, he continues, "I'm wonderin' if you know what a gantlet is?"

Dash considers the question. When he only comes up with a style of gloves, he's confident that isn't what Vasquez is referencing and slowly shakes his head.

Vasquez responds, "Way back in time, in the old country, a gantlet was a way for newcomers to be tested as worthy for joinin' a people's clan. If the fella was strong enough to survive the gantlet's abuse, then he was deemed suitable."

Dash lets this sink in. All the incidents, from the moment he fled for his life to his spontaneous decision to go west and then his unlikely survival, flash before him with new light.

"Here's my thinkin'," Vasquez continues, "you've been runnin' the West's gantlet. Each of the trials of your westbound trip was a test of your strength and determination. Can't say if the West is done with you, but, my Lord, she's doled you some terrific punishments."

Dash doesn't argue with his assessment but wonders just how much longer he will get punished for doing the right thing.

"I'll leave you to your thinkin', Dash. Just remember, yours is a new life. Not to say it's goin' to be easy, but you'll never be what you were. A man your age taking on the responsibility of a baby is goin' to change you. But Bridger sees somethin' in you. I'd take full advantage of his teaching. It could be your future."

In February, a warm wind blows out of the southwest and no one is immune to its tease. The deep-drifted snow against the fort's balustrade melts appreciably in just that one day, signaling an end to the long winter, even if this particular event is a fraud. Caught by the wind's lure, Vasquez announces he, Smudge, and Fred will make the trip to Salt Lake City with the idea of restocking the fort's necessities. The trip will take them a week on snowshoes with the hopes they will find a freighter who will sled them back through the drifts.

Dash watches his new friends lumber away on their snowshoes before disappearing into the white blur. He wonders what life in the city would have been like had he, Nora, Violet, and Amalee accomplished the trip they had intended.

Narcissa is stoic for a few days following her husband's departure, leaving Dash to wonder if she is angry or worried about his travels. Neither reason matters, he realizes. Her hands are full with two babies, a two-year-old son, Louis, and a twelve-year-old, Armilda.

One dark, snowy day, Dash arrives to fetch Amalee for the morning, only to find Narcissa in an uncharacteristic mood. The dark circles under her eyes are so alarming that Dash has to bite his tongue against an intrusive question until he can't help himself.

"Narcissa, I can see something is wrong. Is there anything I can do for you?"

After a few moments, her soft voice whispers her response.

"Dash, this is wild country. No one knows what will happen. It's very different than my home in St. Louis. Granted, I lost my first husband there. But . . . but . . . when I look at your little girl,

I wonder about her future. I'm sure Louis has not told you, but I had a son, Hiram, Armilda's little brother. One day, the pair were playing at the creek south of this fort, and the Utes stole him from me. He was only four years old. Since Armilda was ten years old, she outran them and made it back to the fort.

And even Bridger, the mountain man of all men, has suffered a child's loss. His daughter, Mary Anne, was at the Whitman Mission School in Oregon Territory when the Indians, thought to be friendly, showed up and massacred everyone. Joe Meek, another mountain man, had his daughter at the same school, found her mutilated, but they never found Mary Anne. No one knows what happened to her. Just like I don't know if my Hiram is alive or dead."

Dash is shocked into silence.

"All I'm saying, Dash, is to watch out for your baby girl. She's precious. You can never take your eyes off her. Ever."

Dash thinks of how close he came to losing Amalee. At almost six months old, she has completely captured his heart. When he holds her, he nuzzles into her neck, feeling her soft fatness, the folds of her neck and thighs, concurrently abundant and vulnerable. The fullness of her porcelain-toned cheeks makes her eyes squint even when she is not smiling. It makes him laugh. She grins and giggles at the littlest things; her coffee-brown eyes the mirror image of Nora's. When she tires of their games, she snuggles into his arms, laying heavily across his chest where her sweet breath comes and goes in gentle snores.

He feels bound to this child, for more reasons than he could explain to her.

Nearly a month into Vasquez's absence, bells signal an incoming freight wagon. From his chores in the barn, Dash feels his heart skip a beat. He joins the other excited fort occupants as they rush toward the ladened sleigh. When Vasquez dismounts, Narcissa beats the mass and throws herself into his arms. Dash helps the driver, Smudge and Fred unhitch the exhausted mules, their sides still heaving from the journey.

After all is settled, everyone jams into Bridger's cabin eager for information from Salt Lake City and the greater world.

The freighter, Horatio Fontainebleau, uses the most unrecognizable English Dash has ever heard. Relieved to see others struggling to decipher the man's jargon, Dash focuses his attention on the man's thick accent, sloshed together words, and the repetitive use of "g'dam."

Vasquez tells them of his observations about Salt Lake City.

"The talk of the city is Stansbury's report following his overwintering there last year. Them Mormon folks are mighty stirred up, suspicious of the US government. Sayin' the government is primed to drive the Mormons from their newly settled country, just like they was driven out of Missouri in '46. But here's what has Brigham Young spittin' furious, my friend and partner."

Vasquez turns his attention directly to Bridger.

"Stansbury has recommended Fort Bridger as a US military outpost. Young distrusts everything about the US government, especially bein' this close to him. So now he's making accusations against you!"

Perched on his tree stump seat, Dash watches Bridger's expression shift from pride in Stansbury's recommendation to boiling rage.

Vasquez continues, "Young and his people been spreading stories sayin' you lied about what they could expect for a growing climate in the Salt Lake Valley. Accused us of stranglin' trade between the Mormons and the California emigrants by bein' too generous when they stop here—makin' them Mormons look stingy. And you warned Young about how the Utes felt toward white people. There's been some trouble. Young blames you sayin' you armed the Indians in hopes they'd kill off the Mormons for you. I think Young means to run you off and take your land so the US government can't get a toehold in their country."

Dash watches as Bridger forms his thoughts while rhythmically tapping a stick on the fireplace's hearth.

"Sounds like ole Brigham should have listened to my advice on several fronts. Guess some learn best from a hard lesson. I'd been here years before that righteous fella showed up. Brigham can't stand the idea I made peace and have respect from the Indian tribes. Blisters his ears that I know the country better than him, and I picked a better place for my tradin' and livin'. If he means to come and take it, I intend to keep it or die tryin'.

The cramped room builds with tension and Dash is relieved when Blaze asks Horatio for news from California.

"Can tell you them goldfields is makin' some folks g'dam rich. Ships full of seekers are unloadin' in San Fran like beetles with their butts on fire a'scurryin' into them g'dam mountains with nothin' but nuggets in their eyes and no sense in their heads. Some come from g'dam Australia, Europe, and South America thinking they're the one that's gonna make it rich and go back home with his pockets overflowin'. They'll be the first that up and die from not takin' the right gear along.

And women? Cain't find a female, married or not, in five thousand faces. Makes men mean and nasty, it does. Mean because they miss bein' cared for or cared about and frustrated for not gettin' the gold they was promised. Nasty when they're quick to pull the trigger or flash the blade. In some camps, a man's killed every night after a card game or an argument. Had to get out myself—too close to gettin' sliced one night. Just left my g'dam claim and walked away. Weren't no good anyways, just rocks, sand, and silt."

"How long ago did you leave?"

Dash's question makes Bridger grin.

"Ah, yes, our marooned gold seeker turned crack shot, Dash."

Horatio swivels around to give him a visual going over. Dash meets Horatio's gaze steadily.

"Me and my partner were in the first wave in '48," Horatio tells him. "Suffered through a rough winter in the mountains outside of Sonora. Found a few nuggets but weren't nothin' to cover the g'dam expensive supplies in town.

Worked 'til late spring of '49 when I saw somethin' I shouldn't have and got run out of town. More to livin' than bein' wet, cold, and hungry. Took us the better part of summer and fall to get enough coin to buy horses and supplies to cross the mountains headin' east.

Partner disappeared in them mountains during a storm. Left me no choice but to leave him before I froze. Found myself in Salt Lake City among the damnedest folks I ever saw. Spent the winter wonderin' what I got myself into, and then Vasquez here came along and needed a wagon and a driver. Glad to put space between me and them for a while."

Another question draws Horatio's attention away, and Dash leaves the room quietly. On his way back to the storeroom's solitude, he chews on what Horatio said about California. Could it be possible the Yalies are having as much trouble getting to California as he and the Bostonians have had? How probable is it to think the wager money has not even arrived in San Francisco?

Horatio and his endless stories become a refreshing fixture at the fort's communal supper table. Curiously, Dash is drawn to his bold behavior, a contrast to his own quiet nature. Horatio made it clear he will return to Salt Lake City with the fort's bounty of furs as soon as the drifted snow and oozing mud allow.

On one of his prairie inspections, he invites Bridger and Dash to join him. As they walk, Dash asks Horatio, "Where did you learn to drive mules?"

"Learnt from my daddy in eastern Lou'siana. Grew up on a farm in the low country and hauled the harvest to N' Orleans.

Older brothers did most of the freighting, but I got my chance when I was ten, barely could touch the floorboards when I sat on the wagon's bench. Good thing I grew up quick."

"How old are you anyway, Horatio?" Dash asks.

"Nineteen years and a few months," Horatio responds. "You?"

Dash pauses before saying, "I guess I turned twenty-three in September."

Bridger snorts, "Pups! Both you boys are just pups!"

One night, after Dash leaves Amalee at Narcissa's for the night, he is intercepted by Horatio while walking back to his domicile.

"Wonderin' if we might talk about somethin' away from the others, Dash?"

Dash nods and gestures him toward his tiny space. As he feeds kindling into the stove, Horatio launches right in.

"You still thinkin' on California?"

"Honestly, after your commentary, I'm doubting. Originally, I was in a hurry. But now, well, I'll just be glad for me and my little girl to arrive in one piece."

"I suspect the sooner you get there the better, don't you think?"

"I do. But now that I've got Amalee, things are different. She's not likely to make the trip on dried meat and moldy biscuits."

Horatio is quiet until Dash turns and faces him.

"What do you say about you both headin' back to Salt Lake with me? Probably leave in a few weeks, maybe a month. We'll team up and drive over them California mountains together when the g'dam weather breaks. Be the first to the goldfields, for sure."

"I thought you didn't want to go back to the goldfields."

"Didn't say I wouldn't go back to California, just don't think workin' claims is my callin'. Too many g'dam greenhorns doin' that. I can drive freight, know my way around horses and mules.

Lots of ways to make money that don't have nothin' to do with breakin' rocks and standin' in water up to your ass."

Dash looks into the fire's flames as he considers the idea.

"What'll I do about Amalee? Can't take any chances with her."

"Reckon you'll need to find a momma for her. Truth? Ain't no decent women in California; all's either married or soiled. Nothin' in between. But she's a cutie. There's probably someone who'll take her off your hands."

Dash feels anger flash through him, and growls, "Amalee stays with me."

His tone startles Horatio into uncharacteristic silence. When Dash looks up, Horatio's sheepish expression pleads for forgiveness.

"Sorry, Dash, g'dam sorry-assed idea. No papa leaves his baby girl. Not after all you've been through together."

Horatio stands to leave.

"Think on it, Dash. Don't need to know right now. It would be g'dam good to have your company, but I'm not sure 'bout having the little tick along."

Dash decides Horatio's offer is just the opportunity he needs to start his new life and maybe, just maybe, track down the wager. But when he tells Narcissa about their plan, he learns she is just as hesitant as Horatio about having Amalee join them. Only more fierce.

"No, you'll not be taking that precious child into the wilderness. She can stay here until you come back once you and Horatio have been successful. I'll keep her as my own, but I will not let you risk her life while you search for your future."

With no rebuttal to Narcissa's ultimatum, Dash leaves the Vasquez house to inform Horatio of Narcissa's offer to care for the child while they are gone.

"She expects me to come back and fetch Amalee," Dash explains.

Horatio nods thoughtfully before saying, "Alright then. We make two trips. One without your little tick, come back, get her and make another trip, this time goin' up and over them mountains before the snow flies. It'll be good money, count on it."

"How are you sure it'll be so lucrative?"

"It's like this," Horatio replies, "I remember so much about my g'dam trip from California to Salt Lake City—pitiful few souls have done the wrong-way trip like me. And I knowed two things: west of the Wasatch Mountains, there ain't no feed, and the old Humboldt will trick folks to thinkin' there's water forever at first, but that g'dam mangy river up and dies just when the travelers need it most. With not a lick of g'dam grass or water for miles, livestock starts a'dyin', and it's nothin' but death for miles.

So I got no interest in haulin' my belongings to California with an empty freight wagon when there's plenty of room for somethin' useful on the trail. Know what that is?"

Dash shrugs his shoulders before he smiles and says, "Water and feed?"

"That's it, Dash, you got it!"

"So what would our business arrangement be?"

"Well, I got the team, the wagon, and the water barrels," Horatio says.

Dash eagerly adds, "I can buy hay and oats, if there's any to be found after this winter."

"Then I say we're even partners."

Dash silently considers everything before saying, "No time to waste if we're going to be the first to cross in May."

Later, Dash wonders if his disfigurement will cause alarm in Salt Lake City like he knows it would in Boston. It hadn't been of social consequence on the plains since no one knew him before he arrived at Fort Bridger. But in Boston, citizens would react to his visage and look away, maybe even ostracize him.

His mind lingers on the faces and names of those who have become his new family. They had shown him compassion and cared for him in his time of need. Additionally, they encouraged him and celebrated his successes in arenas unknown to him in his prior life. Had he stayed in Boston, he would have never experienced any of this—the good and the bad—and it's unlikely the road ahead will be any less dangerous.

When the young men pass their idea by Vasquez, Dash can tell the man is intrigued. Horatio has an answer for all of his testing questions while Dash sits back and listens to their discussion and becomes more confident in Horatio's business acumen.

After answering the last question, Vasquez offers one last bit of advice, saying, "Boys, this sounds like a good idea, but I'll caution you on one point. By the time you encounter these westbound travelers, they have been stretched to their limit, both physically and mentally. Some will be stronger and you won't have to worry about them. But others will be cracking inside. You won't be able to see it until it's too late. Their desperation will make them lash out some way, maybe pull a weapon unexpectedly. Keep your wits about you at all times. Never underestimate a soul that's withering from disappointment or delusion. They can become downright dangerous."

His words hit Dash squarely. Between him and Horatio, he is sure his experiences give him the upper hand in this kind of knowledge but there's still a lot that he doesn't know about Horatio.

For three uneventful days of westbound travel, Dash listens to Horatio's endless stories, but his mind wanders to the unkept strings of his life. The most recent one, leaving Amalee with Narcissa, still gives him a twitch of guilt, although he was surprised at her unquestioning agreement to his request. Perhaps, he concludes, when he handed her a bag of coins, it helped her decision. But he had made it clear he would move heaven and earth to return for Amalee, and they shook on that promise.

As the wagon rumbles on, Dash marvels at how stress-free the last few days have been and says to Horatio, "It's been a quiet time. In all my travels before Fort Bridger, seems like we couldn't go a day without some kind of tragedy."

"I imagine there was a jinx in your company. A jinx makes it g'dam tough."

"What are you talking about, a jinx?" Dash asks.

"Where I'm from, if there's bad luck that just keeps happenin', there's been a jinx set. And unless someone knows how to break it, nothin' good is goin' to happen."

"How do you know? I mean, how do you know who's got the jinx?"

"Hard to tell. Could be the one what's got the worst luck. Or maybe they've got some kind of look to them. You know, a physical problem."

Dash's mind whips at the statement. He was the only one with any kind of deformity among the original Bostonians. The thought brings a swell of guilt. He couldn't possibly be responsible for the loss of so many of his friends. And why, out of all of them, would he be the one to survive and get tortured all the more by their loss?

"What's goin' through your mind, Dash? You've gone quiet as death."

Not ready to reveal his thoughts, Dash swallows hard.

"Too many things happened. It couldn't have been just one person carrying a curse."

Horatio clucks to the mules while considering Dash's words and says, "S'pose it's over, since you're still here. Amalee is fine, and y'all will make it to California. Given your survivin' all of it, you must be tough enough."

The streets of Salt Lake City are still a muddy slosh when they arrive. Stables and a boardinghouse, in that order, are their primary objectives followed closely by their search for hay and oats. As they mingle with the city folks, any fears Dash may have had about his appearance and being shunned because of it, melt away. Many inhabitants of Salt Lake City are survivors of the long and perilous trek across the plains to their religious haven. Missing appendages, frostbitten or by accident, leave many individuals with limps, halts, or mauled visages. He fits right in.

It takes a month of scouring the city and surrounding farms for their desired cargo. In early May, Dash watches the emigrant wagons trickle in with gathering momentum by mid-month. Dash and Horatio diligently load sheaf after sheaf of hay inside Horatio's woven willow walls that raise the wagon's sides to three times their original height. Bags of oats are stacked to form a low wall in the wagon's bed leaving vacant space for water barrels.

With their final purchases made over the next two weeks, Horatio signals their readiness for departure. But Dash frets over the lack of water barrels and asks why they have not bought any yet.

Carrying a sense of calm about the subject, Horatio says, "Don't worry yer head none. I got the barrels in a safe place."

"Where?"

"Hid them last fall. In a safe place on the trail. We'll get to them before we need to haul water."

Dash watches as his partner's easy grin spreads across his face. He smiles back knowing he's traveling with someone who has traveled the road ahead more than he has—even if only once.

Finally, they begin the next leg of their enterprising adventure. Six days from Salt Lake City, they cross paths with folks merging onto the California Trail from Fort Hall. The collision happens in an open valley southwest of the City of Rocks, everyone vying for livestock forage and straining the local springs. As Horatio negotiates their wagon into a camping space, Dash's mind registers the significance of the chaos before him. Horatio's simple but brilliant plan is all about competition for resources. When the resources run out, they will be the ones to provide, at a cost.

The evening sky features a brilliant sunset, the clouds reflecting the fading rays in hues of pink, red, and orange. Horatio's thrice-tall wagon walls attract attention from the curious folks who ask for an explanation. Once Horatio explains the desolation in front of them and how this wagon load of hay and oats is going in their same direction, he gets nothing more than smug head nods.

He mumbles to Dash under his breath, "Full of themselves, these folks. Don't rightly know what they're in for. Can't begin to picture what the desert looks like. Most of them have been holed up at Fort Laramie or Fort Hall for the winter, so they've got itchy feet. But they're not thinkin' about the other side. Not yet."

The talk around the campfires focuses on the day's travel over Granite Pass, prompting Dash to ask Horatio if they should be concerned.

"It's the other side they should be worried about. It was rutted somethin' fierce last fall. Too many folks and rainstorms made cuts so deep a wagon's axles'll scrape. Can't imagine it's gotten any better over the winter."

An overcast sky greets them the next morning, and teams of horses and oxen jockeying for position pass Horatio and Dash's camp. Rambunctious drivers bawl commands for slower drivers to give way. Clots of family units surge past, with children of all ages walking alongside the wagons or orbiting on horseback. Mothers call out like hens, their squawks directed to those who dawdle. Dash wonders if the children ever get mixed up or left behind.

A stab of longing to see little Amalee's face fills his heart, but he acknowledges Horatio's instinct—too much turmoil dwells in this place to have her along right now. Dash wonders if Widow Wilson and her children from the Baltimore company continue heading west, or if they gave up and went home. If they hadn't turned back, they would have turned out like everyone else in that ill-fated wagon company—dead.

When a crowd of young men on horseback leading equipment-ladened packhorses rush past them, Horatio shakes his head and chuckles.

"If they go too fast, they're goin' to wear down those animals, no doubt. Probably not as bad as those comin' in July, but they gonna learn the hard way. Slow and steady is the way to get there."

Dash marvels that just one year ago he would have been one of those fools as his long-dead best friend's face flashes into his memory. Horseback had been Hugh's chosen method—horseback and moving fast.

Because theirs was a trip of strategy, Dash and Horatio wait to move out until the rush ceases. The trip up Granite Pass is gradual and easy. Horatio's cautions come true on the other side: the descending road fans out wide, and wagon drivers do their best to stay out of the hazardous gullies and ruts.

Dash breathes a sigh of relief when they get to the bottom and water the mules at Birch Creek. Grateful to have Grunt to ride for a change from the hard board seat, Dash lets Horatio lead them to Goose Creek for their evening camp. From his bedroll, he listens to the sounds of the emigrants, suddenly grateful for the chance to take this trip more than once.

The days pass on the trail. They learn the names of different groups, where they are from, and what their motivations are for going to California. For him, California holds the undeniable lure of claiming the race's wager. It's entirely possible the Yalies have claimed it by now, but on the outside chance they haven't, he's got until May of '51 to get there. One year from now.

He feels an unspoken promise to claim that wager, to finish what his Bostonian comrades set out for together. How quickly, he thinks, has he racked up a quantity of promises to keep—one to Lillia, to Nora, and now to Narcissa. He feels dogged determination fill his veins, something that has not always been one of his traits. One thing this trip has altered about him is the realization that calculated determination changes lives.

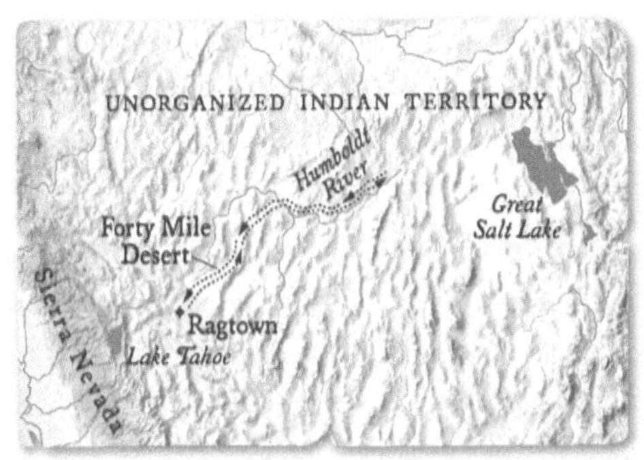

Chapter 16

MAY, 1850

CALIFORNIA TRAIL

When Dash and Horatio run out of things to talk about, the monotony of clattering wagon wheels and clouds of trail dust fill the time. Digging deep for a topic for discussion, Dash asks Horatio how he had come to own the wagon they are driving.

"Grew up freightin'. I was itchin' to get away from my pa, so when the Mexican War broke out, I joined up. Fought in the Battle at Monterrey. Damn awful. When the war was over in the spring of '48, my buddy Clem and I heard about gold in California. Colonel Kearney had them g'dam big freighting wagons to get to California but couldn't take them through the mountains, so we run 'em through the Mexican desert on Lt. Colonel Cooke's new Mormon Battalion wagon road.

"Ran a jerk line on five pairs of mules riding the mule closest to the wagon since there wasn't a bench seat. That wagon road went through four hundred miles of the g'damest country, as dry and hot as a smith's forge. Cooke's desert road had been well-traveled, and we passed hundreds of dead animals, some still hitched. It was a g'dam shame to leave equipment in the desert, but since there weren't no fresh animals, it stayed where it stopped. But I remembered it.

"We joined up with Kearny on the other side of the desert and went on to Mission San Luis Rey and then to San Diego. Hugo and I spent the winter in a g'dam minin' town named Sonora. Had a claim once, but nothin' came of it. Left it in a hurry. Worked the whole summer haulin' goods from the cities to camps tryin' to earn enough to head east. By the time we crossed over the g'dam Sierras, we had the shirts on our backs, blankets, saddles, enough food and water for two weeks, and a horse apiece.

"Havin' not come west over the mountains, we didn't know what to expect. When we hit the top, somethin' happened, and Clem went g'dam sick in the head. Couldn't talk right, went pure delirious. I tried to calm him, but he took his bullwhip and ran off in the night. I could hear him asnappin' it, at what I don' know. Figured he was fightin' off somethin' a hauntin' him.

"I was afraid of fallin' off a cliff, so I stayed put 'til daylight. At first light, I jumped up and started pokin' around for him. Them g'dam rocks weren't no good at leavin' a trail. I called and called, kept comin' back to the campsite to see if he'd showed up. Nothin'. That night, I couldn't think of what to do and was sick with worry. I made a big fire thinkin' he'd see it. But then the weather changed during the night. If I waited, I'd likely die in the snow—the idea plum scared me to g'dam death. I packed our horses and started down the other side hopin' he'd just step outta the trees and say, 'Where you goin'?' But he never did."

Horatio pauses and Dash shoots a side glance to see his companion staring ahead, lost in his memories.

"Passed folks who wanted my horses, but I told them I was headed east and needed them. Glad I didn't let them go. Passed the same death, despair, and abandoned equipment I saw on Cooke's Road, but this time I had two decent animals. When I came up on this here wagon, I knowed it the same as what I drove on Cooke's Road, and it was my chance. There wasn't nothin' wrong with it, just a left-behind. Owner probably rode the animals to California.

"I stripped it to its bed and hitched up my animals to it. Took it slow. Wasn't near as hot, comin' up on the end of September. Made it to water just in time. Wasn't much for the horses to eat but brush tips. Once they got a little stronger, we set out again. I picked up left-behinds here and there, things I figured someone might favor in Salt Lake City.

"Wasn't long before I was in the city with enough to sell and rebuild the wagon to my likin'. Put this bench seat on it, put up woven willow sides instead of their high plank sides, and figured out some skids for the snow. Bought these mules and got to know Vasquez. He saw my fine freightin' wagon and needed to get back to Fort Bridger. You know the rest."

"So that's how you know where there are water barrels?"

"Had lots of time for thinkin'. All kinds of them g'dam empty water barrels were tossed along the roadside. Figured if I was ever back this way, they might come in handy. So, I hid some in a canyon. They're waitin' for us to come get them. Figure they're as good as g'dam gold . . . under the right circumstances."

Just as Horatio finishes his story, they come around a bend and find a left-behind wagon.

"Well, would you lookie there."

Horatio's hoot startles Dash. The wagon had been stripped of mechanical parts, leaving only its wooden skeleton and a few water barrels lying in the dirt. Their usefulness was now lost for their owners, but not on Horatio and Dash. After a quick inspection, they load the barrels into the wagon's bed and drive on.

It is not long before multiple streams converge, and the Humboldt River becomes a reality. As they watch the muddy flow, Dash is suddenly impressed with the river's raging width. Horatio leans in.

"Goin' to have to cross it, just a matter of where."

"Aren't there any ferries?"

"Not in this god-forsaken place! No man in his right mind would run a ferry durin' the g'dam spring runoff. Lucky our load ain't too heavy yet."

They drive along the river's south side with the rest of the wagons, the spring moisture oozing up on either side of the wagon's wheels. The mule's small feet make sucking sounds as they march through the mire. All of a sudden, Horatio pulls out of line.

"There's my mark. I's wonderin' when it'd come up. Dash, we've got to cross now. Them barrels is on the other side."

Dash can't believe his ears.

Now? Here?

His mind flashes back to the many times he had dealt with fickle river water. The ferry on the Youghiogheny. Rescuing Nora from Redstone Creek. The three weeks on the Ohio River, Mississippi, and then the Missouri. Being stuck in the vast plains on a flooded river-created island.

"I'll swim Grunt across. You drive the team," he suggests.

"Fine with me. Goin' to wait so no one follows us."

When the break comes, Horatio marches the mules into the rushing water while Dash follows on Grunt. Before he knows it, Grunt finds his feet in the shallows on the other side.

Once beyond the sight of any passing emigrants, Horatio pulls the mules to a stop. They unhitch and hobble the mules in a quantity of untouched spring grass that leaves Dash in awe. There aren't any other travelers on this side of the river, yet.

Horatio sets off to seek his hidden cache, leaving Dash with the mules. But after an hour, Dash starts to worry. Absentmindedly, he reaches for his rifle, its smooth stock bringing him comfort.

Only a moment later, Horatio bounds out from behind some wild plum trees.

"Don't know what I was thinkin'. Put them barrels in a g'dam near impossible place to reach, but I found them. Let's take Grunt and the mules and put three barrels on each animal. We'll have them hauled in two trips."

"How many barrels are there?"

"Thirty. Like I said, good as gold in the bank."

Fetching the barrels uses up the rest of the day's light. After efficiently rearranging the wagon's load, they make camp for the night, allowing the livestock to continue grazing. When Dash hears Horatio humming optimistically while building their evening cookfire, he shares the sentiment.

After traveling parallel to the emigrant flow for a few days, the wagon train must cross the river to their side. At the top of a sandy ridgeline, Horatio stops the wagon and watches the crossing play out below them. There are moments of chaos as animals balk, but with the help of ropes and strong swimmers, everyone crosses without incident.

As they join the masses and settle in for the night, Horatio lowers his voice and says, "Got three days before there ain't nothin' but alkali and dust in that desert bottom. The river disappears, and there ain't no more water for a long stretch.

"Won't be long before some folks get real interested in what we're hauling. Ain't nothin' but sand, sagebrush, and death for as far as you can see. We'll stop at the last possible clear spring before the desert. Goin' to take us a bit to fill them barrels, maybe half the day."

Horatio's bleak description of the upcoming terrain makes Dash recall the open ground where the mutiny had happened.

That was five days between water.

Following the crowd heading south three days later, Horatio and Dash lag behind to begin to work their plan. They stop at the last good spring before the vast arid valley. While the animals graze and rest, the two men start the arduous process of filling the barrels, two buckets at a time. It takes all day.

"Horatio, the wagon is getting pretty heavy. I'd better ride Grunt when we move out, just to monitor the load."

"Best hope folks get desperate sooner than later. Don't want no wagon trouble."

Horatio's ominous tone rests uneasily with Dash for the whole night.

For the following three days, the sun's rays shine down on them brutally, from sunup to sundown. The water's weight forces more stops to avoid undue strain on the mules. Dash tries not to panic when their plodding progress causes them to lose sight of their original wagon train, but it isn't long before other wagons catch up to them.

After a few more days in the searing heat, they do some business. Some folks buy enough water to fill their depleted barrels, while others are grateful for the forage and oats for their animals. As payments get deposited into the hidden "bank" Horatio has built into the wagon's bed, Dash feels a wave of relief quell his worries. He gives himself permission to think about getting back to Amalee.

One afternoon, a sudden deluge interrupts the monotony of cloudless blue skies. The ground absorbs every drop leaving them to slog through sticky mud. It isn't long before the accumulation on the wagon's wheels forces them to an early stop. When the mules finish their meal of hay and oats, Horatio and Dash crawl into the tarp-covered wagon bed, strip off their wet clothes, and make their bed in the grass hay, drifting off to raindrops pattering on the tarp.

After the best rest since Fort Bridger, Dash emerges from the wagon bed to a glorious scene worthy of a painting. The night's moisture has stimulated the barren expanse to burst into a flamboyant quilt of blossoms. While they wait for the trail to dry enough for travel, Horatio studies their location.

"I reckon we'll get to the Carson River with three, maybe four days more unless we meet up with folks needin' our goods, and they lighten our load enough, so we make up time."

Once the sun is high and the trail dry, they hitch up and set out again. As they round a knoll, evidence of remarkably deep ruts in the trail give way to a gathering of several wagons. Hobbled horses hop about as a woman tends a cook fire—clear signs of a breakdown.

When Dash and Horatio approach, they see a wheel cracked clear through, the flat metal tire bent off the wheel's wooden felloe. The men lift their heads and wipe their brows before approaching the freight wagon. Dash recognizes them as the travelers from the Humboldt as Horatio pulls the mules to a stop.

"We caught a rut. Wheel finally gave out," one of the men says.

"Don't have no parts," Horatio tells him. "You'll have to scavenge a left-behind."

An older man steps away from the others.

"Animals are lame. Could you be convinced to ride ahead and find us a wheel?"

"How much you payin'?" Horatio asks.

"How much you needin' to do the Christian thing?"

"Ten dollars will be about right."

Horatio's price makes Dash twitch, but he stays silent. Quiet blankets the air while the men consider the cost. Finally, the older man speaks up.

"Seems high, but you've come along in our hour of despair. You bring us a wheel and when it fits, we'll pay you for it."

"No sir, you'll pay half now."

"Without knowing of your success?"

"Seems to me you're the one doin' the askin'. If you want our help, you can pay us to scrounge. Half now and half when we return with a wheel."

Horatio's unnaturally firm tone makes Dash's head jerk to see his partner's hard stare trained on the older man.

"Have it your way, son."

The man bows his head and reaches into his coat. Before the motion registers in Dash's consciousness, Horatio pulls his pistol and has it aimed at the man's drawn weapon. Dash feels his jaw go slack in disbelief.

"Sir, you just pissed away my Christian feelin's. Put away your weapon and let us pass. You'll be gettin' your own replacement. Sure there's somethin' a day or two's walk down this g'dam trail."

Handing the mule's lines to Dash, Horatio keeps his pistol pointed at the group. As Dash stares straight ahead and starts the mules down the rutted road, he hears the other men growl at the old man to put away the gun. Horatio doesn't relax his stance or uncock his pistol until they are out of range. After a few minutes of silent traveling, a voice calls out from behind them making a quiver run down Dash's spine. Horatio redraws his pistol.

"Don't shoot, don't shoot!"

Dash cranes his neck and sees a gasping young man gaining on the wagon.

Horatio barks, "Now what you want?"

"We're sorry for the old man. He's startin' to wear down. Temper's gettin' worse as we go. Don't know from one day to the next how he is going to react to things. My ma's sure he's going to kill one of us before California."

"Perhaps someone should remove his firearm," Dash suggests.

"We would, if he didn't sleep with it."

"Here for apologies, or is there somethin' else on your mind?"

"Was hopin' to catch a ride to the next wagon wreck. I'll roll the wheel back, so you're not slowed down. Hope it's not too far—I left without any water."

Horatio and Dash agree to let the young man sit in the wagon's bed and they continue on. When they come to a wagon with a suitable wheel attached to a broken axle, they help the young man get the wheel off, before parting ways in uneasy silence.

Dash breaks the tension after they are underway again and asks, "This is what Vasquez warned us about, isn't it?"

"Yep. People get wrung out watchin' their g'dam dreams disappear, and it makes some of them do the nastiest things. I suppose the old man is mighty tired. He don't know it yet but, there's even tougher trials ahead gettin' over them California mountains. They're goin' to be ghosts and demons before they see the g'dam green hills of California, if they make it that far. Wish I could warn them but don't think they'd listen, anyhow."

After three days in the Forty-Mile Desert, the smell of rotting carcasses is overwhelming. Forced to wear a handkerchief over their faces to keep from retching, Horatio and Dash watch as all living things become desperate. Decomposing animals litter the trail, their despondent owners not bothering to release the harnessed corpses from their wagons. Apparently, it's all the pitiful souls can do to gather what they can carry and resume the westbound march.

It is alarming how quickly their water stores have dropped, and Dash knows Horatio is just as concerned when his entrepreneurial partner chooses to pass up sales opportunities. They can't afford to help anymore. Whenever they pass emigrants, Dash keeps his gaze straight ahead rather than initiate contact.

Ragtown, the closest thing to civilization on the desert's western edge, is disheartening. A collection of deserted shanties and dirty, shredded trader's tents ravaged by the winter weather beckon to them like miserable ghosts. As Horatio pulls the team to a stop, disappointment and fatigue mingle with the hot evening air.

"Them traders ain't made it through the g'dam mountains yet. At least there's water."

Initially, they camp next to the river with everyone else. The tension is palatable when it becomes obvious whose animals have not suffered in the desert passage. Dash knows Horatio is just as worn out as he is, but the fear of someone trying to swap livestock keeps Horatio twitching at every sound and movement. Rest is reserved for the livestock.

After two days in Ragtown, Dash is relieved when Horatio suggests they hitch up and head north—away from the southbound crowd. Not only can they relax from their livestock guard duty, but if they can find it, grass hay will be even more valuable on their return trip. Dash can't believe their luck when, several miles to the north along the Sierra foothills, they find an untouched meadow.

Over the next four days, the two men harvest as much of the meadow grass as daylight allows. They fill their wagon barrels with fresh spring water and sheaves of fresh hay while the mules and Grunt rest. After being gone for a month, Dash allows himself to become buoyant with anticipation for seeing Amalee again.

Two days eastbound in the soul-boring heat of the Forty-Mile Desert and Dash's levity evaporates. They come across party after forlorn party, many afoot now, desperate for news of how much longer they have to endure the desert's travails. They sell half their water supply and a third of their hay at twice the price of just two weeks earlier. No amount of hay will help some of the pitiful animals they encounter.

On their third night eastbound, they make camp early to escape the sweltering July heat. Several westbound wagons arrive and camp nearby. Horatio and Dash welcome the company and are quick to offer their established campfire in anticipation of new conversation.

They watch the small group stagger into position, the men listlessly unhitching the woeful horses. Once the folks are settled and everyone is introduced, the hair on Dash's neck stands on end when he recognizes a Boston accent. He doesn't have to wait long before Horatio learns the man's hometown.

"Did you hear that? Could be a neighbor."

Dash's mouth goes dry as he scrambles for a story that is truthful enough without getting too familiar.

"Boston proper?" Dash asks, reluctantly.

"Quincy's my family home. Family came in on the early ships but not the Mayflower, as fate would have it."

Dash recognizes the famous ship's importance to establishing elite status in Boston's social groups before saying, "My father owns a quarry in Milton but I grew up in Somerville."

"Busy time for the quarries, although less so now since the railroads have switched from granite to wooden ties for their rail beds."

Dash gulps. The man is too familiar with the granite business. But then, no one, including Horatio, knows his true identity, only his alias.

He forces his racing heart and clenched fists to relax as he says, "Been a while since I was home."

Another man speaks up.

"Considering the exodus of so many young men, it's a wonder anything gets accomplished. Hardly enough people to do all the work."

The man from Quincy speaks again. "There've been several complete mysteries of young men who have disappeared in our area. Not a word, not a trace left of them. Parents left to assume they've died or run off to the goldfields. In one particular case, the young man disappeared while on a family errand. Left the woman he was to wed a week before the service. The bride was so ashamed, she left the area with an uncle. The fellow's family published appeals in regional papers with no luck. One has to wonder if there wasn't foul play involved. Do you know of this case?"

Dash is certain this stranger is conveying his personal story, but to what end? Has he been discovered? He wishes he could leave the campfire, but knows it is impossible without replying.

"No, sir. I left when the westward rush started."

"Does your family know of your whereabouts?"

"My family didn't approve of my decision. I'm sure they don't care where I am or how I spend my time."

"That's a shame, son," the man replies, his hard stare at Dash disguised by a sympathetic expression.

Dash clears his throat and says, "Excuse me, the mules need checking."

Walking briskly away from the campfire, Dash's mind clouds with skepticism at the man from Quincy's story. He can't imagine his father had run ads offering a bounty, just like he did with the runaway slaves. But the description of the jilted woman is what lugs at his thoughts. He knew Lillia's uncle was coming all the way from France for their wedding. Would Lillia really have left Boston with him, and accompanied him back to France? While plausible, it is also plausible they sailed somewhere else, like San Francisco.

When he returns to the campfire, Horatio looks up and smiles in the dim glow of the dying embers.

"Suppose we'd best get rested for another day. I like our progress. We're much lighter and we know the soft ground only gets harder the further east we go. Did you see that one wagon at the lead? Them folks have green velvet linin' along the wagon bed's walls. Just like them fancy hotels in N'Orleans. There's a feather bed in there too!"

"How do you know?"

"The husband said the wife's worried about bugs in it. Demands they take time every mornin' after sleepin' and every evenin' before sleepin' to air it out. She gets out a rug beater and beats 'em out."

They both share a chuckle and settle down. But Dash struggles to find sleep. The fingers of his past pry open the al-most-healed wound from Boston. Old voices and phrases haunt him, especially his father's.

Think you're too good to do this work? You're such a disappoint-ment.

In the morning, Dash wakes first and sets to work, drawing buckets of water from their barrels to bring to the animals. At their last slurp from the bucket, he hears Horatio holler and turns to see the folks from the previous night at their fire. Dash hustles back and sees the man from Quincy

"We've discussed it and would like to buy all the hay and oats you have left to sell."

Horatio and Dash exchange glances, while concealing their shared grins. They quickly calculate their return trip's need and determine they had twenty extra sheaves of hay at two dollars a sheaf and a sack of oats for ten dollars. Without batting an eye, the man hands over the coins and the group hauls away their purchases.

After a brief salute, Horatio urges the mules eastbound. Dash is eager to cross the Humboldt River and get to Salt Lake City, but when they arrive, they find the river's volume too high to try the crossing alone. Forced to wait for a westbound company, they make camp. To occupy their idle time, they construct their own raft, wide and long enough for a wagon, made up of their empty water barrels and other left-behind parts. The only thing lacking from their impromptu ferry is a heavy rope long enough to span the swollen river's width.

The construction activity keeps Dash from ruminating on the passage of time, but by the evening of the third day, he admits his anxiety.

"Don't go fretting', Dash. Someone's bound to show up soon."

Just then, the mules' ears flick in unison toward the east. One by one, the silhouettes of eighteen wagons crest the hill in the dying daylight.

The new company's men hail Horatio and Dash at sunrise, and following Horatio's directive, three mounted men enter the river's swirling current along with the necessary guide rope. When the horsemen emerge wet and triumphant, they knot the rope around a large cottonwood tree. The crossing commences after the knot is tested and confirmed by those on the opposite bank.

Dash swells with equal parts pride and relief, as the salvaged-parts raft is successfully flipped and bobs high on the water's surface. On its maiden voyage, the downstream current pushes against it mightily, but the raft holds together.

On the opposite bank, women and children are in the process of their well-rehearsed efforts to lighten the wagons. While the men wait, they lob a barrage of questions at Horatio about what to expect down the trail. Horatio's answers are taken as the gospel truth and Dash realizes they both represent authentic, trail-hardened Westerners. He also can't avoid the emigrant's anxious expressions when they learn of their livestock's perilous future.

For each wagon crossing, two men are required to heave on the guide rope while two more pole from the down-current side for stability and decent progress. The water's force is so powerful that frequent role rotations among the exhausted men are required. By late afternoon, they have only six wagons left to cross but fatigue has set in.

A carelessly loaded wagon's tongue catches in the river current's flow and twists aggressively to the left, sending two men flailing into the water. No one panics and the men swim to shore, laughing at their unexpected dunk. But Dash suspects his raft's stress and doesn't participate in the gaiety.

While the others secure the next wagon for its trip, he inspects the plank groove where the tongue had caught. The pressure had slightly pried up the plank around a knothole. While hardly cause to stop their progress, Dash feels his caution flare. If the remaining wagons are not too heavy, it might hold.

Finally, they come to the last westbound wagon. The afternoon shadows grow long, and Dash anxiously paces with anticipation. The plank has held so far, and once he and Horatio are on the other side, they can get on their way.

But then he hears the men discussing the company's last, massive wagon. Its owner resembles a bull terrier in looks and temperament. Dash is astonished at the man's arrogant tone toward the others, having not participated in the crossing until now. His wife, a short, plump woman, bawls for help from the wagon's interior. As the other women begrudgingly come to her aid, Dash hears a haughty sermon begin on the care of her belongs. He wonders how long the company's women have tolerated this harpy.

When it comes time to load the wagon, Dash is shocked when the wife refuses to leave its interior, relenting only after her husband threatens to drag her out. As she gingerly steps down onto the muddy riverbank, Dash tries not to stare at her pale, tender-skinned feet—and the soft, pink satin slippers upon them.

Everyone struggles to load the wagon, except the owner, who shouts commands from the riverbank. Once levered up onto the raft's deck, the wagon is carefully rolled forward, its rear wheels blocked into place on the raft's opposite edge. Dash feels an ominous chill run through him as the wagon's left front wheel comes to rest squarely on the damaged plank's knothole.

Horatio takes a pole position while Dash and three men grip the guide rope. They begin their pull and pole effort even though sheets of water ripple across the raft's deck at the midway point.

Dash tries to calm his trepidations, but when calls go out from the rope hands for more progress from the downstream side pole men, he flushes with impending dread.

"Ain't got nothin' more to give," Horatio calls out.

When two rope men suddenly shift their grips, the weight adjustment causes the raft's upstream edge to tip into the current—and is caught in a flash. The catch triggers the cracked plank to snap under the wheel's weight and the wagon lists forward into a dramatic tilt. With a mighty splash, the wagon pitches into the river's flow. All the men aboard are tossed into the swirling water. Finding his feet in the river shallows, Dash sees the wagon's tongue anchor into the mud against the raft deck, the acute angle awkwardly supporting the wagon's behemoth mass.

Helpless except to gawk at the partially submerged wagon, the owner squats in the riverbank's mud and stares at his sunken loss as it takes on water, one side floating half-heartedly off the raft's edge. The air echoes with the wife's pitiful screams from the opposite shore.

Dash knows saving the wagon requires a quick response. And yet, given the swift current, lifting the wagon off the raft could mean risking someone's life. After long deliberation, they decide to attach a rope to the raft's downstream side and a lever under the wagon's tongue with the intention of heaving on the lever to release a trapped barrel.

Horatio leads the men in a mighty tug on the attached rope, while Dash and two others strain against the tongue. No effect. Changing tactics, Horatio slacks the rope while Dash's men keep upward pressure on the tongue. A loud crack ricochets through the air and the raft shifts.

Emboldened, the rope men yank again and again. Dash senses a change in the raft's position, and he works madly with the men to shovel mud from around the trapped barrel. After several minutes of shoveling, the rope men pull again, but the trapped barrel and tongue hold fast. Feeling discouragement creeping in with the evening's chill, Dash realizes the culprit in their dilemma is the barrel.

Could it be as simple as changing the direction of the rope pull?

Bellowing instructions, he orchestrates the men into one last yank on the raft's rope. With a mighty, unified grunt and strain, the trapped barrel pops out and the raft releases into the swirling current, freed from its burden. Dash and several men scurry after the raft, eventually tugging it onto the downstream riverbank.

At the glowing fire, Horatio wraps a blanket around Dash's shaking body and offers dry clothes while chattering about their success. After eating a warm meal, Dash leaves Horatio at the company fire, entertaining the travelers with his animated stories.

At the company's outskirts, the darkness engulfs Dash. Only with this darkness does he notice the glow of a solitary campfire hidden by the sandy bank at the river's opposite shore. With all the excitement, it seems no one has considered the wrecked wagon owner's wife. Studying the distant scene, he feels a flash of pity for the lone woman before crawling under the wagon and falling into an exhausted sleep.

The morning begins with the looming quandary of what to do about the massive wagon still wedged tight in the river's mud and constant current. Their only course of action is to push the wagon further into the river, in hopes of dislodging the wagon tongue from the mud. With four pairs of horses ready to hitch on when the tongue is freed, several men enter the water and lean with all their might against the wagon's bed. When the tongue finally loosens, the horses are quickly hitched. After four or five tries, the waterlogged wagon sloshes up the riverbank.

Draining water spews from the bed like a fountain, and the women begin their tactical effort to remove anything salvageable. There isn't much. What the current hasn't taken, the water has ruined. Dash notices few have sympathy when the owner moans about his bad luck.

Horatio and Dash coordinate the effort to reattach the raft to the guide rope. Assisted by the company's men, Horatio loads their wagon, its lightness remarkable to all. Dash mounts Grunt and swims their mules across ahead of the wagon's crossing. As he emerges from the river with the splashing team, he waits for the wagon's arrival just up the riverbank from the lone woman's overnight camp.

Their almost-empty wagon arrives within minutes, and Dash helps hitch the mules to it before Horatio drives the wagon off the raft. Curiosity getting the best of him, Dash leads Grunt up the riverbank's high lip to cautiously peer down at the pile of possessions. He sees her body curled by the cold fire, lying in a peaceful sleep. In the dust, just beyond the gently arched fingers of her pale hand, lies an empty bottle.

Dash looks over his shoulder toward the opposite bank at her husband whose full attention is focused on his saturated wagon.

One of the company's men arrives at Dash's side and grimly reaches down for the bottle, muttering, "Strychnine. She took the whole bottle. She and old Hayes have been at each other's throats since South Pass. No one knew what to do. Figured their marriage was none of our business. She was nasty to the ladies. My wife told me about her sayin' something about a gift her mother had given her, if the situation became overwhelmin'. I guess this must have been it.

Hayes thinks money can fix everythin', but it can't help him now. That wagon ain't goin' to last him—metal's been wet too long. It'll rust up in no time. I best take care of business and give him the news."

Dash watches the man cross the river on the raft and tell Hayes of his wife's circumstances. When Hayes finally shuffles toward the raft to cross to her, he is joined by several other solemn men armed with shovels, clearly showing this is not the first grave dug on this trip.

Once across the river, Dash watches Hayes plod toward the scene, his head hanging dejectedly between his slumped shoulders, the others following at a respectful distance. Hayes bends over to inspect his wife's corpse, and Dash expects to hear a few kind words, maybe some expression of emotion.

After a brief look, Hayes straightens, dry-eyed, and says to no one in particular, "Not made of the right stuff."

In the three days since the Humboldt River tragedy, Dash has silently wished he could erase the Hayes woman's image from his memory. So absorbed in her tragedy, in fact, that he hasn't realized how long Horatio has quietly honored his brooding. One afternoon, Horatio breaks his companion's reverie.

"Dash, I gotta tell you somethin'."

Horatio's abrupt statement makes Dash's eyebrows arch questioningly.

"Them folks, they were mixed up for sure, but most of them were normal. They were grateful to us for helpin' them."

"Oh? I'm not sure we were too smart to help them, Horatio. We lost time. And then . . . that woman? I'll never understand that."

"Me neither, Dash. But just so you know, they were grateful to the tune of . . ." he fishes around in his pants pocket until he produces a handful of coins, ". . . to the tune of twenty-two dollars. One from everyone, except the wrecked wagon. That ole man paid us five dollars for our trouble."

"When did they pay you?"

"They paid me the night before we parted ways. I was goin' to tell you, but you'd already gone to sleep. And the next day, that awful thing happened. Since you've been stewin' I figured I'd wait. Decent of them, huh?"

Dash nods as he considers everything.

"Where's that put us, money-wise, for this trip?"

"Well, without breakin' out the bank, I'm guessin' we're somewhere around six hundred."

Dash stares at his partner in disbelief. Horatio returns his gaze before they both crack big grins of agreement and Horatio says, "Alright, then, back to Fort Bridger."

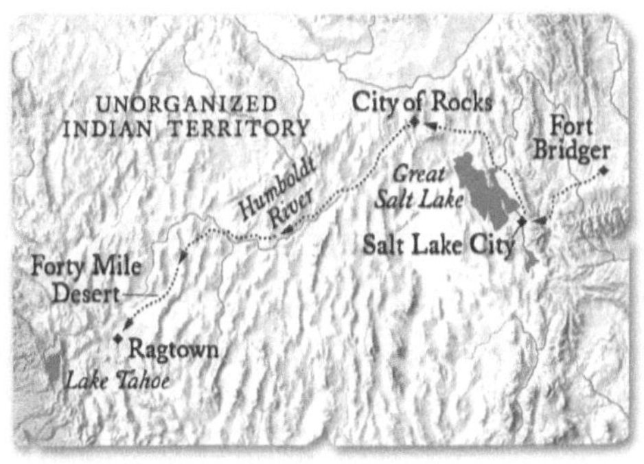

Chapter 17

JULY, 1850

FORT BRIDGER,

UNORGANIZED INDIAN TERRITORY

At sunset, Fort Bridger comes into view. Dash and Horatio had been gone for just short of two months. Where there had been oozing mud and melting snow-drifts, the camping area outside the fort's balustrade was alive with activity from three different emigrant companies. When they pull through the fort's gate, the cramped interior echoes with the ring of the blacksmith's hammer and people calling out to each other.

Dash takes in the bustling scene with anticipation, searching for Amalee, thinking to himself with a warm feeling of pride, that he kept his word to Narcissa.

"Dash, I cain't believe your not off that seat a lookin' for your little one!"

"I sure am eager to see her, but I don't want to leave you with all the unharnessing."

"I can do this fine. Get on in there and see your baby girl!"

Dash hops down, his boots sending up a cloud of dust on impact. When he knocks on the Vasquez cabin door, the door swings open and Louis engulfs him in a hug.

"You boys made it back! Wonderful! You need to see Amalee. She's changed a mite since you left."

Dash nods and steps through the doorway. He sees Narcissa sitting with Amalee and Mary Ann on either side of her, a spoon in each of her hands, both poised to a child's open mouth. The children sit in identical chairs, their food strategically placed for the most efficient process. Their three-year-old son, Louis, sits close by feeding himself, oblivious to the production going on across from him.

When Narcissa glances in Dash's direction, a clatter of slaps on the tabletop reprimand her tardiness. Narcissa grins as she shoves a heaping spoonful into each child's mouth before she stands to greet him.

"Look who's here, Amalee. It's your papa, baby girl!"

Amalee pauses to study Dash, glancing in his direction. Her dark oval eyes are as enchanting as always. When she doesn't respond to his presence, Dash feels surprised, not anticipating she might not recognize him. Narcissa wipes the food from Amalee's face with her apron and hoists the child to her hip. With a joyful smile, she brings Amalee to him.

"She's beautiful, isn't she?"

Grinning, Dash takes Amalee.

"Hello, my little lady. I sure have missed you," he says, lifting her up and giving her a kiss on the nose. It surprises him how deeply felt his words are.

Then to Narcissa, he says, "I see you've been feeding her well."

"She's a hearty eater. I suppose it's one of my flaws, but I do love a chubby baby. They stand a better chance if they're well nourished."

Narcissa returns to Mary Ann to repeat the cleaning process. Dash notices Amalee surveying him cautiously until he sticks his face into the nape of her neck and blows against her skin. That makes her squeal, and he knows she remembers her papa. Because that's what he is, he realizes. He's all she's got, and she doesn't know anything different for a father, or any parent, for that matter.

She attempts to grab his beard with a fat little hand. When he clutches her fingers, the grit and calluses of his hand close over the smooth whiteness of her skin and he's embarrassed by his road grime.

"I need to wash up before I hold her much more. It's been a long trip."

"But you're back in one piece. We can't wait to hear of your adventures. Louis and I need something new to talk about after all the incivilities of this place. I'll get started on some supper. You boys must be tired of trail food."

Agreeing, Dash goes directly to the barn to help Horatio finish with the mules. As he walks, he wonders at Narcissa's words, *after all the incivilities of this place.*

When the men finish their chores, they wash up at the water trough before hurrying back to the Vasquezes' home. A piece of mirror hangs casually on a string from a nail in the trough frame and, curious, Dash picks it up. The man looking back at him is a stranger. His face, that which is not covered in long whiskers, is tanned to a dark brown. With his hat off, he sees a distinct white line at mid-forehead from his hat's placement.

But what captures his stare is the left side of his face. The eye socket that once housed the wandering eye he had kept patched now holds his eye straight and true. But the bone around his eye and his cheekbone had healed in a rippled and dipped way giving him a contoured profile, the skin slick with shiny scar tissue. When he slowly turns his head to the right, he is as he remembers. The view of his left profile is deformed . . . and hideous.

No one said anything to him about how he looked. No one had shrunken back in horror, not even when he was in Salt Lake City. Horatio never said anything . . . does that mean it doesn't matter? Would his mother even recognize him? And if she did, would she still want him? He doesn't wonder about his father.

Dash releases the mirror and washes his face and hands with vigor. Horatio, who had dunked his whole head under the water, slings his long-wet hair around and laughs.

"Ain't a full bath but feels mighty good gettin' the grime off, don't it?"

"I need a shave. I don't like my whiskers."

"I imagine that can be arranged. Narcissa will have somethin', I'm sure of it."

They find Amalee and Mary Ann playing on the floor, the pair now crawling confidently. When Amalee sees Dash, she makes her way toward him, pulling herself up on his chair while chattering in an unknown dialect. Narcissa arrives with his supper.

"She's so close to walking, I'm sure it'll happen while you are traveling."

Speaking over Amalee's ruckus, Horatio asks, "What do you think she's got on her mind?"

Narcissa places his dinner in front of him and says, "I believe she's inviting herself into your lap, Dash."

Dash picks Amalee up and sits her on his knee. Quick as a flash, Amalee puts her fat little hand right in the middle of his mashed potatoes. Narcissa bolts toward them and whisks Amalee away.

"No, huh-uh, young lady, not at my table. You can play with Louis and Mary Ann while we finish our supper."

When Narcissa returns to the table, she says, "I apologize, Dash. She is still young but you're going to have to hold a hard line with her manners. She has a powerful mind of her own."

Smiling to himself, Dash thinks, *as did her mother.*

Their meal is filled with food and stories. In the name of good taste, Dash leaves the Humboldt River tragedy out of their telling. They learn Brigham Young has spread vicious rumors about Jim Bridger, accusing him of arming the Ute and Snake Indians, who are forcing Mormon settlers off their lands.

Narcissa puts generous slices of apple pie in front of the men before scooping up Amalee and Mary Ann for bedtime kisses. When it is Dash's turn to kiss her goodnight, Amalee hesitates again. Her puzzled expression brings on a round of adult laughter and she joins in, like she knows why they are laughing. When Narcissa leaves to put the children to bed, Vasquez turns his attention to the young men.

"Imagine you boys are too road weary to talk of your next trip. Maybe in the morning. Do those goldfields still hold the lure they once did, Dash?"

"At this point, I doubt there's any gold left."

"Gold, as we know it, ain't the only way of makin' it big in California," Horatio adds. "There's plenty of other g'dam things that'll score the same money and not as back-breakin' as pannin' or sluicin'. This trip's done proved it."

"The rich man will always be the one who answers a need."

Vasquez's words strike a chord in Dash.

Both men are right. Horatio has taught him the importance of knowing people's needs before they are aware of them. In a twisted and foul way, he admits his father was doing the same thing for Kinkade. But the future Dash wants is to be a force of good in the world, given his second chance at life. It is unexplainable to him why he has survived when all the others succumbed, and his eyesight has been restored in a freak accident.

No, it is time for him to use his new gift for good, not harm.

Over the next two weeks, Horatio's effort to feed his mules short of foundering pays off and they regain their athletic physiques. He and Dash make several trips into the distant hills to harvest hay, scything one day and bundling the next. They are only satisfied when the hay is mounded high and tightly tarped in the wagon bed. After supper that night, Horatio lays out the next step.

"We'll have to go into Salt Lake City to find oats. Hope there's still some around after all these folks," waving his hand toward the emigrant camps.

"Don't you worry," Vasquez says. "Most of these travelers aren't going to Salt Lake City. Most head right up to South Pass and over. That's what's got Brigham Young so worked up. Says Bridger's takin' away business by promotin' his trading post too aggressively."

"You think they'll sell to us?"

Vasquez coughs.

"Just don't tell them you know me or Bridger. They'll be eager to sell, probably goin' to have to pay more than in May, though. Or maybe they'll be eager to get rid of what they got before the harvest. Who knows?"

Narcissa shows Dash the clothes collection she has put together for Amalee. When she adds other important items for Amalee's care, Dash is impressed if not slightly overwhelmed. He had no idea a child needed so much.

"Dash, there's something else. I took apart Amalee's basket after she arrived. It was ruined with the baby's waste, but I found things in the basket's lining before throwing it in the fire. I made a new storage packet for the things . . ."

Her voice trails off as she quietly hands a tied buckskin packet to Dash.

"I admit I looked through the items," she says, "but, honestly, I don't know what to make of the contents. Seeds, I think, but I'm unfamiliar with them. And there are written notes in a language I don't know. And then there's the cameo and a few other of your wife's personal items, or perhaps her mother's."

Dash takes the pouch, his hands shaking slightly at the weight of what this discovery means. It's all Amalee has left of her mother, the hopes and dreams Nora left behind.

"Thank you, Narcissa. I will pack this with my things to keep it safe."

Back in his storage room, Dash sits before the wood stove and gingerly unties the thong holding the leather pouch closed. The first thing he sees is the cameo pin. Setting it aside, he slowly rolls the pouch open while admiring Narcissa's delicate stitches that have created a secure folded pocket at the pouch's lower edge. Once unfolded, he sees several small, waxed envelopes, folded and crinkled at their edges. Opaque enough to not be able to see, he lifts them from the pouch and examines them, pressing them between his thumb and forefinger. Certainly seems like small seeds, just like what Narcissa said.

Several folded sheets of paper sit snugly in the pouch and when he removes them, he sees a foreign script decorating the pages. Squinting in the low light and holding the paper close, he studies the script carefully, assuming it's a dialect from Nora's people back in Ireland.

A few pieces of handmade lace, a small string of glass beads, and a hair comb complete the contents of the pouch. Dash gently returns everything to its place, then slowly rolls the pouch up, reties the leather thong, and places it in his saddlebag with what remains of his sparse personal belongings.

The night before they are scheduled to leave, they celebrate Mary Ann and Amalee's first birthdays. Narcissa makes a special cake piled high with wild strawberries. They sing the birthday song, delighting both girls. Mary Ann silently grins at the celebration, but Amalee enthusiastically joins in with loud squawks while slapping her little hands on the table.

Once Amalee is in bed, Narcissa pulls Dash aside and solemnly asks, "Perhaps you and I can take a walk?"

Dash nods, her tone making his heart suddenly pick up its pace.

Stepping out into the dusky light of the hot July evening, Narcissa says, "Dash, making this trip with Amalee is going to be quite an undertaking for you."

Trying not to show any emotion, he says, "Go on, Narcissa."

"I've been married to two men for a total of twelve years. Neither were suited for childcare, especially for a girl baby. I doubt you're much different."

Before he can voice an objection, Narcissa continues.

"My best advice is to join a wagon company with a family in it. Amalee is uniquely suited for getting along with others. Negotiate a way for her to be with a family with other children to play with and they can help you care for her. Don't think you can do this alone."

Dash quietly considers her words before saying, "Thank you for your advice, Narcissa. I will do my level best to find help for her along the way. And thank you for everything you have done for her, for us. Your willingness to nurse her in the early days and care for her while Horatio and I were gone . . . I'm indebted to you and Louis. None of us know what the future holds, but I will always be ready to help if I can."

When Narcissa hands Amalee up to Dash in the wagon the next morning, the child's face is bright and cheerful. He notices tears in the woman's eyes and he gulps a silent prayer that Amalee is ready for this adventure.

As Horatio eases the mules out of the fort's walls, it occurs to Dash that this is the first time he has traveled any leg of this long trip twice. At least he knows what to expect. That should make it easier to adapt to having the baby along. But he has kept his promise to Nora and now, to Narcissa. He is determined to do right by Amalee too.

From her perch on the wooden bench between Horatio and Dash and shielded from the hot sun by a broad bonnet, Amalee babbles at everything they pass. At their midday meal, Dash lets Amalee crawl around in the grass where she quickly demonstrates her mobility. In a blink, she strays outside his vision and when he finds her, she is contentedly tasting several rocks at the road's edge.

Horatio laughs.

"Narcissa would be havin' a fit about now."

In Salt Lake City, Horatio doesn't waste time getting to a feed store for the oats. As Vasquez had hinted, the price had gone up since May, but both men know the oats' value on the trail. Once ten sacks of oats are stuffed into the water barrel and hay sheaf-ladened wagon bed, they leave the city and head north.

Three days later, they intersect the California Trail. Narcissa's directive to find a traveling family is sufficiently impressed into Dash's mind. As they join the flow of westbound travelers, he takes a keen interest in the wagons' occupants. He is discouraged to find so few families with children.

On their fifth day, they stop for a meal with a company from Indiana, its even-tempered captain welcoming them without hesitation. Out of nowhere, a little girl appears at Dash's side and asks if Amalee can play. Dash picks up Amalee and follows the child to her family's wagon.

"Ma, look what I found on the trail!"

The woman turns, her expression telling Dash this is not the first time her four-year-old daughter has brought her a trail treasure and watches the mother's expression shift to eye-widened surprise.

"Well, Deedee, this is the cutest thing you've drug home yet!"

Introducing themselves, Dash learns that Paul and Eliza Townsend and their daughter Deedee are from Marietta, Ohio.

"Floated past Marietta on a flatboat on my way west. Didn't stop, though."

"It is a blessing to have your little one play with Deedee during our rests. Go ahead and tend to your wagon. She'll be fine with us."

"Thank you, ma'am."

Dash leaves and helps Horatio water the mules at the creek. When he returns, Amalee and Deedee are in high spirits in the wagon bed. He picks Amalee up and Deedee tugs at his shirt.

"Mr. Dash, can Amalee play again?"

"Sounds good, but make sure your ma and pa are agreeable. Amalee can be a handful."

Deedee nods soberly.

"Ma and Pa don't like me leavin' the wagon, but it's hard when there is nothing to do or no one to play with."

The next few days pass with Amalee spending more and more time with Deedee. Dash can't believe his good fortune. As they approach the Humboldt River crossing, he is relieved when Eliza offers to look after Amalee during the crossing. He is nervous and shares these thoughts with Horatio.

"Dash, it's August. The g'dam high water has passed. Bet we can drive the wagon across without it coming halfway up our wheels."

"A bet? No bet from me. I just hope you're right. It'd be a refreshing change not to get soaked."

True to Horatio's prediction the river is low, and the wagon train barely slows to cross. Horatio takes on the guiding role and helps direct the wagon teams toward the shallower areas. The event is shocking in its contrast to the last time. That evening by the campfire, Horatio tells the grisly tale from their last crossing leaving everyone aghast at the tragedy.

When Dash fetches Amalee before bedtime, she greets him with a bright, "Da!!" Surprised by her sweet name for him, he scoops her up and nuzzles her neck.

Eliza quietly motions him away and says, "Dash, the girls play so well together, I'm wondering if Amalee might spend more time in our wagon."

Dash's heart leaps at the idea as he says, "If it wouldn't be a burden, I'm grateful to you for looking after her."

"As grateful as I am to have Deedee occupied, I assure you."

Dash hoists Amalee to his shoulders for their walk back to their wagon and whistles a tune while doing a little jig, his antics dissolving Amalee into a frenzy of delighted giggles.

"Now that we're in the desert, it'd be best for all livin' things to travel at night."

Horatio's idea is met with sighs of relief. Everyone relaxes to repair and prepare for the coming endurance test. Without even a bush for cover, the men work in the shade, while the women and children hole up in their wagons or under tarp lean-tos.

With the western sun bright in their eyes, they set out. The instant the sun disappears behind the horizon, a flush of cool air washes over them and Dash hears singing coming from some wagons. After five hours of traveling in the dark, folks call for a break. When Dash checks in on Amalee, he finds Deedee protectively holding Amalee's hands from above as she stomps in the dust.

"Look Mr. Dash, Amalee is getting ready for walking!"

Eliza joins him as the girls parade before them.

"She's a strong one. It won't be long, and you'll have a runner on your hands."

Dash feels a hint of powerlessness wash over him, as Deedee looks up and grins.

"Don't worry, Mr. Dash, I'll take real good care of her. She and I can go out on treasure hunts together when she gets better at walking."

"You'll do nothing of the kind, young lady. Now that we're in the desert, you mustn't stray from this wagon train, especially with Amalee. You could be lost and die of thirst before we find you. No more treasure hunts until we're in California, understand?"

A cloud of disappointment washes across Deedee's face as she mumbles, "Yes'um."

The desert's night chill has its desired effect, and the company agrees to travel for three more hours using the waxing moon's light for guidance.

The wagon train's travel is uncomplicated for the next week, much to Horatio and Dash's pleasure. They are in the sink of the Humboldt, the wide-open expanse of the river where the last of the water oozes out of the ground in stinky mud pools. The water is rancid, and Horatio cautions the travelers not to be tempted to drink it. He charges the Indiana company less for their water reasoning that the sooner the water load is lightened, the easier it will be for his mules.

Their hay supply has also become a popular item, the trail's shrubs having been completely denuded by the starving livestock preceding them.

Horatio shares that if they keep their pace, they will arrive at the Carson River in four days. Dash knows this is the most desperate time of the trip. The August heat has made the stench of dead animals lining the wagon trail even harder to bear, and everyone covers their faces trying, and failing, to thwart the sickening smells.

As the Sierra Mountains grow closer, some ignore Horatio's advice for slow and steady progress and push ahead. He shakes his head in disbelief as the spaces between wagons stretch to irregular half-mile gaps.

He growls, "Fools. They may make it to the g'dam Carson River without anything dyin', but the animals will be plum wore out for climbin' mountains. No mind. They ain't listenin' to nobody now."

At their last camp before completing the desert crossing, they celebrate with singing and music from a traveler's fiddle and accordion. Everyone is relieved to be west of the dreaded Forty-Mile Desert. After praising Horatio's advice and unique perspective for their success, he is quick to caution them.

"Folks, we've got another hundred miles along the foothills headed south before we get to the canyon. From there, another hundred miles over the mountains and down the other side to Hangtown. Good news is, from Ragtown up yonder," he motions with a flip of his hand, "there's lots of trading posts along the way. Best know, them traders go through heaps of trouble to get goods over them mountains so they ain't afeared of chargin'."

Restocking opportunities are welcome news, but learning they have only two hundred miles to California contributes to their levity, since most have spent a half-year getting to this point. Dash chooses not to dwell on his traveling time. Watching Amalee and Deedee dance and giggle around the campfire, he realizes he feels happiness, true happiness, for the first time in years.

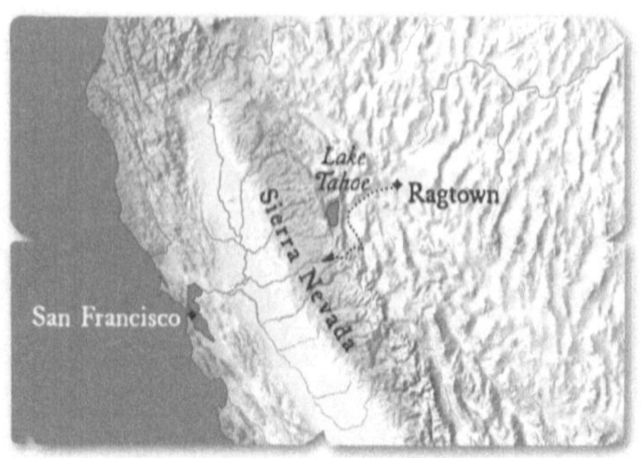

Chapter 18

AUGUST, 1850

CALIFORNIA TRAIL

Ragtown is a vision of entrepreneurial activity now that it's late August. Dash marvels at how the dilapidated tents and shanties they found in June have been rebuilt. While they have no need of the vendors, Horatio and Dash relax, while the Indiana company shop and have repairs made at a blacksmith's forge.

To kill some time, Dash perches Amalee on his shoulders to see the sights. One vendor has stick candy and Dash buys a celebratory piece. He takes the candy to Deedee, knowing she is old enough to enjoy it.

Deedee thanks him with a grin and a hug to his thigh, saying, "I'll share it with Amalee when she needs the most distracting, I promise."

The company stays in Ragtown for two days, but it isn't long before everyone is itching to get down the trail. Traveling south-bound, they follow the Carson River and its clean-flowing water. After four days, the Carson Canyon comes into focus and the enormity of its challenge hits them like a sledgehammer.

"The days of travelin' on sand are gone. Rocks of all sizes make up the trail now. We'll be liftin' wagons over and around boulders their same size. We'll use ropes and levers, and the men will have to join the animals if we're goin' to make it over the top. One wagon at a time in many places. The trail begins along the river, crosses several times and, after roughly five miles, we'll come to where the valley opens up. We'll make camp there. No stoppin' 'til we get to the valley."

As Horatio paints a mental picture of the mountain's trail, Dash watches the expressions of the company's men. This part of their journey presents them with an entirely different set of ob-stacles. While some faces harden from the challenge, others pale.

Once she finishes nibbling on her biscuit, Dash lifts Amalee from his lap to the ground, expecting her to plop down when he releases her. But instead, Amalee maintains her balance and turns toward Horatio sitting nearby. Taking timid yet deter-mined steps, she stumbles in his direction. He hoots at Dash, who catches the big moment from the corner of his eye, just as she plops into the grass at Horatio's side.

Deedee excitedly orbits Amalee in her next attempt and Eliza nudges Dash.

"Congratulations, you are opening a new chapter with her. Mobility will be a blessing and a challenge with Amalee. But you can count on us to help as we can."

Dash smiles his gratitude but his mind whirls with the im-plications of Amalee's mobility. While recognizing his life might be easier, her sudden freedom brings a new level of concern for her safety.

Horatio's warning proves true when the Indiana company arrives in the Sierra foothills, the soft desert dirt now replaced by a rocky road paralleling a raucous river. Horatio encourages his mules as they struggle against the wheels' resistance on rock edges and ruts.

They inch through the canyon, and by late afternoon they arrive at Horatio's promised valley. Relieved, everyone makes camp, but Dash finds it hard not to stare up at tomorrow's route clearly etched into the mountain's side. Horatio catches his glance.

"It's called 'One Mile Mountain,' and it'll take all the strength and ingenuity we got. If we're lucky, we'll get all the wagons up it in one day. But there's always the chance we might spend a night separated. Things is about to get interestin'."

At dawn, Horatio leaves Dash with the mules' lines to organize the climb. When he returns, he is quick with his statements.

"The children can't stay in the wagon. Too rough. Can't risk losin' them if the wagon gets away from us. Goin' to ask Eliza to haul them on her hip to the stoppin' point and wait."

When Dash nods, Horatio jogs off to the Townsend's wagon. Paul slaps his horse's rump and drives to the front. Dash watches as Eliza dutifully gathers up Deedee and Amalee to join Horatio's lead group of men. He feels a twinge of protectiveness flare, his newly cultivated paternal instincts making him doubt if he shouldn't have insisted that Amalee stay with him. The feeling passes when he acknowledges his role of successfully driving a wagon will take all his concentration. Amalee is better off with Eliza.

Behind the walking group, Paul drives his wagon forward, now harnessed with several more teams of horses. Echoes of shouts and calls from the first wagon boom from the surrounding canyon walls, as the wagon disappears around a bend. Dash takes solace in knowing their fading calls signal their progress up the mountain.

After several more wagons, it is Dash's turn. He eagerly enters the tight canyon and finds the road's incline immediately. A faint-hearted soul might entertain the thought of turning around, but retreat is no longer an option. The trail's left side is solid granite, while an ever-deepening river chasm falls off to the right.

After three hundred uphill yards, the mule team needs encouragement. Everyone does what they can to spur them on with whistles and hoots until the team pulls their wagon to a level spot for a brief rest. The men take up positions as human brakes. A job, that if not done well, could find them crushed under a backward careening wagon.

At Horatio's signal, the wagon lurches forward followed by gasps of relief from the brakemen's lips. The mules strain and pick their way along the rocky trail; no creature's footing is too secure in the rocks and ruts. They endure three more stops, three more bracings, and everyone gasps for air. At the last stop, Horatio gives them the good news first.

"The end's just beyond those boulders dead ahead. The bad news is there's a granite slick to cross with no good footholds. The mules are too smart to go where there ain't nothin' to hold onto."

He grabs the lead mule's headstall and, with his encouragement, they get the wagon over the slick and into the meadow. Dash eagerly leaves the mules to Horatio and rushes to the Townsend's wagon. The little girls sit surrounded by their rag dolls. Amalee sucks on a bit of the hard candy he had given to Deedee, and he laughs at the mess.

"Mr. Dash, see how good Amalee is being? Ma says after seein' me take such good care of Amalee, I might get another brother or sister of my own soon."

Dash glances at Eliza, who blushes and shrugs as she hands him a day-old biscuit.

"Tell the other men they can have the same, if they care to visit."

Everyone works diligently with the remaining wagons and when the last arrives, a mighty cheer goes up from the company, the echoes ringing off the canyon's walls. Their arrival has taken the whole day, but Horatio offers them reassurance.

"There are parts ahead where we'll have to bust our guts again, but they'll be in shorter bursts. The worst is behind us."

Dash twitches awake. His muscles have cramped painfully in the night. He pokes his head out of his blanket's protective cover and sees nothing but white. Low-hanging clouds whisper through the camp making a dramatic sight. They are in a cloud!

Struggling to his feet despite the protest of his leg and back muscles, he carefully avoids Amalee still curled up in her bedroll and peeks through the wagon's cover. One look around tells him he is not alone. He walks to the camp's fire where Horatio is already mapping out the next section of travel.

"Best to wait 'til it's dry, too slick for them animals. Red Lake is sittin' at the base of two summits. Once we get to the lake, we'll camp and rest before we push over the top. When we're on the downhill side, we'll be pullin' them wagons by their tailgates to slow them down. But," he says grinning, "not so many rocks. Nice and gradual, not so g'dam steep."

The postponement brings a flood of relief to the company. Dash returns to the wagon to haul Amalee, blankets and all, to the Townsend's wagon. Deedee has created a blanket fort for the day's play and as he walks away, he hears the two girls chattering like chipmunks.

Dash uses their furlough to search for more grass for the animals. Success comes around the bend and while the animals eat their fill, he surveys the sky for any hint of a break in the weather.

The break never comes. At the midday meal, some voice their disappointment, but Horatio quiets their concerns.

"Just as well. The animals need rest. The next climb, while shorter, is steeper. It'll take the same effort as yesterday."

After inventorying their hay stock, Horatio and Dash decide to harvest grass, in case there is nothing at Red Lake. Sacks in hand, they venture across a rocky barrier to a beckoning green meadow.

The traveling is difficult. While picking their way across the sprawling stone field, Dash notes the sharp, angular rocks. He knows if anyone were to slip against them, the damage could be crippling.

Once through the slide, they cut handfuls of the virgin foliage with their knives, working their way along the meadow's outer edge until their sacks are almost full. As they come around a boulder pile, a sight stops them dead in their tracks.

There, propped up against the south side of a boulder, sits a skeleton. Its clothes hang from the bones in flimsy shreds, patches of dried skin and tuffs of hair remain on the skeleton's exposed parts. Fragile finger bones still grip a bullwhip's handle.

Dash is shocked when Horatio suddenly and silently backs away, a look of horror on his pale face, leaving Dash to study the skeleton alone. He hesitates to disturb its restful pose but notes the skeleton's outstretched legs, now only bones covered in thinning cloth. Then he notices a tear in the fabric. Two bleached and shattered bone ends protrude from the tear, speaking to the break's severity. As the haunting afternoon mist swirls between them, the skeleton's repose, while gruesome, shows calm acceptance of the inevitable.

With a break like that, the man would have had no alternative but to face the fact that his adventuring days were over. Of all the death he's seen on this trip, Dash finds this to be the least disturbing.

He leaves the skeleton in his chosen position—the mountain's watchman—to find Horatio. Picking his way back to the camp alone, it is as if his partner had sprouted wings in his rush. Once back in camp, he is relieved to see Horatio's sack of grass propped against one of the wagon's wheels. He searches the encampment, around the campfire, among the other men and horses, with no success. Figuring Horatio may have set out to scout tomorrow's route, Dash uses the last bit of sunlight to head up the trail.

After thirty minutes of climbing in the increasing dusk with no luck, he returns to camp to form a search party. At that moment, Dash sees Horatio's bowed figure against a boulder's windless side. A ghostly chill passes through him when he recognizes how similar Horatio's pose is to the skeleton's. A bloodcurdling shriek meets Dash's touch.

"Dash, what you tryin' to do?"

"I've been looking for you for hours!"

Horatio is quiet for several minutes, his eyes downcast, his head roving back and forth, like he is chasing something. Dash has never seen his partner act like this before.

"I had a nightmare only two nights past. I saw that g'dam skeleton. Saw him clear as day in just that place and just that position, right down to the g'dam whip in his hand. I panicked because I remembered what happened in my nightmare. The skeleton snapped that g'dam whip at me and told me I was next, since I'd left him on the mountain."

"It's your lost partner?"

"Yep. Recognized his whip. My dream told me I might find him in these g'dam mountains. I wasn't one to place too much power on dreams, but now I think different."

Dash sits down next to Horatio and says, "At least now you know what happened to him. His shinbone was snapped in two. He must have fallen while walking in those sharp rocks."

Having lost so many traveling companions on his travels, Dash knows there isn't anything comforting to say to Horatio. Instead, with a strong hand, he squeezes his friend's shoulder conveying his sympathy.

"Best get back," Dash says. "Everyone is wondering where you are. I almost started a search party."

"Now, why would you go and do that?" Horatio says, squinting at Donovan.

"You're kidding, right? Without you, none of us knows where to go or what to do. You have been our leader through this stretch of the trip, and we've been welcomed into this company like part of their family because of you. We all need you, Horatio."

Horatio is quiet for a few moments before whispering, "Well, I'll be g'damned."

Eager to get back before dark, Dash rises and asks, "What did you find when you came up this trail?"

"Ain't goin' to be easy. This g'dam weather has got to break before we can start, that's for sure. Around that bend, there's more boulders than a mangy dog has fleas. Goin' to need to empty the wagons 'cause the men's goin' to have to lift them without the horse's help. Don't remember it bein' this g'dam treacherous, but I was goin' downhill and not thinkin' right. Did a lot of stupid things tryin' to find Clem. To think he was right there so g'dam close."

Despite their skepticism toward Horatio's assessment, the Indiana company's doubts evaporate when they see the scratched-out trail twisting through a chaotic scramble of boulders, shale, and scree flows. Resigned to lightening their wagon's loads to manually lift them over the rough patches, the men turn back to the wagons.

Approaching their camp, they find several new faces at the campfire. Five travelers huddle around the warmth, their life's possessions strapped to their backs, their feet wrapped tightly with rags. The company's women whisper that the shoeless troop had come up on them quietly. They had looked half-starved and delirious, so the women fed them while praying their men would return soon. The Indiana company leader sent the women to unload the wagons before confronting the travelers.

"Where you boys from?"

One, who Dash takes to be the youngest in the group, looks up.

"Originally from Iowa. Had some bad luck. Your womenfolk are kind to feed us. Be on our way now that you're breakin' camp."

Dash watches the young man flash a subtle hand signal to the other four men. Without a word, they rise, heads bowed, never making eye contact with anyone. Dash feels a tingle of suspicion rise.

Paul Townsend asks the five men, "How are you getting up the trail in your condition?"

The same young man answers.

"Heard tell of a footpath that takes out from here and avoids the climb of the main trail. Supposed to cut three days off the trip and get us to the next trading post. By your kindness and God's mercy, we should make it."

With that, the young man flashes a flurry of signals and the strangers spin on their heels, leaving without a word. They march a short way up the trail before disappearing over the edge and into the woods.

Walking back to their wagon, Dash sighs with relief while Horatio whispers his doubts.

"Somethin' not right about them men. Not lookin' at us, no talkin'. Either they's mute folks or they've got somethin' up their sleeve. My feelin' says it ain't somethin' good. Make sure you got your rifle ready, in case we need some black powder persuasion."

Dash agrees their demeanor was all wrong. Too weak to raise their heads but then strong enough to rush down the trail. He takes Horatio's suggestion, checks his rifle, and slips his arm through its strap, settling the weapon onto his back.

Meeting up with the other men, Dash notices a loaded musket has been left for the women as a precautionary measure. He hears Amalee call out.

When he turns, she and Deedee are waving and his heart lightens at the sound of her small voice, "Bye, Da!"

His quick wave promotes a further flurry of calls and waves, and he smiles at his tender feelings for this little one who considers him her father.

After only a short distance, and as Horatio had predicted, the road becomes too difficult for the animals to drag the wagon. The team is unhitched and driven ahead. The wagon is lifted and pushed up and over impeding boulders by the brute strength and the hands of men. The twisted trail forces the men to awkwardly manipulate the wagon, gaining only inches at a time. Once able to re-hitch, they face the last obstacle: a quarter-mile-long snow shoot chiseled out by preceding emigrants through a twelve-foot-tall avalanche flow.

After two excruciating hours, the first wagon reaches Red Lake. They drive the wagon to a safe spot and unload the mules' packs into its bed. While clearly fatigued, the men feel the need to get back to the women, especially after the morning's events. Leaving two guards, they rush back down the mountain trail.

Now familiar with the trail's challenges and aided by previously placed ropes and levers, the company leader's wagon progresses much faster. Triumphant cheers herald their arrival at the lake. As they catch their breath, the company leader breaks out a whisky flask.

"Just a little token of my appreciation and for added strength for the next trip."

After a quick swig, the men decide to spend the night divided, Horatio and Dash agreeing to camp below with the Townsends. They also decide the company's only two-wheel cart will be their day's last effort. Leaving the company leader's wife to prepare the evening meal, the men brace their feet in the trail's scree, their talk buzzing with the next day's strategy until a musket's boom echoes off the mountain valley's walls.

As the sound still reverberates, Dash follows the men creeping toward an overlook.

Even from three hundred yards away, they recognize the shoeless vagrants, the talkative one holding the shotgun on Paul and Eliza while the other ragged men raid their wagon.

Horatio whispers, "Dash, glad you got your rifle. This ain't good."

Dash retrieves his rifle and loads it. Rather than observe the activity, he calculates the distance and wind for how much gunpowder to use in his shot.

He asks, "What's happening?"

"They're still there. The talker uses hand signals to get the others to do his bidding. They're deaf, sure of it. None are makin' a sound. They're stuffin' sacks full of food. Nobody's hurt but the talker's been holdin' the gun on Paul and Eliza the whole time. No sign of the young'uns."

When Dash peeks over the boulder, his heart almost stops. Amalee and Deedee, in their bright white bonnets and calico dresses, are meandering toward the wagon camp, oblivious of what's happening.

Horatio sees the girls at the same time and sucks in a ragged gasp. The little girls come around the wagon, Deedee holding something in one hand, while towing Amalee along with the other. One of the ransackers jumps out and snatches Amalee away from Deedee's grasp. He loops his arm around the toddler's waist and totes her like a surprise bonus, the child's wails of supreme disapproval clanging off the canyon walls. Dash's soul rattles.

The gun-toting leader signals and Amalee is passed to him. Then Eliza calls out, but Dash can't understand her statement. He watches as Eliza reaches for the flailing child, substituting herself once Amalee is safe in Paul's arms. Dash realizes she has traded herself for his child!

Protective anger pulses through Dash's system. The newly burdened thieves hurry down the same trail they had taken in the morning, the leader falling into the rear position while prodding Eliza ahead of him with the musket.

"Can't let them get away," Horatio whispers.

Hoping for a better view, Dash skitters to the overlook's outer edge. From this vantage point, he sees their narrow footpath. It is well-worn and zigzags away from the wagons, down through the undergrowth, before disappearing into the darkness of pine trees.

The approaching evening's dusk leaves him little time. Resting his rifle's long barrel on a granite boulder, he lines up the rifle's sight and calculates the angle and the bullet's momentum. The key to this shot is to hit the marauder while missing Eliza. He waits for the first man to disappear into the pine trees, followed by the second, third, and fourth. When Eliza comes into view, he knows the fifth man is prodding her from behind. Confident of his range, he slows his breathing, expels the air in his lungs, and lightly strokes the trigger.

The explosion's thunder crackles through his nerve endings. Black smoke swirls in a gentle updraft of mountain air and obscures his vision. When it clears, Dash stands and stares at the scene unfolding below him. His bullet had found its mark. The marauder had fallen forward when the bullet's momentum hit him, his now-dead weight toppling onto the unsuspecting Eliza.

Dash watches as Paul arrives at her side and flings the dead man's arm and torso to the side. Eliza, covered in another man's blood, makes no effort to stand. She sits up and holds her head. Paul lifts her over his shoulder and hauls her back up the footpath, not stopping until he reaches their wagon.

Dash follows Horatio and the others as they rush down the slippery trail. When they arrive, it is clear Eliza is alright and being cared for by the other woman in the company.

Suddenly seized by panic, Dash grabs one of the men's shoulders and asks, "Where are the children?"

The man points toward the Townsend's wagon. Two pairs of little eyes emerge from under a deep pile of blankets, their blinks slow and disbelieving. Satisfied, Dash turns back to the crowd. His eyes meet Paul's steady gaze.

Paul says, "She's going to be alright. The bullet grazed her head but shredded her right ear."

Paul goes on to tell their story.

"They snuck up on us. The talking one had the gun before I could grab it and started pointing and waving his hand to the rest of them. They went right to the wagons to grab food. I tried reasoning with him, but when he shot the gun into the air, I figured I'd shut my piehole."

"What did they want with the baby?" Horatio asks.

"No idea. Eliza's mothering come out and she traded herself, told him she could cook and care for them; the baby would just be a burden."

"She's better off than if they'd have got her to theyselves, Paul. If they'd got her too far down that trail, we'd a been hard pressed to get her back before they'd have messed with her."

No one replies to Horatio's statement. Instead, they turn to Dash, whose pulse quickens in the face of their judgment. Paul speaks first.

"Thank you, Dash. Those men wronged us all. This is what happens when a fella chooses to break the law—take a chance on someone being a mighty fine shot from a distance. Hope you don't mind me asking, where'd you learn to shoot like that?"

"Bridger," Horatio cuts in. "Yessir, last winter when Dash was stuck at Fort Bridger, Jim Bridger himself taught him how to make the long shot. Said directly to me he ain't never seen no greenhorn take to shootin' like Dash. Got a natural gift for it."

"You hadn't shot a rifle until last winter?" Paul asks, astonished.

"I didn't have any need to know before then," Dash says. "Cities don't have the need for folks to take the long shot. But it seems like me and this rife are designed for each other. Paul, I'm awfully sorry for Eliza's ear."

Before Paul can reply, Eliza's voice cuts into the men's conversation.

"Not another word, Dash. I knew what I was doing. I was afraid, but your bullet saved my life, I'm sure of it. My ear will heal. I'll come up with a new hairstyle."

From behind him, Dash hears one of the company's men ask an important question.

"Is anyone else here nervous about the others coming back for their missing comrade? Without him, they don't stand a chance of surviving, which could make them even less concerned about doing something stupid. I didn't see any of them carrying weapons, did any of you?"

Nervous glances passed between the group until Horatio says, "Bein' deaf and mute is surely a death sentence in this country. By now, they must know somethin' happened to their leader. They's either scared witless, resigned to dyin', or thinkin' on how they might return for more thievin'. Best sleep light tonight. No tellin' what they'll do but we ain't givin' them a chance to cause more mischief."

Dash adds, "I didn't see any other rifles but it's hard to believe that they are not carrying knives and other easy to hide weapons. I'd feel better if we set up a guard for the night, maybe two-hour shifts so some can get a block of sleep."

Agreement to Dash's suggestion comes in the form of a series of low grunts before the men leave to retrieve the corpse. As each man passes by Dash, they offer their hand to him with solemn gratitude. When they return with the body, everyone inspects the gruesome sight. The lead ball's impact had passed through the neck, severing his jugular vein and answering their question about where all the blood covering Eliza had come from.

The sight of the dead man, a life he had personally taken, makes Dash's stomach turn. He rushes away to puke in the nearby bushes.

After a time, Horatio appears at his side, whispering, "Hey, now. You did the right thing. Folks can't just pull a gun on other folks, steal their food, take a hostage, and expect to get away with it. No sir, you done the right thing for our company."

"I suppose you're right, but I could have so easily hit Eliza."

"Eliza knew there was a chance she could die anyway, if not by your efforts to rescue her, by what them men might have done to her."

When it's time to bed down for the night, Dash tries to put Amalee in the Townsend's wagon bed, but she clutches fistfuls of his shirt and whines, "Daaa."

"Amalee, I'm here along with Paul and Horatio. After your sleep, we're going up the mountain to a beautiful lake. But you need to snuggle down with Deedee."

Easily distracted, the two little girls settle into their nest of quilts before Dash leaves the wagon and checks his rifle one more time. He notes the clear night sky is bright with stars contrasting with the camp's thick tension. Despite their shared fatigue, guards are posted, but no adult lays their head down without a gun at their side.

As the sun crests the mountaintops, they bury the body under three feet of stone, the pile blending into the rough, rock-strewn mountainside. They repeat their wagon-moving process from the day before with the last two wagons and the cart, exhaustion slowing their progress. Once all are at Red Lake, they make a lean camp, since much of their food staples had been stolen. Following a meager meal, the company give themselves up to overwhelming fatigue.

Their final push over the summit's unforgiving rocks and thin air takes all they have, mentally and physically. Willing themselves over the last steep incline in the day's last light, they drive downhill to make camp in the pine and fir forest next to a snow-fed stream. Dash inhales the forest's sweet perfume, so grateful to be rid of the desert's stink.

He and Horatio draw first watch, drinking coffee to stay alert. The stars make their appearance in the darkening western sky when Horatio starts the conversation.

"I knowed a man back home who could pick off a deer at two hundred yards. I never could get the knack for distance. Bridger give up any secrets?"

"Not necessarily secrets, but to take a deep breath, exhale completely, and squeeze the trigger when your body is at its stillest. The squeeze has to be as gentle as a caress on a woman's breast."

Horatio's head jerks up, his eyes wide.

"Well, there's my problem! I ain't never done that part!"

Dash, sensing a moment for levity, says, "You mean breathe out so far you are completely still?"

"Naw, Dash, the other part. You know cuz you're Amalee's daddy and knowed what her momma felt like, but not me, nope, ain't had the experience. Yet. Been lookin' at them girls in the dance halls, but I never had enough money for funnin'."

Horatio's bold admission nudges Dash toward his own truth.

After a brief contemplation, he says, "Horatio, I need to admit to something. I've let everyone believe what they wanted to believe but you need to know. I'm not Amalee's father. Her parents were . . . her father, Ace, was barely a friend, more of an acquaintance I had hoped would become a friend, but cholera took him on the Mississippi. Amalee's mother, Nora, and I . . . well, I'm not sure how to say it. Ace had asked me to get Nora and the baby to safety if anything happened to him. I was honoring his request just fine until the wagon mutiny before Fort Bridger. You know the rest."

Horatio lets the words sink in before speaking into the complete darkness, "Nobody's goin' to learn different from me, Dash. You're her 'Da' and that's how it's going to stay. But I got to tell you one thing: I admire your courage and keepin' your word to her parents. No one can tell you're not her daddy."

Horatio would never know how cherished his words were to Dash. For a brief, flashing moment, he contemplated telling Horatio about Lillia and the wager, but decided to revel in the glow of Horatio's words for a few days before taking the risk of tarnishing them so soon.

Chapter 19

SEPTEMBER, 1850

WESTERN SIERRA MOUNTAINS, CALIFORNIA

California feels like a new world. As they descend, they see distant rolling hills cloaked in golden yellow, divided by dark veins of tree-lined gullies. The air smells of warm, fertile ground in contrast to the sterile sand and rocks of the desert they had just crossed. Even the light is different. It gives everything Dash sees a golden aura and he now understands the spell this place casts over people.

The Indiana company's camp discussions are filled with anticipation from those who are joining family members, while others still kindle hope of finding gold. For most, eagerness for the future builds with each passing mile. In contrast, Dash feels his inner coil winding tighter and tighter. Each mile brings him closer to knowing if the race wager has been claimed or not.

Hangtown is the decision point for those turning north to Centerville and Grass Valley and those continuing west to Sacramento and San Francisco. The company makes camp on the city's outskirts, their final supper together blessed with abundant greens and fresh vegetables purchased from a sparse collection of farmers. The campfire chatter is jovial, yet the somber reality of their imminent separation sets in.

After supper, Dash asks Horatio to take a walk while Amalee and Deedee have one more night together in the Townsend's wagon. As the pair set off down the dusty road, Dash struggles to find his words.

"Horatio, you know I was supposed to be in California about a year ago, right?"

"You told me."

"Well, there are a couple of unknowns waiting for me in San Francisco, especially since I'm so late."

Dash explains the wagered race between his group of friends from Boston going overland and the group from Yale going around Cape Horn.

"I'm the only one left from the Boston team. For all I know, the Yalies have arrived, answered the courier's newspaper advertisement, and are long gone into the hills. But I can't stop hunting until I know for sure. It's too much money and I've paid too much of a price."

Horatio's expression tells him his partner agrees.

"It's a true-life treasure hunt, ain't it? I can't believe you got that kinda money waitin' for you! But you could be outta luck. So, what's your second unknown?"

"Back in Boston, I was engaged to be married. A week before the wedding, I learned my father and brothers were secret bounty hunters and white slave traders. I knew nothing of it until my father sent me to carry out an exchange of young Irish immigrant children to a loathsome pervert who wanted to teach them 'the pleasure arts.'

"I was sent to a tenement house to pay the children's desperate mother for them and then was supposed to deliver them to the man. But when I arrived, the mother had just died. I couldn't do it. I intended to take the children to a relative in Baltimore. But to do that, I had to steal the money my father had given me to buy them.

"The reason I joined my friends and the Bostonian team on their westbound race was to escape my father's wrath and get the children to safety. It seemed like the perfect opportunity.

"But to this day, I can't forgive myself for what I did to my fiancée. She was a fine woman, the equal of which I likely will never find. I sent her a coded note with my explanation and apology. It was all I could think to do at the time. I asked her to meet me in San Francisco. I don't know if she ever made the trip or not. I don't know how she possibly could have—"

Horatio is painfully quiet until he looks Dash directly in the eye.

"Your tellin' me you expected a woman—a city woman even more—to up and leave her family with only a g'dam coded note a week before you was gettin' hitched? Ain't no woman in my world who'd a done somethin' so foolish."

Dash watches as Horatio closes his eyes and shakes his head.

"And tell me it ain't so, Dash. I sat there and listened to that ole boy from Boston tellin' that story. I listened and pitied the family, pitied the broken-hearted woman, and you're him? You're the g'dam low-down dog who made the woman leave her family disgraced because her man ran out on her?"

"I am, I did, but I wasn't going to admit it in front of those folks. Listen Horatio, my father and brothers prey on women and children, and I had to get those kids to safety. When we got to Baltimore, their aunt had left to go west just days before. I left them in a church orphanage, which was the best option given their circumstances. I know it wasn't right or fair to leave Lillia. She might have even come with me if I would have had time to ask, but I had to run. If my father or brothers had caught me, I believe they would have killed me. You have to know I've changed. I don't resemble, in any way, the man I was eighteen months ago."

Horatio shifts his weight back and forth in the road dust. Without a word, he turns on his boot heel and heads to the encampment. After a few steps, he stops and reverses. He marches up to Dash and glares into his face.

"So, you're tellin' me your woman could be in g'dam San Francisco? That she's cut from tough enough cloth to make this trip," he spits as he flails his arms, "all by herself? No g'dam man to protect, support, or guide her? All . . . by . . . herself?"

Dash replies earnestly, "Honestly, I've been thinking about that. The story we heard from the Bostonian was that she left with her uncle. Maybe she convinced him to sail to San Francisco with her."

"That'd take a smooth talker, smooth like an ivory-handled pool cue. I sure don't know a woman who can convince someone like that. And you've been ridin' by my side for how long? Since April? And you just now think this is somthin' you oughta share with me? Don't know what is more interestin' to me right now, Dash, the treasure or the woman. Both have got me intrigued. And you're the only one who knows about this in the whole world. You's g'dam somethin'." His voice trails off before he walks away.

After a few minutes, Dash also heads back to the encampment. As painful as his confession had been, he is relieved to no longer have sole ownership of his secrets. When he quietly beds down under the wagon, Horatio is there but has turned his back on his partner.

Dash doesn't sleep that night. He frets over Horatio's reaction and the immediate consequences for both him and Amalee. But even more, he worries about finding out the answers to what has been driving him westward. He is so close now.

That night, for the first time since Fort Kearney, he dreams of Lillia. Maybe Horatio's reference to being as smooth as an ivory-handled pool cue spurs his memory. He dreams about her way with words, her keen mind for sorting out details, and then her ability for assembling them in ways that fit her needs. He feels certain she made the trip to San Francisco, but he wonders if it's possible she has changed as much as he has.

When the sun crests the Sierra peaks at dawn, Dash turns over to check for Horatio's prone form only to find him gone. Dash scrambles out from under the wagon and scans the encampment. He sees Horatio brushing his mules. Absorbed, Horatio only looks up when Dash approaches.

"I have to apologize to you, Horatio. I'm sorry for keeping things from you. I've been living with them so long, they've just become part of me. Looking back on it, I'm grateful I didn't ask Lillia to join me. This way, at least she's alive."

"Well, now," Horatio says, an agreeing shrug passing from one shoulder to the next, "I reckon you been torn up for a while now. For my part, I'm sorry for comin' apart at you when you was tryin' to get the story out. I believed you was somethin' different and what you said last night messed with that. I ain't done a whole lot a good in my life, though, so I can't be the judge of you. But we've made good partners."

Dash winces at Horatio's use of past tense, each word feeling like a bee sting. He hangs his head in defeat, certain Horatio has made up his mind.

"I suppose we ought to figure out how this is going to work, your wagon and mules. Maybe I could buy one from you and . . ."

"What are you talkin' about?" Horatio hollers. "You goin' somewhere?"

"Well, I just figured you were done with me. Trust is important."

Horatio turns back to the mule and brushes the animal's loose hair clouding the morning light's sparkle.

"You figured wrong, Dash. You tol' me you did them things. What you did to your girl was wrong, sure enough, but you ain't been nothin' but decent to me. You're a good friend and an honorable man to little Amalee. I believe this trip has impacted you some, so you got new ideas to work on."

"I appreciate that," Dash says.

"And if you think I'm goin' to let you look for that treasure without me, you're wrong; wrong as a horsefly on a weddin' cake, wrong!"

Both men laugh knowingly at this. Then Dash turns serious again.

"But what if my search is fruitless?" he asks. "What if Lillia and the wager never even made it to California? There's a gamble in this, Horatio, and while it's something I've taken on myself, it's a lot to ask of someone else. Unless, of course, you knew you'd have a cut of the wager."

Horatio concentrates on his brushing, but raises his eyebrows at the mule's shoulder, waiting for Dash to continue.

"So, what would you consider a fair cut for helping me find the wager money?"

"After all you went through, splittin' it would be too much. But I'd consider sixty/forty a decent enough share."

Dash instantly sticks out his hand in agreement.

Deedee and Dash walk side by side from the Townsend's wagon to Horatio's. Dash's arms are full of the accumulated blankets and clothes, while Deedee's arms are strained to bursting with a doll collection, which she has determined are all Amalee's favorites. Her face has tear streaks, and she sniffs loudly. Dash searches for comforting words.

"Deedee, you've been a mighty good friend to Amalee. Your folks have done so much for us. I'm beholden to them and you. I expect that, God willing, we'll cross paths again."

Eliza arrives with Amalee on her hip along with a napkin full of biscuits.

As she sits Amalee next to Deedee, she asks her daughter, "What's going on here?"

"Mr. Dash is sayin' we're goin' to see them again because God is willing it, and you and Pa have done so much for Amalee that he's holding on to you."

Deedee's muddled interpretation of his words, followed by her self-confident grin, makes everyone smile, even though Eliza's expression holds a hint of confusion.

She tousles her daughter's hair playfully and says, "Dash, Amalee is a special little girl. Paul and I hope some of her has rubbed off on this little one. Even though she's young, we're amazed at how fast she learns. And a happier child I can't imagine ever meeting again."

"I reckon it won't be long before Deedee has a little brother or sister who's just as smart and will be a wonderful playmate," he tells her and gives her a hug.

The Indiana company mounts up but today is different. Hands are shaken, waves made, and when the captain gives the signal, the wagons fall into line. Dash and Amalee sit on Grunt, next to Horatio's wagon, and wait their turn. He knows the company will pass through Hangtown before he and Horatio turn westward, while the rest will continue northbound toward Grass Valley. Reins in hand, Horatio turns to Amalee.

"Ready for San Francisco, little lady?"

She smiles and waves at the mules.

"Go, go, mooles!"

Final waves come as Horatio and Dash peel off the line. Amalee enthusiastically waves to Deedee and Eliza as they turn away. Dash sees the glee in her face and wonders if she will ever see these people again. He is suddenly grateful to say goodbye without the tragedy of death accompanying the event. He has seen so many comings and goings since he left Boston that he has a new appreciation for enjoying and learning from folks and nurturing a friendship in their moment together. One never knows if the encounter will be the last time.

With no one to slow their pace and a decent road to travel on, Horatio and Dash make excellent progress through the rolling hills and farms of the open countryside. Dash asks where all the miners are, and Horatio points at the mountains toward the north and south, explaining the differences in the two mining districts.

"Most of the easy findin' is over. If gold's on a fella's mind, he's got to get to the mountains. His food comes from here. Folks are makin' their money feedin' and supplyin' them that's breakin' their backs in the mountain's rocks and rivers. That's why I think there's more g'dam money to be made in haulin' and supplyin'."

They try to formulate a plan to find the wager's courier and Dash explains about the newspaper advertisement. When Shingle Springs comes into view, he and Amalee pull aside at a mercantile, while Horatio and the wagon continue down the road.

After securing Grunt to a hitching post, Dash balances Amalee on his hip, walks through the open door, and tells the shopkeeper, "I'd like to buy a newspaper, sir."

"Comes out tomorrow. It's a weekly, and I ain't got one of last week's left. You just rollin' into town?"

"Yessir. On our way to San Francisco."

"Goin' the wrong way if gold's what's on your mind, son."

"We've got other things to look into and San Francisco's the place to start."

"You'll have to take a steamer from Sacramento. No good roads all the way to the city, just river travel."

Dash thanks the man and leaves, bouncing Amalee into the saddle before mounting up, his mind cogitating on how they will take a steamer to San Francisco. After catching up to Horatio, he explains this news and is surprised when his partner doesn't even pause in his response.

"S'pose we best break into our bank."

That night, on the banks of the American River, Horatio loosens the nail on the bank's bottom plank, while Dash holds their wooden water bucket beneath it. Amalee squawks in surprise as the coins clatter loudly. They pour the money out onto a blanket and begin to count, Amalee gleefully running her pudgy little fingers through the piles of gold and silver coins.

"Nine hundred and eighty dollars all told," Horatio announces. "That's the total amount of the three crossings plus the extra money we got for the river crossing in July."

"We did well, didn't we?" Dash smiles as he shakes his partner's hand.

The next morning, they stop at a place called "Five Mile Station." Horatio tends to the mules, while Dash takes Amalee inside for a second attempt at a newspaper. Minutes later, he returns with the newspaper under one arm and Amalee squawking like a cornered chicken. Horatio's glance asks the question, and Dash hollers his answer over her screeches.

"She saw the candy. I got a newspaper. Let's go."

Dash barely has Amalee hoisted up to Horatio when the shopkeeper arrives with a stick of candy in his hand, offering it to Amalee with a wide smile on his face. Dash thanks him and takes the candy.

"If we ever come to the point of starving, Amalee is our food ticket. Folks will do anything for her. You should've seen what I turned away before this."

"She could come in mighty handy, alright."

Swatting the mules into action, Horatio grins at Amalee who triumphantly shows off her stick candy, pink drool oozing from her mouth. Once settled, Dash opens *The Daily Union* and scans the advertisements. The news is filled with announcements of ship arrivals, reports of new claims, crimes, and city gossip.

With the sunset scorching their faces, they come upon a boardinghouse across the street from a stable and yard. Dash and Amalee get off the wagon's seat to arrange for rooms. With Amalee, his saddlebag, and his rifle, Dash's arms are too full to open the boardinghouse door. As a large woman rounds the porch corner, she sees his struggle.

"Oh my. What have we here?"

Dash lowers Amalee to the floor where she stands, gripping his pant leg.

"I'm hoping you have a couple of rooms for board. I've got a friend stabling our mules and the wagon. One room for him, one for my girl and me."

The woman doesn't answer. Dash follows the woman's gaze that's focused on Amalee. Suddenly, the woman scoops Amalee into her arms and swabs the candy's sticky residue from Amalee's chin with a dishcloth. When the woman whisks Amalee down the hallway, Dash follows until he feels a gentle hand on his arm.

Dash turns and looks into the kind eyes of a gentle soul who says, "Sir, she's harmless. We lost our little one a while back. Yours is the first young one my Bess has seen since. We're hoping another is on its way soon, but until then, well, she's just lovin' on your baby girl. Nothing to fear in her. Bob Bunlin's the name."

"I'm sorry for your loss. We've just come in from the east. Looking for rooms while we arrange for a steamer headed to San Francisco. We've been told we'll find one in Sacramento."

Bob shakes his head.

"Been a tough year for Sacramento. There ain't much left, not after the terrible floods in January past. Most of the city was underwater for quite a while. About the time they got it built back up, a round of fires came upon them and swept through the city along the river. Lost the entire embarcadero. There's been riots too. Lucky for you, about all they have are steamers. Last time I was in town, there were three docked, greenhorns scurrying off them like rats with their tails on fire."

Dash shuffles his feet and asks again, "Any chance of those rooms?"

His question snaps Bob back to reality, and he scans the ledger book.

"Yes, sir, we have two rooms. We could figure out a little bed for your girl."

Dash's ears perk to singing coming from the kitchen. Bob hears it, too, and whispers, "Haven't heard that in a while."

Horatio stomps up the porch stairs and pulls the door open. Dash detects something is wrong, just as Horatio announces his problem to anyone who will listen.

"Things have changed since I been gone, yes sir. Ain't no allowances for folks no more."

"What are you talking about?" Dash asks.

"I'm gettin' charged for everything from hay to poop here. They won't take the wagon unless I pay to park it. Says if it's taking up space, then it's space they can be makin' money on. But ain't no one else usin' the place; just my mules and a wagon. Rest of the place is empty. Acted like I was a second-class citizen when I dusted up at their price too."

Bob sighs. "Those fellas, the Woutons, are hard dealers. I think you ought to bring your wagon and mules to our barn, and we'll figure out a price to board the mules. Don't worry about the wagon. There's plenty of room for it in our yard."

Horatio undergoes an instant transformation.

"Mighty grateful. I only paid for the one night. Figured there'd be somethin' better than that cheatin' situation. First thing in the morning, we'll go down and fetch them back."

Their meal is the finest since Narcissa's at Fort Bridger. Amalee entertains the other boarders, while Dash and Horatio tell stories of their journey from Salt Lake City. Dash asks more questions about steamers and ships from the east and one boarder offers his opinion.

"Likely that if you was meetin' a ship from Boston or New York, they'd have disembarked in 'Frisco before boardin' a smaller steamer to Sacramento. Folks is always findin' one another. Two people will pass, stop, back up, and stare before sayin', 'Rufus, that you?' Next thing you know, there's smiles and handshakes, drinks, and laughin' even though real life ain't much to laugh about. They've found someone familiar and that's all that counts."

Dash's heart surges, and he wonders if it will be the same when he encounters Lillia.

Bess is delighted to watch over Amalee while Dash and Horatio set off to explore Sacramento. The flood and fire devastation is obvious, but the citizens have shown a determined spirit to rebuild. Hoping to strike up a conversation with a local, they stop for a meal in the city.

When nothing comes of their plan, Dash feels a wave of doubt wash over him.

Horatio says, "Don't fret now, Dash. There's goin' to be somethin'. How about we pay a visit to the local newspaper office? They should be familiar with names and circumstances better than most."

Above the front window of the newspaper's office, "The Daily Union" is painted in neat, black letters. When they walk in, the overwhelming smell of ink and paper fills the air.

Through the clank of machinery, a hearty voice calls out from the back, "Hello, boys. I'll be right there!"

After a few minutes, a tall man leaning on a cane appears in the doorway.

"Name's William Chamberlain, editor and owner of this paper. What can I do for you?"

"Have you seen any San Francisco newspapers advertising for a group from Boston?"

Chamberlain's facial expression changes to a frown.

"Not lately, but I picked up a newspaper around the first of the year with a curious advertisement to that effect. The wording alluded to them knowing who they were. It stirred my curiosity, but since I knew nothing of it, I disregarded the whole thing—until now. Are you one of them?"

Without acknowledging his question, Dash blurts, "That'd be January?"

"Yes, but there've been two fires since my visit. I have a recent copy of the *Bee* here somewhere. Ah, yes, here it is," Chamberlain mumbles as he searches through a stack of papers on a back table. "This is dated July 16."

Dash scans the paper. When he finds no mention after a few minutes, he sighs in frustration. Chamberlain pats him on the shoulder.

"Don't lose hope. Perhaps funds were limited."

"Or" Dash says, "someone has already arrived and answered the ad."

"If you don't mind me asking, what is this all about?" Chamberlain asks.

Dash sighs again before explaining, "There was a winner-take-all wagered contest to see who could get to California first. I took a crooked route and may have lost out on the payoff."

"Mr. Chamberlain, how far is San Francisco?" Horatio asks.

"By steamer, it'll take a day. Most leave early to avoid navigating at night. You fellas on foot or horseback?"

"A freightin' wagon."

"The city has a powerful need for wagons. I can promise you'll be busier than a cat chasin' rats if you make the trip."

"Somethin' to consider, ain't it?"

Dash nods to Horatio, his mind racing to analyze their options. Shaking hands with Chamberlain, they leave for the riverfront, where Dash hopes they'll find real answers to their questions.

They learn they have three days to wait for the next steamer. While the charge will be hefty, they can afford to take the mules with them. The next question is what to do with Amalee. Dash doesn't hesitate.

"She goes with us."

"I don't know, Dash. It ain't the Humboldt desert, but we's goin' into another kinda wilderness. This one's got all manner of scallywags. Don't like havin' baby girl mixed up there."

On their way back to the boardinghouse, Dash almost makes up his mind to leave her when he hears Bess's voice sing out, "There he is! There's your daddy! I told you he'd be back soon."

She holds Amalee, whose full cheeks have big, beaded tears sticking to them. Dash leans in close and scoops Amalee out of Bess's arms.

"What are all these tears about?"

"Oh, little miss thought she might try to find you, so she helped herself to the front doorknob. Didn't like it when I told her she couldn't leave the house."

Bess pokes her finger into Amalee's fat tummy and continues.

"You're just in time. Supper's ready. You boys wash up and I'll get Amalee settled into her chair."

No, thinks Dash, *I'm not leaving her behind. That is one goodbye I am choosing not to make.*

Three days later, Dash, Amalee, and Horatio board a San Francisco-bound steamer with Grunt, their four mules, and the freighter wagon. The trip on the river, while only a day long, holds them in rapt wonder as the steamer winds its way through the grass-covered hills that seem to roll right to the river's edge.

A warm, late-September breeze fondles the dry, golden grasses with an invisible hand, the movement casting a spell over Dash. He remembers Hugh's explanation of the zephyr breeze and how many times it has accompanied him on his journey. Now, so close to his destination, his eyes brim with the absolute improbability of him being the one to arrive.

It had been eighteen months since he left Boston and Lillia behind. Hugh's fatal accident, along with the loss of all his Boston companions. A year has passed since Nora had been lost over the cliff and left him with little Amalee. In that time, he had recovered his sight, learned to shoot a long-barreled rifle, and successfully traveled three times across the Great Basin. He had developed a deep friendship with Horatio and an enduring love for a baby girl, not of his fathering.

Improbable barely describes it.

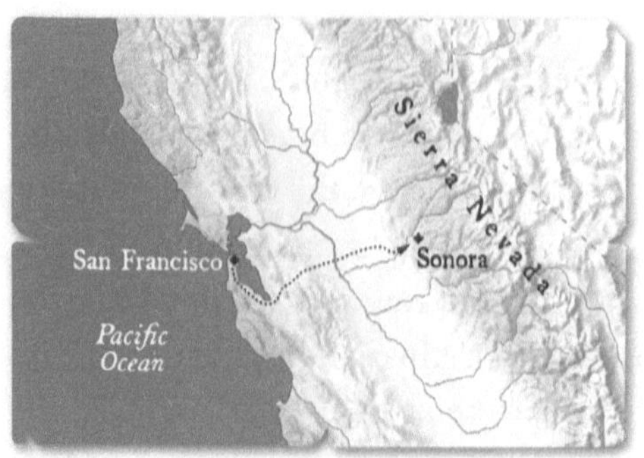

Chapter 20

SEPTEMBER, 1850

SAN FRANCISCO, CALIFORNIA

Disembarking in San Francisco is a bigger challenge than either Horatio or Dash could have expected. Once the mules were harnessed to the wagon, Grunt tied alongside, and the trio in place on the wagon's high seat, Dash lets out an exhausted sigh.

Horatio notices and agreeably says, "I hear you, partner. Things in this city are even more chaotic than I remember. Never did come in from the river, though. Maybe it's always been like this. We need to find a place to hunker down and get our bearings."

They travel slowly away from the Embarcadero inland, asking for boardinghouse and stable referrals as they go. Finally, they come upon a large boardinghouse across the street from a stable and know they have found the spot. Pulling their wagon into the stable, they are swarmed by potential customers interested in hiring.

Leaving Horatio to sort things out, Dash slings Amalee onto his shoulders and crosses to the boardinghouse. Their late afternoon arrival has Amalee cranky, and while she had been entertained by the steamer trip, she is not shy in communicating her impatience for eating.

Successfully arranging for two boardinghouse rooms, Dash doesn't wait for Horatio to get something for Amalee to eat. By the time Horatio joins them in the dining room, Amalee has finished her meal and is rubbing her tired eyes.

Horatio barely sits down before saying, "Chamberlain was right! I got ten names of folks who need my wagon to move goods. There's more hauling work here than we can ever dream of gettin' done in daylight! We need to talk about how we want to go about this, Dash."

Sliding a room key toward Horatio, Dash says, "How about you eat your supper while I settle Amalee down for the night? We can meet in your room to discuss what we'll do tomorrow. I'll knock once I know she's asleep."

After such a big day, Amalee snuggles into the soft sheets of the room's bed and Dash has to wait barely ten minutes before her soft snores fill the room. Careful to make no sounds, he leaves her and taps lightly on Horatio's door. Once inside, the two men form a plan, which includes buying a current newspaper and Dash's visit to the San Francisco Port Authority to check ship manifests for the courier's arrival, and for Lillia.

According to their plan, Horatio takes on the first of three jobs he contracted for the next morning and Dash gathers up Amalee and heads for the Port Authority building. Passing through the streets, he is surprised by how they are potholed and unkempt, not a cobblestone to be found. Humans and livestock commingle their refuse in the same streets. Structures of canvas and wood—the most economical and abundant—are under construction everywhere despite the charred evidence of a recent fire.

Dash develops a powerful yearning for the wild and open world of Fort Bridger just as they arrive in the open park off the waterfront where the Port Authority building sits. The park and its green grass expanse are a welcome retreat from the chaos of the streets.

Letting Amalee off his shoulders to stretch her legs, Dash is struck by the jumble of cultures mingling in the streets. Mostly men, it seems the world's ethnicities have descended upon this place with the same goal—instant riches. He remembers one of Horatio's lectures:

"Them Mexicans and Chileans been minin' their own g'dam country for hundreds of years. White folk learned minin' from them and once it got figured out, whites kicked them off their claims. And them Indians, they got treated bad by everyone."

Shouldering his way through the crowd, Dash arrives at the Port Authority building. Given the low doorway, he lowers Amalee from her perch and enters, almost gagging at the sweltering stench of confined humanity inside. Working the room until he finds an official, he inquires about passenger lists from the arriving ships. The man beckons Dash from the common area to a more private room, closes the door, and dramatically presses himself against it.

"I prefer days with less chaos. Now then, what ship list are you looking for?"

"I'm looking for a ship and a passenger, but not on the same ship."

The official's stern stare is startling.

"We've seen four hundred ships and thirty thousand people in the last year through this city, sir. Can you tell me the ship's origin, at least? Perhaps its expected date of arrival?"

"The ship was the *Night Call* out of New York City, left in April 1849. The passenger likely left from Boston around the same time."

"Well, that's a start. If the ships weren't lost as they crossed the Horn, and they started in April, the earliest they would have arrived is November. So, let's begin there."

Removing a volume from a shelf and placing it on the table in front of Dash, he explains how to decipher the ledger. He finishes with, "If you don't find it there, December's log is here," pointing to the volumes stacked neatly on the shelf. "Now, I'll leave you to it and join the throngs of idiots, I mean, emigrants."

After the official firmly pulls the door behind him, Dash settles into a chair, positioning Amalee on his knee. As he bounces her up and down, he begins with the November ledger. Twenty ships arrived from New York City, but only eight from Boston. Neither the *Night Call* nor a passenger named Soilleux are listed anywhere.

He retrieves the October ledger. When no trace of either name is found, the venom of discouragement pulses through his veins. The *Night Call* may have been delayed. But Lillia? Had she left from a different port, perhaps New York City, or north of Boston?

He reviews the list and finds several entries for Beverly and Newburyport. He scans the ship's names registered to Newburyport: "*Glorious*," "*Bold Wonder*," "*Gold Star*," and "*Ornery Agnes*."

He stops, his finger jerking at the last name's oddity. All the other ships had regal names, but the *Ornery Agnes*?

Dash chuckles when thinking of the woman who must have inspired such a name, if she really existed. Out of curiosity or, perhaps, the need for distraction, he reads the entire entry:

Captain: Rupert Eagleton. Crew: 12. Passengers: 13. Primary cargo: Ice.

His finger travels across the page further and sees that the ship also had canvas and citrus from Chile for a merchant in San Francisco. Before he gets to the passenger list, he hears the door swing open and realizes Amalee is no longer on his knee. Racing out the door, he finds her, scoops her up, and returns to the ledger room where he decides to call it quits for the day.

On their way back to the boardinghouse, they pass an establishment with a large window facing the street. To his shock, Dash sees Horatio facing him, his hands holding a fan of cards. The other men around the table are intensely focused on their own cards.

Taking Amalee off his shoulders and settling her on his hip like a practiced parent, he enters through swinging doors, clearly a saloon replete with red velvet and dancing girls. He approaches Horatio.

Leaning down, Dash hisses, "What are you doing?"

"Just havin' a little fun. But see that fella opposite me?"

Dash cautiously raises his gaze to a grizzled face, the man's hat pulled low but not low enough to hide a wide jawline fringed with reddish-brown whiskers and tanned skin stretched tight across his facial bones.

"Yeah, so?"

"He's the mangy scoundrel who forced me off my legal claim. Rafael Eagleton. Thinks he's goin' to take me at cards just like he took my claim. I aim to take it back."

"I didn't know you knew how to play cards."

"My Pa was teachin' us ever since our hands got big enough to hold a full hand. Taught us strategy and even more important, he taught us how to read faces."

"What are you using for money?"

"I'll use my own part, not touch yours. You don't need to worry about that. You got my word, partner."

Dash regards the others around the table before shifting Amalee away from the group and saying, "Good luck, and keep a clear head."

A barrage of pounding on his room door makes Dash leap from his bed to make it stop. When he cracks the door open, Horatio falls into the room with gasps.

"Dash, I'm in trouble. Got behind. Did some big talkin' and poor thinkin'."

In hopes of keeping Amalee from waking up, Dash shushes him before hissing, "What are you talking about?"

"I lost a heap of money. All of mine and I reckon some of yours."

"How'd you lose it?"

"Well, I got to winnin' for a while. Even won my claim back, but then Fate turned her back on me and I started losing big. Finally, it was just me and him, that wily Eagleton fella. I laid it all on the line: my money and the g'dam claim right along with it, along with boastin' about doublin' the pot. I was bluffin' for sure, but when he laid down his cards, I knew I was caught short."

"How much did you lose?"

"Twice what I had. I talked fast, gettin' creative about settlin' up. Offered an all-or-nothin' option, if he'd consider a shootin' contest. I was relieved when he agreed to settlin' the debt that way, says it'll be more fun than beatin' me to smithereens. When you win, he'll forgive my debt, even though he's still keepin' my g'dam claim."

Having been around Horatio so many months now, Dash is familiar with his partner's fast talk, but it takes him a moment to replay the last sentence before he understands its implication.

"Did you say *I'm* in a shooting contest?"

"A shootin' contest, Dash, and I know you're the man goin' to win it too."

"The long shot?"

"That'll be part of it."

"You don't have me killin' anyone, right?"

"Naw, I might have put you in a tight spot but wouldn't ask you to kill, no sir."

"When's the contest?"

"As soon as we get to Sonora."

"What?"

"It's hard to tell what he wants more—to know how good a shot you are, or if he's just after the money I owe him."

"And what am I going to do with Amalee while I'm traipsing over the California hillsides with an angry miner bent on out-shooting me?"

"We'll be with you, and I'll watch over her. It's the least I can do, considerin' you're goin' to save our money, not to mention my life, most likely."

Dash doesn't know which he is more disappointed about: learning Horatio has a weakness for gambling, or that he has chosen this very moment to shine a light on his character flaw. But he has no choice. They are partners, and he never would have gotten this far if it hadn't been for Horatio's know-how and ingenuity.

"Why Sonora?"

"Eagleton fancies himself as a great shot but wants the contest to be in his world, not the city."

"How long to get to Sonora?"

"If we go by horseback, it'll take three, maybe four days. We'll have the contest, set everythin' straight, and be back to continue our treasure hunt."

Dash considers the timeline. It would mean another week away from getting answers, all to save Horatio's backside. He must get their money back. He has no choice.

"What kind of shooting are we doing?"

"Don't know. Reckon you'll do some of all kinds."

"How am I supposed to know when I have won? Or lost, for that matter?"

"Don't say 'lost.' Can't lose, Dash. You just can't."

Four days later, they arrive in Sonora just before sunset. Along the way, they had camped under Rafael Eagleton's watchful eye, who seems concerned Horatio might try to slip away. Similar to the rough trappers at Fort Bridger, Amalee has charmed the rough man, her smiles and sounds softening his hardened facade.

Horatio, however, is as jumpy as a cricket in a bed of coals. Dash has never seen anything but confidence and swagger from his partner, so he is puzzled by his behavior. Something isn't right.

Sonora is a rough town. Dash wonders aloud about where they will stay.

Eagleton says, "Y'all are stayin' at my place. Got plenty of room."

"That's kind of you, but I've got to think of my little one."

Eagleton brushes off Dash's objection.

"Don't fret about the child. We'll manage her care."

Continuing on the dirt road that bisects the town, Dash hears bawdy music coming from several establishments. Women hang from open windows, their effects announcing their profession. Leaving the town, they climb into the rolling, tree-covered hills where the streams have been scraped of what little wealth they held. Horatio leans toward Dash with an interesting gleam in his eye.

"We're goin' toward my claim. I remember it like it was just yesterday."

"But it isn't yours anymore, right?"

"Nope, had it the other night and lost it again, g'dam stroke of bad luck."

After several miles of riding into the woods, they come upon a valley with a clearing nestled next to a stream. The water splashes as it rushes against the stones and grass-covered banks that guide its liquid path. Dash looks around for the same kind of damage they had seen along the other waterways, but this one has not been molested like the others.

He asks Eagleton, "Why hasn't this stream been worked?"

"Oh, we took what it had, but once we knew it was played out, we set it right, so we'd have clean water," Eagleton replies.

They round a bend, and the encampment spreads out before them. Not since Bridger's fort has Dash seen such a well-organized arrangement of dwellings. Rafael lets out a shrill whistle as they ride toward a corral. A large cabin door opens revealing a beautiful woman, her dark hair falling in a graceful arc on either side of her face. Her expectant smile lights up when she looks in Rafael's direction.

When Dash sets Amalee down in the grass, the woman gives out a squeal of delight as she hurries to the group. Amalee looks up and grins at the stranger. In broken English, the woman asks to hold her.

"Sure, but she's covered in road dust, ma'am."

Dash's statement falls on deaf ears. The woman hoists Amalee to her hip. As she walks away leaving him holding the sack full of Amalee's clothing and blankets, he hears the woman ask Amalee about her dolly.

Rafael comes to Dash's side and says, "I told you your child would be cared for here. She is my wife, Marie Claire. She'll watch over Amalee while we commence with our business. It's almost dark. We'll eat and rest and get to the contest in the morning."

"Where's all the others?" Horatio asks.

"Went back home. Had business. May or may not be back sometime in the spring. You miss them?"

"Oh, no, just wonderin'."

Dash glances at Horatio. Since they had arrived in Sonora, his partner's face had paled, but after this news, the color returns.

After a delicious supper, Horatio, Dash, and Amalee are given their own cabin for the night. After such genuine hospitality, Dash struggles to understand why Horatio is so threatened by these folks. He decides to get to the bottom of Horatio's problem before tomorrow's contest.

In the dim light of the cabin's dying fire, Amalee is curled up in her blanket nest and the men are laying side-by-side on bedrolls.

Dash asks, "Why are you so uncomfortable around Rafael. What's he got on you?"

"When I first got to California, me and my partner sailed down the San Joaquin River to Stockton. Rafael and his brothers came off the same ship. We all came to Sonora together."

"So, what's the problem?"

A long, uncharacteristic silence follows until Horatio finally says, "I ain't tol' you everythin'. By February of '49, it had been mighty cold and the men were crotchety. Lots of fights and shootin', lots of men died over a hand of cards or sayin' something wrong. Every mornin' there'd be a row of corpses piled outside the saloons. With the cold and snow, buryin' was slow, so bodies piled up and lost their humanness—no name, kin, or nothin'.

One night, I was playin' a hand and before I knew it, it's just me and a couple other fellas in the place. When I left for our claim, a g'dam snowstorm had blowed in, and the ground got covered with pancake-sized flakes. I came around a corner and seen a couple of them Eagleton brothers messin' with bodies in the dead pile. Must have stared too long. When they know'd I was watchin', one stopped and came over and asked, 'What are you starin' at? They ain't goin' to need it no more.' I started to leave but before I could, the other one hollered out, 'This one ain't dead! I cut him an' blood's flowin'!' and them boys raced off."

Dash soberly absorbs the story and reconciles, "You were the only one to see what the Eagletons were up to, and they knew it. They figured you might tell somebody, so they decided to scare you off? If harvesting men's parts was common practice, why did they care about you seeing them?"

"I suppose it offends a man's sensibilities. I laid low for a couple months, tryin' to wipe my memory. One night I heard somethin' in our camp. I looked out the tent, got my head snapped back by my hair and a knife put at my throat. Some old boy growled, 'You best scoot. Ain't no good goin' to come from flappin' your gums about somethin' you think you might have seen. Leave your claim and stay alive. Stay and you ain't worth more than what's in that creek.' So, Clem and I saddled up and headed out—left our whole caboodle behind. Kept my mouth shut tight until last night."

"Do you know if the castrated fellow lived?"

"Saw him a few days later walkin' away from the hills. I thought about stoppin', but I figured he had enough on his mind, although I always wondered what became of him. Tell you what, Dash, I've been real watchful of my parts ever since."

Dash considers Horatio's story, but one thing doesn't add up.

"Horatio, after all that, why did you sit down at the card game in San Francisco and get me and Amalee into it?"

"Honest, when I seen him sittin' there, I felt like maybe I could get even for him forcin' me off my claim."

"Are you certain Rafael was involved?"

"I know'd it was them Eagletons doin' the cuttin'. I know the sorry fella walked away—not havin' his family jewels didn't end his life. Nobody died that wasn't already dead. But, it violated a code of trust. Never could figure why we got run off. Suppose I figured if I could win back my claim, I could get some answers."

"Seems out of character for you, Horatio."

"You're right, Dash. Just had a weak-headed moment. Won't happen again."

The following morning, the men gather in the meadow, and Rafael lays out the simple ground rules of the contest. Taller and stouter than Dash, Rafael is dressed the same way he was at the card table, down to his low-brimmed hat, except he is clean shaven.

Rafael's deep voice growls, "I pick the mark and fire first. For your shot to count against Horatio's debt, you have to hit the same mark. Ten shots total. Miss one shot and the contest is over."

Initially, the marks are stationary—tree branches and knotholes. Rafael makes his mark, and Dash matches him every time. Then come more complicated shots like hitting a rock so it falls from its cliff face. Once again, Dash answers the challenge.

After the eighth successfully matched shot, he knows Rafael has to be worried about losing. Trudging along a hillside, Rafael stops abruptly and whispers, "In the tall grass, see them? A flock of turkeys. One for me, one for you."

Dash follows the man's pointed finger to a shallow bowl in the hill where the turkeys are spread in a line foraging for grasshoppers. If he is to match the challenge, he'll have to fire a split second after Rafael as the birds will scatter at the first shot. He raises his rifle and sights toward the flock's perimeter. When Rafael fires into the flock, Dash pulls his trigger less than a heartbeat later.

Blue gun smoke swirls into Dash's eyes, blinding him for a moment. When it clears, Rafael is missing. Already at the death scene, Rafael has removed his hat and is scratching his head. When Dash arrives, he sees why Rafael is perplexed—three birds lay on the ground, two on the perimeter.

"Well, I'll be . . ."

Dash maintains a nonchalant expression.

"Looks like you'll be eating turkey for a while," he says.

"What are you going to do for an encore?" Rafael demands.

"Whatever it takes to release Horatio from his debt."

"Let's see what comes up on the way home," Rafael responds, as he hauls the turkeys up by their feet.

At the compound, they come upon freshly set fence posts each topped with a tin can. Rafael puts down the turkeys with a grin.

"Looks like Marie Claire has plans for target practice. Shoot through all five of those cans with one ball and the debt is clear."

Dash loads his rifle and lines himself up, noting a light breeze blowing to the right. He knows the impact with each can will cause the lead ball to shift slightly in its trajectory. He aims for the left of center-most spot on the first can and hopes for a gentle nudge from the wind.

When he fires, he hears the staccato ping of each can singing as they flip into the air. He sets down his rifle and stares at Rafael, a wave of relief gushing through his body. Rafael nods in silent agreement and picks up the turkeys.

"You been shooting long?" Rafael asks.

"Just a short time."

"How'd you come to be so accurate?"

"Bridger gave me some pointers. Suppose that helps."

"Horatio told me you learned from Jim Bridger, but I didn't believe him. We hear unbelievable stories about him."

"Had to spend the winter at his fort. There isn't much else to do in that howling wind, especially when you're hungry."

"You'd never shot before then?"

"No, I was raised in the city. No need for the skill there."

"What city?"

"Around the Boston area."

"I was raised in Newburyport. In this country, that makes us neighbors."

Dash is hit at that moment with a wave of recognition. Eagleton. Newburyport. The ship with the funny name. They had to be related.

"When did you get to California?" he asks Rafael, trying to sound casual.

"Me and my brothers were delivering a cargo to the US Army off the coast of western Mexico in September '48, when the word got out about gold being discovered in California. We figured we had as good a chance at it as anyone. We convinced my oldest brother, the ship's captain, to sail north so we could have a look around. He warned us we couldn't stay long. We disagreed. We rowed ourselves to shore and abandoned him. By the time we got here to Sonora, the winter had settled in and there was nobody but natives around.

We didn't speak their language, but we learned the rules early on. We made our claims and set up our operation when there was no one around to get in our faces. We built our cabins and took turns working the stream. There was plenty of gold, and we worked hard to make sure we had gathered it all."

"Must have been pretty tough to work the streams during the winter," Dash says, laying his bait. "Horatio says it was pretty cold and wet."

"Horatio been talkin'?"

Dash notices the abrupt shift in Rafael's voice but answers his question.

"He's told me of your early relationship, how you all traveled from Stockton together in the fall of '48. Said he and his partner were workin' the streams a couple of hills over from this place. Had a pretty rough winter, especially when the rush of Mexicans showed up. Said things got a little tense."

Dash knows his words have struck a nerve when Rafael lets an uncomfortable pause settle into the conversation before he speaks.

"Them Mexicans and Chileans were not far behind us and, as it turned out, neither were the French. We were pretty much the only Americans until about a year ago. Most white folks decided to stay north around the American and Sacramento River drainages. Things started building up around here in the fall of '49.

"When the government implements the Foreign Miners Tax, it will move some Mexicans and others out, even though, I'll admit, we're just as foreign as they are. It sure takes the pressure off the stream work. I'll give them one thing—those fellas know how to get the gold. We watched and copied their methods. Haven't done bad for a family of sailors!"

A friendly, almost comradely, slap on Dash's back accompanies Rafael's remark.

They walk into the compound to see Horatio's eager face along with Amalee standing at his side. Dash keeps quiet, leans his rifle against the cabin's wall, and takes Amalee in his arms.

"How'd he do?" Horatio blurts out anxiously.

"Well, there's one thing you didn't lie about and that was the shootin' ability of your partner. Want him around when there's trouble."

"Never know, he might make it his occupation since the gold is quittin'," Horatio says.

"Is there a chance of that?" Rafael asks, cocking an eyebrow.

"I'm just spitballin'. He don't cotton to the idea of killin' folks. Just huntin' for game and such."

"Good to know. Horatio, you're off the hook. Scoot out of town and take your sharpshooter with you. If you don't find your way back, it'd be just fine."

They gather their things and saddle up, Rafael returning a sack of coins to Dash specifically. Marie Claire kisses Amalee several times before handing the child up to Dash. They leave the compound on the same trail they had come in on, riding in silence until they're on the other side of Sonora and Dash figures there's enough distance for their conversation.

"Horatio, after your story last night, I could hardly sleep. Why would someone want a dead man's scrotum?"

"I know it seems like a right nasty thing but, when there's men crawlin' all over the hillsides, their eyes glazed over for the lust of gold, certain civilities get tossed. Like I said, I cain't say I ain't never done nothin' to be ashamed of, but I won't ever stoop that low."

"But why not figure out somethin' else to use? Anything."

"When you're scavengin' for flakes and gold dust, a canvas sack leaks the fine particles through the stitchin'. Mexicans started usin' ram's ball sacks until there weren't none left. Made some afraid of losing his own."

"But . . ."

"More and more men kept arrivin' and the demand was fierce. It was absolute insanity."

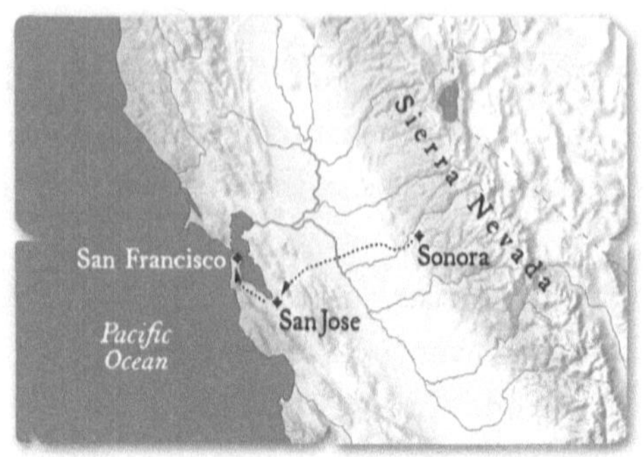

Chapter 21

SEPTEMBER, 1850

SONORA, CALIFORNIA

Given that the mules' boarding costs had been paid for a full month before they left San Francisco, Dash, Amalee, and Horatio ride due west from Sonora rather than rush back to the city and its chaos. Their casual return to the Pacific Coast might have been considered sightseeing by some but, in truth, it was a dogged exploration for opportunities.

After all their time traveling, Amalee is comfortable living outdoors, and late September weather in California is quite pleasant. They catch fish in streams and shoot turkeys for their supper. They buy produce and dairy goods from newly established farmers. Everything seems abundant compared to the life in San Francisco.

Following a month of nonchalant travels, they arrive in San

Jose, a day away from San Francisco. Dash finds the climate comfortable and the pace of life easy. Without mentioning his observations to Horatio, the idea of homesteading in this place begins to germinate.

Deciding to clean up and sleep in a proper bed for the night, they find a boardinghouse, and each buys a hot bath. In the parlor after supper, Dash settles Amalee into his lap and picks up a newspaper. Horatio settles into a chair next to them.

Reading aloud, he starts with reports of California's statehood and the state government's efforts to get established and ratify a constitution. His mouth goes dry when he comes to the reports of a cholera outbreak in Sacramento. Warnings have been issued for the downstream San Francisco waterfront where, it is anticipated, the disease will show up first.

"Don't like the sound of that, at all. Little Miss, time for bed," Horatio says, standing and lifting Amalee out of Dash's lap.

Before they walk away, Dash announces, "How about exploring this area for work and staying away from the city crowds?"

"I wouldn't mind the idea, one bit," Horatio replies and leaves Dash to his paper.

When Dash turns to the last page, he instantly reads the lettering in the lower right-hand corner.

Could it be?

He reads the advertisement again before rushing up the stairs, two at a time. Outside their room, he tries to compose himself but can't keep his hands from shaking. Opening the door, he looks in cautiously. Horatio has Amalee's nest of blankets arranged on the floor and peers over his shoulder at the door.

"Da's here, close your eyes now."

Horatio looks up and registers the look on Dash's face before whispering, "What? What is it? What's happened?"

Dash's shaking finger points to the small corner ad and he whispers, "There's an advertisement."

Horatio grabs the paper from him but asks, "What does it say, Dash? Come on, spit it out!"

Dash focuses, wanting to absorb the full meaning of each word, and says, "Notice: The Boston vs. Yalie wager has arrived. Come to . . ."

His eyes glaze over the address as his mind jerks away. He checks the date of the paper. It is the September 26 edition—only one day old. A current of energy runs through his fatigued brain as he assesses the implications of this discovery. No one has claimed it. Can he be the only one left?

"Dash, Dash, partner, talk to me." Horatio is a man possessed with action and asks, "Where do you have to meet the fella with the winnings?"

"There's an address here in the paper."

He watches Horatio's expression as he weighs the timing of their actions against his concerns about the hazards of being in a city about to be hit with cholera.

"Here's an idea, Dash. We get some sleep—if that is even possible—and then we hightail it back to the wagon and the mules and get to findin' your man. Once we claim your winnin's, we get the hell outta there."

"At dawn. Let's leave at dawn."

Once the October morning's feeble light burns off the low-hanging fog in the streets, the two men rouse Amalee, watch her eat breakfast, and then they saddle up and head north. Horatio sets a brisk pace, although with the news of cholera, Dash insists they stop along the way for food, filling their canteens from fresh springs as they go.

By early evening, they arrive at the livery where they had left the wagon and mules. Choosing to hunker down in the wagon's bed rather than find a room, the trio fall into an exhausted sleep from the day's travels.

The next day, Dash pulls out the newspaper advertisement to ask the livery man for directions. The man wags his finger toward the north.

"Chestnut and Taylor streets, they're in that general direction."

Still unfamiliar with the city, they drive for several blocks before frustration sets in. Horatio jumps off the seat and asks for help. He returns several minutes later, his expression a mixed message of emotions.

"What did you find out?" Dash asks.

"A couple of things. Neither of them good, I'm afraid."

"Go ahead, then."

"The cholera is sure enough here, on this side of the bay. This fella told me folks started comin' down with it a week or so ago. They're tryin' to get things under control, but there's plenty of folks who have died."

"What else?"

"This fella says the corner of Chestnut and Taylor is in ruins. After the last fire, no one rebuilt on account of legal trouble."

Dash drops his head in frustration. But then an idea pricks his thoughts.

"Let's pay a visit to the newspaper office that printed the advertisement. They could tell us who placed the ad and where to find him. It was just a few days ago, and we should be able to track him down."

They pass buildings scarred by fires, some still smoldering. They learn the City Hospital had burned, but all the patients had been saved from a horrible death. Arriving at the corner of Taylor and Chestnut, they have confirmation of the ruined building. Dash asks a passerby about the location of the newspaper office and is directed to a glass-fronted building two blocks away.

Horatio waits with Amalee on a bench outside, while Dash enters the building hearing the rhythmic clattering sound of metal-on-metal presses. The receiving counter is a simple wooden plank set on a pair of sawhorses. From the dark interior, a young man emerges, wiping his hands on an already ink-stained apron.

"Good day. How may I help you?"

Dash retrieves the advertisement's folded page.

"I need to know who has been paying you to print this advertisement. We went to the location and there's nothing."

The young man looks from the ad to Dash with studying eyes.

"He said someone would figure it out. Although, I'll admit to you, I think he's hoping no one will."

"Wellingham?" Dash asks.

"Yep. He's been placing this ad every two weeks for a year."

Dash runs through his mental calendar. Wellingham arrived while he was recovering at Fort Bridger.

"Do you know where I can find him?"

"Nope," the young man shrugs. "Comes in at the end of the month to pay for his two ads. Told me he would be free of his obligation in May '51. He has big plans to invest in local real estate. I hear all kinds of 'big plans,' but this fellow seems to have some kind of stake in a claim or something of that nature."

"Why would he send someone to a building in ruins?" Dash asks.

"Told me if anyone found the building and still had enough drive to come back to this office to search for him, they'd be the right person. In the early months of his advertising, he got tired of the wrong ones making a claim. He decided to put a little goose into the chase."

"Do you know where I go from here?"

"All Wellingham said was, 'If anyone shows up here, tell them they will find me at the Jenny Lind Theatre every Wednesday night.' But the Jenny Lind burned down a few months back. They've just rebuilt her again. I ran an ad for its reopening. Mr.

Wellingham should be attending the show this Wednesday. Suppose you'll have to wait for a few days."

After getting directions to the theatre, Dash thanks the young man and leaves. Back at the wagon, he shares his information with Horatio.

"What we goin' to do for two g'dam days waitin' for the theatre to open?"

"We aren't going to wait."

"What? We aren't goin' to claim the prize?"

"No, I'm saying we aren't going to wait until Wednesday. We're going to track him down before then. I've come this far. I'm not giving up until I have the money. Waiting means flirting with cholera."

Something comes over Dash. Now he knows he is the first to claim the wager and all that stands between him and the money is Wellingham. And it sounds like Wellingham has begun to spend the money before it is his, even if it's only in daydreams.

His idea is to explore around the Jenny Lind Theatre on the hunch that Wellingham would be living in the general vicinity. Horatio drives the team toward the waterfront. As they drive around the block, Dash examines the people they pass, trying to recall anything about the man he had met over a year and a half ago.

They stop to rest the team along an open area where Horatio takes Amalee for some exercise. Dash holds the mules' reins and observes the waterfront's activities, watching people closely, trying to judge if cholera is present. He does not detect it. Then he hears the call.

"Doctor Gibbs, come quick. He's in here."

A woman's voice trills through the area's din beckoning a man wearing a stylish stovepipe hat and carrying a doctor's satchel. He quicksteps down the dirt road and Dash watches the man stop at a squatty structure just three doors away.

Curious at first, he decides it is none of his business and refocuses his attention on Amalee playing in the late afternoon sun.

But there was something about the woman's call.

His contemplations are interrupted when two women hurry away from the same door where the doctor had entered. Shortly, he sees the door open again and the doctor emerges, although Dash notes the man's slumped shoulders, his step slack and defeated.

Horatio and Amalee return to the wagon, but as he trades the reins for Amalee, Dash feels an odd compunction to understand the event's circumstances. Asking Horatio to wait, he steps down from the wagon. Nearing the structure's door, he sees a sign swinging in the light breeze. His eyes strain to read it, and when he does, his mouth parches.

"Howard Wellingham, Esq."

He imagines their meeting, the shock on Wellingham's face when Dash arrives without his eye patch but with his new visage.

"Sir, may we help you?"

A woman's voice startles Dash from his thoughts. He refocuses and recognizes the two women from earlier. Close now, it is clear they are sisters, their tawny blonde hair and hazel eyes so similar one might guess they were twins, except for the care lines of an older sibling. Dressed in clean but utilitarian clothes, they hold their postures the same, tilt their heads similarly, and each stare at him with obvious concern.

"Perhaps."

"Do you have business with Mr. Wellingham?"

"Actually, I do have business with him."

"Oh sir, we are distressed to tell you, but Mr. Wellingham has passed. Just within the last hour. It is not safe to enter. The doctor warned us to stay away. It is the cholera. The doctor told us to notify the authorities so the neighborhood can understand there is a victim among us."

Stunned, Dash's body involuntarily folds onto the top step. As a tearful surge of frustration and self-pity wells in his eyes, he feels a warm hand on his shoulder.

"Sir, we are sorry for your loss. Will you share a cup of tea with us as we also mourn our friend?"

Dash looks to the wagon and Horatio waiting there, Amalee sitting on his lap flicking the mules' reins in playful imitation. Speechless, he can only stare, the implications of Wellingham's death rolling over him in a violent wave. He nods in Horatio's direction.

"I . . . I . . . have . . . I have a friend and child."

"They are welcome too. Follow us. There is a livery close by for the animals."

The women set out and Dash walks in a parade of stumbles back to the wagon.

"Horatio, we have a problem."

"Is it with them ladies? Because if it is, I can't see as they could present much trouble."

"Follow them. We have an invitation and a problem at the same time."

Dash pulls himself up to the seat and Amalee gleefully scrambles into his lap, as he continues, "Wellingham died of the cholera an hour ago. These two ladies have invited us, as fellows who have business with Wellingham, to a cup of tea to mourn his loss."

Horatio gapes but flicks the mules' lines and turns the wagon to follow the brisk strides of the ladies block after block. They stop at a building with the word "Laundry" painted neatly over the door, and the older sister points Horatio to the livery adjacent to their building. The younger woman inserts a key, and two women enter while Dash and Horatio drive the wagon to the livery and make arrangements for the animals. Once their possessions are secure, they return and knock on the laundry building's door.

A moment later, the women welcome them into the business area of the building—a neat arrangement of counter and shelves holding stacked bundles wrapped in paper and tied with twine.

Dash notices a decorative name tag draped on each for quick and efficient service. The older sister shuts the door behind them.

"We've not introduced ourselves. I'm Sarah Browning, and this is my sister, Hope."

"I'm Dash and this is my little girl, Amalee. Horatio here is my business partner."

"Follow us, please."

Sarah leads them down a narrow hall and into a kitchen area complete with a stove, several ironing boards, and multiple heavy irons sitting on the stovetop next to a heating kettle. Offering them a seat at the table, Sarah looks directly at Amalee, and with a mischievous smile says, "While we wait for the water to heat, would you like a piece of cake?"

"Cake! Yummm!" Amalee near-shouts.

The ladies smile at her enthusiastic response as Horatio concurs.

"Yes'um, that'd be mighty fine."

"So, how is it you know Mr. Wellingham?" Sarah asks.

Before he answers, Dash considers that these women were complete strangers only an hour ago and, while his reply won't relay the truth, it's not a complete lie, either. This moment calls for delicate strategy. The whole truth can be told when he knows them a little better.

"He was an acquaintance from back East. I was looking forward to seeing him when I got to San Francisco."

"Did you come by sea or by land?"

"By land."

"How long have you been in California?"

Horatio cuts in, "Dash is new in town, but I been here since '48. I tried my hand at pannin' before I learned it ain't as easy as some folks would have you think."

Sarah nods her head in agreement.

"That is what we are hearing from our customers. Some say the gold has dried up."

"The easy stuff is long gone, yes'um."

"What do you do for a living in California, now that you aren't prospecting?"

"We're freighters."

Hope arrives with the cake and Amalee lets out a howl of joy and starts banging on the table, like she had done at Narcissa's,

Dash is quick to say, "Patience, Amalee, you'll get some. But you must not yell."

Hope set the plates of cake in front of the men and continues the conversation, despite Amalee's outburst, saying, "There's a mighty need for labor and hauling in this city."

"We've had so many fires and tremors and now cholera. I have to believe the Almighty might just be tellin' us this isn't the paradise we had hoped it would be," Sarah adds.

Dash's curiosity gets the best of him when he asks, "Where are you from and why did you come to San Francisco?"

The two sisters share a look. Sarah nods for Hope to explain.

"We were foolish. We're from a farming family in Vermont. Our Pa treated us like indentured servants, so we ran off and boarded a ship thinking California would give us a better life. We had some trouble along the way, but then our fortunes reversed, and we got financial help to start this laundry. Now we care for ourselves without the control or protection of men. Forgive my directness. I believe in speaking plainly."

Dash glances at Horatio after Hope's bold statement and sees his partner quietly pondering the women's story. Turning back, Dash asks the question that has been dominating his thoughts since they met.

"How did you know Wellingham?"

"He arrived on the same ship we did last October," Sarah replies.

Following a thoughtful pause, he says, "I knew him when he worked in banking. Is that what he came to California to do?"

Without hesitation, Sarah answers, "I understood he was on

official business, a courier. Said he had to deliver a trunk to a group of men involved in a race. Recently he had begun to believe he was going to be the beneficiary of the trunk, since no one had shown up to claim it. We're doing such big business with the laundry that he had offered to help us expand, once the money was his. With each passing day, and no one claiming the money, it became easy to start planning—if only in our imaginations. Now, well, he never told us where he stored the trunk. It could be anywhere."

"You ain't got no idea where the trunk is?" Horatio sputters.

"No, he talked of putting it in a bank, but then he worried he couldn't trust them. Lately, there have been runs on banks. He fussed about that money all the time, felt an obligation to make sure it was used like it was supposed to be, that is, until he could have it for himself, and us," Sarah said.

Between bites, Dash asks casually, "Why wouldn't the trunk be in his house where he could keep an eye on it?"

"We thought it would be there, too, but we searched the place before calling Dr. Gibbs. There's talk that once someone dies, valuables seem to go missing when the authorities move in. We figured the trunk was better with us since we knew the rules associated with it. But we never found it. His place is tiny, so it was obvious it wasn't there. Most perplexing."

Still trying to mask his agitation, Dash asks, "What happens now? I mean to his body and his house?"

"Dr. Gibbs called the coroner to collect the body for disposal in the morning. I imagine his dwelling will be quarantined for a while. Not sure how long before we can get in again."

"Forty days." Dash replies, "Quarantine is for forty days. Did he have any family to return his things to?"

"No, he was alone. Rather an odd bird," Hope replies.

Dash helps Amalee finish her cake, trying to formulate a plan in his head. Finally, he says, "Ladies, thank you for your hospitality. I wish we'd arrived in time to renew my friendship with

Wellingham. Despite the circumstances, it has been a delight to make your acquaintance. May we ask permission to return your hospitality?"

The young women exchange looks before Sarah answers, "That would be most welcomed. And we wish you the best of luck in finding freighting work."

As they step from the building, Horatio starts in.

"You're jus' goin' to leave?"

"What'll you have me do, Horatio?"

"Tell them gals you are the lone survivor of the overland team, a course!"

"Listen, I'm not proud to have not been completely truthful with Sarah and Hope. Given what they've told us about Wellingham and his precious trunk, they aren't likely to trust that I'm the last to claim the wager and not just taking advantage of their information. Wellingham was my only validation. That's as lost now as the trunk. Additionally, he basically promised to help them personally once he acquired the wager. Why would they not be suspicious of me? It's not human nature, Horatio. And we would squander our connection to them. After hearing their story, I feel like we need to come up with a new strategy."

"How's this?" Horatio starts. "Cholera be damned. We go over there and search the place with our own eyes. Really turn it upside down. If there ain't a trunk, we're all in the same boat."

"A boat with a slow leak. I don't like the idea we would poke around in a quarantined place, Horatio. Too much of my life has been altered because of cholera. Forty days will give us time to become better friends with the girls. Then maybe we can get them to go with us, so we don't look like looters."

"Hmm . . . that means December, don't it? Plenty of time to get to know Sarah and Hope. I like the idea of that, Dash. I like it plenty."

Chapter 22

OCTOBER, 1850

SAN FRANCISCO, CALIFORNIA

Despite their concerns about cholera and curiosity about Wellingham's mysterious trunk, Dash and Horatio decide to focus primarily on befriending the Browning sisters. They find a boardinghouse for themselves which is adjacent to a livery for the mules but both are quite a distance from the laundry. It becomes clear that caring for Amalee limits the kind of employment they can pursue, so Dash asks Sarah and Hope if they wouldn't mind looking after Amalee so he and Horatio can take jobs hauling and delivering.

"I do expect to pay you for caring for her, Miss Sarah."

"We would expect so. Say, fifty cents a week?"

Dash considers her number briefly because it's a little on the steep side.

His hesitation spurs Hope to slide a glance at her sister before saying, "Make it a dollar a week, and we will not only care for Amalee in the daylight hours, but we'll also prepare supper for all three of you."

Dash nods in quick agreement, and a deal is struck.

Following a full day's work, the men arrive at the laundry for their supper. They hardly enter the door before Amalee begs to be picked up. She takes Dash's scruffy face between her fat little hands and holds it, so they are nose-to-nose as she gives him the day's report. Once finished, she wiggles out of his arms to visit Horatio with the same story.

As the adults become more familiar, Dash's original motivation for keeping the sisters as friends shifts. Sarah takes a liking to Horatio, and Dash believes the feeling is mutual. Because of her care of Amalee, he and Hope spend more time together. Despite not finding time to continue his research at the Port Authority, Dash remains distant, his promise strings—however faint—are still attached to Lillia.

November's arrival finds Horatio and Dash busier than they have ever been. They have a regular circuit of clients who have them hauling from the waterfront to warehouses, from warehouses to markets or storefronts, and occasionally work sites. Their payments are in coins and taken immediately after the delivery has been made. It's a policy Horatio implements with stoic deliberation.

By the first week of December, the cases of cholera are few, and the city of San Francisco lifts the quarantine on buildings, including Wellingham's. Horatio is quick to point out that it is time to do their exploration.

"I know, Horatio. Let's talk to the sisters tonight at supper. Maybe we can make it an event instead of sneaking around. At this point, I've come to believe it is better to make it sound like we are helping them find their treasure rather than trying to wrestle it away when I'm helpless to prove my identity."

After a long pause, Horatio concedes, "That's mighty big of you, Dash. Especially after all you've been through. I'll go along with you, but it tears at my heart knowin' the wager is rightfully yours."

"I'm not giving up just yet," Dash says, smiling ruefully.

Hope and Sarah are pleased to have Dash and Horatio help them reinvestigate Wellingham's place, and a thorough search turns up nothing but a few documents.

The disappointed foursome returns to the laundry where Hope says sadly, "I suppose stumbling onto the trunk was too good to be true. At least we found some important papers he had left behind. We can care for those until it is time to hand them over."

Sarah takes a handful of envelopes to a cabinet and stores them in a ledger without anyone giving them a second thought.

Before winter began, San Francisco residents demanded that the city council upgrade their main thoroughfares. One of the most important projects is a proposed plank road from the market district of San Francisco to the agricultural area around Mission Dolores. Hopelessly stalled by lack of finances and politics, construction on the project does not get scheduled until March.

Through the winter and in anticipation of the road construction, Horatio and Dash join several other hired wagon teams to haul heavy loads of sand and brush from the southern hills to the waterfront. Slowly but surely, sandy hillsides are flattened to allow for a reasonable road grade. Wagonload after wagonload gradually fill the water's edge, an area destined to become build-able space by land speculators.

The work is hard and slow, but Horatio and Dash take pride in their daily progress. Compared to Fort Bridger, the San Francisco winter season is mild and, oftentimes the men find themselves in shirt sleeves by midday. It is during one of these times when Horatio notices his partner's changing build.

"I don' know what's got into you but you're a changin' some-thin' fierce. At Fort Bridger, you was a slim one, but now I don' hardly recognize you for the bulk in your shoulders."

It is true. Dash, while having shed his soft, Boston physique well before Fort Bridger, has noticed remarkable development in his musculature and goes through several shirts and pants over the course of the winter.

"I don't understand it either, Horatio. I'm just keeping up with you. I suppose it's eating the sisters' good food. We should give them credit for keeping us off the bean and bacon diet we lived on after leaving Fort Bridger."

"Yessir, them girls have done right by us, haven't they?"

"Sure have," Dash agrees.

Once the road construction starts in March, Dash works on the survey and inspection crew, his sharp mind learning how to use the instruments and making grading calculations quickly. He en-joys helping the contractor overcome obstacles in creating the road. And there are many, including the bogs that routinely suck eighty-foot pilings into their depths.

The months pass quickly, and it is May 1851 before the men know it. On a rare day off, they take the sisters and Amalee on a picnic, to thank them for all they have done. Horatio's affection for Sarah has become glaringly obvious, and while Dash hasn't made the same bold moves toward Hope, there are subtle hints of a growing bond between them.

Ever since arriving in San Francisco last September, Dash would observe women walking along the city's boardwalks, hoping to spy Lillia. Now, after months of disappointments, he doesn't even bother with a glance. Lillia and her memory have all but faded away, and he has to reconcile that she had not taken up his desperate request to meet him in San Francisco.

He decides it is time to move on.

Following work the next day, Dash and Horatio arrive at the laundry at the usual time. Amalee grabs Dash's pant leg and tugs for his attention, her big brown eyes bright with excitement.

"Show you, Da, show you."

"Show me what?"

"Sof' spot."

He looks at Hope for interpretation.

"She's been occupied by it all day. And she took her nap there. I think she has bigger plans for tonight. You best see it."

He and Hope follow Amalee as she totters to the building's back room, her shoulder-length crimson curls bouncing glee-fully. Rounding the doorframe, Dash discovers a laundry bag draped over a chair as a canopy for a generous pile of empty bags arranged into a comfortable nest.

"Me seep."

"This is where you had your nap today?"

"Yes an' dis night."

"You want to sleep here tonight?"

The curls bounced in the affirmative. Dash looks at Hope, who shrugs indifferently to the idea. Sarah calls them to supper.

Picking up Amalee, he whispers, "We'll decide after supper."

When Hope and Sarah show no resistance to Amalee's wish, Dash agrees and acknowledges that one less stop would make their morning easier. After giving Amalee a parting hug and kiss, he and Horatio leave for the boardinghouse. On the street, Horatio stops and looks around.

"What's such a cold wind doin' blowin' at this time of year?"

"It probably isn't anything. After such a mild winter, I guess we aren't used to the chill."

"Not sure I like this northern climate. I'm startin' to miss the heat and wet of L'usiana.

Sometime in the early morning hours, Dash wakes to the pungent smell of burning wood. Initially worried that the boardinghouse is on fire, he vaults for the room's door. No smoke in the hallway. Stumbling to the building's front door, he sees other boarders already outside gaping northward. The not-so-distant glow of dreaded fire reflects against their faces. Calculating how close Sarah, Hope, and Amalee might be to it, Dash turns to see Horatio approaching, rubbing watery eyes.

"Is it close to the laundry?"

"Hard to tell but its likely that the flames are headed their way," Dash confirms, stepping off the porch into the gale of cold wind.

Following him, Horatio asks, "Know anythin' about fightin' fires?"

"Nothing more than to do what I'm told. If water needs hauling, give me a bucket. The more hands the better. But it's the girls we've got to get to first."

"We'll get them somewhere safe and then help fight the fire," Horatio agrees.

As they sprint through the streets, Dash's imagination runs wild with panic-filled images of Amalee in danger. The wind pushes the smoke into his eyes and down his lungs, but he keeps running.

It does not take long for the men to arrive in the midst of the fire's roar. Firemen appear pulling a contraption that pumps water from a reservoir. The firemen's hoarse voices yell directions while men and women shriek to each other as they rush from their homes. Explosions from various incendiary items punctuate the air. Fighting through the chaos, Dash and Horatio turn up the familiar alley between California and Sacramento streets and then onto Front Street. They are close, but so is the fire.

When they approach the laundry, the flames are shooting high in the sky. Straining to see through the smoke, Dash makes out the silhouette of the laundry, dark black against the fire's brilliant glare. Coming closer, the two men feel the fire's heat on their faces as they search around the building. Before entering the laundry, Dash sees Sarah filling a bucket with water from a catch basin before scrambling up a ladder and splashing it on the laundry's roof.

"Sarah!" Horatio screams, but the roar of the fire stifles the word before it reaches her ears.

Racing toward her, Dash grabs her shoulder as she comes off the ladder, her face streaked with sweat and grime. Frantic to keep up her efforts, she initially shrugs off his hand, but after recognizing the two men, she throws herself into Horatio's arms.

"Where are Hope and Amalee?" Dash asks urgently.

Rushing to hand them buckets, she pants, "Right after we heard the alarm bells, I sent them and our important papers to Mission Dolores to be as far away from the fire as possible. Keeping your baby girl safe was more important than saving the laundry. We agreed she would bring Amalee back in a day or so."

Unable to keep from visibly sighing with relief, Dash says, "Good. Now we can focus on keeping the laundry from burning to the ground."

Taking up a bucket a piece, the men follow Sarah's lead and continue to throw water on the building. The fire continues its unrelenting march from one building to another, the wind whipping the flames into twisting curls that lick up the street's structures. When the fire is directly across the street from the laundry, Dash is sure their efforts are doomed.

A gust of wind sends a firework of sparks and embers cascading over the frenzied trio and Dash ducks against the scorching shower. When the smell of singed hair makes him reflexively pat his head, he turns to see Sarah's blouse and hair bun smoldering.

"Horatio!" he yells. "Get some water on her!"

With a quick motion, Horatio sends an arc of water directly at Sarah and drenches her with a direct hit. So absorbed with her rescue efforts, the deluge brings Sarah to a sudden shocked standstill, her mouth gaping in surprise.

"Thank you!" she yells at him over the fire's roar before rushing toward the water basin to refill her bucket.

"I'm not sure we are going to save it!" Horatio yells, grabbing her hand and starting to retreat.

As the fire's heat drives them to the other side of the building, Dash sees the dry wood of the building's walls begin to darken against the intense heat and knows that if the fire gets any closer, the wood will spontaneously ignite.

And then he feels it. The air suddenly clears and the gusts driving the fire's flames and sparks toward them now pushes at their backs. Speechless at the wind's reversal, the three friends can do nothing but watch the fire's fury blow back on itself. Without fresh fuel, the inferno withers into smoking, smoldering piles of debris.

Hugging each other with relief, Horatio is the first to say, "I ain't never been so scared of anythin' in my life! G'dam, that was close!"

The wind's sudden shift is nothing less than astonishing. The buildings on the street's northern side smolder in ruins while the buildings on the southern side stand triumphantly. Sarah, her loosened and wet hair hanging around her face and shoulders, wears the dull expression of a weary survivor as she watches the fire diminish.

Slowly, she looks up at the men and says, "Now that the laundry is safe, we should see what we can do to help."

"Before we do that, I think we need to take a look at your arms and back. Those embers probably burned through your blouse enough to burn your skin," Dash says.

Horatio adds, "Besides, just because the fire's out, it still needs time to let the hot spots die back before we start haulin' the mess away."

Both men's points give Sarah enough relief that she nods with resignation. Going inside the laundry, she leaves them to inspect her upper body and give them a report. After several minutes of waiting, she returns, her hair restored to its usual tidy bun and some bandages wrapped around her forearms peeking out from under a fresh blouse.

Looking up at her expectantly, Horatio's expression shows his true concern before he says, "What's the damage?"

"Nothing that won't heal with a little care and time. Just a few blisters on my arms, but I will keep them clean and protected so they will heal quickly enough," Sarah replies, before adding, "I think we have earned a rest. How about you both make yourself comfortable upstairs and I will lie down in the laundry room for a little while?"

Dash looks at Horatio and says, "I'll give it a try but I'm not sure my nerves will let me just yet."

"I'll have no trouble with a little shut-eye," Horatio answers.

A few hours later, they are up and hungry. Sarah fixes a quick meal before saying, "We need to see if we can help anyone who wasn't as lucky as we were. I'll lock up and then we can go together to fetch the wagon and team."

Agreeing, the trio leave the laundry and walk to the south where there is no devastation. Once on the wagon's seat they head the team north toward what they are sure will be a difficult scene.

Portsmouth Plaza is ruined. Stunned residents wander from one burned-out shell to another, wailing for survivors. As Horatio's wagon passes by newly constructed brick buildings, thought to be safe in a fire, they notice they've become like ovens and observe rescue parties grimly removing burned bodies.

At her first opportunity, Sarah hops off the wagon and offers to help a mother by holding her small children, while the mother searches their charred home for anything useful. The men watch in pitiful silence.

"Are you here to help or gawk?" a deep voice shouts from the shadows.

"Whatever you need," Horatio responds.

"We need the rubble removed. Makes no matter where you start, just start. Watch yourselves, though. Things may still be hot."

Leaving Sarah to tend to those in need, they chose a corner building, one with easy access to the street. They pull the wagon up close, and other men with tools toss and heave debris into the wagon bed. Dash throws himself into the work, desperate to ward off the anxiety around when he'll next see Hope and Amalee.

Consumed with their efforts, the men work the entire day hauling and dumping wagonload after wagonload to the city's outskirts. They make twelve passes before night falls. Exhaustion forces them to sleep under the wagon's bed rather than return to the laundry with Sarah.

On their first dump run the next morning, and the early eastern morning light in Dash's eyes, he sees carriages arriving with aid from Mission Dolores. He wants news of Hope and his baby girl, but the carriages pass them by too quickly.

They work all day and through the night, resting only for donated meals and water breaks. Business after business employs them to haul off the refuse, and rather than lose out on a job, they stay in the city another night eating food provided by aid workers.

Having never witnessed it before, Dash is amazed at how quickly businesses are being rebuilt in this ill-fated city.

When they finally drag themselves to the laundry the following evening, Dash's heart melts at the sound of Amalee's excited voice squealing, "Da, Da, Da!"

He swoops low and picks her up in a flourish, her face straining against the force and her mop of unbridled crimson curls flowing out behind.

"Amalee, I missed you."

As she rubs her hands across his beard's scruff, she wrinkles her nose.

"Miss you, Da. You dirty, Da."

"Cleaning up after a fire is dirty work."

Hope walks into the room, her apron streaked with the telltale signs of the laundry business: wetness and soot stains from other peoples' fire-damaged clothes.

"Thank you, Hope, for taking Amalee. I knew she'd be safe with you when Sarah told me."

"Getting to Mission Dolores was not easy. Little Miss is heavy, and I had to stop to rest several times. It took us most of the night, but we made it to a boardinghouse. It was providence, though. After resting for the day, who should walk in at supper time but the Captain and Mrs. Eagleton! It was incredibly good luck. They gave us a ride back to town in their buggy. We had a great time bouncing along. When we arrived and found Sarah here, the building and our business undamaged, well, we have been celebrating ever since."

"Buggy fas', Da."

"Did you get to ride in a buggy, Amalee?"

"Yes, Da, it was fas' and bouncy. Missope and me laughed."

Throwing her head back, the child lets out a loud giggle snort that makes the adults laugh, in spite of themselves.

"Yes, buggies are fast and bouncy. Not like Uncle Horatio's wagon."

Amalee nods. Then she says, "Da, need a bath. You smell bad."

"Well, since you said it like that, I'll clean up some."

Dash puts her down and grabs a bar of soap and a towel. Horatio had already made himself respectable and sits in the kitchen while Sarah stirs a pot on the stove, their conversation low and intense.

"I just can't get over two things, Sarah. First, how much area burned so quick and second, how them folks is already rebuildin', after just a couple days!"

"Every day they wait to rebuild, the longer it takes money to start flowing again," Sarah replies.

"They're not wastin' a moment."

"Whatever you're stirring sure smells good," Dash says as he passes by.

Sarah smiles and nods.

"Thank you. Did you hear it was the Eagletons who brought Hope and Amalee back from Mission Dolores?"

Dash stops in his tracks. Hope had said the name, but it hadn't registered with all of Amalee's excited babbling.

The men exchange startled looks.

"Captain and Mrs. Eagleton. Hope and I arrived in San Francisco on Captain Eagleton's ship, and Mrs. Eagleton is our financial partner in the laundry."

Dash shakes his head and continues to the washroom, their conversation within earshot.

"Where'd she get the money to spend on a business?" Horatio asks.

"I imagine it was hers to do with as she wished."

"Ain't no woman I grew up with had no money of her own. My pappy took the egg and butter money my ma made and told her it was to help repay him for all she'd cost him early on."

After a long pause, Dash hears Sarah say tersely, "What kind of upbringing did you have that a woman would cost her husband so much money?"

Dash finishes washing, then dries off and returns to the kitchen. He sits at the table and Sarah fills his cup with coffee but doesn't offer Horatio more. She leaves the pot on the table and silently leaves the room. Dash sees his chance and leans across the table.

"Well, what's all that about?" he asks Horatio.

"I suppose I said somethin'. Probably crapped in my nest with Sarah."

Dash asks, "What exactly did you say?"

"I just said that in my part of the country, a woman don't have no money of her own. It all goes to the man of the family to do with as he sees fit."

"Well, Horatio, you're in a new country. I'd guess independent women like Sarah and Hope might take exception to the idea of forfeiting their hard work's compensation to anyone."

"But who's got the job of protectin' her? Feedin' her? Puttin' clothes on her back?"

"Right now, she does it all by herself. If you're thinkin' of courtin' her, you better be sorting out the idea. She's not going to let you come around and take away her new personal freedoms, no matter how much she might like you."

"How come you understand her notion?"

"Remember that woman I almost married? She's like Sarah, strong and smart. She doesn't need any man to make her way."

"And you was goin' to marry her knowin' that about her?"

"I was. And I would still if I ever see her again . . . if she forgives me. Two big 'ifs.'"

Sarah returns, her voice choking with atypical emotion.

"You should know, Mr. Wellingham's place burned to the ground."

"How do you know?" Horatio asks.

"I took the Eagletons to it, seems they had some business together."

The two men share a look before Dash says, "I hadn't even thought to look."

After three weeks of clearing fire debris, Dash and Horatio prepare for the plank road's continued progress toward Mission Dolores. Once Dash finishes with the road's measurements and calculations, he returns to the manual labor of shoveling sand into wagon beds. The late-May warmth has pushed any memory of winter's chill behind them and sweat stains the laboring men's work shirts.

When Horatio pulls out with his load, another wagon master backs in. Dash sets his flat-nosed shovel into the sand just as two riders pull up next to the wagon. Their animal's hooves skid to a dramatic stop, and the commotion halts the shoveling.

One of the strangers calls out, "Lookin' for a fellow named Dash. Anybody know of him?"

The road boss hollers back, "Who's askin'?"

"Name's Eagleton. Need his help—him and his rifle, to be exact."

"He's right here. Take your talkin' out of the way of progress," the road boss barks as he points in Dash's direction. "Don't think you can chat all day. We've got a road to build."

The strangers dismount from horses provisioned for spending many nights on the trail—and their saddles bristle with several holstered weapons. Dash approaches, adjusting his hat against the sun's glare to see if he knows them.

"Dash, I'm Luca Eagleton and this is my brother, Giorgio. You won a shooting contest with my brother, Rafael Eagleton to settle a debt in Sonora 'bout October of last year. Remember?"

Dash nods solemnly at the memory.

"Your shootin' impressed my brother. Got a bad situation and we need some assistance. Been sent for a travelin' judge but he's nowhere to be found. Rafael suggested you might be our alternate for justice."

Dash studies the men, their resemblance to Rafael Eagleton becoming clearer with each passing moment, except neither have the coarse complexion of their brother.

"What kind of trouble?"

"We'll explain on the way. Could you come?" Giorgio asks.

Dash thinks of all the reasons he can't fulfill the men's request and comes up empty. His hesitation is misinterpreted.

Giorgio says quickly, "Don't fret about price. We'll make it worth your while."

"I don't have my horse here. I'd have to go back to town for it and my rifle. I also need to make some arrangements. Judging by your horses' load, it's not likely I'm getting a ride from you. We'll have to wait until my partner's next wagon load."

"We'll wait in the shade, out of the way," Luca says.

Nodding in agreement, Dash returns to shoveling, and before too long, the wagon is full of sand and moves out. Another wagon takes its place, gets filled, and moves away before Horatio's wagon pulls up empty. While the other men fill it with sand, Dash explains the situation to Horatio.

"See, Dash, I told you. Your shootin' is going to be important. I knowed it, yessiree. Don't you worry about Amalee. I'll keep her company."

"Thank you. I'll ride back with you, and then we'll fetch Grunt before going to the laundry for my saddlebags and rifle."

Dash motions to the Eagleton brothers, who take up their positions, and asks Horatio, "Do you recognize them?"

Horatio's expression pales before replying, "Yep, more Eagleton brothers."

"But they weren't here during our shooting contest with Rafael, which might mean they've all returned from Boston."

"I reckon you're right. There's more of them than ticks on a dog."

Once they load the wagon and Horatio is ready to pull out, Dash tells the road boss he'll be gone for a week, but Horatio will continue the loading jobs.

"You expect to find your job here when you come back?" the road boss asks, skeptically.

"I hadn't considered you wouldn't need help, but if someone shows up and wants the work, give them my job."

Turning away, Dash motions to the brothers before taking his place next to Horatio and heading toward the city.

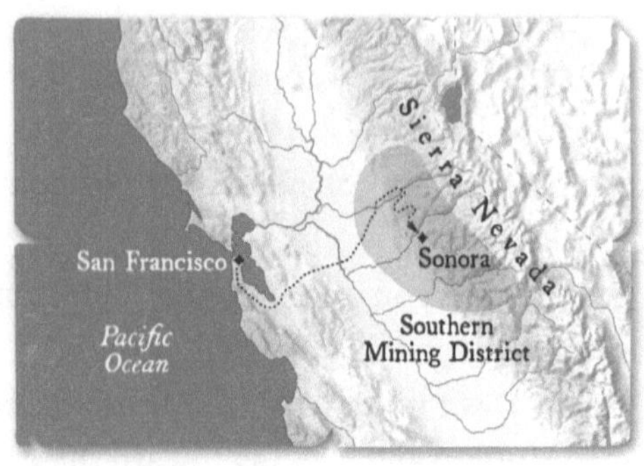

Chapter 23

MAY, 1851

SONORA, CALIFORNIA

The two-day climb into the southern goldfields is every-thing Dash hoped it would be—the cool, clean air and the thick stands of trees providing shade from the heat building in the lowlands. Green grass and flowing streams are around every corner, along with camps of all sizes and types.

Enormous sluice boxes line the waterways, their troughs flowing with the powerful water current. Men diligently attend to the wooden sluice boxes, methodically scooping shovel loads of river gravel and mud in hopes that gold will drop to the corru-gated bottom and catch against the wooden ridges. He remem-bers Horatio's words, *Lots of ways to make money that don't have nothin' to do with breakin' rocks and standin' in water up to your ass.*

Along the way, Dash learns the circumstances of him being sought. He listens carefully without asking too many questions.

His ears perk up when Luca says, "My brother, the captain, and his wife are traveling incognito to all the camps to educate the men about the false tax collector."

Dash asks, "Why would a woman get involved in this kind of business?"

"Oh, our sister-in-law is an excellent debater. If there's any kind of negotiation, my brother wants her quick mind involved. And she's not the helpless type. She knows how to defend herself, and she has a weapon for close combat none of us had ever seen. She's even killed a man with it. No, she's perfectly suited to participate in this kind of situation."

When they ride into a Mexican camp later that afternoon, Giorgio asks the camp's leader, without dismounting, if the tax collector has arrived yet. The man replies in broken English, and when he finishes, all the surrounding miners cheer loudly, "*Viva Dona Perla!*"

Not knowing any Spanish, Dash leans in and asks, "What did they say?"

"The plan when I left Sonora was my sister-in-law had left a pearl with the camp's leader as a collateral promise their tax money would be returned to them. They've hung the name Dona Perla on her. It sounds like the tax collector was here this morning and my brothers and sister-in-law confronted him and his cronies, forcing them to leave without making a collection. This Mexican camp sent a couple of riders ahead of my brothers' party to alert other mining camps to not pay their taxes when the collector shows up. They're hoping a united effort by all the miners will defuse the situation before things go too far."

"How do we know where they are?"

"I know their route if they followed it. We'll have to check at each camp."

After visiting three camps and each reporting the group's passing, Luca, Giorgio, and Dash are just leaving the last camp when they encounter a fast-moving horse coming toward them. The rider's serape distinguishes him as a Mexican and, when the man sees the trio, he jerks his horse's head up and slides to a stop. His eyes wild with fear, he starts babbling until Luca holds up his hand.

"*No savvy, señor.*"

"Dona Perla . . ." the man utters and then motions to demonstrate a hanging.

"Where?" Dash asks.

The man turns in his saddle and points his finger over his shoulder.

Giorgio demands, "How many men?"

The man holds up two hands, fingers spread wide.

"Go for help. As many as can ride."

Clearly getting the gist of Luca's demand, the frantic man flails his legs against his horse's belly and the animal leaps forward. Dash follows Luca and Giorgio down the trail, formulating a plan, but he isn't sure if the Mexican's motion means the hanging has happened or is still ongoing. In either case, urgency is required. Outnumbered by ten to three is long odds. He thinks of his time with Bridger and wishes he had the man at his side. Bridger's advice rings in his memory.

Take your time to find the right spot to sight in. Always try to be on higher ground for the best view. Game will always have two escape routes. A cornered animal will find a route you wouldn't consider, includin' right at you.

"Which of you is the better shot?" Dash asks.

Luca looks at his brother, who acknowledges him with a quick shrug before Luca says, "I can hit where I aim."

"Good. We might stand a chance after all."

Continuing down the trail with increased urgency, they come upon a crusted blood pool.

"Someone has gotten shot. If they could walk, there would be a blood trail. Or they've hauled them off. Look around."

They split up, one going uphill, one going downhill, and Dash staying on the trail. After only a few seconds of looking, Luca hails, "Over here!"

Dash and Giorgio rush to his location and stare at the body of a Mexican miner, who had been shot in his midsection and left to bleed out in the bushes. Luca takes off his hat and swipes at his hair anxiously.

"This is not a good sign. They were probably ambushed."

They ride for another fifteen minutes, their senses on high alert. And then, as they round a corner in the trail, they hear voices coming from a box canyon on the right. The trampled grass and bushes suggest a mob has ridden into the canyon.

"Giorgio, you stay here while Luca and I get above for a better look. If we can get an advantage, we are going to take it," Dash says.

Dash and Luca circle back and look for a path to the top of the canyon. At a safe distance, they dismount and tie their horses in the trees for cover. They unholster their rifles, gather powder and lead balls, and cautiously move toward the commotion. For the last ten yards, they belly crawl to the canyon's edge and peek over. Dash hears two distinct voices arguing. A woman's voice cuts through the afternoon air with remarkable clarity, while the man's deep voice rumbles and slurs his responses.

Luca whispers, "Look there. They've got the wagon backed up under the tree and three nooses hanging empty. Looks like no one's been looped yet."

Dash considers their options. They're easily forty feet or more above the wagon. From this distance, he can clearly see the wagon's horses.

By the sound of it, there is some kind of trial going on and Dash whispers, "Is this the tax collector?"

"Yep, that's him."

The man's voice rises to a shout from below them, his words too muddled for Dash to discern. It's the woman's voice, its pitch and intensity carrying clearly to Dash's ears.

"At least I'm not a scoundrel passing myself off as a credible law officer. Your time is coming. You see just three of us, but more are aware of your misdeeds. It's only a matter of time before you are brought to justice!"

At once, Dash realizes he knows the woman's voice. It's Lillia. But, no, that's impossible. Or is it? If she and her uncle had boarded Captain Eagleton's ship bound for San Francisco, the captain would have had to be blind and stupid to not fall for her. He wants to hear the story, but for now, he has to make sure Lillia and Captain Eagleton live to tell the tale.

Dash hears the male voice bellow, "I've heard enough out of you, woman!"

A long pause follows before the same voice calls out, "Boys, string 'em up!"

Dash and Luca watch as the bound trio are led to the wagon and shoved into its bed, the men and woman fighting against their captor's rough handling. Just then, Dash hears rustling sounds behind them and quickly turns to see the tattered hats of miners coming up over the hill. They fan out along the canyon's rim and peer over the edge.

"OK, Luca, here's how this is going to go. We don't have a clear shot except at the horses. If we take the horses out, the wagon isn't going anywhere. But our shots have to be simultaneous. When we drop them, maybe our Mexican friends behind us can overpower the tax collector and his accomplices. Hopefully, Giorgio is quick to cut down your family members before too much chaos breaks out."

Both men sight their guns, load them with the required amount of powder, and tamp the lead ball down their rifle barrels. They take their positions. Dash lies on a flat rock, and Luca positions himself a few feet away on a tree stump. Both men make their final sighting adjustments.

By the time the gunmen are ready, the uncooperative victims have the nooses over their heads and tightened around their necks. Wincing at Lillia's rough treatment at the hands of the outlaws, Dash forces himself to concentrate.

"Luca, you take the horse on your right, and I'll take the left one. They're standing perfectly to be dropped by a heart girth shot."

"I'll do my best, Dash. Good luck to you."

The tax collector's whistle lances through the thickened afternoon air and Dash takes aim, gently caressing the rifle's trigger. He squeezes it and feels its action against his shoulder, the smoke from the gunpowder forming a blinding fog in front of his eyes. He hears Luca's shot fire a split second later.

From over their shoulders, the miners let out an inhuman yowl as they bail off over the canyon's walls. Through the astringent blue haze of gun smoke swirling around his face, Dash strains to focus. The ground below him comes alive with movement as the Mexican horde descends on the white men. Sighing with relief, he sees the two horses have crumpled in their harnesses without taking a step, their life's blood pulsing onto the ground from identical bullet punctures.

His attention is drawn to the wagon's bed and the three people standing stalk still, watching the surrounding confusion. He sees the tax collector and his cronies being mauled by the assault of miners, their arms and legs quickly tied, and the men left to flail on the dry ground.

From his side, Dash feels Luca approach, swatting him on the shoulder and meeting his gaze with a wide grin and hooting, "We made the shots, and not even a step forward!"

Just then, through the turbulent swirls of dust and shouts of defiance, Dash sees Giorgio wielding a knife, its blade flashing quickly and the hanging ropes fall limp. He drops his gaze to the grass-covered hillside, lost in his thought until Luca beckons him to follow.

"I think my brothers would like to meet the man who saved their lives. Besides, we owe you a fine sum, I'd imagine. Do you have a price in mind for your sharp shooting?"

Dash straightens before saying, "A price. I haven't done this before, except to settle the debt between Rafael and my partner. Going to rely on you and your brothers to decide what that shot was worth to them."

"Come on then, let's get our horses and go find out," Luca says and turns away from the scene below.

He skips down toward the trees where the horses are tied. Dash follows, his mind in a turmoil. Grateful to have saved lives, he is mentally unprepared for what to say or how to act. But each step brings him closer to finding out the truth about the last nagging question he has harbored all the way from Boston.

One thing is certain; if the woman is Lillia, she has married another. Now isn't the time to be devastated. Too much has happened in the last two years for him to lose confidence in his new persona. She isn't the only one who has revelations.

Luca mounts his horse and trots it through the canyon's opening. Dash leads Grunt, allowing the energy from the shooting to diminish. Upon entering the canyon's opening and the chaos there, he hears several shots fired and instinctively crouches low. A vindictive cheer rises from the miner mob, and he sees they have shot the tax collector.

Luca, well ahead of him, has dismounted and strides confidently toward the Eagleton brothers. From his distance, Dash only recognizes Rafael, but he sees a tall, mustached man embracing a woman. Bringing himself upright, he takes a deep breath and works his way through the crowd of milling miners toward the Eagletons.

He watches as the mustached man releases the woman and grabs Luca by the shoulder. He pulls Luca into a tight hug before engaging in an animated conversation. After several exchanges, he sees the woman step forward, then look up at the man Dash assumes is her husband. Following a brief, wordless trade of expressions, everyone scans the area in his direction.

Dash's steps slow at the scrutiny. Standing beside her husband, he sees Lillia's gaze fall on him. She studies him carefully, her expression a mixture of confusion and disbelief followed quickly by a warm softening and the familiar smile he remembers.

Through a thunderous cheer, he watches the tall man step forward and say, "I'm Captain Rupert Eagleton, the oldest brother of the Eagleton clan, and damn glad to make your acquaintance. To say my wife, brother, and I owe you our lives is no exaggeration."

Gripping the captain's offered hand, Dash feels the taller man wrap a bear-like arm around his shoulder and spin him to face Lillia. She continues to study him wordlessly, unabashedly searching his scarred face.

After all the time that has passed, all the practiced conversations, and all the explanations he knows he has to make about so many things, he says, "Hello, Lillia. It's so good to see you again."

No one is more surprised than Dash when Lillia rushes toward him. When she throws her arms around him and embraces him with a stout hug, he tentatively returns the gesture, his eyes locked on the captain when he does.

Speaking into his ear while still holding him tightly, she whispers, "Oh, Donovan, I can't believe it is you! I was beginning to lose hope of ever seeing you again. And now you are here, saving my life and that of my husband. There are not enough words to express my gratitude."

It takes a while for the buckboard to be unhitched from the dead horses and replaced with new horses before they can haul the dead tax collector and his living cronies back to Sonora. Dash waits on Grunt, watching the miners harvest the wagon horses' meat. He sees Lillia staring at the process.

He rides up alongside her and says, "Nothing goes to waste here. Every bit of the animal has a use."

"Don . . . Dash, I can't believe it. How long has it been?"

"First thing, Lillia, I'm Dash to everyone here. Second, I've counted the months since I left Boston. It's been just over two years since I left you."

Before she bows her head, he catches a glimpse of Lillia's warm smile. Several minutes pass and she raises her eyes to meet his, her expression filled with confident admiration as she says, "I kept your secret from your father as you asked, even kept it from my parents so they wouldn't have to face him dishonestly."

"I put you in a terrible situation. I have so much to explain."

"You do," she agrees. "But I do as well."

"You're married," Dash says, observing the captain riding toward them.

"I am. That's just part of the story."

Captain Eagleton rides up and says, "We're ready to head back to Sonora. How about you two bring up the rear?"

Dash, his stacked hands resting on the saddle horn, casually lifts two fingers in acknowledgement of the captain's suggestion. The captain turns, whistles shrilly, and waves at the wagon of bound accomplices now being driven by Giorgio. Dash and Lillia watch as the buckboard lurches forward awkwardly and the remaining Eagleton brothers turn their horses to follow before taking their position on the trail.

Dash struggles to start their conversation and is relieved when Lillia says, "I spent many days and nights being confused and angry at you for leaving me. But honestly, your departure forced me to do what my intuition had been telling me to do all along. Your disappearance steeled my nerve to leave Boston and its suffocating culture. I've found who I truly am. Now that time and events have passed, I can say I'm grateful to you."

Dash lets her statement wash over him before replying, "I, too, have found a new life here. I can't imagine returning to the life my father expected of me."

"Along the way, I found Rupert. I hope you have found someone too?"

"I've . . . well, I've been hesitant to commit, because I . . . I did so poorly by you. My note contained an unrealistic request, and I didn't want to betray you twice."

"Is she here in California?"

"She is. She and her sister run a laundry in San Francisco."

Dash watches an odd expression flash across Lillia's face. She appears shocked when she asks, "Which one, Hope or Sarah?"

Dumbfounded, Dash stammers, "H. . . Hope. But, how do you know?"

"We sailed together from Valparaíso on Rupert's ship. Wait, are you the friend with the little girl? I can't remember her name."

"Amalee. Yes, she's mine. I mean, she's not mine by fathering," he adds quickly. "I adopted her from a woman whom I met on the overland trip. Oh, Lillia, we need more time to tell this right."

"I agree. But perhaps if you start with how you came to have two children by your side when you first met Howard Wellingham?"

"You know Wellingham too?"

"He sailed on Rupert's ship as well—on our first passage from Newburyport. I was with Uncle Sebastian. Howard said he needed to beat the race's teams with the wager, and Rupert's ship was his best option. About the children?"

Dash shares the details of the family secret he discovered and the horrible circumstances where he found Molly and Quinn, along with the decision to save them. All culminating in the need to steal his father's money and leave her with only a coded note of explanation.

"I knew you had taken money from your father. He came to our home and pleaded to know where you were. After how he had treated you in my presence, I knew you had hit him in his soft spot, his treasury."

"I was in a panic, Lillia. I feared he would hunt me down, and well, it's hard to know with him. I couldn't take the children to where he asked me to, so I ran away. For the longest time, I believed I should have asked you to come with me. But, after having survived what I have, I'm relieved I didn't. You might have died like all the others."

A long pause follows until Lillia sighs and says, "What's done is done, Dash. So, who is Amalee's mother?"

Dash unfolds the story of his brief friendship with Ace, of pregnant Nora, and how, by St. Louis, he had lost not only four of their seven team members but Ace as well.

Lillia holds up her hand to interrupt him, "At a women's meeting last spring, my mother heard a young man telling of his experience being injured by a passing steamboat explosion. He told of a race to the goldfields and mentioned your name. My mother was so distraught that she got apoplexy. It paralyzed her left side, but once she learned that I already knew the race, she started an immediate recovery."

Startled at Lillia's revelation, he asks, "How did you know I was in the race?"

"We sailed past the *Night Call*, or her remains, when we came around Cape Horn. Wellingham needed help writing condolence letters to the families and asked for my help. I used the race ledger and discovered your name on it, rather, my nickname for you."

Dash folds his hands across the saddle's horn and explains, "I used the nickname because I was afraid my father would track me down. I took it as my own when I became the last living member of the overland team. No one knew any different, and it was my last chance to start a new life. By the way, I learned you had left Boston with your uncle. I just didn't know where you had sailed."

"How?"

"My partner and I were driving a freight wagon eastbound

across the Great Basin, returning to Fort Bridger last July, and a fellow from Quincy recounted the story after it had been printed in a Boston newspaper and the advertisement my father had placed. He mentioned the woman had left the city."

"Uncle Sebastian caught his own kind of gold fever, and we set out for California with a load of canvas to sell. That is when I met Rupert, Wellingham, and the Browning sisters. But I still have to ask, are you truly the only one left from your overland team?"

"Yes. Wellingham died and without him, no one can verify my true identity. Besides, he hid the trunk somewhere and we could not find it."

The topic of the lost trunk throttles their conversation until Lillia says, "I know where the trunk is. Wellingham bequeathed it to me after he died, since no one from the overland team had shown up."

"I arrived at his doorstep shortly after he died."

"Really?"

"That's when my partner, Horatio, and I first met Hope and Sarah."

"Sarah mentioned someone named Horatio helped her save the laundry in the last big fire."

"I was there too. Hope took Amalee away to keep her safe."

"We met Hope and Amalee in an inn by Mission Dolores just last month."

The two stop their horses and stare into each other's eyes, marveling at how closely their lives had entwined, despite everything. That is when Lillia gets a good look at the scars running along the left side of Dash's face.

"What happened to you?" she asks.

Dash is surprised at how painful the memory still is. Clicking his horse to continue walking, he figures out how to consolidate what went into the unlikely recovery of his left eye's sight.

When the story, with all its tragic details, comes out, it leaves Lillia gasping, "Oh, my God, Dash! How are you still here?"

"I wish I knew, Lillia. So much of my survival and recovery is improbable. I owe my life to so many strangers. Especially at Fort Bridger, their kindness was overwhelming."

Dash elaborates on Jim Bridger's efforts to coax back the use of his left eye and teaching him to shoot, the Vasquezes' devotion and care of himself and Amalee and, ultimately, how Horatio came into his life while at Fort Bridger.

When he finishes, he sees that Lillia is still contemplating his story and asks, "Do you mind if I ask you a question?"

"Not at all, go ahead," Lillia replies.

"Luca told me his brother's wife killed a man with a unique weapon. Did you really kill someone?"

Lillia becomes pensive as she mulls the memory of killing in order to prevent him from setting the *Ornery Agnes* on fire in the middle of the Pacific Ocean before she begins.

"His name was Coopton, and we picked him up in Valparaíso on our first trip to San Francisco in August '49. He deceived us all with his congenial and docile behavior, but once on the ship sailing north, he became irrational and demanding. He said he caused the wreck of the *Night Call*. I had climbed the mainmast with Rupert to see the heights, and below us, we spied him gathering materials to set the ship on fire. I tried to decoy him while Rupert got into position to stop him. When Rupert tried to subdue Coopton, he put up a horrible fight. After I saw Rupert being bested, I rushed through the smoke and used my weapon to save him."

"Wouldn't Coopton be committing suicide by setting a ship afire in the middle of the ocean?" Dash asks in astonishment.

"He lost some of his sensibilities due to the loss of, as Hope and Sarah put it, his 'family jewels.' Seems there was some kind of event in the winter of '48 when he was accidentally castrated."

Dash pulls Grunt abruptly to a stop and gasps. He says, "Horatio believes the Eagleton brothers might have been involved in an event like that. Could they be the same?"

"They've never breathed a word of it to me."

"My advice?" Dash says with raised eyebrow, "Don't bring it up. If it is the same situation, you took care of the problem. One last question. Why did the miners refer to you as Dona Perla?"

Lillia smiles fondly at the name as she says, "Rupert and his brothers salvaged a whaling ship west of the Sandwich Islands that had a secret cargo of pearls hidden in the barrels of whale oil. Sebastian and I reclaimed them and now he is in France selling them for what I hope will be top dollar. I saved a few special ones for my pleasure. When we had to come up with something valuable enough to show our sincerity to help the miners, I used my pearls as collateral."

Smiling at the conclusion of her explanation, Lillia asks, "How is it that you know Rafael Eagleton well enough to have him ask his brothers to find you in case they couldn't find the traveling judge?"

Dash acknowledges her question and begins to tell her about Horatio's history with the Eagleton brothers and the gambling debt that forced Dash into a shooting contest with Rafael. When he finishes, he sighs deeply before slowly shaking his head.

Lillia asks, "What is it, Dash?"

"I just can't believe what we've experienced in the last two years."

"It is all so remarkable, isn't it?" Lillia admits. "I owe you my life, the life of my husband, and his brother. I'm so grateful to you, Dash. And I'm glad to know you again. You should know, Rupert and I have a son, Justus, named after Rupert's father. It sounds like he is a year younger than Amalee. Maybe we could introduce them at some point?"

Smiling, Dash says, "I know Amalee would like that. She is a very happy little girl, despite all the difficulties she experienced in her early days. And Hope is going to be shocked to learn our history."

Lillia turns serious and says, "You were my best friend for a time—nearly my only friend back in Boston. And more than that really, but I am so happy we have both met our true loves. The love you and I shared was something real and true—no disrespect to that—but we were younger. It was love between two hopeful and desperate dreamers. We've both seen the world now and learned who we really are, and who we are meant to be."

Her words bring the sweet release of the guilt burden Dash had been carrying for so long. And yet, there was more to say to her, and he takes a deep breath before beginning.

"Lillia, while I need to apologize for what happened in Boston, I want you to know I'm grateful for your friendship during those difficult years with my father. You made me believe in myself, and I was better than he let me think I was. We could have made it, a marriage, I mean. Now we know neither of us would have been satisfied living there. That said, I'm not as confident as you are that I have learned who I am. But I have survived somehow through so many close calls that I must be meant to accomplish something."

"Perhaps use your Morse code?" Lillia asks.

"It could be useful here. Right now, though, I've got to think about my immediate future and my life with Hope and Amalee. I'm pretty sure Horatio and Sarah are smitten with each other, so if I were to suggest a double wedding, I can't imagine I would get an objection from either of them."

"I couldn't agree more," Lillia replies, her expression lighting up with an enthusiastic grin.

Chapter 24

JUNE, 1851

SAN FRANCISCO, CALIFORNIA

Two days later and after hours of catching up with Lillia, Dash returns to Hope and Amalee. Dash had set a fast pace and Grunt had accommodated him. His conscience is free and full of light after two years of doubt, guilt, and self-condemnation. The only thing he has to think about is Hope.

As he thinks of her, warmth fills his chest. He remembers how her hair falls from its plait, coming loose in a fringe around her face. He knows she doesn't care, impatiently pushing it back throughout the day. She is hardworking and strong, an able partner to build a home together, a new life.

He wants to take care of her. He'll work hard, so she can sit down now and then. He imagines picnics and days by the ocean, with Amalee playing in the sand. That's the other thing: Hope loves Amalee. He can tell from the way she tickles Amalee after a bath and then snuggles her into her lap before bedtime. And who knows, maybe they will have children of their own and give Amalee brothers and sisters to boss around.

"You ain't lyin', are ya, Dash? Dropped them horses without them takin' a step? Can't even imagine it!"

Horatio's open disbelief matches the expressions of Hope and Sarah, as they all enjoy Dash's tale around the supper table that night. Up to this point in the story, Dash hasn't shared who he rescued but then says, "You're not going to believe what happened next."

Dash looks at all three of them, one at a time, and sees that his suspense-filled words have had the desired effect.

"When I went down to see who Luca and I had saved from hanging, turns out it was Captain Eagleton, Lillia, and Rupert's brother, Donatello!"

Gasps of surprise come from the women, their hands flying to their mouths to cover the exasperated expressions. Horatio's grin is wide with disbelief and awe. No one says anything for a long while forcing Dash to continue.

"Horatio, I've already told you about Lillia, my ex-fiancée that I left behind in Boston but for Hope and Sarah's benefit, here is a quick summary. I had to leave Boston because I discovered that my father and brothers were selling destitute Irish women and children into the illicit sex slave trade. I couldn't join Lillia and her family to my family once I knew that about them. I stole a large sum of money from my father and joined the race to California with my friends from Harvard, but it meant that I had to run for my life. Wellingham was the courier for that race's wager, but you know that. I learned from Lillia that she sailed with her uncle on a ship captained by her now husband, Rupert

Eagleton, along with Wellingham. They picked up the Browning sisters in Valparaíso. But here is the really important news."

He pauses for dramatic effect, and Sarah says with disbelief, "There's more? I don't know how I'm going to keep all of this straight!"

Horatio nods with anticipation, clearly his interest still heightened.

Dash looks straight at him and says, "They know where Wellingham buried the wager money!"

It takes a moment for the weight of his announcement to be processed but once it is understood, everyone in the laundry's kitchen erupts with whoops and cheers.

"They know? What kind of luck is that?" Horatio's voice warbles.

Dash adds, "Lillia told me Wellingham bequeathed it to her when he thought no one was going to claim it, and he was dying. Hope gave Lillia Wellingham's letter as they returned from Mission Dolores after the fire. They went to where his house was only to find it had burned down in the recent fire. Rupert has an idea of just where it is buried, and once we clear the debris away, we're all going to meet next week to dig it up."

"If that don't beat all!" Horatio says, his expression an odd mix of gladness and chagrin.

Up to this point, Hope hasn't said a word about Dash's story and explanation, her reaction more muted than Sarah's. When he looks at her expression, he can tell she is troubled but doesn't want to pry into her feelings in front of Sarah and Horatio.

"How about we rent a buggy tomorrow morning and go to the beach in San Jose with a picnic lunch?" Dash suggests.

"Pic-nic, pic-nic," Amalee chants while she slaps the tabletop.

Sarah and Hope exchange looks before Sarah says, "If you can find a buggy for all of us, we'll put together the lunch."

"Sounds like fun to me," Hope adds with a slight smile. "It would be good to explore San Jose. Everyone speaks highly of it."

"Alright then, first thing in the morning, Horatio, Amalee, and I will secure a buggy and meet you ladies here with your picnic lunch."

On their way back to the boardinghouse with Amalee bouncing along on Dash's shoulders, Horatio springs the question Dash knows he has been aching to ask.

"Did they pay ya?"

"Not yet. That'll come."

Horatio's disappointment at Dash not receiving compensation for his work is clear, but what Horatio says next is truly unexpected.

"Well, you've been gone for five days, and some things have happened at the job."

Dash stares silently at his partner, prompting him to continue.

"It's like this. It seems some of the boys we were workin' with took an exception to you dartin' off like you did. They complained to the boss and, well, when they came to me and I got my neck out of joint. I told them off. It got us fired. Sorry, partner."

Speechless, Dash quietly lowers his chin to his chest.

"Don't you fret none, Dash. Me and Sarah been scoutin' options all over town. Got some good ideas but need to go look at a few with you along so's you see what's out there. Good news is there's plenty o'work for fellas like us not afeared to do haulin' and shovelin'."

Dash is quiet for a moment as he considers Horatio's words. Finally, he turns and starts walking again.

When Horatio catches up, Dash says, "Actually, Horatio, I'm not worried, at all. I have had plenty of time to think on my travels, and I've come to my senses. Hope and Sarah are good hardworking women who, if we court them right, might consider us for husbands."

"Lordy, Lordy! I been waitin' for you to turn the corner on Hope! And I agree. Hope and Sarah are mighty fine ladies. But them girls have developed a tough skin when it comes to men. They get men slobberin' all over them when they come for their laundry. We's got to put a shine on us, somehow. Make 'em know we's serious 'bout courtin'."

"What do you say we get out our best clothes, take baths, cut each other's hair, and shave off these whiskers?"

"All by tomorrow mornin'?"

"How serious are you about convincing Sarah she should have you?"

Dash's question brings a long pause.

"A bath first thing in the mornin' is a mighty strange idea. And my best clothes is the ones that has only a couple o'holes 'stead o' five or six. Think they'll even notice?"

"I'll bet they notice us trimmed up and clean shaven before they say anything about our worn clothes."

"Heck, Dash, I think we ought to go 'bout it right now. I'll see if they'll draw the bath while you put Amalee to bed. What do you say?"

"I say you're a man on a mission. If they'll do it, tell them we want two hot baths. I'm not sharing your dirty water."

As if Fate had blessed their idea for her own enjoyment, the boardinghouse owner agrees to draw two baths, and the men work on changing their appearances. Back in their room, they light a candle to cut each other's hair and shave each other's whiskers. When they finish, both young men stare at the other.

"G'dam, Dash, them scars ain't nothin' no more. Just gives you some interestin' character."

"What about you, Horatio? I've never seen you without whiskers. Sarah isn't going to believe her luck when this fair-faced man shows up tomorrow. Glad you thought to do this tonight. We'll get a good night's sleep knowing we don't have to rush through our beautification in the morning. One thing we do need to consider is what if Amalee doesn't recognize us?"

"Lord Almighty, I didn't consider our little lady. We're goin' to have to spend a little time lettin' her get used to us 'fore we leave to get Sarah and Hope."

"With Amalee being the only familiar face between us, we'll need her to vouch for us before the girls agree to a buggy ride, for sure."

"We ought to give a stab at sleepin' but, honest truth, Dash? I got me a swarm o' butterflies swirlin' 'round at the idea that we's goin' to court them girls. Meetin' up with 'em tomorrow seems different, don't it?"

"Yep, we're turning a page, for sure."

The waves' salt spray billows across their faces as Dash, Amalee perched on his shoulders, and Hope walk along the beach in their bare feet. Screeching seagulls, waves crashing, and Amalee singing to herself are the only sounds Dash hears while he waits for Hope's reply to his gently presented question, "What would you think about getting married?"

He feels distressing tension swell in him at Hope's long pause. Finally, she says, "Do you know how many proposals Sarah and I get on an almost daily basis?"

"I'm sure you get quite a few."

"We do. Not because they love us, because they're lonely. We've learned to be polite but direct in our denials. After what I learned last night about your engagement to Lillia and sudden departure, I'm trying to figure out what to say."

Dash takes a few steps and then turns to face her squarely before saying, "Lillia and I were rescuing each other from lives we hated. She from the constrictive social limitations on women and me from my despicable father. We loved each other and would have made it work had our marriage happened, but clearly, she found her true love in Captain Eagleton. I am telling you now I believe I have found mine in you. Would you marry me?"

Taking her chin in his fingers, he lifts her face to his and sees tears welling in her eyes. Unsure why, he whispers, "What is it? Is the idea that bad?"

"No, Dash. It's not that. I've just had to put bars on my heart. Honestly, the minute you and little Amalee arrived on our doorstep, the day of Wellingham's demise, I knew I wanted to be your wife and mother that child. Don't ask me how. I just knew."

"So, that is your answer? Are you saying yes to my proposal?"

"Yes, but I have one worry. What happens to Sarah? We're bonded tight."

Dash looks over her shoulder at where they left Horatio and Sarah on the picnic blanket. While not completely sure, he thinks he sees them embracing.

"I happen to know the same question I asked you, has been asked of your sister."

Quickly looking back, Hope spies the same embrace before whipping around to look into Dash's eyes. She flashes his favorite animated expression and says, "Gosh, Dash! You boys really know how to surprise us!"

"I think she said yes, don't you?"

"Ah, she's been sweet on him about as long as I have been on you. Something about your working hard and caring for little Amalee like you do. Made both of us consider you boys differently."

With that, Dash swings Amalee off his shoulders, her fat little feet squishing into the wet sand as she toddles toward a pile of shells. Taking Hope in his arms, he feels her stout warmth press against him, her reciprocating touch confirming their intention before they gently find each other's lips.

Gathering Amalee, they saunter to the picnic blanket, but before they reach it, Sarah stands up and runs to Hope, their expressions equally joyous. Hugs and little giggles of delight come from their gleeful dancing, leaving the men laughing at the display.

"So, ladies, when shall we have the event?" Horatio asks.

"As soon as we get our dresses made," Sarah replies.

"Where shall we have the ceremony?" Dash asks as he takes Hope's hand and smiles. "I believe the Eagletons might be willing to offer their ship, if you like the idea."

Both women gasp and Hope says, "They held their wedding there. It was so beautiful. Remember, Sarah?"

"Oh, we can have the ceremony at sunset, just like them. Really, do you think they would let us, Dash?"

"Given your relationship? I have no doubts. We just have to make sure the captain isn't sailing the ship somewhere. Horatio and I will do the asking when we dig up the wager trunk."

Dash and Horatio greet the Eagleton's rented buggy from the Browning laundry's front porch a week later. Horatio races to Dash's side to make introductions and to formally meet Lillia.

Politely, Lillia says, "It's very nice to meet Dash's business partner. He has told me about your skills and adventures getting to California from Fort Bridger."

"And you, ma'am. To think you are our girls' business partner! With all the miles between us, we got that tie to bind us," Horatio replies.

Rupert's expression shifts and he asks, "Did I hear you say, 'our girls'? Does that mean what I think it does?"

Dash bows his head slightly and says, "Yes, you heard right. We both proposed to Sarah and Hope last weekend when I got home from Sonora. And, remarkably, they accepted!"

"What do you mean, 'remarkably,' Dash? We're fine catches.

Goin' to do right by those ladies, we are," Horatio states with sincerity.

The sound of the front door slamming and Hope's gleeful screech cause Dash and Horatio to step back, allowing her to rush past, while handing Amalee to Dash on her way. Touched by the friends' warm embrace, Dash has only a moment to consider their unique friendship before Amalee starts wiggling in his arms.

"Buggy! Ride, ride!"

Sarah arrives and hands Horatio the picnic basket, saying, "We thought we'd take a picnic lunch with us today. Who knows what kind of time the digging is going to take?"

Groaning at the basket's weight, Horatio says, "Good idea, Miss Sarah. Might be downright starved after all the treasure huntin' we're goin' to do."

Dash sets Amalee down and says to Rupert, "Horatio and I have spent time clearing the debris from Mr. Wellingham's lot. That'll make today's work a little easier on our backs and might give us a quicker resolution."

"Thank you!" Rupert replies. "After what we saw the last time we were here, I was concerned about finishing in one day."

With that, the men load the buggy with the large picnic basket and three shovels. Dash notices the women whispering to each other until Lillia says to Rupert, "Why don't you take Amalee and go ahead? Sarah, Hope, and I will walk with Justus so we can talk along the way."

Nodding in agreement, Rupert flicks the buggy horses' lines and sets out. Amalee, her scarlet curls escaping from under her bonnet, sits between Rupert and Dash while Horatio bounces along in the back seat holding the picnic basket.

When they are out of sight from the women, Rupert asks, "Have you decided on a date for your marriage ceremonies?"

Horatio says, "Might as well make it soon! There ain't nothin' to wait on except the girls making their dresses."

"We want to ask if it would be possible to have the ceremony aboard your ship, Rupert?" Dash asks, adding, "Hope and Sarah have described your wedding with Lillia as the most beautiful they've ever seen."

"Of course, we would be delighted to host the weddings. I might be able to persuade the preacher I used to make a return visit. If this is what you want to do, the weddings must be before August, as I am scheduled to leave for Astoria on the first."

"Golly, the girls best not take too long making their wedding dresses!" Horatio exclaims.

At Wellingham's lot, the men get right to work, leaving Amalee to play with her dolls in the buggy while they sweat in the hot June sun. After Dash and Horatio's debris clearing, the area is ready for Rupert to make a guess at the location of Wellingham's office. Working with enthusiastic vigor, the men begin their challenge.

It isn't long before the chatter of female voices makes them stop and lean on their shovels.

Rupert suggests, "I don't know about you boys, but I think we should open the picnic basket and take a rest."

The men enthusiastically agree to his suggestion and make their way through the debris toward the buggy. They find the blanket spread wide, Justus, and Amalee sharing one corner, while Sarah and Lillia arrange the lunchtime offerings on the opposite corner. Dash arrives in time to see Amalee offering a pickle to Justus.

"Are you hungry, Amalee?" he asks.

"Oh, Da, Missope has pic . . . pic . . . piclies. One for you?"

Grinning at her cuteness, Dash says, "Sure, Amalee, I'll have a pickle."

It doesn't take long to devour the picnic lunch. The women

fold the blanket and pack the basket into the buggy while the men return to their excavation.

The women watch casually as the men continue their search, but all jump when Horatio yelps, "I hit something!"

Working quickly, the men clear away the sandy soil. Dash runs his fingers along the trunk's outline, digging out the ends until they locate the handles. With a great heave, they yank the trunk from its earthen hiding place, revealing the rusted padlock.

Rupert says, "I remember Wellingham had it padlocked. It's a good sign no one has tampered with the contents."

Lillia whispers loudly, "Rather than break the lock off for all eyes to see, let's take it back to the laundry and open it in private."

With renewed energy, all six adults and the children pile into the buggy and rumble through the streets toward the laundry. Once inside, Horatio uses a hammer and chisel to break the trunk's padlock, ceremoniously sweeping his hand toward Lillia to do the honors. She takes a deep breath and makes an announcement.

"Before we open it, I've been thinking we should split the contents among the three couples here. The funds will benefit all of us in our different life avenues. Considering all the lives lost, the wager will honor them by being used in diverse and positive ways."

Each adult casts glances, but no one objects to her proposal. Lillia lays her hands on the encrusted trunk lid, and Dash feels a drop of sweat run down his temple. His mind flashes to Hugh and then to each of his traveling companions. He still can't believe he is the only one of them all, including the Yalies, to survive the trip. He knows what it cost him to win the race, get access to the trunk, and now he remembers the contents inside.

Lifting the lid, everyone presses against Lillia—their curiosity too much for manners. She reaches into the trunk and extracts its entire contents: the race ledger, an envelope, and . . . sand.

"What the . . . ?" Rupert growls.

Sarah and Hope gasp in unison, "How could he?"

"What's in the envelope?" Dash asks stoically.

With shaking hands, Lillia removes the folded letter from the envelope. Dash watches as a perplexed expression crosses her face, followed closely by one of resolution. She unfolds the letter and mouths the words from the page with no emotion.

> *Lillia,*
>
> *If you are reading this, I have succumbed to something terminal—either natural or human. You know as much as anyone; I have a fatal flaw. You and your uncle fanned its flames to life on the ship. I tried to overcome it, but the demon of gambling owns me. Please remember my better points.*
>
> *Admiringly,*
>
> *Howard Wellingham, Esq.*

Dash stares at Lillia as she raises her eyes to his. No one speaks when he turns and walks to the laundry window, staring into the distance. He hears Rupert say, "I have no words. Howard had his weaknesses, but I didn't realize excessive gambling was one of them."

"Perhaps he was lonely," Sarah says, her eyes full of tears as she continues, "he approached me on several occasions. I just didn't have a good feeling about him. I should have been more sensitive."

Dash hears Lillia say, "No, Sarah, you trusted your instincts. I, too, can attest to Howard's peculiar streak."

Hope joins Dash at the window and takes his hand, saying, "It doesn't matter. We'll make our way. It might have been easier with the money, but we'll be happy in our work together."

Suddenly overwhelmed by her confident words, Dash takes Hope in his arms, their embrace forming a bond of trust in their future together.

Chapter 25

JULY, 1851

BENICIA, CALIFORNIA

The July sun slips slowly down the distant hills of San Francisco and the surrounding cities. From the deck of the *Ornery Agnes* docked at the Benicia Barracks, Dash watches the sun's golden glow as Barnabas, the ship's cook, lights the many candles lining the ship's railing. Lillia had out done herself with local flowers and greenery made into garlands that wind themselves around the helm's stairs.

Horatio, standing opposite him, wears a new white shirt, pants, and boots matching his own. They procured the list of food Barnabas had asked for, and the smells coming from the ship's galley made Dash's stomach growl.

He sees Amalee emerge from the passenger's quarters dressed in green and wearing a head wreath of white flowers and pink pepper berries while holding Lillia's hand. Initially, Dash watches as his little girl slowly steps toward him. His heart flushes full when Amalee sees him and trots toward him before jumping into his arms.

"Amalee, look what I have," Dash hears Barnabas ask from behind him.

The stick of candy he uses as a lure causes her to wiggle out of Dash's arms and follow the cook over to stand off to the side by Lillia.

"How much longer do those ladies need, anyway?" Horatio asks impatiently.

"Not long now," he replies and directs Horatio's gaze toward the passenger's quarters' door where Rupert is emerging, Hope on his right side and Sarah on his left. All the surroundings blur when Dash sees Hope in her wedding finery. Her gentle smile warms him as she approaches. He feels his face flush.

Stopping in front of the men, Rupert gives each woman to her betrothed before joining Lillia as the preacher begins. He states the roles for the husbands and wives before pronouncing the couples married. Each couple exchanges a kiss and a long hug before turning to face Lillia and Rupert.

"Congratulations! Barnabas, let the festivities begin!" Rupert calls out.

Mouthwatering dishes of all kinds line the dining table. Barnabas, ever the proud uncle, brings Amalee and Justus to their parents once all the food is served. The children add their excitement to the party, sampling all the food on their parents' plates.

The preacher tells tales of his life, and Horatio tells his own stories. Before long, Rupert stands and holds out his wineglass for a toast.

"To the new couples. May they have years of joy and prosperity. May they have peace in troubled times, and may they bring children into the world."

Horatio whispers to Sarah loud enough for Dash to hear, "I like the idea of having a passel of little ones, don't you?"

Sarah blushes and pecks him on the cheek.

Dash begins his toast, "To the Eagletons who have blessed us with this lovely place to celebrate and the promise of future friendship."

As everyone raises their glasses, Dash looks toward Lillia and raises his glass acknowledging her and Rupert before taking a sip.

Horatio says, "While you're standing, you goin' to tell them our good news?"

Dash bows his head and looks around the table before saying, "On a recent trip to explore San Jose as our new home, Horatio and I met a man leading the effort to get a telegraph line established between San Francisco and Marysville via San Jose and Stockton."

Horatio interrupts, "And when he learned Dash knows Morse code, he jumped at the chance to get us involved."

"Yes, but it is a project in its infancy," Dash continues. "They need funding and state support, which could be a year out. We would be part of the construction process initially, but we could work ourselves into other, less-taxing roles once it's established."

"That's wonderful news, Dash and Horatio!" Lillia exclaims.

Sarah quickly adds, "We will keep the laundry going until we get established into homes of our own. In the meantime, the boys will continue to do freighting work."

"All very exciting news," Rupert says as he smiles at the young couples.

Horatio asks, "What about you, Captain? What plans do you and Lillia have coming up?"

Dash sees Rupert pat Lillia gently on the back before saying, "You know I sail with the Army on August 1. But, Lillia, would you like to share your news?"

Dash witnesses an atypical blush rise in Lillia's cheeks before she says, "As it happens, Rupert and I will welcome our second child in November!"

"Hooray!" Sarah and Hope exclaim in unison.

"Which means I will oversee the construction of a proper stone home in Benicia while Rupert is away. Also, we are speculating on several land lots. We are anticipating Benicia becoming a major California city."

Dash braces himself when he hears Horatio say, "Gosh, Lillia, you can do all that without Rupert around to help you?"

Smiling at his partner's naïveté, Dash hears Rupert say, "Once you get to know her, Horatio, you'll learn there is very little Lillia can't do on her own."

Dash laughs with the rest of the party knowing the truth of Rupert's words.

"That said, I have one more toast to make," Rupert says, standing once again.

Dash sees Lillia's expression shift to being curious about what her husband is up to.

"I must offer a toast, with my most sincere feelings, to Dash and his ability with the long shot. Without you, my new friend, Lillia and I would not be here now. I am very grateful to you, knowing of your trials and losses along the journey west, that you willingly came to our rescue, just in the nick of time, and your shot was true."

Dash sees tears flowing down the women's faces as the captain's heartfelt words have their impact. He knows he, too, has words to say but finds them difficult at first.

"I have no words of explanation except to say that it feels good to be able to contribute to making a difference in this world. My life wasn't always this rewarding."

"Here, here!" the group cheers.

Settling into more quiet conversations, the party breaks up. Grateful that Lillia had offered to let Amalee stay on the ship until tomorrow afternoon to let the new couples have time away from the responsibilities of life, Horatio and Dash had made reservations at the American Hotel in Benicia for the night. Dash watches as Amalee takes Justus's hand, and the two little ones make their way toward Lillia and Rupert's quarters where Amalee has spent the day building a pillow fort.

Dash scans the scene before him. It's been a little over two years, yet it feels like a lifetime of change. Despite everything, he is in awe of his happiness. As the warm, westbound breeze threatens to blow out the last of the candles, he smiles as he hears Hugh's voice say clearly, "It's the zephyr wind. It's a good omen, chum."

Author Notes for The Gantlet

This is a work of fiction. While most names, characters, businesses, places, events, and incidents are either the product of my imagination or used in a fictitious manner, my stories weave around actual events and places. I do have some historical figures represented, but all of their interactions with my characters, including dialogue and activities, are the product of my imagination. Otherwise, any resemblance to actual persons, living or dead, or actual incidents or events is purely coincidental.

During my efforts toward accurate research, I was continuously taken aback by how similar the mid-nineteenth century's social, global, immigration, financial, technological, and political issues parallel the first quarter of the twenty-first century. I created a blog on my website, www.jjameswheeling.com, to delve more deeply into the different areas of what life was like in 1849–51.

I have read multiple diaries and accounts of the emigrants traveling west, their preparedness and their trials. I did not use one particular journal or diary to make up the overland part of the story, instead choosing to describe the travelers in my story as an amalgam of many individuals and their accounts.

I have tried to travel to many of the settings in the story, but I have not been able to float on a flatboat down the Ohio. Many of the places that existed in 1849–51 have either been torn down, built over, or repurposed, so experiencing them is a real challenge.

Below please find the lists of places, events, historical figures, and common practices used in my story.

Places that existed in 1849–51:

- Fort Hill was located in the modern Financial District of Boston known for its tenement housing that many immigrants found their way to when they arrived.

- The Lowell Railroad Line was built in 1842 to move people and goods between Boston and the mills at Lowell. It runs through Somerville and is still a commuter rail line as well as housing today's Green Line light rail, five new subway stops, and a multiuse corridor in the old track bed.

- The Old Colony Railroad operated from 1845 to 1893 and connected Boston to Fall River by way of Plymouth. The train operated from Boston Kneeland Street Depot located on the corner of South and Kneeland Streets.

- The Bank of Albany was located in New York City and was one of the major banking entities in the nineteenth century for the eastern seaboard.

- The Abiel Smith School for Free Blacks was a segregated school in the Boston area established in 1835.

- The Baltimore & Ohio Railroad ran from Baltimore to Cumberland, Maryland.

- The National Road was the first highway built entirely with federal funds after being authorized by Congress in 1806 during the Jefferson administration. Construction commenced in 1811 in Cumberland, Maryland, and closely paralleled an old military route. By 1818 it had been completed to the Ohio River at Wheeling, Virginia (modern West Virginia). Before the funds ran out, the road pushed through Ohio and finished at Vandalia, Ohio, in the 1830s. It was the first road in America to be macadamized. McAdam was a Scot who brought the paving technique to America that consisted of hammering smallish stones into place across a roadbed that fit tightly together enough to create a smoother surface compared to cobbles or dirt.

- Frostburg, Grantsville, Fort Necessity, and Uniontown were all towns or stops along the National Road in Pennsylvania.

- Brownsville, Pennsylvania was a major emigrant stopping point for supplies and materials in 1849.

- Wheeling, Parkersburg, and Ravenswood, Virginia (West Virginia didn't become a state until 1863), were all cities on the Ohio River that existed in 1849.

- Marietta, Ohio; Lexington, Louisville, and Paducah, Kentucky, are all cities along the Ohio River that existed in 1849.

- Louisville was the center of slave trade in the mid-nineteenth century and is credited with the phrase "being sold down the river" as an expression for literally being sent to New Orleans but also the expression for hopelessness and loss.

- On February 2, 1848, the Treaty of Guadalupe Hidalgo ended the Mexican-American War and gave the United States much of today's American West, including California, western

Colorado, the southwestern corner of Wyoming, Utah, Nevada, western New Mexico, and almost all of Arizona, for $15 million dollars and the assumption of $3.25 million of Mexico's debts. Mexico also gave up all claims to Texas.

- All of the territory west of the Missouri and Iowa borders was referred to as "Unorganized Indian Territory" in 1849.

- From 1670 to 1870, Rupert's Land was used to describe the Hudson Bay watershed, which encompasses much of what is now called Canada. Named after the cousin of King Charles II of Great Britain and Ireland in 1670 to honor his cousin, Prince Rupert, the first governor of the Hudson's Bay Company.

- The California Trail started from either Omaha or St. Joseph on the Missouri River and ran through modern day Kearney, North Platte, Scottsbluff, Casper, and South Pass to the City of Rocks and Elko, then along the Humboldt River, through the Forty-Mile Desert toward Carson City and the Sierra Nevada mountains and over to California. There were also bypasses to Salt Lake City and Fort Bridger as well as numerous cutoffs along the way. Traces of the emigrant trails from Salt Lake City and South Pass still exist with historical markers to give explanation.

- Fort Kearney, Fort Laramie, Fort Hall, and Fort Bridger were all either military posts or trading posts in 1849.

- The "Short Cut" between Fort Laramie and Fort Bridger that I use in the story was known to a few under the name "Cherokee Trail." It was never part of the California Trail because of its lack of water. I was able to confirm its existence from a rancher who helped me locate it on a map and stated that it was enough of a trail that they use it today to move their cattle.

- Utah became a territory on September 9, 1850, and encompassed all of present-day Nevada and Utah, the southwest corner of Wyoming, and the entire western slope of Colorado.

- Cooke's Wagon Road was established by Philip St. George Cooke and the Mormon Battalion during the Mexican-American War. It eventually became known as the Southern Trail and was one of the first routes between New Mexico and California.

- Mission San Luis Rey was a former Spanish Mission located in modern Oceanside, California, and was known as one of the most prosperous and had the largest population of all the missions in California in the mid-nineteenth century.

- The Humboldt Sink, Forty-Mile Desert, Ragtown, One-Mile Mountain, Red Lake, Hangtown (modern day Placerville), Centerville, Grass Valley, Shingle Springs, Five-Mile Station, Sacramento, San Jose, San Francisco, Sonora, and Benicia were or are all real places.

- California is the only state to ever bypass territorial status and go directly to statehood on September 9, 1850.

- Water lots were approved by Governor Kearney early in San Francisco's development. They entail taking sand and materials from other road building activities and hauling them to the tidelands between Clarke's Point and Rincon Point in an effort to create revenues for the new city. Many of the wharves and buildings constructed on those sights were very unstable.

- The Mission Plank Road was constructed over very swampy and sandy land to connect Yerba Buena (San Francisco) to Mission Dolores. It started construction in November of 1850 and finished by the spring of 1851 at a cost of $96,000.

- Portsmouth Plaza now known as Portsmouth Square was the first park in San Francisco when it was Yerba Buena in the early nineteenth century and was renamed in honor of the USS Portsmouth, the American ship that captured the city during the Conquest of California.

- American Hotel was one of several hotels in Benicia in 1851.

- Originally conceived in 1850, California Telegraph Company was granted an exclusive franchise to run a telegraph line between San Francisco and Marysville by the California State Legislature in 1852.

- Events that actually happened that I used in my story:

  › The race to California actually happened, but it started between two groups of young men from Marietta, Ohio. Inspired by it, I moved its start to Boston.

  › While steamboats on the Ohio, Mississippi, and Missouri rivers had been operating since the early 1800s, they faced many hazards, including hidden waterlogged trees and surprise shoals produced by shifting currents. Mechanically, steamboats were very susceptible to boiler explosions, and my research on steamboats is loaded with grizzly examples of death and destruction from mismanaged boilers exploding with little forewarning. I did not use one event for the explosion in Parkersburg but chose to amalgamate several examples of the kind of destruction that happened when a steamboat's boilers exploded.

  › Flatboats, with their simple and economic construction, joined steamboats, keelboats, and simple rafts on the Ohio River. Mostly constructed in Pittsburgh and Wheeling, the flatboats floated with the current and brought goods like barreled pork, potatoes, apples, wool, and lumber south to New Orleans. Once they arrived there, the goods were sold along with all the lumber that made up the flatboat and the flatboat operators found their way home. Carrying their wealth, these flatboat operators were preyed upon by river pirates and road thieves, making their successful return home to pay off their debts less than guaranteed.

› The Great St. Louis Riverfront Fire happened on May 17, 1849, when a steamboat caught fire, became unmoored, and caught in the Mississippi River's current, spreading its fiery destruction to steamboats tied up to the river wharf all along the banks of the Mississippi. The fire spread into St. Louis' riverfront properties destroying many businesses and residences.

› Cholera was a real and present problem during the summer of 1849. Originally traced to ships from Europe coming into the port of New Orleans, the invisible killer and how it spread was a mystery at the time. It traveled up the Mississippi River, across to the Ohio and Missouri Rivers and killed hundreds. So many died that people resorted to creating mass burials called "Cholera Pits" to deal with the volume of bodies.

› The summer of 1849 is recorded in diaries as being very rainy in the Midwest. It is difficult to know for sure except by diary account.

› Sacramento was very prone to flooding due to its proximity to the confluence of the American River and the Sacramento River. It also experienced its fair share of fire damage due to the use of flammable building materials.

› The San Francisco fires on December 24, 1949, and May 5, 1851, both happened and were just two of many that plagued the temporary housing of San Francisco until they started building with bricks.

› The San Francisco Fire of May 5, 1851, was driven by a rare and extraordinary northern gale that drove the fire into the heart of San Francisco's business district until, unexpectedly, the winds turned back on themselves. Many thought the wind's change was a miracle.

• Real people, things or organizations woven into my story:

› "Missing Friends" was a pamphlet by the Catholic Church in all the major cities along the East Coast during the mass immigration of Irish and other Europeans.

› Bounty hunters and river pirates were a very real and present danger for travelers in the mid-nineteenth century. Bounty hunters, employed by southern slave owners, prowled all the byways, be they water or road, searching for suspected runaways. The runaways could be indentured servants from Europe, black slaves, or even freed black people who could not prove their status who were abducted and sold as slaves. River pirates preyed on river boat operators returning to their businesses in the North after selling their wares in New Orleans.

› The "Buckeye Belle" was a steamboat on the Ohio and Mississippi rivers in 1849.

› Colonel Stephen W. Kearney was a one of the foremost frontier officers in the United States Army and contributed to the Mexican-American War, along with helping to establish the military presence in the western territories when emigrants began to move west. The outpost, Fort Kearney, was named after him. He was also appointed the governor of the newly occupied territory of California in 1848 and was instrumental in the development of San Francisco's business district, including approving the practice of creating "water lots."

› Jim Bridger and Louis Vasquez, as well as Vasquez's wife, Narcissa, were partners in the trading post known as Fort Bridger.

› Jim Bridger had a Native American wife of the Flathead tribe, Cora, who gave him a daughter named Mary Ann and two other children before dying. Mary Ann was killed while in captivity after the Whitman Massacre in Walla Walla. Bridger remarried to a Ute woman named Chipeta who died in childbirth while having a girl they named Virginia. He quickly married a third time, to a Shoshone woman he named Mary to help with the newborn. Mary had three more children and raised them in Missouri where Bridger moved them to be safe from the Mormon threats at Fort Bridger. All in all, he lost two wives and a daughter in the wilds of the American West. All of this is referenced in my story through Narcissa Vasquez and her fear of living in the wilderness and protecting her children.

› Joe Meek was another fur-trapping mountain man and a good friend to Jim Bridger.

› Brigham Young and the Mormons did emigrate to the Great Salt Lake area of Utah in 1847 trying to find a place to live outside of the control of the United States where they had experienced harassment and death for their religious beliefs. Unfortunately, the Treaty of Guadalupe Hidalgo in 1848 included the Great Salt Lake area and made it part of the United States.

› Tensions between Jim Bridger and Brigham Young were real and well documented.

› The *Daily Union,* the *Sacramento Bee,* and the *Alta California* were all newspapers being published in California in 1849.

> There was a corrupt sheriff in Tuolumne County, California, in 1850–51 who did collect taxes from the English-illiterate miners even though the Foreign Miners tax had been repealed in 1850. I decided to dispatch him, but I do not know if that is how he met his demise.

- Practices and beliefs at the time:

  > "Seeing the elephant" or "Chasing the elephant" were common phrases used to describe people who had fallen under the gold rush's spell and were going to California and leaving everything, and everyone, behind in their quest for riches.

  > No one understood germs, contagion, or the importance of cleanliness, so diseases like cholera ran rampant.

  > Cyanide, strychnine, and arsenic were all easily accessible poisons in the mid-nineteenth century. I found stories of all three used by individuals on the California Trail who had reached their wit's end.

  > I found stories of the harvesting of dead men's scrotums for use as gold sacks in the Yukon Gold Rush specifically but believe the practice could be plausible wherever the pressure of gold fever, scarcity, and survival exist.

Acknowledgments

Since these are my first publications, I'd like to acknowledge a few important lights who, over the many years of learning to write and get my story out, have encouraged and supported me.

First, Will Grey who taught the courses on writing fiction and non-fiction for Fort Lewis College's Continuing Ed program. His last words to me were, "We are going to see your name in lights one day." Those few encouraging words have kept me going.

Louise Powers-Ackley, my seventh-grade French teacher and a really good friend. Louise was the very first person I shared my story with thirteen years ago. She is a trooper. I know now that manuscript was a mess. But she waded through it and gave me enough positive feedback to keep the fire burning.

My North Carolina Lake Logan Writer's Group who changed my life by helping me find my voice. Jenn Browning continues to encourage me and be my "English teacher lady" when I don't know what to do with grammar.

Liz Trupin-Pulli came into my life with a bang at a Women Writing the West conference in 2016 and gave my ignorant self a break by agreeing to read my manuscript. After a few pages, she stopped and provided me with a list of editors. For the next eight years she coached me, represented me and furthered my knowledge of the writing profession.

To my first editor Bill Greenleaf, my New York editor Andra Miller, my copy editor Candace Sinclair, and my proofreader Sean Strain, thank you for your insights, perspectives and encouragement. Bill told me that learning to write is like learning to play an instrument. After all these years, I now understand.

To the team at Mayfly Book Design, Julie, Ryan and Jess, I am so grateful that Fate brought us together on the day I decided to self-publish my stories. It was the good omen that proved I needed to take that next step. Your insights and professionalism brought Matt Kania of Map Hero into my life and his work blesses each of these stories.

So important in these last few years is the sanctuary and friendship I have found with Suzanne Zerbe-Erickson. She gave me a quiet place to be away from my ranch life to write. She reads my manuscripts and offers valuable feedback. She mothers me after I lost my own mother and has given so much kindness and encouragement. I have a hard time putting my gratitude into words.

To Bill Brown who taught me how to shoot a rifle and handgun just to experience the sensation in order to put it into words for my characters, thank you for your time and enthusiasm.

My husband, Joe. We've been married for thirty-nine years and these books represent a new adventure for both of us. We have gone through the early married chapter, the corporate chapter, the children chapter, the homeschool chapter, the farm and cattle chapter and we are now onto the publishing chapter. There were tough times along the way but we knew and trusted each other so we made it. I am grateful for his love and support. Our daughters, too, for their patience on family trips when I had to stop at one more museum or historical marker. Just one more.

And then there's my greater James family whom I live next to, work with and for, and are partners with in our family agricultural land. I can credit them for teaching me to trust my instinct and believe in myself. Ours is a dynamic, competitive and complicated family structure held together with a firm commitment to being stewards of our land and our family legacy.

There are so many others who have been my cheerleaders, never forgetting to ask about how the book is coming along, what can they do to help and eagerly awaiting the release. I can't mention all of you but I hope you know how much you mean to me.

Without you all, it would have been easy to get frustrated and give up on this project. These books represent well over a decade of perseverance and prayer. Thank you.

About the Author

J. James Wheeling lives on the James Ranch in Durango, Colorado. The mountains surrounding her home are rich with stories of the miners, railroads, and ranchers who settled in the Animas Valley after the Brunot Agreement was signed with the Ute Indians in the 1870s.

Raised on the ranch, she graduated from Colorado State University where she met and married her husband before living in five major American cities. They returned to the ranch to raise their children where she taught herself to be a chemical-free produce farmer. She homeschooled her daughters, ran the produce farm, was a 4-H leader, dance and swim mom and helped escort the local livestock judging team across Colorado. She works beside her husband and extended family to steward their land using regenerative practices as well as marketing grass-fed beef directly to the consumer.

Her curiosity about American history has her dragging her husband to museums across the West in the off-season. Her best writing ideas come when she is working in her vast flower beds. She has two new son-in-laws and two corgis.

You won't know the whole story until you read both books!
Available now wherever you like to buy your books including
the James Ranch Market in Durango, Colorado

Sneak Peak

HERE'S WHAT I'M COOKING UP

NEXT FOR DASH

It's October,1853. Dash Truepenny and Horatio Fountainbleu have just helped finish the first telegraph in California from San Francisco to Marysville. Dash begins to wonder if there is a chance that Molly and Quinn are still in the Baltimore orphanage where he left them. What if he could unite them with Amalee, her only cousins? Does he dare venture into Boston to visit his mother and sister? Or is the risk of being discovered by his father and brothers too much?

At the same time, Lieutenant John W. Gunnison is on a government survey expedition trying to find the best route for a transcontinental railroad. Everything is going smoothly until they get to Utah Territory where a tense impasse is happening between the Ute Indians, westbound emigrants and the Mormons. What happens next creates even more tension and begins a new chapter of distrust and deceit in the territory.

By April 1854, Dash finds himself employed by a Army expedition disguised as a livestock resupply effort to the westernmost

Army post in Benicia, California but is actually on a mission to get to the bottom of what happened to Gunnison. Forced to spend the winter in Salt Lake City, he witnesses men who hardly interested in justice but rather their own agendas. He also learns the difference between white man's justice and Native justice.

What happens when the three cultures collide and Dash and his family are in the middle? Will he be pressed to use his long shot in the name of keeping the peace? What role will Hope play in helping to find a reasonable solution to the predicament they find themselves in?